OFF TO BE THE WIZARD

OFF TO BE THE
WIZARD

Scott Meyer

47NORTH

Text copyright © 2014 Scott Meyer
All rights reserved.

Printed in the United States of America.

Published by 47North, Seattle
www.apub.com

ISBN-13: 9781612184715
ISBN-10: 1612184715
Library of Congress Control Number: 2013947607

Cover design by: InkD

OFF TO BE THE
WIZARD

The following is intended to be a fun, comedic sci-fi/fantasy novel. Any similarity between the events described and how reality actually works is purely coincidental.

1.

Terror.

Martin Banks enjoyed science. As a child he read about people who made huge, world-changing discoveries, and he had wondered what emotions he would feel if he ever discovered something really earth-shattering. Now he had made just such a discovery, and he was surprised to find that the answer was absolute bowel-loosening terror.

Martin didn't consider himself a hacker. He didn't like the image that the label implied. Sure, as a teenager he'd experimented with the whole pose, but found that rebelling against everything all the time was just too exhausting. It was like an emotional treadmill. It never ended and never got you anywhere, because when you live in a state of constant open rebellion, the *powers that be* disregard you. So, Martin decided that he wasn't a hacker. He was just a guy who really liked monkeying with computers.

Martin was spending the evening his usual way, poking around the internet, seeing what he could get away with. The TV droned away in the background, providing ambient light, occasional distraction, and the illusion of human contact. He knew that many of the things he was doing were technically illegal, but he kept his tampering strictly harmless. That way, the authorities wouldn't bother with him as long as more destructive perpetrators were roaming free. He told himself that, but he was too smart to really believe it. That didn't stop him from waking up his computer every evening and seeing what he could see.

This night he was poking around the servers of a cell phone manufacturer that had been in business since the 1930s, when they made AM radios the size of post boxes. He hadn't done anything particularly bad. He didn't have to force his way in. Anyone with a working knowledge of network structure and a willingness to look at a tremendous amount of stupefyingly boring information could have found the file.

It was the kind of file nobody would ever look at. Five terabytes of plain ASCII text characters. Even its name made Martin sleepy—*repository1-c.txt*. The moment that Martin thought, *No sane person would be interested in a file like that*, was the moment he decided to give it a look.

He figured it would take far too long to download, so instead he chose to access it directly using a terminal emulator. When it opened, the file appeared to be an endless series of huge, discrete blocks of data. The individual chunks were massive tangles of numbers tossed with rare pieces of recognizable text. He might have disregarded the file entirely if not for the fact that many of the numbers appeared to be changing constantly. He double checked. This was his default text editor, and it hadn't, as far as he knew, been updated to allow this sort of thing. But, there it was.

The first thing Martin always did when he found some new data file was to search for his own name. It may seem egocentric, but Martin wasn't worried about that. He had spent a lot of time thinking about himself, and had come to the conclusion that he was definitely not self-absorbed. He searched for "Martin

Kenneth Banks." Usually a word search on a simple text file took no time at all. Plain text is easy for a computer to work with. Due to the sheer size of the file, though, Martin's search for himself took nearly ten minutes. It finally found his name lodged toward the back of the file.

He spent over an hour peering at the data, and eventually was able to tease out some recognizable information. Whoever had made this file knew a lot about him. He was irritated to find his height was wrong. It wasn't labeled *Height*—it was just the number. But it was unmistakable. Five feet, eleven inches. It was wrong in that while that might be how tall Martin was if you went to the trouble of measuring him, he'd been putting six feet two inches on every form he'd filled out since high school. He edited the number and hit save. He spent a few moments looking around at various numbers in the file, then got up to go to the bathroom.

Martin stretched his arms, stood up quickly, and felt a terrible discomfort in his groin. It was like someone had grabbed the waistband of his jeans and pulled upward. These were his favorite jeans. They'd always been a little tight (he liked pants that constantly reminded you that you were wearing pants), but they never caused him anything like this sort of discomfort. He looked down at his waist. His belt was right where it usually sat, but the inseam of the jeans was definitely riding higher than usual. Also, now that he looked, the hems were slightly higher on his ankles than he'd remembered.

Weird, he thought, as he pulled his pants down a bit and walked into the bathroom. While absentmindedly taking a leak, he glanced over at the mirrored front of the medicine cabinet. He saw dust building up on top of the medicine cabinet and thought that he should really clean up there. He didn't dust that spot often, because he couldn't see up there. He stared at the dust, letting that thought sink in until he realized his aim had drifted and he was urinating on the wall.

The whole time he was cleaning the wall behind the toilet he was laughing at himself. When he was a kid, occasionally he'd have to leave the house at night to fetch something from the car for his parents. He would always think about how weird it would be if some horrible monster was chasing him, and by the time he returned to the safety of the house he would be in a dead sprint with his stomach tied in knots. Then he would laugh, because it was ridiculous to think that a monster would be chasing him in his front yard on a well-lit street in the suburbs. This, he knew, was no different. His pants rode up. It probably meant he was gaining weight. Not a good thing, but nothing to freak out about. And the medicine cabinet had probably settled a bit, or one of its support screws had torn free of the drywall, or maybe he was imagining the whole thing. Sitting around all night in a dark apartment with the TV and computer screens providing all the ambient light is bound to affect your perception after a while.

When the wall was as clean as it was going to get, he turned his attention to the medicine cabinet. It was still fastened firmly to the wall and didn't appear to have moved. He could still see the dust-covered top, and furthermore, he was pretty sure he had always been able to look himself in the eye when he looked at the cabinet's mirrored front. He remembered the mirror cutting him off about halfway through his eyebrows. He was looking in the mirror now, and all he could see was his nose. He looked at his feet again to reassure himself that he was barefoot. Then he just stood there, being confused.

Finally, Martin left the bathroom. He turned on every light in the apartment. He walked out to the living room/kitchen/dining room of the apartment. It was all one space, but you could tell the kitchen was a different room, because there were appliances in it. You could recognize the dining room because there was a cheap chandelier hanging from the ceiling over the spot where the architect clearly wanted Martin to put a table and chairs. Instead, the chandelier hung at eye level in empty space behind Martin's desk chair. Martin scanned the room and told himself that he'd always been able to see the top of the refrigerator, and that he was only noticing it now because it was so dusty.

Enough of this, Martin thought. He went to the bedroom closet to dig through his toolbox. When he moved out of his parents' house, his uncle Ray had volunteered to drive the rental truck. While watching Martin and his friends carrying Martin's belongings from his comfortable seat in the air-conditioned cab, Uncle Ray noticed that Martin owned no tools. Martin told him, "I've always lived with my dad, so I've never really needed tools. While you're noticing things, have you noticed that you sitting there in the cab of the rental truck with the motor running and the air conditioning blasting is costing me a fortune in gas?"

Uncle Ray said that he had noticed, and that it was fine, and didn't bother him.

Later, Uncle Ray gave him a fairly well-stocked tool set as a housewarming gift. The tool set came in its own toolbox. Martin told him, "Thanks! Uh, did you notice that the toolbox is pink, and says *Her First Tool Kit* in sparkly letters?"

Uncle Ray said that he had noticed, and that this was also fine, and didn't bother him. Good old Uncle Ray. That guy was unflappable.

Martin returned from the closet with a pink measuring tape and a tiny pink plastic carpenter's square. He grabbed a pencil and stood with his back to the jamb of the bedroom door. He placed the carpenter's square on his head and carefully made a mark where the square met the wall. Martin smirked at himself for wasting his time like this as he ran the tape measure up the wall to the mark. He leaned in close to read the measuring tape.

The mark met the tape just a touch above the six feet, two inches mark.

He repeated the process and got the same result.

He thought, *Clearly I've gradually grown three inches over the course of the last few years, and only noticed it now, right after changing my height in a weird text file I found online. That's normal.*

Martin sat at his computer and looked at the file while he thought. He wanted to just start changing things to show himself how silly he was being, but he also wanted to close the file and pretend he'd never found it, so he just sat there. After twenty minutes of this he decided he had to prove once and for all that he was being stupid. The cursor was still at the same place he'd left it, at the height notation. Martin edited six feet two inches to read six feet one inch.

He walked back to the bedroom door. He stood straight and tall with his back against the door jamb. He carefully placed the square on his head and marked its location with the pencil. He methodically ran the tape measure up the wall, taking care to make sure it was plumb, and noted with great interest that his height now measured six feet one inch tall.

He measured himself again. Five times. He'd have tried a sixth time, but his hands were shaking too badly to make a legible mark.

He sat and stared at the TV for about an hour. He had no idea what was on, and he didn't care. He walked back to his computer, re-edited his height to five feet eleven inches and closed the file. He went into the bathroom and splashed cold water on his face.

He looked himself in the eye in the medicine cabinet mirror.

He went to bed. Not to sleep. To bed. Every light in the apartment was still on, as were his clothes. He lay there and thought about the implications of what had just happened, and that was when he felt the terror. Everyone who paid any attention to science fiction, or for that matter to science, eventually came across the concept that reality as we knew it was a computer program. That people were subroutines. That we weren't biological organisms clinging to a ball of rock hurtling around a ball of fire suspended in a sea of nothing, but that we were simulated organisms attached to a virtual ball of rock, located in an unfathomable program that could be a game, a weather simulation, or even a screensaver.

Well, not a screensaver, Martin thought. *Any society advanced enough to produce a program this sophisticated would have long since developed a monitor that didn't burn in.*

Once Martin's mental state had downgraded from terror to severe agitation, he saw the irony of the situation. Since the beginning of recorded time, man had debated the nature of existence. The greatest thinkers spent their entire lives wrestling with fundamental questions. Even basic discoveries like the wheel and the lever had made profound differences in mankind's existence.

Now Martin had proof of exactly what we were, and the means to change things instantly, with almost no effort. Martin had, with one accidental discovery, become the most important figure in human history, and he desperately wished he could take it all back.

Martin looked at the clock. It was 3 a.m. He'd been lying there, staring at the ceiling and staving off panic, for six hours. He got up, downed two sleeping pills with a double shot of bourbon, turned off the lights, and eventually lost consciousness.

2.

The alarm went off at seven. Martin was still under the influence of the pills he'd taken, so while his eyes were open and his body was moving, his brain was not. He showered. He brushed his teeth. He shaved. Usually his brain would have slowly come awake, but Martin was actively choosing not to think. As he walked through his apartment, his eyes locked on the shaky pencil marks on his bedroom doorjamb. He stared for a moment, grimaced, and then shut his brain down again. He made coffee and toaster waffles. He glared at his computer as he ate. He read the news on his smartphone this morning. It felt safer that way.

He drove his hatchback to work. When he got to his building, he didn't remember anything about the drive. He sat in his cubicle and shuffled paperwork. At quitting time he realized he could remember almost nothing about his day. He had drifted through it in a haze. He walked to the parking lot, sat in his car, and looked at himself in the rearview mirror. This couldn't go on. He resolved then and there that he would spend the rest of his life pretending that the file didn't exist.

He drove home as fast as he could and immediately turned on his computer and opened the file. He'd reasoned that he couldn't pretend that the file didn't exist unless he figured out exactly what it was.

He searched for his name again, and again found the chunk of data that defined his existence. He knew where his height was, but the other useful metrics proved harder to define. His intelligence, his percentage of body fat, his strength, and his level of health were all impossible to quantify objectively, regardless of what people pitching diet plans said.

He found his weight, but dared not change it. He reasoned that weighing less didn't mean necessarily being less fat. He could easily render himself less dense. He could imagine his parents attending his funeral, being asked how their son had died and having to admit that nobody could explain it, but he'd somehow spontaneously become a foam.

Martin took a different approach. He pulled up his banking app on his smartphone and looked up his bank account balance. He searched for that number in the file and found it immediately. He took a deep breath, moved the decimal point one place to the right and hit save.

He refreshed his banking app. His balance read $835.00.

SUCCESS!

He felt a pang. Not a pang of conscience. He hadn't stolen money from anybody. He'd created it out of thin air. The money hadn't existed. Now it did. The way he saw it, he'd done the world a favor! The pang was fear. He knew this was too easy, and if the authorities found out what he'd done he would be punished, even if it wasn't technically against the law. Martin knew that the burden of proof was on the accuser, so anybody who attempted to prosecute him for electronic bank fraud would have to demonstrate how he had done it without accessing the bank's computers. Furthermore, he reasoned, there are two parts to any theft: taking a thing away from its owner, and keeping it for yourself. Martin wasn't taking anything from anybody, so he figured it wasn't theft, or at least that he was fifty percent less likely to get caught. It was flimsy reasoning, but it was good enough to let him sleep. He moved the decimal point back one space and walked away from the computer for the night.

Again, he watched TV without ever noticing what was on. Again, he lay in bed without going to sleep. Again, he resorted to over-the-counter sleep aids and inexpensive bourbon to get the rest he needed.

The next day was Friday. He sailed through work like the *Flying Dutchman*. The ship was moving, but nobody was at the helm. His supervisor was concerned that Martin was acting strangely, but he was getting more work done than usual, so she chose not to interfere with a good thing.

Martin realized that he couldn't ignore the file. What he'd learned he could not *un*-learn. He was just going to have to show some willpower. He put a great deal of thought into all the things he should not do. Things that might be possible, using the file, but would probably lead to no good. Having spent all Friday collecting dangerous ideas, that night when he sat at his computer, he had no shortage of things to try, and a whole weekend to try them in.

3.

First, Martin selected the entire chunk of data that he now believed was essentially him, and copied it to a separate file, which he encrypted and copied to the storage card on his phone.

The second thing Martin did was move the decimal on his bank account three digits to the right. He considered making himself a millionaire, but why risk it when he could make himself a thousandaire anytime he wanted?

I have to be careful, he thought. *I don't want to screw this up.*

At first he wondered how something as complex as a human being could be encapsulated in a chunk of data that was small enough to be managed, but once he calmed down and thought about it, he could see how it might work. He saw that the file was a list of parameters, but not detailed descriptions. He could see the code that defined his heart. He verified this by taking his pulse and watching the numbers fluctuate in real time. The numbers made no sense to him. They might not make sense even to a cardiologist, but they changed predictably in time with his pulse. The code described what the heart was doing, and the ways in which it might differ from other people's hearts, but not what it, as a heart, was. It was as if somewhere else there was another file that described human hearts in detail, and every person's data referred to that to render their specific heart. The same went for all the other organs, although this was much less interesting to him once he realized that he had no access to the fundamental structure of his body, and could not, for example, transform his skeleton into an unbreakable metal.

There were other shortcuts built into the system as well. He ran a search for his current longitude and latitude. He understood the notation thanks to a brief flirtation in his late teens with geocaching, and had access to the actual numbers thanks to his smartphone. When he found his exact coordinates in the file he decided to move around and see if they changed. He walked backward slowly while peering at his monitor with an ever-increasing squint. The numbers appeared to be changing as he moved. So, instead of tracking each person's absolute position in space, the system tracked them in relation to the Earth. After the coordinates there was a number that he saw was his height above sea level. Martin jumped, and though it was hard to read the screen while jumping, he could see that the number changed while he was in midair, then returned to its starting point by the time he landed.

Martin knew what he had to do next. If he didn't try, he'd wonder for the rest of his life.

No, that's not true, he thought. *I'd wonder until I eventually broke down and tried it anyway, so I might as well try it now.*

He hunched over the desk without sitting, swallowed hard and increased his altitude notation by one foot. He exhaled slowly.

"Now we see if I can fly," he said out loud to posterity, posterity in this case being his empty apartment. He hit the enter key.

Instantly he was one foot off the ground. Just as instantly, he was falling one foot to the ground. Slightly less instantly his full weight came down hard on the floor and his desk, jamming both of his wrists and twisting his right ankle. He was almost able to remain upright, but eventually fell backward very hard into his desk chair, which bent permanently from the strain and knocked the wind out of him. As he sat, trying to get the air back into his lungs, he could hear his downstairs neighbor hitting her ceiling with a broom and yelling at him to quiet down.

Okay, Martin thought, *I can't fly, but I can fall whenever I want.*

Martin turned his attention back to the longitude and latitude. He took his smartphone to the far corner of his bedroom and noted the GPS reading. He returned to the computer, sat down, and entered the coordinates. He took a deep breath, hit enter, and he was in the far corner of his bedroom. His feet were on solid ground, but the rest of him was in a seated position with no chair beneath him. His weight came down on his tailbone. It didn't break, but it felt like it wanted to. He took a moment before he got up and walked back to the computer. The downstairs neighbor was hitting the ceiling even harder and yelling even louder. He pictured her trying to get her damage deposit back, claiming the hundreds of broom handle marks had been there when she moved in. This made him smile.

He now knew he could teleport. He also knew that he had to put thought into how he'd do it, or he could seriously hurt himself. Again, he looked at the GPS app. He picked a spot about a mile away, a place that would be well lit, but where nobody would see him: the side parking lot of a Boston Market franchise. He entered the coordinates, stood up, bent his knees to absorb any shocks, extended his arms slightly for better balance, gritted his teeth, and hit enter.

He was in the side parking lot of the Boston Market. He was glad that he hadn't changed out of his work clothes when he got home, and that his wallet was still in his pocket. He wished he'd kept his shoes on, and his keys in his pocket, but you can't have everything. He lived in Seattle, so he was grateful that only the pavement was wet and not the air itself. His computer was still back at home, so he couldn't simply teleport home. Instead, he walked home, eating a bad Boston Market meatloaf sandwich, thinking about what he would do next, both about the file and his spare apartment keys, which he'd left with his downstairs neighbor.

Who better? He thought. *She's always home. She pays close attention to what's going on.*

His wrists, ankle, and tailbone hurt, but the walk home and the ruining of a good pair of wool socks were totally worth it, both for the time it gave him to think and for the look on his downstairs neighbor's face.

"Why are you being so loud up there?" she asked.

"What do you mean? I wasn't home. I walked to Boston Market. See?" he said, holding up his sandwich wrapper and his now-empty drink cup. "It's exactly one mile away, so I've been gone a while."

"You could have driven."

"If I had my car keys, I'd have my apartment keys."

"Why aren't you wearing shoes?"

He looked at his feet.

"I like to walk quietly. You know that."

"How do I know you didn't buy that food earlier, then just bring it down here now?"

Martin chuckled. "What makes more sense, that I ate some fast food, saved my trash, deliberately made a bunch of noise, then locked myself out of my own apartment just to come down here and lie to you for fun, or that I simply decided to walk a mile without shoes to eat at Boston Market?"

She had no answer, because neither option made any sense. Martin returned to his apartment a tired but happy man.

He minimized the file for a bit and went to the Android smartphone app store. With some effort he found a combination of emulators that could pull up the file on his phone. No more walking home, or really, anywhere.

He had one more item on his mental to-do list.

He spent quite a while searching before he found the fields for the date and time. He was past being surprised to find these entries in forms he could easily understand. He figured the program had just passed these concepts on to the people it created as a short cut. Why spend cycles creating new notation systems when it can just give people ones it already knows will work and get on with rendering trees?

He looked at the time notation for a long time. It was, essentially, the world's most accurate clock. The numbers seemed off until he realized it was Greenwich Mean Time.

He was going to try time travel. He couldn't *not* try, even though he was terrified of the whole idea. He carefully added thirty seconds to the time notation, hit enter, and ... nothing happened. He double checked. The time notation hadn't accepted his input. He tried again, with identical results.

Martin let out a long breath, and said, "It's probably just as well."

A voice from the corner of the room said, "Try going back in time, not forward."

Martin jumped, then looked toward the source of the voice. He saw himself standing in the corner, holding his smartphone, which Martin was also holding. Martin was looking at himself. Not a picture. Not a reflection. He was seeing him.

He'd expected himself to be better looking.

They stared at each other for a moment. Finally, time-traveler Martin spoke. "I said, you should try going back in time, instead of forward."

Original Martin was too busy freaking out to listen, and didn't catch what Future Martin said.

"What?" Martin asked, snapping out of it.

Future Martin shook his head. "Great, now I'm confused."

"*You're* confused?!"

Future Martin looked irritated. He muttered something under his breath as he tapped at the smartphone in his hand. He looked up once more, made eye contact with Original Martin, and disappeared.

Martin walked over to the spot where his double had stood. No scorch marks or anything. Martin didn't know what he expected would happen to the area someone time traveled into, then away from in quick succession, but he knew he expected more than nothing.

Martin looked at his phone and saw the file's time field, ticking off the seconds. He quickly subtracted about thirty seconds from the time and hit enter.

The world around him did a fairly fast dissolve between *now* and the dusty memory that was the world half a minute ago. He saw Past Martin standing in the middle of the room, absorbed in his phone screen, looking disappointed.

Past Martin exhaled and said, "It's probably just as well."

Martin felt sorry for Past Martin. *I looked so sad,* he thought.

"Try going back in time instead of forward," Martin suggested helpfully.

Past Martin was badly startled. He looked at Martin with genuine panic in his eyes, which quickly cycled through incredulity, amazement, and, to Martin's lasting dismay, disappointment.

Great, Martin thought. *I'm dumpy looking, and easy to read.*

Martin decided to try again. "I said, you should try going back in time, instead of forward."

Past Martin opened and closed his mouth a couple of times. Finally, he managed to ask "What?"

Martin was not impressed with himself. "Great," he said, "now I'm confused."

Past Martin looked genuinely affronted. *"You're* confused?!"

Martin gave up. "Fantastic," he muttered as he reset the time. "I'm the first man in history to meet myself, and I learn that I'm an ugly idiot."

Martin hit enter, and watched his former self disappear as he returned to the moment after he left.

That didn't go well, Martin thought. Upon reflection, he should have expected it. First meetings are always awkward, even if you're meeting yourself. *Next time should go smoother. I'll have a better idea how to behave, and how to react.*

Martin heard a quiet *ahem* to his right. He looked, and was not surprised to see himself standing there, smiling at him.

"I'm you, an hour from now," he said. "Wanna play some heads-up poker?"

4.

The next morning Martin woke up with a hangover. He hadn't drunk much while playing poker with himself. Just a few beers.

The first round, when he was Past Martin, he lost badly. Then he went back in time and played through it all again as Future Martin. To be honest, he wasn't that into the second round at first and had mainly gone back and offered to play out of a sense of obligation. Then he started winning, because he could remember some of the hands Past Martin had. Any game is more enjoyable when you're winning, although in the end he broke even. He shuffled off to bed, as tired as he'd ever been in his life, but with his brain firing at full steam. He thought about what would have happened if he'd won the first round of poker, then come back and won again. Was that possible, and if so, where would the winnings come from? Could he create infinite wealth by losing at poker against himself? Of course, he could create infinite wealth anyway, by simply moving a decimal point in the file.

He eventually realized that if he was going to get any sleep he was going to have to force the issue, so he downed his now nightly cocktail: two sleeping pills, and a shot of bargain-brand bourbon.

Now it was morning, and he had a hangover.

He sat at his desk, eating toaster waffles and drinking coffee while he stared at the file. The night before had been a dazzling rollercoaster of discovery, but the morning after was, as usual, a grim slog through the bumper-to-bumper commute of reality. He had proven that the file was a tool that could improve every aspect of his life. His aching feet, twisted ankle, and jammed wrists, as well as his ruined socks and his confused neighbor, all proved that he could also ruin his life if he continued to act without thinking first.

He had already decided not to change his body anymore. Until he understood the file much better, it was too dangerous. Better to just create money and buy a health club membership, or plastic surgery if needed. He had also decided that rather than add a huge amount of money to his bank account, he would occasionally add small amounts. He hoped this would help him evade detection.

He could fly, briefly. Really, he could place himself in midair for a moment before he fell to the ground. He had an idea of how to fix that, but it wasn't his first priority.

He could teleport. This was amazing, but also very dangerous. Happily, his clothes had teleported with him. He reasoned that the file, or the system that used the file, must define your clothes and the things in your immediate possession in relation to your location, just like it tracks your location in relation to the earth. That was a relief. Martin didn't want to have to explain to the police why he had materialized naked in a public place. Really, he didn't want to explain to the police why he had materialized at all. He needed to make sure if he was going to teleport someplace, that in addition to having the right longitude, latitude, and altitude, he would need solitude. He needed a landing zone where nobody would see him.

Lastly, he could go back in time and return to his starting point, but he couldn't go forward beyond that. He reasoned that this was because the past was a known state, but the future had not happened yet, and was unknowable and unreachable. He didn't know for sure, and likely never would. The point was, he could go back in time, and return to the present. Essentially, he was just teleporting to another time as well as another place. So, the parameters he needed were longitude, latitude, altitude, solitude, and ... time.

The only way he could do all of these things was to access the file. He could access it from his computer and now from his smartphone. Public computers were out of the question. He couldn't install the software he'd need to securely access the remote computer that hosted the file. It looked like his phone was going to be his primary means of access to the file from now on, so he needed to make sure he didn't transport himself any place that the phone wouldn't work, or he'd be stuck. He pulled up his carrier's coverage map. It was now a map not only of *reliable* high-speed data access but also of the places where Martin had God-like powers over time and space. That shouldn't have felt limiting, but it did.

I can instantly travel anywhere I want, he thought, *on this map of the continental United States, as long as where I'm going is in one of the red blobs. The dark red blobs. The lighter ones are iffy.*

For the first time since finding the file, Martin Banks thought before he acted. He made a list of things he needed to do before he could proceed, arranged them in a logical order, and started working down the list.

He searched the file for his phone's serial number and model name. He was relieved to find them. He was afraid that the file would cover only people, but that clearly was not the case. The file was immense (much larger than even the huge listed file size) but not infinite, and he wasn't sure it was large enough for all people and all objects, but there it was, an entry for his phone. The entry wasn't very large. He supposed, as with people, that mass-produced items like phones didn't need to be described in detail for every copy. Instead, each copy had an entry that described how it differed from others of its type, but the full description of what made it a phone resided in a separate file somewhere else.

He spent some time making a rudimentary smartphone app to automatically edit the file. He found the phone's battery level. In the file it was accurate down to five decimal places. On the phone it was totally inaccurate unless you installed a separate app, which only gave you the reading in whole numbers. He verified that he had the battery level by checking the file against the battery app, then playing a juice-hungry game on the phone for five minutes. He rechecked the battery level and was sure he had the right field. He set the experimental app to run in the background, resetting the battery level to one hundred percent every ten seconds. He played the game again for another five minutes. Afterward, the battery was still full.

After an hour of searching, copying, and pasting, he had modified his phone to always have seventy-three percent battery remaining (one hundred percent would have looked suspicious). This would save him from needing a bunch of spare batteries and carrying them in a bandolier like Chewbacca.

He also made his phone always broadcast to and from an area that was covered by three separate cell towers and two power substations, no matter where the phone was actually located. It was an intuitive leap, but Martin now understood that the radio waves produced by the phone were just as artificial as everything else, and could also be manipulated, and if he could specify where the signal was broadcasting from, he could also specify when. Time, after all, was just another number in the file.

He had a harder time trying to reason his way through time travel. In the cold light of day, Martin could see he'd been incredibly reckless in even attempting it. He'd also been incredibly lucky. In theory, once he'd gone back in time, there would have been two of him being described by the file at the same time, which you'd think would result in some sort of error, which would be a bad thing. It hadn't, though. Martin had reasoned that there was a program somewhere that accessed the file and used it to render the world, and that the moment he was experiencing at any given time was as far as this theoretical program had gotten.

As for travel to the distant past, if reality really was a computer program, then it always had been, which meant that the file had always existed. It was strange to think that the file predated the invention of computers, but it only predated the human invention of computers. Whoever or whatever had created the file had clearly invented computers long before whatever program Martin was experiencing was written.

If the file had always existed, then, in a sense, everything in the file had always existed. So really, the only reason Martin hadn't been around through all of history is that the program hadn't been given a reason to render him there, and now Martin knew how to give it that reason.

Martin couldn't prove anything beyond the existence of the repository file, but that was enough. He thanked himself for about the millionth time for having learned to program computers, and got to work. When the weekend was over his app was good enough for the moment.

The app had three tabs. The first tab's icon was a dollar sign. It told him his checking account balance and allowed him to quickly change it. The app made the necessary edits to the file automatically.

The second tab's icon was a compass. It used a popular mapping program's A.P.I. to display a satellite map of the Earth. He could zoom in to look at an area, select a spot and the app would input the coordinates and altitude into the file. A heartbeat later, he would be there. There was also a dialog box where he could enter a date and time. If he didn't specify a date and time, the app kept him in the present. There was a button to take him back to wherever and whenever he was when he last time traveled. A temporal undo button, if you like. Handy for if he found himself someplace he didn't want to be. He also had a list of places he'd teleported to and from. He could mark certain places and times as favorites to make it easy to get back to them.

The third tab was labeled "?!" That tab had three buttons. The first button's purpose was to prove to people that he had the power he now had. If he hit it, the app would add three feet to his altitude. The button was labeled *Hover*. He hadn't figured out a way to alter his altitude and have it just stay altered, so instead his app would re-enter the change ten times a second, keeping him in the air until he hit the button again. He tried it, and the experience was unpleasant, but nothing he couldn't handle. The second button said *Home*. One press would take him back to his apartment. The third button was bright red and said *Escape*. Martin had given that one some thought.

Martin was sure that nothing he'd done was immoral. He hadn't hurt anybody. He'd just helped himself. He was also pretty sure nothing he had done was illegal. Who writes laws against bending space and time to your will? But he was also certain that if anybody ever found out what he was doing, he would be in big trouble. If he was lucky, they'd just throw him in prison and keep his discovery for themselves. If he was unlucky, he'd be dissected as an alien. He knew that if things went south, he'd need an escape plan. He tried to think of someplace he could go where no government or corporation could find him. He knew that in this day and age, that was a problem, but he also saw that was the answer. *This day and age.* He could escape to the past, and nobody alive today could touch him.

He knew that the things the file allowed him to do would seem like magic to anyone who witnessed them. If he was going to escape to a point in the past, it should be a time when magic was believed to exist. That way, instead of people yelling, "Magic! It must be some kind of trick! Let's beat him until he tells us the secret," hopefully they would yell, "Magic! I've heard of that! I've never seen it in person, though!"

The trick was finding a time and place where the next sentence wouldn't be "Let's burn him!"

He tried to think of an example from history of a magician who had been revered. The only names he came up with were Houdini and Merlin. Houdini died after he was punched in the gut by a fan. That didn't seem promising. Merlin was King Arthur's wizard, and also probably fictional. Even if a real person had been the germ of the legend, he certainly hadn't had any powers. He was probably just a shaman who was good at looking mysterious. He had parlayed that into a life of some prestige and a legend that had lasted until today. *That'll do,* Martin thought.

Sure, life in the Middle Ages probably wasn't very pleasant, but there was nothing saying he had to stay there. It was just a safe place to go and chill out. If it turned out to be a nightmare, he could always jump further forward in time until he found someplace he liked.

He did a little research. Very little. He didn't expect to ever use the Escape button. He just wanted to have the option. First he looked into the idea of trying to become Merlin himself. *Someone has to do it,* he thought. That idea died ignominiously within the first minute of his research. Nobody knew for sure when, where, for how long, or indeed if Merlin had lived. The one thing all of the scholars seemed to agree on was that if Merlin or any of the characters from the Arthur legend had existed, they probably did so in the sixth century, not a particularly pleasant time to be alive. Martin let that idea go. Instead, he ran a search for the phrase *the best time to live in Medieval England.* The third result in the list was a link to the Amazon page for a book entitled *The Best Years to Live in Medieval England,* by Gilbert Cox. Martin read the product description:

> In this, his seminal work, popular historian and television presenter Gilbert Cox makes his case that the period between 1140 and 1160, placed as they were, after the Battle of Hastings, before the Murder of Thomas Becket, and well before the Black Death, was the absolute best time to live in Medieval England.

Good enough for me, Martin thought. He split the difference and set the escape date for 1150, and the place for Dover, because the white cliffs were the only geological landmark in England he could think of. He considered Stonehenge, but he didn't want to materialize in the middle of a bunch of Druids.

It was only a precaution. He made the Escape button, but he hoped to never use it.

As it happened, he used it within forty-eight hours.

5.

Martin was happy to go back to work. After being cooped up in his apartment all weekend, thinking complicated thoughts and wrangling computer code, it was nice to get out and be around people, even if he was just doing data entry. He was still sitting at a computer, but it required no real thought, and he was alone in his cubicle, but that's not really being alone. It's just private enough to lure you into a false sense of security, and get you caught scratching yourself somewhere you shouldn't.

He drove to work, his car a sunny little island of calm in the middle of the swollen river of misery that was the morning commute.

Martin was done worrying about the philosophical implications of his discovery. He had finally come to see it like this: some say the universe was created by God, and we are powerless pawns to his whim. Some say the universe was created by random chance, and we are powerless specks in a vast, indifferent ocean. Martin could prove that the world was created by a computer program, which made no difference, because who created the program? God? Random chance? He hadn't answered the question, he had just pushed it back one step. The difference was that people weren't powerless pawns or powerless specks. People were powerless subroutines, or at least everyone was but Martin! Powerlessness didn't seem so bad when you only saw it in other people.

Martin had the easy air of a man with a plan. He would continue to live as he always had, but with no money problems and the ability to go wherever he wanted on his days off. He would live a life billionaires would envy. Total freedom and total anonymity, and the best part was that he didn't have to change anything. All he had to do was keep a low profile, and there was no profile lower than the one he already had. He would keep his current job, keep his current car, and keep his current apartment. None of them were great, but they could change in time. For now, the way forward was to stop all progress.

As he walked into the cubicle farm, it looked different to him. A week ago he saw it as a fluorescent-lighted, beige-walled abattoir for the human spirit where he had to spend most of his time. Now he saw it as a fluorescent-lighted, beige-walled abattoir for the human spirit where he *chose* to spend most of his time. It was like a corporate-drone fantasy camp.

He sat smiling at his desk, humming as he took papers from his inbox, entered the pertinent information from the form into the proper field of the database, then deposited the form in his outbox.

He went to the break room. A woman he had known for two years without learning her last name was staring at the water cooler. Her first name was Becky. She had a pale complexion and limp, dishwater-blond hair that somehow perfectly matched her faded, threadbare business suit. *In its way, it is a cohesive look,* Martin thought.

"How are you?" Martin asked.

"Bored," she replied.

Martin said, "I know, right? Everything about this place is breathtakingly dull, isn't it?"

"YES!" She looked around to see if anyone else was listening, but they were alone. "Have you ever found yourself hoping, just for a second, that you'll get into a car accident?"

"TOTALLY!" Martin said, louder than he'd intended. "Because it would be interesting!"

"Yeah, nothing where anybody got seriously hurt. I don't want that," she explained.

"No. Just hurt enough that you get to go to the Emergency Room."

"Hmmmm. Maybe ride in an ambulance and have two beefy guys in uniforms help me. A broken arm is the sweet spot. You need immediate attention, and you get out of work for a couple of weeks, but you're not debilitated or anything...." She trailed off, lost in her fantasy.

They stood in silence for a minute.

"Well," she said, "I have to go back to work."

"I guess you do," Martin said. "They don't pay us to stand around talking."

She smiled. She had a great smile. Martin had never seen it before. She said, "They certainly don't pay us enough to justify doing our jobs," as she left the break room.

And she's a manager, Martin thought. *If I work really hard, I might get promoted to her job someday.*

At noon, as everyone else was going to lunch, Martin was carrying a cardboard box full of his belongings out to the car. Quitting wasn't nearly as difficult as he'd imagined.

When his supervisor asked why he was going, Martin said, "I'd rather do something that makes me happy."

His former supervisor smiled the smile equivalent of a middle finger. "Well, with an attitude like that, we don't want you."

His plan was already destroyed, but Martin saw it was a stupid plan. Keep doing something that made him miserable so he could fit in with the miserable people. What he should have tried to do was find some happy people to fit in with. Maybe he could go back to school. He'd hated college so much that he'd dropped out, but that was when he believed his future was riding on it. Maybe now that he knew it was meaningless he'd enjoy it.

When he returned to his apartment, he saw it as if for the first time. White stucco walls and a beige carpet. If you looked at the floor in broad daylight, you could see the traffic pattern. Faint wear tracks traced the routes from the bed to the bathroom to the kitchen to the computer to the couch.

It was time for a lifestyle upgrade. He knew it wasn't necessary, but on a deeper level he knew he needed it. He'd been good, hadn't he? He'd known about the file for almost a week and he hadn't done anything with it to benefit himself. Yes, he had put eight thousand dollars into his bank account, but he could argue that he'd earned that money by discovering the means to procure it. Besides, he already had that money. Even if getting it was wrong, spending it now wasn't. It was just the logical conclusion of an act he did days ago. In a sense, it was already done. He made a quick mental list of things he wanted to replace. He figured eight thousand dollars would go pretty far.

A day later he reflected that it *had* gone pretty far. All the way to the checkout line at IKEA. He had carefully selected his purchases to stay under his eight thousand dollar budget, and had just managed it. Looking at the pile of flat-pack, he knew he couldn't carry it home in his car. He pulled out his phone, looked at his now single-digit bank balance, adjusted it up to five thousand dollars, and went to rent a truck. Sure, he could have waited for IKEA to deliver his furniture, but having so much stuff delivered at once to such a small apartment might have looked suspicious, and worse, would have required patience.

By five p.m., his new furniture was in his apartment waiting for assembly. His old furniture was sitting on the pavement behind a thrift store. The truck was returned to the rental agency. Martin settled in for a night of serious furniture assembling. He went to the closet and pulled out Her First Tool Kit. He looked at it in his hand.

By six p.m., Martin was back with his new tool kit, a massive metal case full of sockets, wrenches, screwdrivers, even a saw. He also had a drill he could use to drive screws.

As he assembled the furniture, he mused that unlimited money was like a superpower. It allowed one to do almost anything. Hire a plane to make you fly. Hire a truck to carry heavy things. Hire doctors to keep you healthy. Hire mercenaries to vanquish foes. You could pay someone to do anything, and at the end of the day, you were responsible for having gotten it done.

He still hadn't decided what to do with his life. He wanted it to be something of which he could be proud. Maybe he'd create a comic book. Hire a writer to flesh out his ideas. Hire an artist to draw it. "Rich Man: He Pays People to Serve Justice." It was an idea.

By 11 p.m., he was exhausted, and he slept without assistance for the first time in a week. The next morning he arranged his new furniture. He started installing his computer on his new desk. He put the 18-inch monitor on the desktop. He put the dusty CPU tower under the desk. He started to hook up the tangle of wires, then he laughed at himself for being so stupid.

The closest electronics store opened at eleven. At ten past he was walking to his car with a new high-end, all-in-one computer that looked like a huge monitor with a keyboard attached. Soon, it was hooked up and purring like a kitten, and his old computer was running a utility to completely erase the hard drive. He turned his attention to his entertainment center.

Martin looked at the large TV cabinet he had purchased, and the smallish TV he had owned for years. An hour and a half later he was pulling into his parking space with the new TV he'd bought at the second-closest electronics store (going back to the same one would have looked suspicious). He was so excited that he got careless removing the TV's box from the rear hatch, and ripped the headliner of his car. *Damn*, he thought, *I wonder how much that'll cost to fix.*

Buying a new car took longer than buying a new TV. He had saved some time by not making any attempt to negotiate. He'd simply excused himself to use the restroom and adjusted his bank account so he had the down payment. The dealership's sales team seemed stunned when he returned from the restroom and asked if they could hurry this up. He was proud that he had the forethought to get a payment plan. He could have paid cash, but that would look suspicious. This way, he was building a credit rating, which would make him look more normal on paper, and in the end it was all money he was creating out of nothing anyway. Who cared if the interest rate caused him to spend more of it?

Also, he could have gone nuts and bought a Ferrari or something, but he hadn't. He just got another bright-red hatchback. The sport model. It had a stripe, got to seventy-five miles per hour an eighth of a second faster, and the tires wore out faster while only costing twice as much to replace.

He drove home with a dopey grin on his face. He threw his jacket in a heap in the passenger seat and passed the time on his drive home playing with the car stereo at every red light.

Martin Banks felt pretty smart, right up until he pulled up to his parking space and saw two men in dark suits. Martin was startled, but reminded himself he had done nothing illegal (as far as he knew), and that there was no reason that these two men would be there for him. For all he knew, they wanted to tell him about God. He got out of the car and made eye contact with one of the men (it was pretty much unavoidable). The man smiled.

"Hello, Mr. Banks. Nice car."

Martin's heart clenched like a fist. His mouth went dry. He looked at the men as if through a long tunnel.

"Do you want to talk to me about God?" Martin asked.

"Not unless he paid for the car," the man answered.

6.

They took my phone, Martin thought. *It never occurred to me that if I got into trouble they would take my phone.*

Martin sat alone in an interrogation room that looked like it could have been made by the set designer from a bad TV show. The only thing that saved it from being a total cliché was that if this were a set, the chairs would look cooler. They'd be stainless steel or something. Instead he sat on a beat-up wooden chair that was probably older than he was. He was still wearing his weekend uniform: baggy cargo pants, faded polo shirt, and sneakers, although they had confiscated his belt and his shoelaces. Again, cliché.

The two men had introduced themselves as Special Agents Miller and Murphy, then informed Martin he was under arrest, cuffed him, and stuck him in their unmarked car, which Martin didn't mention was parked illegally. The ride to the station was horrible. Martin figured being under arrest and riding to a police station would always be horrible, but in his case it was worse than for the typical perp. He knew he could easily escape. All he had to do was get his phone out of his pocket, open the app, hit the button, and he'd be at home. He'd be handcuffed, but still, one problem at a time. He considered fleeing for a moment, but decided against it. Martin knew what he had done, and he knew it would be very difficult to prove, or even explain without sounding crazy. If, however, he disappeared from the back seat of a police car, that would be easy to explain.

We arrested him. We put him in the car. He escaped.

Martin figured that the method of escape would be seen as a minor detail, unless they somehow figured it out, in which case Martin suspected he'd spend several months answering questions and the rest of his life regretting the answers he'd given.

So Martin decided to bide his time, and was pretty happy with that decision right up until they booked him. The first step of the booking procedure was to remove his handcuffs, which he'd liked. The second step was for him to empty his pockets, and that was when Martin knew he was doomed. As reluctant as a man walking to the gallows, he handed over his wallet, his keys, and his phone. The rest of the booking procedure was a blur. Then they'd put him in a holding cell and let him sit there for about an hour. Now he was in the interrogation room.

Special Agents Miller and Murphy came in and sat across the table from Martin. Miller was tall and muscular, with a receding hairline. Murphy was average height and doughy, with unruly brown hair. They both looked happy. Miller silently read papers in a manila folder with Martin's name written theatrically on the tab.

Eventually Miller closed the folder and put it on the table.

"Mr. Martin Banks," he said, "we're going to ask you a few questions. The more quickly and more honestly you answer, the sooner we can all go home."

Martin considered this. "So, I may be going home tonight?"

"Oh definitely, Martin, you're going to go home tonight. But, bear in mind, jail might be your new home."

"Ah," Martin said.

Miller continued. "See, my partner Murph and I aren't from Seattle. Heck, until today Murph had never been to Seattle, isn't that right, Murph?"

"That's right."

"See, we had to fly up from L.A., on no notice, because of you. That's where we live. L.A. Hey Murph, why do you live in L.A.?

"Because I hate rain."

"*He hates rain,* Martin! So you can imagine how happy he was to have to come to Seattle in October! You happy, Murph?"

"Nah, I ain't happy."

"He's not happy, Martin! You got anything to say about that?"

Martin stammered. If he were any more off balance he'd be lying on his side. "I'm sorry?"

"Murph doesn't want your apology, Martin! He wants answers! If you answer Murph's questions well enough, we can go home tomorrow, and maybe get some sightseeing in before the flight. Would you like that, Murph?"

"Yeah, I'd like that."

"Murph wants to go sightseeing, Martin! Maybe see the Space Needle, or that market you got where they throw great big fish around for no reason. Murph's seen it on the Food Network about a thousand times."

"Oh," Martin said, mostly out of reflex, "if you do go to the fish market, right next to it there's a little shop that sells the best tiny donuts. You don't wanna miss out on that."

There was a silence so thick you could lean on it.

"Why," Special Agent Miller asked, almost too quietly to hear, "because we're cops?"

"NO!" Martin said, an edge of desperation in his voice. "They're just great donuts! A little machine makes them fresh, and they … give them to you … in a brown paper bag."

"Shut up about the donuts! Murph doesn't want your donuts! Murph wants you to answer his questions!"

"Then when's he going to ask a question?"

"Shut up, Martin! I'm asking the questions here!"

"That's kinda my point."

"Shut up! Shut up! *Shuuuuuut uuuup!*"

Miller sat down and panted for a while. Murphy just stared at Martin. Finally, Special Agent Miller continued.

"Look, kid. We're Treasury Agents. Until recently, we used to investigate bank fraud, and we were good at it."

"Too good," Murph said.

"That's right, Murph, too good. We were so good we got promoted to a special task force. A small task force. Elite, they call it. How many agents are on our task force again, Murph?"

"Two."

"Two agents: me and my partner, Murph. I'd say that's pretty freakin' elite. We investigate the bank fraud cases where nobody can figure out what the fraud was, even the bank that got defrauded. That means that before we can start solving a crime, we gotta figure out if there was a crime at all. That's why we're here, Martin. To try to figure out if you've committed a crime."

They sat in silence for a moment.

"Have you committed a crime, Martin?"

Another silent moment passed.

"No."

"Good! Glad to hear it," Miller said. "Perhaps you can tell us how you managed to put five separate sums of money, totaling more than twenty-three thousand dollars, in your bank account without making a deposit or a transfer."

Martin had never stopped to add up all of the cash he'd *created*. "Wow, that's a lot of money."

"Not really," Special Agent Miller said. "Normally, it takes more than a hundred thousand to get our attention. It was the number of times money just showed up that made the bank suspicious."

This news did not make Martin happier. *I'm screwed*, he thought. *The jig is up. All the way up. Even if I get out of this, they'll be watching me for the rest of my life. My best-case scenario is that I get to go back to my life the way it was, only now I'm unemployed and gave all of my furniture to Goodwill. At least I can buy it back for cheap. It won't come to that, though. They'll pin something on me. I'm going to prison. I can't see how I can get out of this.*

"So, you gonna tell us, Martin?"

Martin had been so absorbed in his misery he'd nearly forgotten the men in the room with him. "Pardon?" he asked, startled.

Special Agent Miller smiled. "My partner Murph and I were wondering if you'd tell us how you got all that money into your account without depositing, transferring, or even earning it, as near as we can tell."

Martin perked up instantly. "Oh! I'll do better than tell you. I'll show you! All I need is for you to bring me my smartphone."

Agent Murphy stood up, and with a bright smile, said, "Will do. I'll be right back."

7.

Martin materialized in his apartment with his thumb on his phone app's home button, the police evidence bag containing his wallet, belt, and shoelaces in his other hand, and a big smile on his face. The smile faded as he fell to the ground, again landing directly on his tailbone. He cursed himself for not having had the foresight to stand before he teleported. Luckily, the federal agents searching his apartment didn't see him fall. They only heard him hit the floor.

The agent sitting at Martin's desk searching the new computer slowly turned around. He and Martin made eye contact for a moment, then Martin sprinted out the front door. As he passed the bedroom, another agent peeked around the corner. Martin raced out the door and made for the parking lot, cornering as best he could in his unlaced sneakers. He was happy to see they hadn't towed his new car yet. He got in and tore out of the parking lot as quickly as he could, narrowly missing a bedraggled old man on a beat-up bicycle.

He knew where he was going, and happily, it was only a couple of miles away. That didn't leave him much time to think, but he'd have all the time he needed to think soon, possibly too much. Now was the time for action.

He looked in the rearview mirror and was not surprised to see two dark, unmarked cars with flashing lights concealed in their grilles closing on him. He sped up, not even entertaining the notion of getting away. He just needed to keep them from getting in front of him. Martin knew he was going to escape. Where he was going to escape to and where he was going to escape *from* were the questions.

He didn't want to teleport out of a moving car. He'd made a big enough mess without risking injuring or killing someone. He also didn't want to teleport with anyone watching. He knew that Murphy and Miller had likely recorded his first disappearing act, but one video of an inexplicable event, witnessed by the two men who made the video, and who would be embarrassed to have let a kid in his mid-twenties escape, would probably look suspect. If he also disappeared in a public place with multiple federal agents watching, that would be hard to explain away. Martin hoped he would get a moment of privacy to grab the things he needed and think about where he wanted to escape to.

Martin continued driving the speed limit. He figured that as long as he didn't seem to be a danger to anyone, his pursuers wouldn't risk public safety to stop him. Whatever he was going to do, he needed to do it quickly. The two unmarked cars were now accompanied by at least three squad cars, all with their lights flashing and sirens blaring. He was only a few blocks from his destination, and if he didn't do something to put some distance between him and his pursuers, he'd never get away.

Martin's shiny red hatchback led its loud, ugly parade through the quiet suburb where he grew up. Martin blew through a stop sign. A ticket for a moving violation was the least of his worries. He pictured his sentencing. Twenty years for bank fraud, followed by traffic school. *All the more reason not to get caught,* he thought.

He got an idea that he hated immediately, but it was the only idea he had. There was only one turn remaining before he reached his destination, a ninety-degree left onto the street where he grew up. He had always avoided using his phone while driving, but in this case he made an exception. He pulled up the app and hit the tab with the compass on it. The phone displayed a satellite map of his surroundings. He selected a spot fairly close to where he wanted to be. The final turn loomed. His thumb hovered over the screen as he floored the gas pedal of the brand new car and aimed it for a huge tree he used to walk past on the way to school each morning. He glanced at the phone in his right hand, making sure his thumb was going to hit the right spot. *If I time this right*, he thought, *I get away. If I don't, maybe they'll chalk it up to texting while driving.* The car jumped the curb, and in the last second before hitting the tree, his thumb hit the screen.

It was a workday in the suburbs, so nobody was outside to see Martin appear in the middle of the street in a seated position, suspended a foot off the ground. Martin fell straight down to the road beneath him. Again, his weight landed on his still-healing tailbone. As he fell, he heard the surprisingly hollow crunching noise of his car hitting a tree two blocks away.

He scrambled to his feet and peered into the distance. He saw what was left of his car wrapped around the base of the tree. He smiled as he saw the police vehicles pull up to the wreck, all sense of urgency drained out of them. The federal agents who had torn his apartment to shreds stepped out of the black, unmarked cars and ran to the crumpled wreck to see if Martin needed a doctor or a coroner. Martin's happiness didn't last long. It was shattered by a blasting car horn from behind him. He spun and saw a green minivan approaching. He had forgotten that he was standing in the middle of the road.

He lunged to the side of the road, looked back to the wreck, and his worst fears were realized. The agents heard the horn, and had clearly recognized Martin even at this distance. They were pointing in his direction and scrambling back into their cars. The minivan's driver, a mousy woman with a pinched face, gave Martin the stink-eye as she drove past, but Martin never knew it. He was already sprinting across a yard and into a specific house, his chosen destination.

＋══════＋

Walter Banks sat on a large sofa in the living room of his home, a split-level ranch in the suburbs of Seattle. He was watching a rerun of an old sitcom. Back when he was working, he thought the show wasn't worth his time. Now that he and his wife were retired (him from Boeing, her from a desk job at the school district), and the kids were grown and out of the house, he had more time to spend on TV shows. This, he was learning, was not a good thing. He didn't know the name of the show he was watching, but he did know that it adhered to the standard sitcom template. Below-average-looking guy, married to stunningly beautiful woman, is unhappy.

His wife, Margarita (who was roughly equal to him in attractiveness, but who had made him very happy) was in the kitchen, doing whatever it was she was doing this week. If you asked her what her hobby was, she'd call it crafting. Crafting was a broad term, and every week she had some new thing she was making out of some new thing he wasn't allowed to throw away anymore, or which he had to go to the craft store and buy with her. They'd stand in the aisle of Styrofoam balls, which was next to the aisle of big sheets of cardboard, and across from the aisle of fake ficus trees. It was the ficus trees that confused him. *What could anyone possibly make out of those?*

TV wasn't holding his interest, so Walter went to see what his wife was up to. She was sitting at the kitchen table with her back to the entryway. A large part of the table was covered with newspaper. On the newspaper, blobs of white clay were sitting, spaced evenly. As he got closer, he was confused by what he saw. He kissed his wife on the top of the head.

"Margarita, what are you doing?"

She turned and showed him what she was working on. "I'm sculpting little geoduck clams! We can send them to our friends who live in other parts of the country. A little piece of the Northwest," she said, holding up the one she was working on so Walter could appreciate it.

Walter asked, "That's a clam?"

"It's not done yet. I'm doing the necks first, and when they're dry, I'll do the shells."

In the distance, they both heard the sound of multiple sirens, getting louder very quickly. Walter walked toward the front window to see what was going on, but got only two steps before they heard the hollow crunch of a collision. Walter went to the window and started to open the curtains, but the front door burst open, and their youngest son Martin burst into the house. Martin slammed the door shut and locked the deadbolt. He had a plastic bag in one hand.

"Son…" was all Walter had time to say before Martin had spun around and hugged him so firmly that it squeezed the breath out of him.

"Dad! Mom! I need you to know two things," Martin said. He released his father from the vise-like hug and advanced on his mother. He paused, confused at what his mother was holding, then hugged her much more gently than he had his father. "Just remember, I love you, and it isn't true."

He released his mother and walked toward the hall that led to his old bedroom.

"It's not true that you love us?" His mother said, in a quiet, confused voice.

"What? No! I love you. Something else isn't true."

"What isn't true?" his father asked. He had to shout, as the sirens were very loud now.

Martin looked at the front window. He saw the color of the police lights filtering through the drawn curtains. He said, "You'll see soon enough." He took one last look at his parents, then said, "I'll be in my room." He walked into his boyhood bedroom and closed the door behind him.

Martin felt bad for dragging his parents into this, but he knew they'd be fine. No evidence tied them to anything illegal, because there was no evidence of anything illegal. He'd securely wiped his old computer, and he hadn't done anything with the new one. He was taking his phone with him. His parents could afford a lawyer if it came to that, but there might still be a way to keep them from needing one. He needed time to think.

Peeking out the window of his old bedroom, which looked out on the front yard, it was clear he'd get no time to think here. The two unmarked cars and three squad cars were crowding the street, lights flashing. The agent who had been monkeying with his computer saw Martin through the window and smiled. Martin wrenched the curtains closed. His eyes darted around the room.

He dove for the closet. Any second he'd hear the agents pounding on the front door, and then he'd only have a few moments of freedom left. He saw what he was looking for in the closet and he snatched it up, tucking it under his arm with his wadded-up jacket.

Well, here goes, he thought. *Soon, I'll have all the time to think I need.*

As quickly as one would rip off a bandage, or jump into the deep end of a cold swimming pool, Martin pulled out his phone, opened the app, and pressed the Escape button.

8.

In the distance near the horizon, a bank of clouds was casting a shadow over what Martin couldn't quite believe was France. Here, though, the sky was a pale blue with only a few clouds thrown in as if to add texture. The sea roared as the sea always did, but it was a distant, hollow sound. Distant, because despite the fact that this spot was only a hundred feet or so from the edge of the land, the actual point where sea met sand was at the base of a dizzying, chalk-white cliff.

Here, on top of the cliff, a steady breeze blew the wild scrub grass and forced the sea birds to work for every inch of progress they made. On one side the horizon was nothing but clouds and sea. On the other, the horizon was all gentle rolling hills and trees. Martin would have found it all very restful, if he hadn't known he was so utterly screwed.

He sat on the ground right there where he had materialized and allowed himself to freak out. He alternated between panic, tears, and shame, waves of each rolling over his brain in random order and for indeterminate stretches of time.

More than anything, he felt stupid. So very stupid. All he'd had to do was lie low. That was the whole plan. Two words. Lie low. So simple, but clearly too complicated for him.

After a while, he started thinking instead of just feeling. He was in a mess. The first order of business was to figure out how to fix it. He listed his problems.

No job.

No cash.

Bank account almost certainly frozen.

Wanted by the police.

Parents aware of the first four items on this list.

No food.

No shelter.

Exiled to Medieval England.

That established, he tried to prioritize the problems in order from least to greatest, and then spent an indeterminate amount of time feeling panic, shame, and sorrow again.

Clearly, choosing which problem was worst was not productive. Instead, he tried to figure out which was the most urgent, which clarified things. He needed food, and he needed shelter. All of the other problems were part of one big ball of problems. If he could make the ball of problems go away, the food and shelter issues would be a piece of cake, but he didn't know how to do that.

His first impulse was to go back to his apartment, before the chain reaction of stupid decisions started, but he didn't think that would work. What would he tell himself? "Be careful, or you'll screw this up?" Past-him already knew that. In fact, he remembered thinking almost those exact words. Also, if he were going to go to the future to warn past-him, wouldn't he have already done it? When he went back in time to tell himself to go back in time, and to play poker, his first experience of it was of seeing himself appear from the future, not of getting the idea to go to the past. If at any point in the future he were going to go warn himself, at some point before now he would have been warned by himself.

Martin was angry with himself for not stopping himself from doing the stupid things he had done. He knew this was not rational, but he was beginning to suspect that rational thought was not his strong suit.

For whatever reason, warning himself was not an option. He'd have to find some other way to fix the mess he'd left behind in the future, and since he had no idea what that would be, he'd have to bide his time here, in the past. That made the food and shelter problems clearly stand out from the rest, and for some reason, that made Martin feel better. Also, he didn't have to worry about messing up the space-time continuum, because if he was going to, he already had, long before he was even born.

Okay, he thought, *I know what my problems are. What are my assets?*

He had his clothes. This was not a promising start, but there it was. His shoes were still unlaced. He dug the laces out of the plastic evidence bag Agent Murphy had handed him when he'd asked for his phone. As he laced his shoes, he continued down the list. He had his clothes. He had a jacket. He had his phone. He had his wallet, full of plastic cards that were useless except as bookmarks. He had his car keys, which were equally useless here and in the future, now that the car was totaled.

He could stay in this time, go back to his time, or try any time in between. He could transport anywhere on the globe, but he'd have to be careful. He had picked the White Cliffs of Dover because they would be there. They had existed for millions of years, so they were a safe landing zone. Even that wasn't quite true, he saw. He had picked a landing spot about thirty feet from the cliff edge, but he had materialized over a hundred feet away. This might have been an error, or continental drift, or perhaps the cliff had eroded. Maybe it was a bit of all three. In any case, Martin couldn't guarantee that any geological feature would be where his mapping program said it was. He had considered picking a mountain peak as a landing zone, and now he was glad he hadn't. Imagine materializing in midair, thirty feet to the left of the peak. He shuddered at the idea. He could still teleport anywhere, but he'd need to be careful.

He was in Medieval England, which was both a problem and an asset. He had chosen this time and place as his escape hatch because he spoke English, and the people believed in magic. He could hover and teleport to prove his so-called powers. Heck, the phone itself would look like magic. He could just show it to people and they'd be convinced. His clothes would look strange. His manner would seem strange, and his English wouldn't be quite the same as the local dialect, which might just make him seem otherworldly. He had the plastic bag the agents had put his belongings in. The locals certainly would never have seen anything like that.

Lastly, he had the thing he'd rushed home for, aside from seeing his parents one last time. He held it up to look at it, and was delighted that in his senior year he'd chosen to go to a Halloween party as Draco Malfoy from the Harry Potter movies. At the time it was just an excuse to bleach his hair, which hadn't worked out, but now he had a dark robe with a snake sewn on it, and a magic wand. He tried the robe on. He'd gained weight since high school, but the robe wasn't too tight. Well, it was too tight, but it wasn't *too* too tight.

He turned his back to the ocean and started walking. The plan was to find people, convince them he was a wizard, get food and shelter, then lie low while he made a plan. It was a simple plan, and it would work this time. He knew how *not* to do it.

Yes sir, he thought, *I'll just lie low. First step: find a bunch of people and convince them I have magic powers.*

9.

After an hour of walking, Martin crested a small hill. He hadn't covered as much ground as he'd hoped. Walking through wilderness, even when it's devoid of trees, takes more time and effort than walking on a sidewalk. He was irritated that nobody had ever mentioned this fact to him, but after some thought he realized that people who walked in undeveloped areas in his time did so mostly for fun, and if that was the case, having to spend more time doing it wouldn't be something they'd complain about.

It was getting late in the afternoon. Soon it would be evening, and while he knew that people had slept outdoors for millennia, he'd never done it himself. He had no idea what could attack him in the night, but he'd seen enough movies to have some ideas. Wolves. Highwaymen. Evil queens. He spent a lot of time thinking about being attacked by an evil queen. It actually didn't sound so bad. At any rate, he did not like the idea of spending the night outdoors. He knew that if things got really bad he could go back to his own time, but he was still in big trouble there. Here, he was alone, tired, and hungry, but at least he wasn't being actively pursued. Besides, if things didn't start to look up here, he had all the rest of history to go to. He figured he'd give this time and place a shot and see how he liked it.

He squared his jaw, and thought, *Martin Banks: Time Tourist.*

He reached the top of the hill and saw what might be a road in the distance, near the tree line. He figured it would take another hour at least to reach it. He could see a long way, and there were no other people anywhere. He pulled out his phone, made a quick estimate of the distance to the road, and a few seconds later he was standing in the middle of it. *This was more like it.*

The road was a set of two ruts that had been reinforced enough to effectively become one large rut. In one direction the road disappeared into the woods. In the other it continued in open grassland along the edge of the woods, allowing Martin to see nearly a half-mile of empty road. He didn't know which direction would lead him to a village first, but he did know which direction he could travel more easily. A few seconds later, he was a half mile down the road.

He spent the next half hour leapfrogging huge chunks of land. There were a lot of large, clear sections of road he could teleport past. In a few places the road disappeared around a bend, but he'd see it reemerge in the distance, so he'd jump to that spot, cutting who knew how much distance from his journey.

He was getting discouraged that he hadn't seen any other people when in the distance he saw what appeared to be two men on horseback riding towards him. They were still hundreds of yards away. He started walking toward them. He hoped to at least find out how far he was from the nearest village. As the distance between them slowly closed he could see more detail. They were either men or powerfully unattractive women. They had swords. *Honest-to-God SWORDS!* He could tell they had seen him. They didn't seem concerned. They weren't speeding up at all, and neither was Martin, but the distance between them seemed to be closing much faster than before, and each second brought new, unwelcome details. Their clothes were made primarily of leather and a fabric that looked scratchy. The colors were mottled, and by mottled he meant stained. The worst part was that they were both smiling.

Martin knew that if they tried anything, he could hit the Escape button again, and it would take him back to the cliffs, but all of his progress would be lost. He opened the app, hoping he wouldn't need it. He'd lived in the city long enough to know that to show any fear was the absolute worst thing he could do. He forced himself to smile and to walk faster toward the two.

As he got closer, their smiles faded. *Maybe they think I'm gonna attack them,* he thought. *I'm wearing a wizard robe.* He didn't want them to attack preemptively. He meant them no harm. He only wanted information about the nearest village. Martin decided to act friendly.

"Hello!" Martin yelled, waving casually with his right hand, but holding his phone with the left, his thumb hovering over the Escape button.

The men leaned in closer and spoke to each other. They were about a hundred feet away now, and could really get a good look at Martin. Martin could also see them. He noticed that the two men shared three eyebrows and three working eyes between them, but the distribution was not uniform. They stopped their horses.

Maybe hello *was too modern a word,* Martin thought. *They don't know what it means. I should be careful what I say.* He tried to remember how people greeted each other in ye olde times.

"Hey! Hail! Greetings!" he yelled, waving energetically.

The two men seemed unnerved. They glanced at each other, then spurred their horses to an instant gallop. They passed

Martin, giving him as much room as they could without riding into the woods.

"Salutations! Um, well met! What-ho!"

The man who passed closest to Martin (one eye, two eyebrows) gritted his also non-traditional number of teeth and dug his heels into the horse's flanks again. Once they were past him, the men fled at top speed. Martin turned to watch them go, and saw that a horse-drawn wagon was approaching him from behind. *It must have been in a part of the road I bypassed,* he thought.

The two men passed the wagon without giving it any apparent thought. Martin watched the wagon's approach, wondering if the driver would be afraid of him too. The wagon was drawn by a single horse, and there appeared to be a single driver with no passengers. The driver seemed small and was wearing a hood. He couldn't see if anything was in the back of the wagon, which stopped ten feet short of Martin.

At least this guy doesn't seem scared of me, Martin thought. *I wonder what his eye to eyebrow ratio will be.*

The driver removed her hood and said, "Good day."

She had brown hair, roughly but not inexpertly cut to shoulder length, and wide-spaced brown eyes. Martin noted a lack of makeup, which seemed odd to him until he took a half second to think about it. *I'm going to have to get used to that,* he thought. Her cloak was like a large hooded poncho, but with sleeves. It was charcoal gray over a long skirt the color of oatmeal. All of her clothes looked very soft and very warm. She was making eye contact, and was smiling, which he found promising. Her teeth were whiter and straighter than he'd expected a medieval wench's teeth to be.

"Uh, good day!" Martin replied, then stared at her for a moment, unsure what to say next. The woman stared back.

During his walk, Martin had thought about what demeanor he should maintain with the people he met in this time. He had settled on wise, mysterious, and commanding. In short, *wizardly.* This was his first chance to give it a shot.

"Good lady," he said, in a voice that was louder than he'd intended, "is there a town or a village nearby?"

She continued to look him square in the eye and smile while considering her answer. Eventually she said, "Aye."

"Ah," Martin said. He looked back down the road the way he came, then looked up the road the direction he was heading. "Is it far?"

She said, "No, I expect to be there before dark."

Martin looked at her horse and wagon. The horse was smallish, but seemed healthy. The wagon looked primitive but sturdy, with wheels that were solid wood disks. Most important, the horse and the cart were both pointing in a specific direction. He pointed the same way. "The village is this way, then?"

"Aye."

"All right then. I guess I'll see you there. Okay. Um. Good evening."

Martin took a step. The woman said, "Would you like to ride with me? The road can be dangerous, and I would not mind the company of a wizard."

Well, now we're finally getting somewhere! he thought as he pulled himself up onto the bench next to her. The cart started moving. It was not a smooth ride, but it was far better than walking. He decided to try to listen more than he talked. He wanted to take in information, not give it away, but the young woman driving the cart seemed content to ride in silence. She was still smiling. She just wasn't talking. There was information Martin needed, and if he was going to get it, he'd have to start the conversation.

"How did you know I'm a wizard?"

"That is a wizard's robe, is it not?" she asked, not turning to look at him.

"Indeed! Indeed it is! Yes," he said. "Indeed."

They lapsed back into silence. After a time, Martin decided to try again.

"I appreciate your offering me this ride, but aren't you at all afraid to be in the presence of a wizard such as myself?"

"No. If we are attacked, you'll likely be quite useful," she said, still staring straight ahead.

"Oh, I understand why you'd be less afraid *with* me, but aren't you at all afraid *of* me?"

"Nay," she said, "I'm just a seamstress and tailor. I have nothing to interest a wizard, just needles and thread. And I needn't worry about you ravishing me. Everyone knows wizards are celibate."

Martin didn't like hearing that. He changed the subject. "So, what can you tell me about the village we're going to?"

"It's the place where I live. It's not a mere village, but a good-sized town. Leadchurch, it's called. I'm sure you've heard of it. It's quite famous."

"No," Martin said, remembering to use his grandiose voice. "I've not heard of it. I'm new to this land."

"Oh, interesting," she said, taking her eyes from the road to look at him for the first time since the ride began. "Where are you from?"

Time to try the cover story, he thought.

"The east," he said. "You said Leadchurch was famous. What for?"

"The church, of course. 'Tis a fine church, clad entirely in precious metal."

"What precious metal?" Martin asked, his curiosity piqued.

"Lead. What else? A precious metal indeed! Most useful! We had to import it from the north country. Pilgrims come from far and wide to gaze upon the church at high noon. It's a dazzling sight. The grayest thing you've ever seen. Some mark its exterior with their thumbnail. Children often lick its surface, but we try to discourage that."

"So, is there much work for a wizard in Leadchurch?"

She mulled this over. "I'd say so. Mind you, there's a wizard in Leadchurch already, but if you can prove your magic is equal to his, I bet you can keep food in your belly."

"Splendid! I can't wait to see it." He paused. "I'm sorry. I haven't introduced myself. My name is Martin."

"And I'm Gwen," she replied.

They came to the edge of town. It was the most abrupt town edge Martin had ever seen. There was nothing but sparse woods, then a meadow, then a tight grouping of rough-hewn buildings with thatched roofs. Some had timber frames; others seemed to be made from piles of stone. Gwen stopped the wagon in front of a very noisy two-story building. There was a sign hanging over a door that had a painting of a tree stump.

"This is where we part, Martin." Gwen said, turning to face him. "This is The Rotted Stump. Here you'll find food, a bed, and plenty to keep you entertained. If you ever need any new garments made, or alterations to your robe, please keep me in mind." She reached into the bed of the wagon and produced a long stick with marks cut in it at regular intervals. She held it up to his arm, clearly measuring his sleeve.

He thanked her and climbed down out of the wagon. His feet had barely touched the ground when she pulled away.

The town looked exactly as he expected a medieval English town to look, except much more pleasant. The road was not a sea of mud, but a sort of large, loose gravel. He suspected that on a rainy day it got a little sloppy, but not much worse than some country driveways he'd seen. The buildings were small and made of wood, stone, and thatch, but they weren't shanties. There was even some glass, which surprised Martin.

The lack of lighting was the main thing that differentiated them from modern buildings.

Dusk was fading into night, and there was light in the windows, but it was dimmer and more uneven than he was used to. It looked like the entire town was having a romantic evening in. The people walking the streets seemed healthy and happy. No obvious cases of severe scoliosis. People weren't scurrying in fear. It was a normal town, full of normal people, living without technology.

Martin turned to face the inn. He listened to the sounds. Lively chatter was coming from the building, but he heard no anger or violence in the sound, which was reassuring. He took a moment to get his thoughts in order, then entered the inn.

10.

At first glance, the inn was everything Martin expected, but different. It was dark, but not grim. All of the light came from candles, but there were a lot of them. The tables and chairs were similar to what he would call picnic tables and benches, but still, totally recognizable to his modern eyes. There was a bar, but it was more of an extra-large table. The bartender was a heavy man in a dirty tunic. His right arm was missing just above the elbow. On his bar there was a wooden box with rough metal hinges. The cashbox, Martin assumed. Next to the barkeep's stool, there was a barrel with the lid on, but slightly askew, and the handle of a metal ladle sticking out.

The customers were mostly men (though not by a very big margin), mostly large (and that included the women), and mostly drunk, but there were no fights in progress, and no sense of menace. *It's just a bar,* Martin thought. He felt comfortable enough to continue.

Martin said, "Excuse me," in a loud, clear voice. All sound ceased instantly and every head turned to look at him. Someone groaned.

"I'm sorry to interrupt your evening," Martin continued, "but I just wanted to let you all know that I'm a powerful wizard."

The bartender turned to a young boy standing near the barrel and said, "You'd best get Phillip." The boy nodded and sprinted out the back door.

"Who's Phillip?" Martin asked.

"Local wizard. He'll want to welcome you." The barman replied. Martin heard a few quiet chuckles from the back of the room. He was pleased, though. This charlatan who was calling himself a wizard would come in, spout some mumbo-jumbo and do some stupid trick. Then Martin would show them real magic. He'd start small, show them the plastic bag, then move on to the smartphone. If he needed the big guns, he'd levitate, but he didn't want to use that if he didn't have to.

"So, you wanted us to know that you're a wizard. Now we know. What of it?"

"I was thinking that if I demonstrate my powers, you might give me food and a place to sleep for the night."

"Hmmmm." The barman stroked his stubbly chin with his left (and only) hand as he rose and walked to Martin. "Interesting offer you make, young master wizard. I'd think if I were a powerful wizard, I'd offer to *not* demonstrate my powers if I was given what I want, if you see what I mean."

"I'm not trying to threaten anyone!" Martin said.

"And you haven't! You've just barged in and asked for free room and board without doing us the courtesy of threatening us with your magic."

"I'm sorry," Martin sputtered.

"As well you should be. You don't just prance into an inn and demand free food and a bed simply because of who you are. It's not done! Look at Gert." The bartender turned to the back of room. "Gert, come 'ere."

A woman at the back of the room took a long time getting up from her seat. She rose at normal speed, but there was so much of her that it still took a long time. Once she was up, she walked quickly to where Martin and the innkeeper stood. Again, she moved at normal speed, but her stride was so long it took only a few steps. Gert smiled benevolently and put a hand on Martin's shoulder. The sheer weight of it made Martin squirm. She was all muscle—her fingers were stronger than most men's arms. Martin looked up into her mammoth eyes. They looked sad. The look in her eyes said that she would not enjoy hurting Martin, and she would not enjoy it soon.

"Are you looking at Gert?" the innkeeper asked.

"Yes, sir, I am."

"Good. It might not surprise you to learn that some people used to call her Big Gert. People stopped eventually though. As they say, 'Res ipsa loquitur.' Latin, that is. Means 'The thing speaks for itself.' By the way, people also used to call Gert *the thing*. Anyway, Gert is the only person who eats and drinks for free here at The Rotted Stump. Would you like to know why?"

Martin didn't know how to answer. Pete saw his uncertainty and clarified, "You would find out by me telling you a story, not by Gert demonstrating her methods."

"Oh," Martin blurted. "Then yes, I'd like to know."

The innkeeper explained, "One day, Gert comes in here and announces, much like you did, that she wants food and a bed. And like you, Gert has powers. Far less mysterious powers than you claim, but powers nonetheless. Where Gert's approach differed from yours is that she just went ahead and demonstrated her power. She demonstrated her power on that table." The innkeeper pointed at a heavy oak table that had been broken in half, then crudely braced and nailed back together. "Then she threatens to continue demonstrating until I give her what she wants. It's in my interest to keep Gert happy by feeding her. It's in Gert's

interest to keep me happy by not causing me trouble, and not letting anyone else cause me trouble. Do you mean to cause trouble,
young wizard?"

"No," Martin said, still looking up at the face of Gert, "I won't
cause trouble. But I can show you something you've never seen,
something that will amaze. That's gotta be worth dinner and a bed."

The innkeeper smiled. "If you can show me something that
will persuade me to give you free food and a bed that isn't you
smashing an oak table with one blow, I will indeed be amazed."

They laughed openly. Gert went back to her seat. The innkeeper stood aside. Everyone was watching Martin to see what
he'd do next.

"Good people!" Martin declared, surreptitiously reaching his
left hand into his pocket. "Customers of The Rotted Stump, mark
this moment well, for one day you will gather your grandchildren
'round and tell them of the day the great wizard Martin the Magnificent showed you ... cloth you can see through!"

He produced the evidence bag from his pocket with a flourish, holding it above his head with both hands. All laughter
stopped. The customers slowly approached Martin and the plastic bag. They had never seen anything like it. He lowered it so
they could get a good look.

"I'll hand it to you, lad," the innkeeper said, examining the
plastic as Martin held it tight. "That is something."

An old man poked at the bag with the end of his pipe, watching it deform under pressure. "Will it hold off water?"

"Yes," Martin said. "It lets light through, but it keeps water out!"

The innkeeper gave Martin a searching look. "Can you make
more?"

"Yes!" Martin said. "I can!"

"I'll tell you what. If you'll make more of this, say a few square yards, you'll have a place to sleep tonight."

"You'll trade room and board for the see-through fabric?"

"No. But I'll lend you a stick and you can make a tent."

A slightly raised voice called out from the door. "Hello, Pete, I'm told I may be of some assistance."

All eyes turned to the door. There stood a man of average height and slightly heavy build. He had a neatly trimmed beard, keen eyes, and the bearing of a man who knew exactly what he was doing. He wore a flowing powder-blue robe with flared sleeves, which was by far the cleanest garment in the building, and a pointed hat that matched the robe perfectly. He held a polished wood staff. At the top of the staff, lashed with twine, there was a curved bottle full of some thick, red fluid, stopped with a cork.

"Aye, Phillip. Thanks for coming," the innkeeper said, smiling. "I believe an introduction is in order. Lad, Phillip here is a powerful wizard and friend of the house, the house being me. Phillip, this lad claims to be a powerful wizard, and suggests that I should give him dinner and bed."

Phillip the wizard bowed. "Always a pleasure to meet another practitioner of the unknowable arts! You have the advantage of me. I am Phillip. What's your name?"

Damn right I have the advantage of you, Martin thought. He had this "wizard" figured out. The friendly words, the confident demeanor, the impressive robe, it was all classic con artist stagecraft.

"Says his name is Martin the Magnificent," Pete the innkeeper said, before Martin could respond.

"Ah, very pleased to meet you, Martin." The wizard bowed again, more deeply. His eyes caught the plastic bag. "Oh, my! What is this?!"

"He calls it *see-through cloth*," Pete said, again cutting Martin off. "Says he made it."

"Indeed!" the wizard said, his eyes wide with wonder. "Might I please see it more closely, Martin?"

Martin didn't want to hand him the plastic bag. Who knew if he'd give it back? He could always zip back to modern times and get more plastic, but if this Phillip person made off with the bag, he'd have given the charlatan another tool to use in conning these rubes into believing he was a wizard. Martin didn't want that on his conscience. He held the bag up closer to Phillip, but kept a tight grip.

Phillip smiled and poked at the plastic with his forefinger a few times. "Impressive! Clearly, you are a wizard of prodigious power, Martin. Tell me, can you make more?"

"Don't bother telling him to make himself a tent, 'cause I already did," Pete said.

"I was sure you'd already covered that, Pete. No, I just wanted to see him produce more of this wondrous material. It's always a pleasure to see another wizard work. Perhaps I might learn something. How about it, Martin? You made this cloth you can see through. Can you make more?"

"Of course I can make more! Any time I want!" Martin said.

"Splendid!"

"But I can't do it while people are watching."

This caused some laughter, but Phillip raised a single hand and silenced it instantly. "Of course I understand. There are things we wizards are required to do that are not for others' eyes to see. It was unfair of me to ask that he conjure more transparent cloth right here in front of us."

Martin exhaled, happy that he had dodged that bullet.

"We shall have to find him a private place in which to work."

Gert threw Martin into a small room filled with casks and slammed the door behind him. It was dark, humid, and musty. Beyond the door Martin could hear the wizard and the innkeeper, his captors, talking.

"He'll have no light in there."

"Oh, he shouldn't need any. They are called the dark arts, after all."

"And what if he can't produce any more of the cloth you can see through?"

"That would mean he's a liar. So, naturally, we take all of his belongings, smear him with dung, and chase him out of town."

Martin had a vision of himself in filthy, torn clothing, fleeing into the woods while Phillip went through his former belongings and happened across his smartphone. It was an awful thought, but Martin knew it would not come to that. Of course, he could just teleport out of here, but then what? No, he had to demonstrate that he was a wizard and shut up this con man. Once that was done, things would be much easier.

Martin turned on the smartphone. Its screen lit up the room.

"I think I see a faint glow under the door!" The innkeeper's muffled voice exclaimed.

"See," the wizard said. "I think we'll find this Martin is quite resourceful."

You don't know the half of it, Martin thought.

✦━●━✦

Walter and Margarita Banks stood, bewildered, in the kitchen of their house in suburban Seattle. Their youngest son Martin had just burst in, hugged them both, and told them, "Just remember, I love you, and it isn't true."

As Martin walked toward his old bedroom Margarita asked, "It's not true that you love us?"

Martin stopped. "What? No! I love you. Something else isn't true."

"What isn't true?" Walter asked.

Martin said "You'll see soon enough. I'll be in my room," and retreated to his bedroom, closing the door firmly behind him.

Margarita and Walter looked at each other, confused. They heard sirens, which were getting louder. Walter slowly started walking toward Martin's room.

"Son," he said, loud enough to be heard through the door. "Are you in some kind of trouble?"

He was almost to the door when it burst open. Martin ran out of the door and back to the kitchen. For some reason he was wearing that stupid robe from his Halloween costume when he was in high school.

Martin ran to the drawer next to the kitchen sink.

"Martin, what's going on?" Margarita asked.

Martin held up a package of cling film. "Do you have any heavy duty? This stuff's too flimsy."

"In the cupboard under the sink. Why are you wearing your Snape costume?" Margarita had to yell; the sirens were very loud

now, as if the police cars had parked on the front lawn, which
they had.

Martin muttered, "It's Malfoy. You always get that wrong,"
as he threw open the cupboard, grabbed two boxes of heavy-
duty cling film, and silently thanked his parents for shopping at
a discount warehouse. He then went back to his old room. He
shouted, "Thanks, Mom!" and closed his bedroom door just as he
heard someone pounding on his parents' front door.

Back in the storeroom of The Rotted Stump, Martin caught his
breath. He felt a fresh pang of guilt over the stress he was causing
his parents. He knew that to them it had been less than a minute
since he burst in their front door, but to him it felt like his parents' home had been under siege by federal agents for several
hours. There was nothing he could do about that now, though.
He had problems of his own.

Working by the dim light of his phone's screen, Martin
opened the two boxes of heavy-duty cling film. He set the rolls
aside while he methodically tore and folded the cardboard boxes
so they could be hidden in his pockets. He doubted they'd be
of use, and he didn't think the people of this time would know
what to make of them, but it felt foolish to leave any evidence
lying around.

Martin stood up and spread his arms. He was wearing his
light jacket under his robe, and when he raised his arms the robe
billowed outward from his sides exactly as he'd hoped. He picked
up one of the rolls of cling film and pulled about a yard of the
film off of the roll. He did not tear the exposed film off. Instead,

he scrunched it into a sort of loose rope and fed it through the arm of his robe. He put the roll of film in the left exterior pocket of his jacket where it would be hidden beneath his robe. He held up his left hand. He could see an inch of the cling film extending out of the cuff. With his other hand he tugged it, and with some effort the film fed smoothly off of the roll and out his sleeve. He fed the excess back into his sleeve. Martin giggled fiendishly as he put the second roll in his right jacket pocket and fed the film through his right sleeve.

Pete, Gert, and Phillip heard a knock on the storeroom door. Pete released the catch and swung the door open. Martin Banks didn't say a word. He acted like he didn't notice they were there. He walked back to the front of the inn's main room and held his arms aloft, with the backs of his hands facing the assembled audience. All conversation stopped.

"I, Martin the Magnificent, the most powerful wizard in the ... place, have been challenged to prove my prowess by producing more of the cloth you can see through. Before I continue, I ask the one called Phillip, can you produce the see-through cloth?"

Phillip stood smiling at the side of the room, next to Gert and Pete. "No, Martin, I admit I cannot. I look forward to watching you do so, that I might learn something of your methods. The day we stop learning is the day we stop living."

Yeah, you're about to learn, you fraud, Martin thought.

"SO BE IT!" Martin bellowed. "I will need two volunteers!"

The audience shrank away from him and tried to avoid eye contact, because that's what audiences do.

Martin said, "You! Yes, you. No, not him, you. Come on, I won't hurt you. Oh, all right then, how about you? No? Come on, I just need two people to help. Okay, you two. Yes, right here in front. Yeah, look at me. Okay, don't worry, you don't even have to get up. Look, just stay there. I'll tell you what to do."

With that settled, Martin again raised his arms with the backs of his hands facing the crowd. "If it's the see-through cloth you want, and proof of my power you require, then I present you with both! BEHOLD!" He put his hands together over his head, grabbed the two stubs of film that were poking out of his sleeves and pulled them, spreading his arms. The crowd murmured. He extended his arm to the two volunteers in the front row, offering them the loose ends of film which extended from his hands. "Pull them, my friends. Pull them!"

The two men pulled on the cling film, handing the excess to the people around them as it emerged from his sleeves. Martin kept up the patter to help sell the illusion. "Yes, pull! Behold! Pull and behold! I produce the see-through fabric as a spider spins silk, only I do so from my hands, not my abdomen!" By the time the rolls ran out, the entire room was draped with wrinkled cling film. The audience examined the film, tugging it to test its strength and trying to pull it flat to look through it.

Phillip looked delighted and Martin was confused. Phillip approached Martin, clapping his hands. "Well done! I honestly don't think it would have ever occurred to me to do that. I really am impressed!" He shook Martin's hand vigorously. "I see a great future for you here. Look, forget getting dinner and a bed from Pete. You'll just end up with fleas, and that's from the dinner."

"Hey!" Pete objected.

"You know it's true," Phillip said, still shaking Martin's hand. "Come stay with me. I've got plenty of room and a big pot of stew. I think we have a lot to talk about."

Martin wrenched his hand free. "I'm not going anywhere with you! You just want me to tell you how I did it. You think it's a trick you can use to fool people."

The warmth drained from Phillip's expression. His eyes darted around the room. "Look," he said quietly, "we both know exactly how you did it, and now I think we should go back to my home and discuss it as two wizards."

"Two wizards?" Martin sneered, "There's only one wizard in this room. One wizard and another guy who's done a lot of talking."

Phillip turned to all the other people in the room. "Look, you've all seen me work. Will someone please set him straight?" Something fascinating seemed to be happening on the floor, or the ceiling, or out the windows, anyplace but where the wizards were standing. *Who knew medieval peasants were so shy,* Martin thought.

"Look, Phillip, if that is your *real name*, I've demonstrated my powers. Let's see yours."

Phillip put an unwelcome hand on Martin's shoulder. "Look, you made some transparent fabric. It was very nice, but don't kid yourself. That's nothing compared to a real wizard's power."

Martin brushed off his hand. "So you say, but I still haven't seen anything to prove it."

"That's the way you want to do this? Really?" Phillip asked. "Okay, I challenge you to a wizard's duel. We go outside, you do something to demonstrate your powers, and I warn you, it'll take more than transparent fabric. Then, if I can beat it, I do.

Then if you can beat that, you do, and we keep it up until one of us fails."

Moments later, Martin and Phillip were standing in the street with a large crowd lining both sides. It was dark, but not so dark that Martin couldn't see the look on Phillip's face, even from thirty feet away. Martin was set to go first, and that was fine with him. He was supposed to start small, but he'd open with levitating. There was no way the fraud could top that. He'd slink away in shame and leave town, most likely. Maybe Martin would get his hut. It sounded nice, and some stew would hit the spot.

He saw Gwen in the crowd. He smiled and nodded to her. She shook her head, walked to Phillip, and said something. Martin couldn't tell what from this distance, but Phillip nodded as he replied. She looked to Martin again, her large brown eyes looking equally tired and disapproving.

"When do we start?" Martin asked.

"Whenever you're ready," Phillip sighed.

Martin pulled his phone out of his pocket. It cast what he hoped was an eerie glow on his face. The crowd silenced instantly. He opened the app. His thumb paused over the *Hover* button. He paused for effect, then pressed the button. Instantly he was suspended three feet in the air. He heard sounds of surprise from the gathered throng, but not quite as many as he expected. He figured most of them were too shocked to speak.

The hover app worked as designed, resetting his altitude back to three feet off the ground ten times a second. He'd tested it briefly in his apartment, curled into a ball to keep from putting his head through the ceiling, but now he was in a standing position and holding his altitude for more than a second or two. It was profoundly uncomfortable. Imagine standing in a bus with no shock absorbers driving over cobblestones at forty miles an hour.

Every joint in his body rattled. His teeth hurt. His brain hurt. He feared he might be sick. He feared the vibration might break his phone, his only means of returning to his own time. He loosened his grip on the phone as much as he dared, hoping to dampen the shaking. Despite all this, he did not land. He had to expose the false wizard Phillip, and that meant decisively demonstrating his superior power. He would stay in the air until Phillip admitted he could not do better.

"BEEEHOOOOLD!!" Martin bellowed, in a voice that sounded like he was yelling through a high-speed fan. Even to himself he sounded like a goat. "Phiiilliiip, caaan yooour pooowerrrrrrs maaatch thiiiiis?" He hovered in as impressive a pose as he could muster with his body ringing with pain.

All eyes turned to Phillip, who smiled, shrugged, and said, "Let's see."

Phillip pointed his staff at the sky. The staff glowed an unearthly blue color and emitted a hum, like a kazoo but with more reverb. Smoothly, effortlessly, Phillip soared straight up, thirty feet into the air, his feet dangling beneath him. The blue glow formed a vapor trail that traced his path through the air. The buzzing intensified as Phillip twirled the staff like an oversized baton. He spun the staff so quickly that it became a disc of blue light warping around him. Slowly, Phillip started rotating. As he rotated faster the blue disc became a blue sphere, which got brighter and hotter until it was burning a brilliant white. Despite it being well after dark, the street looked like it was high noon on the hottest day of the year. A voice so loud that it would have given Martin a headache if he hadn't already given himself one filled the air.

The monstrous voice asked, "What do you think, Martin? How's this?"

Without a word Martin turned and ran as fast as he could. It would have been an impressive display of speed if his feet had been touching the ground. He spun sickeningly and toppled over. He came to a rest hanging upside down at an undignified angle, facing Phillip, still vibrating, three feet above the ground. His robe flapped downward. His feet kicked impotently in the air.

Then Martin threw up.

The white sphere of light contracted to the size of a basketball at the pinnacle of Phillip's staff. Phillip was motionless, floating in the air serenely with his staff held at his side, the ball of white light emanating from its tip illuminating the whole world.

"Thanks for visiting us, Martin," Phillip said in a flat, conversational tone. "I'm sure we'll meet again soon."

Phillip pointed his staff at Martin. The ball of light moved with astonishing speed and hit Martin in the chest. There was no pain, but there was momentum, and because Martin wasn't touching the ground, he slid like a hockey puck, spinning out of control as he flew down the street and out of town, the same way he'd come in. A few hundred feet later he disappeared into the woods. As his back made contact with what felt like a tree, Martin lost consciousness.

11.

Sore. Every part of Martin Banks was sore, including his mood. It felt good to stretch out, though. He opened his eyes just a bit. He saw a wall made up of broad, flat stones mortared together. There was a narrow window made of a very crude glass letting in sunlight, staining it a sickly brownish-yellow color in the process. Martin inhaled. His ribs hurt. There was an aroma in the air. He didn't know what it was, he just knew that he wanted to smell more of it, preferably while eating whatever was making it. It wasn't bacon, eggs, and coffee. It wasn't toast. It didn't smell breakfasty at all. It smelled beefy, with some onion and other vegetables thrown in. He smiled and thought, *It smells like stew....*

Martin sat bolt upright, instantly enraged. Phillip was sitting at the foot of the bed in his blue robe. In his hands there was a large, steaming bowl. "Stew?" he asked, pushing the bowl forward invitingly.

"You! How ... GDAAAAARGH," Martin sputtered with rage. "How did you do that? How'd I get here? How long have I been unconscious? What did you do to me? Give me that stew!"

Phillip laughed and gave him the stew. Martin ate greedily and angrily. He was lying on top of the bedding, fully clothed, but with his shoes removed. Phillip walked over to the corner where a cooking pot hung over a small fire. It was a medium-sized room with stone walls, simple furnishings, and exposed rafters. It was a room imbued with the kind of simplicity that the rich could afford and the poor saved up to get rid of. Homey though it was, the dirt floor and the open fire reminded Martin exactly where and *when* he was.

Phillip picked up a jug and poured some of its contents into a rough clay mug. "Good morning, Martin. I'll answer your questions, but not in order. You've slept about nine hours. Gwen, the young lady who brought you into town, and I went out into the woods to find you as soon as we could after the duel. We found you unconscious, floating about three feet above the ground. You were just lying there, vibrating. It looked like you'd bounced off of a few trees before you came to a stop." Phillip put down the jug and walked toward Martin. "We gathered up all of your belongings. I put everything in a pile over there by the wall. Everything but this." He held up Martin's phone. Martin stopped eating.

"Don't worry, I haven't tampered with it. I know better than to mess with things I don't understand. I pushed the glowing square that said *Hover*, thinking it'd bring you back to the ground. It did, much more violently than I expected." Phillip was now standing right next to the bed. Martin watched him warily.

"Now, your most important question. 'What have I done to you?' The answer, Martin, is that I tried to talk you out of making a fool of yourself, and watched you do it anyway. Then I traipsed through the woods in the dark, gathered your belongings, and snuck you back into town. I gave you a safe place to sleep and watched over you in case your injuries were more severe than they looked, and now I've given you a nice bowl of stew. My point is, if I had any intention of hurting you, I'd have done so while you were asleep, or simply left you alone to hurt yourself. I didn't. That should prove my good will. Agreed?"

Martin nodded, and started shoveling the stew into his mouth again.

"Good." Phillip offered the clay drinking cup. "Have some of this to wash your stew down."

"What is it?"

"Beer."

Martin took the cup.

"That's lesson one, Martin. Don't drink the water unless you've boiled it to within an inch of its life. If you want to stay healthy, stick to wine and beer. The alcohol kills the bacteria."

"What do you mean, *lesson one*?" Martin asked with his mouth full.

"Well," Phillip said, returning to his seat at the foot of the bed, "that brings us to your last unanswered question. *How did I do that*?"

Martin stopped eating.

"Don't stop eating. You're clearly famished. Try some of the beer."

Martin took a large mouthful of beer.

Phillip asked, "Did Pink Floyd ever get back together?"

Martin ejected a large amount of beer through his nostrils. Phillip made no attempt to hide his enjoyment.

"My name is Phillip McCall. I was born in London in 1948. My family immigrated to America in the seventies. I graduated from MIT. In 1983 I was snooping around AT&T's mainframe and I found a copy of the same file I suspect you found."

Martin put down the empty stew bowl. He kept the beer. "So I'm not the first person to find the file."

"No."

"How many copies of the file are there? Has anyone else found it?"

"Many people. We can't know for sure how many. As for the file, there's only one file. What we find aren't copies, just, I guess you could call them 'projections,' ghost images of the one true file that show through into our reality. I think it's some kind of glitch. Anyway, we've proven that changes made to the file on one server instantly affect all other instances of the file in real time."

"Well, the fact that you found the file too certainly explains how you did what you did last night."

"Yes. Sorry. I didn't want it to come to that, but you forced my hand."

"No, I get that. I'm sorry." Martin shrugged. "I feel like an idiot."

"No," Phillip said, "you're not an idiot. You just thought I was."

"The whole past to escape to, and I pick a time and place that's already taken. What are the odds?"

"Pretty good, actually. I assume you read the Cox book."

"What?" Martin asked.

"The Cox book. *The Best Years to Live in Medieval England*, by Gilbert Cox."

Martin dimly recalled the Amazon page describing the book that he had decided to trust after reading its title and the first sentence of its description. "Oh yeah. That book! Yeah, that is what made me pick this year," he said.

Phillip's face lit up. "Good, isn't it? Really makes history come alive. It's not perfect, of course, but it's amazing how much he got right."

"I haven't read it," Martin said.

"Pardon?"

"I haven't read it," Martin repeated.

"If you haven't read the book, I suppose you must have seen the BBC documentary series he made. They ran it in America on PBS."

"No, didn't see it."

"None of it? There were four episodes."

Martin shook his head. "No, sorry."

"Did you read one of his follow-up books?"

"No, I read the title, and a synopsis."

"A synopsis."

Martin shrugged. "Part of the synopsis."

"Ah, yes," Phillip said. "You're an American."

"Was it my accent that gave me away?" Martin asked.

"Partly. The Cox book is what led the rest of us here as well. Once we got settled we went in and set up a script that buys a number of copies every year to keep it in print. We want to lure as many people who discover the file here as possible. All the copies are delivered to a warehouse in Cornwall. I'm sure we've made Mr. Cox's descendants quite rich. You should really read the book, Martin. It makes a good case for this time. Relative stability, good crop yields, the Crusades keeping the violence far away. Good stuff."

Phillip could see that he was losing Martin. "More stew?" he asked.

"Please! You said *we set up*. How many others are here?"

Phillip took the empty bowl over to the stew pot. "Twenty-some. It's hard to say. People drop in and out, go back to their own time, check out other periods in history. That's just the people we've identified, mind you. The ones we met because they chose to come back to Medieval England and be a wizard."

"Hmm. It never occurred to me to go anywhere else."

"Me either. I think that's because we're both white males of European descent. We're in occasional contact with a group of sorcerers living in eighth-century Baghdad, and, of course, Atlantis."

"Atlantis is real?"

"Oh, yeah. Most of the women who find the file end up going there to live. What can I say? Ladies like a man with a swimmer's build."

They sat in silence for a moment while Martin dug into his second helping of stew.

"You were hungry, weren't you?" Phillip asked. "Okay, my turn to ask a few questions. Where and when are you from, Martin?"

"Seattle, 2012, and no, Pink Floyd doesn't ever really get back together. Three of them put out some pretty good albums without Roger Waters, but it's not the same. They did a one-off performance for charity, but then the pianist died, and that was pretty much that."

"Shame. How long have you been in this time?"

"Less than a day."

"You got into an impressive amount of trouble in that time. How long ago did you find the file?"

Martin thought for a moment, then answered, "A week ago."

"And I get the impression from your general lack of prepared-ness that you fled here. It seems you have a talent for getting into trouble. That pocket-sized computer of yours, are they common in your time?"

"Yeah. Almost everyone has one."

"Hmm. The future. Must be great. I accessed the file on a Commodore 64 and an acoustic coupler."

"You should go to the future and check it out."

"You know I can't. You must've tried to go to the future. We all try it. We can't go there because it hasn't happened yet."

Martin furrowed his brow. "Well, I can't, because that's really the future, but your future is the past. At least part of it is."

"From your point of view. Get used to hearing that phrase, Martin, and get used to hating it. From your point of view I'm a walking time capsule from the primitive yesteryear of 1984, but from my point of view, anything beyond the day I left my time and came here has not happened."

"But I'm here, and I'm from your future."

"No, I'm from your past. We're both here in our past, so whatever infernal program uses the file can access this time from its memory and put us here together, but in the eighties, when it processed my life—you, your pocket computer, your clothes— none of it exists."

"Maybe I could take you to the future with me."

"Maybe you could, but you won't. You're not the first person from my future to turn up, you know, and they all start out say- ing, 'Sure, Phillip, I'll take you to the future,' but then later it's all, 'I don't know, Phillip, what if one of us ceases to exist?' and how can I argue with that?"

"That's gotta be frustrating."

"Frustrating doesn't do it justice! All I get are dribs and drabs of information that come up in conversation, most of which I don't understand! Near as I can tell, all of popular culture and most of the English language gets taken over sometime in the early nineties by something called *The Simpsons*. I know this because nobody from that time or later seems to be able to put a sentence together without quoting them, then everybody giggles like idiots, and if I ask them to explain, all anybody ever does is laugh and ask me a condescending question about Bananarama!"

Martin managed to not smile.

Phillip took a calming breath, then continued his questions. "So, what kind of trouble did you get into? Did you get caught manipulating your bank balance?"

"Yes! How did you know?"

"Lots of us get pinched that way."

"Did you?"

"No, I actually managed to keep things together for a year before I was found out. I had a good-paying job I enjoyed, so once I proved that I could change my balance, I didn't have to."

"How did you get found?"

"Well, I had a lot of time to play with the file before I had to flee. I found a little chunk of code that you could append to any variable in the file to make it a constant."

"That's how you could fly so smoothly!"

"Exactly. Instead of having to reset my altitude several times a second, I can just set it for a given height and have it stay there, then I can fly. That's just one of the ways that replacing a variable in the file with a constant can be helpful. It has many more applications, most of which I'll tell you about later. Anyway, I bought a car. Are you familiar with the Pontiac Fiero?"

"Yeah, a little Italian-looking job. Weren't they lemons?"

"Mine wasn't. I found my car's entry in the file and played with it until I found its base rate of decay. I reset it to zero and made it a constant. I also gave it an unrealistic amount of power, because that's what you'd do. And it never ran out of gas."

"Nice."

"Thanks, but it's what got me nicked. A year goes by, and one day I get a letter from Pontiac. It says that mine is the only Fiero in existence that hasn't had to be brought in within the first year for some major repair, and that they'd like to buy it back so they can tear it apart and figure out what they did right. I should have just reset its variables and sold it to them for a huge profit, but I said no. So, Pontiac, being a major corporation, sends a guy to steal it. He's not ready for the extra horsepower and immediately drives it into a wall."

"Was he hurt?"

"Neither he nor the car was hurt. The wall, however, came down directly on the car without even scratching its paint."

Martin chuckled. "That would look suspicious."

"Indeed. I didn't want to explain, so I came here."

Martin nodded. "And found that others had gotten here before you."

"No. I was here alone, just me and the locals."

"So, you were the first?"

"That depends on how you look at it. I arrived in this time first, but someone might have found the file before me, but picked a destination time that hasn't arrived yet. What we can say is that I'm the person from the earliest date that has arrived at this point in the past *so far*. The second guy to arrive, Jimmy, found the file two years after I did, but arrived only two weeks later than me."

There was a long pause while Martin thought about that. Finally Phillip broke the silence.

"Look, Martin ... would you prefer it if I call you Marty?"

"*Would you* prefer to be called Marty?"

"Good point, Martin. Like I said, there are a bunch of us from the future living here. We have a good thing going. We can't let anyone screw it up, and so far you've shown a talent for screwing things up."

Martin tensed. His eyes involuntarily dashed to his smartphone in Phillip's hand. Phillip noticed, and smiled.

"Don't worry, Martin, you're in no danger."

Phillip watched as Martin failed to relax. Phillip smiled and handed the smartphone to Martin.

"Better?"

Martin relaxed. If Phillip meant to harm him, he wouldn't hand him a means of escape. "As I was saying," Phillip continued, "I've lived here over a decade. It's my home, and most of the other wizards feel the same. We can't let anybody mess it up, so we've developed a sort of training program. If you want to stay in this time, you'll hang around with me for a while. I'll explain the basics of how we operate, tell you the rules, and teach you the skills you'll need to make a living as a wizard, which is a pretty cushy life. When I think you're ready we'll go introduce you to the chairman and you'll face the trials."

"If I pass?"

"You know the program you have running on that pocket computer of yours to access the file? We have a program that's similar, but ours has been under continuous development for a decade. It gives us powers beyond anything you've imagined. If you pass you'll have full access and the ability to develop and submit new powers for approval."

"What kind of powers are we talking about?"

"The only power you need to know about to make your decision is the power to lead a life where you're free to pursue whatever seems interesting without the pressure of keeping a job, or paying off a car loan or a mortgage. We live like gentlemen of leisure. Our greatest challenge is looking busy. Welcome to wizarding. Your last hard day was yesterday."

"What if I fail the trials?"

"That's a less pleasant story. We send you back to your own time, and we cut off all future access to the file."

"You can do that?"

"Yes."

"But, what if in my own time I'm headed to jail?"

"Then you go to jail. Sorry, but you made that bed yourself. We're not responsible for what you've done. If it's that bad, we're probably doing a good deed by preventing you from doing more of it. I think you'll pass, though. I looked at your pocket computer program, and the fact that there are no functions that can be used as a weapon speaks well of you. Last night you demonstrated that you can talk the talk of a wizard. You showed a flair for the dramatic and quite a bit of creativity! Thanks for all the cling film, by the way. I told Pete that it was useful for covering food and he tried to make a pot lid out of it. It melted."

"Must've ruined whatever he was cooking."

"Even with our powers, we can't do anything worse to food than have it be cooked by Pete. Look, don't worry too much about the trials. If I didn't think you'd work out, you'd have woken up in your own time this morning."

"You'd do that?"

"We've done it before. Marty, we discovered the file, and we here have devised the shell program that helps us manage it. If we don't police its use, nobody will. There was one guy, Todd was his name. Awful little man. He passed the training just fine, then immediately started doing terrible things. We knew he had fled here to avoid arrest, so we sent him back to his time and cut off his access to the file. Also, just to make sure he didn't evade capture, we sent him to a public place, naked and hog-tied."

Martin imagined himself rematerializing in his old bedroom with no means of escape, the feeling of helplessness as the agents stormed in, the looks on his parents' faces as he was dragged away, their embarrassment at being unable to explain why he'd stripped naked and how he'd hog-tied himself. He couldn't let that happen. Martin held up his phone. "And what if I just flee to another time and place?"

"We'd take that as intent to do wrong, cut off your access, and send you back to your time. Now that we're aware of you, we can edit your parameters without you present."

"Yeah, I suppose you could. What if I refuse the training?"

"We send you back to your own time and cut off your access to the file."

"Just like if I fail the training."

"Yes. We consider correctly answering the question 'Do you accept the training?' to be part of the training. Get that question wrong, and you fail the training."

"Do you train everyone?" Martin asked.

"No. Whoever's closest to where a new wizard appears makes initial contact, then we sort of take turns training people. If all goes well, you'll train someone someday. If we were going according to the schedule, I'd be shipping you off to Norway to be trained by a Magnus."

"What's a Magnus?" Martin asked.

"A wizard named Magnus. There are two of them in Norway."

"How many wizards are there in Norway?"

"Two. But after seeing that display of showmanship last night, I've jumped ahead in line. I want to train you myself. You're going to be sort of a special project."

Martin wasn't sure if that sounded promising or not.

Phillip spread his arms wide. "So what do you say, Marty? Do you accept the training?"

"Before I answer, can I ask a question?"

"Sure."

"If I become a wizard, do I have to be celibate?"

This seemed to puzzle Phillip. "No, you don't have to be celibate. You can be, if that's your thing."

Martin waved his hand dismissively. "Never mind. Forget I asked. Yes, I accept the training."

"Excellent. The first step is to get you a proper robe and hat."

12.

Even though Martin knew he was in Medieval England, it didn't sink in until he and Phillip walked out into the street. Until that point he had seen woods, ocean, and an inn. None of those things had changed much over the last several hundred years. Streets, however, had changed dramatically. The street was narrow. People walked right down the middle of it with impunity, wearing lots of leather and lots of leggings. There were no cars, of course, just horse and ox carts. Rather than smelling of exhaust, the air smelled of manure. It was dirty, smelly chaos, but not the kind he was used to.

Martin was wearing clothes that Phillip had loaned him. A rough woven tunic and heavy pants, fastened with a piece of rope for a belt. He was still wearing his sneakers, but they were dirty enough by this time that nobody took notice.

"Besides," Phillip told him, "people are used to a little strangeness when wizards are involved."

Martin was still sore, but food had helped and the breakfast beer had helped even more. He had many questions, but was trying not to ask them in public, for fear of letting *the locals*, as Phillip called them, know too much. He was finding that with all the new information he had absorbed, all the unanswered questions he still had, and the lingering effects of the beer, he was having some difficulty keeping track of things. "Where are we going, again?"

"To the tailor to get you a robe and hat made."

The tailor, he thought. *There's something important about that. What was it?* Finally it struck him.

"Say," Martin said, using his nonchalant voice, "that wouldn't be Gwen the tailor, would it?"

Phillip stopped walking and turned to face him. Martin's nonchalant voice clearly made Phillip profoundly uneasy. "If you mean Gwen the tailor who gave you a ride into town, and was so alarmed by your arrogance that she came to get me immediately, then watched as you made a fool of yourself and got hurled out of town in a white fireball, then helped me cart your drooling, vibrating carcass back into town, then yes."

Martin put his hands up. "Okay, okay, I get your point. Sorry."

They continued walking. "So, is she your girlfriend?" Martin asked.

"No, she's not my girlfriend. She's a smart, talented young lady whom I've known for many years, and she's got enough problems without some lovestruck young wizard trying to impress her like a medieval John Hinckley, Jr."

"Who's John Hinckley, Jr.?" Martin asked.

"Hmm. I guess that's before your time. Perhaps you'd know him if he were on *The Simpsons*. Anyway, please don't bother Gwen. It's hard enough being a woman and a small business owner in modern times. You can imagine what it's like here."

They came to the door of Gwen's workshop. The only thing that differentiated it from all of the other one-story stone buildings was a small wooden plank next to the door with a needle and thread painted on it with some feminine decorative flourishes. Phillip went in. Martin followed. When Phillip had mentioned "Gwen's Shop," Martin had pictured a shop as he knew them, with a counter, and displays, and perhaps the medieval equivalent of a cash register. Instead, what he saw was a workshop full of bolts of fabric and garments in various stages of construction. There were two small windows at the front of the hut, and really, that's what most of the buildings in Leadchurch were. Huts made out of piled rocks and dead plants. In the corner there was a work table, covered with many pieces of cloth, two of which were partly stitched together with a coarse thread that in modern times would have been considered very small-gauge twine.

Gwen was talking to a farmer holding a small stack of folded garments. Martin was absolutely certain that he was a farmer. The man was powerfully built without being buff. His clothes were clean now, but had clearly been very dirty many times. He looked smart, but talked as if everyone assumed he was dumb. *Cripes,* Martin thought, *he might as well be named Mr. Farmer.*

"Ma'am, you make the best clothing I've ever had," the farmer said. "That's why I come all the way into town so often. But the clothes you make do stretch out over time, and I don't think it's unreasonable to ask you to hem your own handiwork at a discount."

Gwen was wearing the same charcoal-colored hooded cloak she had worn the night before, but now Martin could see that it opened at the front, like an oversized hooded sweatshirt, cut to the length of a trench coat. The hood was pulled back off of her head, bunching up slightly around her shoulders and hanging down her back. Beneath the cloak, she wore a lilac colored dress and her petite black leather boots. She glanced at the door as Phillip and Martin entered.

She flashed her warm, pretty smile when she saw Phillip. Her smile chilled a bit when she saw Martin. She took the stack from the man, shrugging. "Sam, you're a good customer, and an honest man, so I'll hem these for free this time, but this is a good heavy fabric, and I promise, it does not stretch with time."

The man pointed at the bottom of his dull brown tunic. It was a little long, as were the sleeves. "Then how can you explain this?" he asked. Gwen seemed to be at a loss.

Phillip said, "I've often thought that most of the men's shirts in this town would be a bit shorter and would fit a bit looser if Gwen hired someone else to do her measuring. Someone men aren't so inclined to impress with their posture and flat gut," then added, "Good morning, Gwen. Sam."

"Good morning, Phillip." Gwen said. "Good morning, Martin. How are you feeling today? Magnificent, I trust."

Sam looked at Martin, astonished. "Is this the evil wizard you vanquished last night, Phillip? I'd heard you slew him and reduced his body to vapor."

Phillip explained that he had reconstituted the vapor into a purer, less evil version of Martin, much as one would distill mash into liquor. This, Sam understood. He thanked Gwen, mentioned that he was off to the cobbler, because his boots were causing him discomfort, and left.

As soon as Sam was gone, Martin said to himself as much as to Phillip and Gwen, "I may have overplayed my hand last night."

"No," Gwen said. "It was very impressive. I'm sure it takes a powerful wizard to make their flying spell continue to work even after they've been knocked unconscious."

"Yes, look, I want to apologize for my behavior. I acted stupidly. Thanks for the ride into town and for helping Phillip come get me."

Her smile warmed again. "You're very welcome, Martin. We all make mistakes."

"Maybe I can make it up to you by taking you to dinner sometime?" Martin ventured.

Her smile cooled again. "Maybe not. What brings you here, Phillip?"

"Martin here is going to be my apprentice, for as long as he lasts. He's going to need a proper robe and hat."

She stood and picked up her measuring stick from the work table. "Good. That thing you were wearing last night was doing you no favors." She spent the next several minutes holding the stick up to various parts of his anatomy and mumbling. Finally she stood and asked Phillip, "Wizard robes and hats are pretty simple. I can have it done in a week or two. I'll need you to come back for a rough fitting in a few days. What color and fabric would you like?"

Martin raised his hand. "It's my robe. Shouldn't you ask me that?"

"What color and fabric?" she asked Phillip.

"Whatever you like, Gwen. We trust you," Phillip replied. Gwen smiled in a way that made Martin want to disagree with Phillip.

As she took a few last measurements by laying her measuring stick along, and at times jabbing it into, parts of his body, Martin asked, "Last night, why did you tell me wizards have to be celibate?"

"I didn't say they had to be. I just said they were," she said without looking up. "Celibate is celibate, whether it's deliberate or not."

A few minutes later Phillip and Martin were back on the street, walking past the townsfolk going about their business.

"Look," Phillip said, "I'll forgive you that one because I remember what it was like to be your age, and being interested in Gwen just means that you have taste, but I'm serious, from now on if I tell you not to do something you have to not do it. That includes hitting on Gwen. If you're to be my apprentice, then that means I'm your master, and I need to be able to trust you to do what I say."

"You're right. I'm sorry. I wasn't thinking."

"Good. I'm glad to hear you say that, because after watching you for less than a day I'm ready to issue my first official command as your master."

Martin braced himself. "I'm ready."

"Okay. Apprentice, I command you to... *think*! Being a man of action is fine, but you need to think before you act."

"That's...."

Phillip held up a hand. "Stop! Did you think about what you're about to say?"

"No."

"Then take a moment. Think about what you were going to say, what you have riding on my continued good will, and how I'm likely to react to the words you were about to let fall from your mouth like a partially chewed mouthful of spoiled cheese."

They stood in silence for a moment as the pedestrians passed them by. Finally Phillip broke the silence. "Have you thought about it?"

"Yes."

"Do you still intend to say whatever it was?"

"No."

"Excellent! You have pleased me, my apprentice! Well done! I'm delighted at the prospect of all the marvelous things you're not going to say in the future! You know, the less you talk, the more people assume that what you're not saying is important."

They walked on in silence for several minutes. Finally Martin spoke. "So, *master*, where are we going now?"

"Marty, you don't have to call me master."

"Good."

"A simple *sir* will do."

Martin thought, and did not respond, which delighted Phillip to no end.

"We're going back to my shop. You can't really do anything until you're outfitted properly, so for the rest of the day you're going to watch me work."

Martin thought for a moment, then said, "I didn't realize you had a shop." And after another moment, "Or work."

"We'll discuss the secrets of our profession in detail when we get to the shop. Just remember that nothing in a wizard's life is what it seems."

Martin decided he'd have to be content with that for now. As they walked, Phillip pointed out the important landmarks of the town of Leadchurch. The blacksmith. The bakery. The butcher shop. He didn't need to point out the church. It looked like any other mid-sized Gothic cathedral, except that it was covered in lead. They watched for a few moments as pilgrims devoutly touched the church and came away amazed at how dirty their hands were.

"The real show is at noon," Phillip said. "Bishop Galbraith comes out and tries to stick a magnet to the side of the church. It never sticks."

"What does that prove?"

"That the church is covered in lead."

"But anyone can see that. And besides, it doesn't really prove anything! Magnets don't stick to a normal church, either. That doesn't mean they're covered in lead."

"True, but the church here in Leadchurch is different from other churches in one very important way."

"What's that?"

"It's covered in lead. You see, faith doesn't have to make sense. If it did, it wouldn't be faith, it would be logic. As wizards, faith is our most important tool."

Just around the corner they came to Phillip's shop. It was a two-story wood and stone building situated with its back to a steep hill, giving the impression that the building was built into the hill. It had a thatched roof and a sign over the door that said *Wizard*. On the door, a small sign simply said *out*.

"Why don't you live here?" Martin asked as they approached the shop.

"Various reasons," was Phillip's reply as he opened the door and entered, Martin following behind him. The front room of the shop was small, with a low ceiling, and was cluttered with weird-looking knickknacks. There were statues, bowls, jars of fluid, jars of powder, and sparkly rocks. In one corner there was a small work table and a set of shelves. The shelves looked like an oversized spice rack, but along with the spices there were some live plants and a few dead, dried animals. On the table there was a mortar and pestle. In the other far corner there was a doorway blocked by a curtain.

Phillip closed the door behind them and lit an oil lamp. "Now we can talk freely. I'll try to answer your questions as best I can. If I forget something, please remind me."

Phillip stood in the middle of the room and spread his arms. "All this is just set decoration. Most of it is stuff I found in the gutter. The only power anything in this room has is the power to confuse. As you learned last night, it's not enough to just turn up, claim to be a wizard, and ask for food. People have to think you're earning your keep. As long as people are sure you're doing something, they don't worry too much about what. I take the occasional gig just for show. Every now and then I appear out of thin air, just to remind people who I am."

"So, you don't have to work?"

"No more than a stage magician has to wave a wand and say *abracadabra*."

"So, what kind of work do you do?"

"You'll see. I have an appointment for later today. But first, let's finish the tour." Phillip swept aside the curtain leading to the next room and beckoned for Martin to follow.

The second room was dark. Thick, dark fabric hung from the walls. On the fabric were crude finger-painted markings and symbols. To the people of this time, they must have looked quite mysterious. Martin recognized many of them: the prism from the cover of *Dark Side of the Moon*, Icarus from the Led Zeppelin album cover, and the Van Halen logo were all instantly familiar. At the back of the room there was another door, partially obscured by the curtains. In the center of the room was the stereotypical crystal ball on a table, only the ball seemed to be partially recessed into the surface. A cloth covered the table and extended all the way to the floor. "Pretty nice, huh?" Phillip asked.

"Yeah. I bet this is pretty convincing," Martin said.

Phillip nodded. "You haven't even seen the best part." He walked around to the far side of the table and sat down. He was just visible in the dim light filtering in around the edges of the curtains. There was an audible click, and suddenly a blue light emanated from the crystal ball, illuminating Phillip's face eerily from beneath. The light pulsed and flickered irregularly.

"That is really cool."

"You don't know the half of it. Come look at it from this side."

Martin carefully walked around the table until he stood behind Phillip. He looked into the crystal ball and there, distorted in the glass, he saw a blue light and white letters that said:

**** COMMODORE 64 BASIC V2 ****

64K RAM SYSTEM 38911 BASIC BYTES FREE

READY

Martin laughed out loud. Phillip smiled broadly and pulled aside the tablecloth. There, mounted on a tray beneath the table, was a Commodore 64 with the power light glowing red. Next to it was a box with two circular appendages rising from its top, cradling the handset from an old-school dial telephone. They shared a good laugh. "Wait, you haven't even seen the best part yet! Go back around to the other side and sit down."

Martin sat in what was presumably the customer's seat. Phillip's face, the crystal ball, and the hand-painted glyphs were the only things his dark-adjusted eyes could make out.

Phillip paused and said, "Now watch, as I summon the demons!" He lowered his eyes, then there was a soft clicking noise which Martin instantly recognized as a keyboard. There was a distant, horrifying screeching noise, followed by what could have been the distant tolling of some horrific bell, then a growling shriek of a thousand damned souls. The sound subsided and the crystal ball pulsed blue and white for a moment before settling into a brilliant white light.

Phillip looked up from the crystal ball. "I am now connected to CompuServe!"

When they stopped laughing, Martin shook his head. "I can't believe you leave this stuff here and live somewhere else. I'd want to guard the computer 24/7."

"I have good reason to live away from my work."

"Which is?"

"That there's almost no real work. Our main job as wizards is to convince people that we're doing important, mysterious things all the time. It's not hard, but the downside is that when people don't know what you do, they don't know what you don't do. If I flipped that sign on my door around to say *in*, within twenty minutes some gormless dung-sifter would be in here asking me to magically sift his dung. Even without turning over the sign, soon, I promise you, someone will come knocking just because people saw us come in. The last thing I want is people getting the impression that they can call on me day and night to *magic away* all of their problems. They need to know that when I'm home I'm not at work, and when I'm at work I have more important business to attend to."

"So our main job is to look busy."

"Yes, and sometimes it takes more effort than actually being busy."

"But still, is it wise to leave the computer…."

"You should get into the habit of calling it *the oracle*, or *the all-seeing eye*, anything but *the computer*. You'll just confuse people."

"And calling it gibberish won't?"

"Oh, it will, but it will confuse them in the way we want it to."

"Fine. Do you really want to leave *the fount of mystical wisdom* unprotected?"

Phillip nodded sagely. "Martin, you see this door behind me?"

"Yes."

"Walk through it."

Martin sensed a trap. He carefully walked around the table to the door. Phillip turned around in his seat to watch. Martin reached his hand out to open the door. His hand nearly touched the hunk of rope that passed in this time for a knob and stopped. His hand couldn't quite reach the door. It was as if an invisible pane of unbreakable glass held him at bay. He explored with his hands. The barrier completely covered the doorway.

"If we ever get tired of being wizards, we could make a killing as mimes, eh?" Phillip said, standing up. He gently pushed Martin aside, then opened and walked through the door. Martin tried to follow, but couldn't. Phillip came back. As he came through the door, Martin could see a staircase beyond, leading upward. Phillip reached down and turned off his Commodore 64. The crystal ball went dark. Phillip walked back out to the main shop. "If I'm not here, nobody can come into the shop at all. I hope people try, to be honest. It adds to the mystique. If I'm here, as many people as can fit can come into the shop or the crystal ball room."

"Can I set up force fields like that?" Martin asked, his eyes wide.

"You'll be able to do it after you've passed the trials."

"How many people can go upstairs?"

"Only me."

"Why? What's up there?"

"Nothing."

"No, seriously, what's up there?"

Phillip lost any trace of a smile. "Oh, *seriously*! You're asking me *seriously* what's upstairs? Then I'll tell you. There is *seriously* nothing upstairs."

"Nothing, or nothing you want to tell me about?"

"From your point of view, those are the same thing. Now, if you're finished wasting our time over nothing, we have work to do."

"You said we didn't really do any work."

"No, I said we work at looking busy. You want to do something every day. Preferably, it'll be something easy that you can make a big deal out of." Phillip made sure his powder blue pointed hat was on tight. He grabbed his staff. There was a knock at the door. "Ugh, never fails. Someone always shows up right as you're trying to get going. You ready?"

Martin looked himself over. "I don't think so."

"Perfect! You're an apprentice. You're supposed to look confused. Follow my lead," Phillip said, and pushed the door open.

A small, filthy man stood there, preparing to knock again. Phillip practically toppled him over. "Oh, sorry, Hubert. I'm in a rush!"

The man held up the dirtiest hands Martin had ever seen, beseeching Phillip. "Please sir, it's about the dung."

"I know it is. Look, Hubert, we've been through this. I can't use my powers to sift the dung for you. I have other matters to which I must attend."

"But Master Wizard, the dung...."

"Yes, you've told me. In the future you'll know to check the dung's viscosity before you agree to sift it."

Hubert looked lost. "Viscosity?"

"Yes, you know. Its … you've been in the dung-sifting business your whole life. What word do you use to describe how easy or hard it is to sift a pool of dung?"

"Ah, you mean its *siftability*."

"Yes. I suppose I do. I have to go now, Hubert. My apprentice and I must help contain an ancient evil."

Hubert turned to Martin. "Oh, Mr. Phillip has an apprentice!" He attempted to shake hands with Martin. Martin, for his part, had never in his entire life wanted so badly to not shake a hand. He considered bowing, but that would only bring his face closer to the hand. He was so off balance that he just blurted out the first thing that came to mind.

"Do you really sift dung for a living?" Martin asked.

"Oh yes, the business was passed on to me by my father," Hubert replied.

"You must hate him."

"Oh yes, very much!"

Phillip growled loud enough for everybody to hear, "Come, apprentice, we must contain the ancient evil!"

Hubert said, "You just said that."

Phillip grabbed Martin's hand, said, "It bears repeating," and pointed his staff toward the sky. Like a shot Phillip and Martin left the ground and sailed off beyond the rooftops.

"Do we have to hold hands?" Martin asked.

"Oh, grow up."

13.

Once the shock of taking flight and of holding hands with another grown man had subsided, Martin really enjoyed flying. It was much smoother than his rudimentary hover program. They zoomed over the rooftops until they reached the edge of town. Now they were gliding along over the forest about twenty feet over the treetops.

Martin was trailing along behind Phillip in a posture that suggested he was hanging by one hand, but in truth, he didn't feel his weight at all. Gentle wind resistance had pushed him back but his grip was in no danger of failing. Phillip was holding onto Martin with his left hand. His right was extended before them, holding his staff at the midpoint and extending its two halves to their sides like wings. Martin watched. It became clear that Phillip was steering by tilting the staff.

"Is this as fast as we can go?"

"We can go much faster, but if you get above thirty-five miles an hour, the wind becomes unpleasant. Besides, we aren't going far."

The rest of the trip was spent in silence. Before he agreed to training, Martin had seen a brief sample of what Phillip could do, and of course, he was keen to avoid going back to his time to deal with the small army of federal agents converging on his parents' house, but this was the first thing he'd seen that made him actively want the training. He wondered how long it would be before he learned to fly, and what other things he would learn.

The trees ended and a patchwork of small farms spread out before them. They veered to the left, lost some altitude, then came to a gentle landing next to a rundown stone hut with a shaggy-looking thatched roof. "All right," Phillip said, straightening his robe, "don't say a word. Just follow my lead and do as I say. This won't take long."

Phillip knocked on the door. From inside there was the sound of yelling, a cat hissing, and objects falling. Slowly, the sounds got louder. Finally the door opened, revealing an old woman. She was small and thin-boned, but she didn't look fragile. She seemed to be made of twisted wire and beef jerky. Her dress was the color of mud, and she was barefoot. A cat was perched on her shoulder, deploying every claw it had to stay there, hissing nonstop.

"Hello, Miss Abigail, how does this day find you?" Phillip asked slowly and loudly, smiling like a used car salesman. Her reply was loud and made up mostly of vowel sounds.

"I see," Phillip said. "I'm told that you have need of my services again." She nodded and emitted more vowel sounds, punctuated with a few sprays of saliva. The cat hissed its agreement.

"Your goat again, I assume?"

This time the vowels were yelled at greater volume and the saliva was launched with more force. She gestured wildly, flailing her arms while the hissing cat tried desperately to keep its perch.

"Of course, I'll be happy to help. I'll let you know when it's done," Phillip said. She nodded, the cat hissed, and the old woman shut the door. Phillip turned back to Martin. "There, the worst is over. Follow me." Phillip walked around to the back of the house. There were two patches of ground surrounded by rough, wood fences. A gate connected the two fenced areas. The gate was open. In one pen there was a goat, standing still, staring at Phillip and Martin.

"What now?" Martin asked.

"Now we move the goat from one pen to the other. Usually the goat moves to the other pen on its own, but every now and then it refuses, and Miss Abigail sends one of her neighbors into town to get me. I got word yesterday that I was needed, so here we are."

Martin shook his head. "So, when you said we were going to contain an ancient evil, you meant we were going to put a goat in a pen."

"No, I meant we were going to do what Miss Abigail wants so she won't come into town herself to get me."

"How will the townsfolk react if they find out that Miss Abigail is the ancient evil?"

"They know Miss Abigail. I expect they'll thank me. Now, on to business. Marty, how would you go about moving that goat?"

"Well, we could go in there and shove it. Could be that just trying would scare it so that it flees into the other pen."

"Yes, but I suspect Miss Abigail tried that. No, she sent for a wizard, so we have to be sure to move the goat the way you'd expect a wizard would." Phillip held his staff with one hand and pointed at the goat with the other. In a deep, booming voice, he said, "Levi objekto!" Slowly, he raised his hand, and the goat lifted into the air, staying in perfect alignment with his hand. Phillip moved his arm smoothly, changing his aim from the airspace above one pen to the airspace above the other, and the goat moved through the air. It would have been almost majestic if the goat weren't flailing its legs wildly and bleating at the top of its lungs. Phillip started lowering the screaming, squirming goat, then stopped short.

"Martin, would you please go close the gate? If I put him down and the gate's still open he'll just run back to the other pen." Martin climbed over the fence, keeping an eye on the levitating goat. It was impressive just how constantly and loudly the goat could bleat. As he closed the gate and tied a slipknot in the rope that held the gate shut, he heard Phillip laugh and the bleating getting louder. He turned and saw that the goat was gliding up behind him, a whirling tornado of hooves and teeth. Martin fled, and the flying, murderous goat followed him seemingly against its will. Martin realized that Phillip was using the goat to chase him around the pen.

Martin yelled, "Dude! Not cool," as he vaulted the fence. Phillip put the goat down as gently as he could, but it was difficult to do while laughing. "I really don't appreciate being treated like that," Martin said.

"That's all right. I appreciate it more than enough for both of us."

Martin shook his head. "I don't know, man. The goat didn't seem to like that."

"You wanted to go in and shove it by hand. Would that be more fun for the goat? Or you, for that matter?"

Martin conceded the point.

Phillip went back to the hovel's front door and knocked. There was a distant, dismissive-sounding shout and some hissing. Phillip yelled goodbye through the closed door and soon they were back in the air.

"So, what now?" Martin yelled over the wind as they flew above the treetops.

Phillip yelled back, "We're done with work for the day. Everyone saw us leave on important business. Miss Abigail can tell people that we levitated her goat, if anyone can understand her. The illusion has been maintained. If we weren't in training, we'd be free to take the rest of the day off."

"So we're going to start my training, then?" Martin asked, not bothering to hide his excitement.

"Yes," Phillip said as he steered them to a landing in a clearing. "Step one is to find you a staff."

They spent nearly an hour poking around the undergrowth looking for a fallen branch that was tall enough, thick enough, and straight enough. It was a pleasant way to spend a day, and they fell easily into conversation.

"Preferably, you want it slightly thicker at the top, with a good place to mount some sort of mysterious object," Phillip said as he poked through the underbrush with the end of his staff.

"Like that bottle of red stuff on yours. I was going to ask you what the deal was with that."

Phillip held his staff by the end and extended it so that its top and the corked bottle were closer to Martin's face. "When the locals ask me what it is, I tell them it's a vial of dragon's blood. Since you're asking, I'll admit that it's a salad dressing cruet I bought in a department store. The red stuff is Tabasco sauce."

"Really?"

"Really. If they don't believe it's dragon's blood I pull the cork and let them smell it. That usually convinces them. One time I got caught putting some on my dinner. I thought I was in trouble, but everyone just thought I ate dragon blood, so in the end it helped sell the image."

They lapsed into silence for a while before Martin spoke again.

"What can you tell me about the trials?"

"Not much. Sorry. If I tell you what the trials entail, you'll only concentrate on those parts of the training, and it's never a good idea to teach to the test. All I can tell you is when you're ready we will go see the chairman, there will be a feast in your honor, all the wizards who can make it will attend, then the next morning, you will face the trials. If you pass, you'll be given full access to our shell program and you'll be a wizard."

"And if I fail, I get sent back to my time without any access to the file."

"Yes, but focusing on failure just makes you more likely to fail. *When* you succeed, you'll have tremendous powers and the freedom to go anywhere, and do almost anything you want."

"Almost anything?"

"Yes, as I said earlier, we sort of self-regulate, but there are certain things that are taboo. We'll cover all that later. We don't want to get ahead of ourselves."

Martin reached down into a bush and pulled up a likely-looking stick. "How about this one?"

"Not straight enough."

Martin threw the stick back. "So, who's the chairman?"

Martin thought Phillip hadn't heard him and was about to repeat the question when Phillip said, "Jimmy's his name, but the locals call him Merlin."

Martin was thunderstruck. "So, there really is a Merlin?"

"No! There really isn't a Merlin! There really is a Jimmy, who found the file two years after I did and turned up in this time less than a week after me. I got here and found that they already had the Arthur legend and Merlin, so I just made a nice low-key life for myself in Leadchurch. Jimmy makes a beeline for London and becomes the court magician and advisor to King Stephen. Stephen had just lost Brittany to the Plantagenets, so he was willing to listen to suggestions. Eventually Jimmy convinced him that the Arthur legend was actually a prophecy, and talked him into changing the name of his son, the heir apparent, to Arthur. Since the kid's name was Eustace, he didn't argue. Then, to top it all off, Jimmy changed the name of London to Camelot."

"He can't do that!" Martin shouted.

"Well, don't tell him that when you meet him. He'll be very disappointed, since he already did it nine years ago."

"But, we can't just change the past like that!"

"Martin, we can't not change the past. In theory, everything we do has an effect, whether it's a small thing, like talking to a tailor you meet on the road, or a big silly thing, like introducing an inn full of peasants to the marvels of cling film."

Martin blushed a bit. "Yeah, I guess I wasn't thinking."

"I know, we talked about that. Thankfully, you are thinking now."

"And I'm horrified."

"Yes, that's how I know you're thinking."

"So, Phillip, how are we going to fix it?"

"Fix what? The timeline? The space-time continuum? Gnarly, unfillable plot holes?"

"Yes. All those things!"

Phillip sat on a conveniently placed log. "They don't exist." He indicated a spot on the log next to him. "Have a seat. This is pretty heavy stuff."

Martin sat beside him.

"You knew time travel was possible, which means you tried it, which means you almost certainly met yourself."

"Yes."

"Thought you'd be taller, right?"

"Yes."

"It's a cliché for a reason. I'm sure you figured out that cause always preceded effect from your point of view, so you couldn't really mess up your own future."

"Yes. So that's how it is with the timeline, eh? We can't do anything that messes it up because we've already done everything, right?"

"There are two answers to that question. *We don't know,* and *No, certainly not.* There's still a lot we don't know about the file and how things work. Most wizards spend their spare time trying to figure things out, and it can be a full-time job if you let it be."

"Most wizards?"

"Some of us have other projects."

"Is that what you have upstairs in your shop? A project?"

"I told you, there's nothing up there. Don't change the subject. Anyway, when I came back here, I was extremely careful. I knew my actions didn't seem to make any difference to the timeline, but I didn't want to take any chances. Then Jimmy shows up and starts changing huge things willy-nilly."

"What happened?"

"Aside from Jimmy and me having a huge argument, nothing. Martin, nothing we do seems to affect the future at all. In the last ten years the entire country has called London Camelot. All of the official dispatches, all of the ledgers all say Camelot, yet if you go back to your time, you'll find Camelot's still a myth and London's still London."

"How's that possible?"

"We just don't know. Some think that something happens later that erases all of this from history and puts things right. Whatever it is, in the future it's already happened, so we see the fixed reality, but back here it hasn't happened yet, so we're free to muck about all we want."

"That's a good explanation."

"But it's not true, and I'll tell you why. Predetermination. If that explanation is true, it means that everything we do was set in stone hundreds of years before we were born. It means we're not individuals, just robots running through pre-programmed responses, and I can't accept that."

"But the whole reason we're here is that we've proved that we're algorithms in a computer program."

"That may be, but I'm an algorithm with free will! Any time someone claims I don't have free will I shout *shut up* at the top of my lungs, because it's totally out of character for me, and it proves I have free will."

Martin thought about this for a moment. "You shout *shut up* every time?"

"Yes."

"That proves nothing. If you do it every time, then yelling *shut up* is a pre-programmed response."

Phillip thought about that for a moment, then replied, "SHUT UP, SHUT UP, SHUT UP!"

Martin smiled while Phillip caught his breath. "Got it out of your system?"

"For now. So, that's one explanation, which I don't buy. The other explanation is that when we go back in time past a certain point, the program, whatever it is, creates a parallel instance of the past for us to go to."

"So, this is an alternate reality."

"I think so."

"Wouldn't we be able to go to the future then?"

"Not beyond our own source time. The idea has its problems, and there's a lot we don't know, but it does explain why we all seem to go to a few specific points in history. The program already has this place set up, so it sort of influences us to come here instead of some other place."

"But doesn't that suggest that we don't have free will?"

Phillip gave Martin an icy stare. Martin put up his hand. "Sorry, I'll shut up."

Phillip stood up and stretched. "Top man. In retrospect, a certain amount of chronological pollution was inevitable, really. I first noticed it when one of the locals told me the weather sucked. I didn't even notice at first, then I freaked right out for a while."

"But just for a while."

"Yeah, well, it didn't seem to hurt anything. Quite the opposite. As I told you, there are wizards like us living in Baghdad in the seven hundreds. Well, when you look around you, this all looks as you expected Medieval England to look, but I can tell you that we aren't supposed to have glass windows until centuries later, yet here they are, and I'm mighty glad of it."

"But, don't you see how wrong that is?" Martin said. "You've made the past...." Martin couldn't find the word he wanted. He eventually settled on "inauthentic."

"I'm not going to pretend you don't have a point, Martin, but like I said, a certain amount of chronological pollution was inevitable. We try not to deliberately change the past, most of us at least, and when there is a change we can't smooth over, it's not really the end of the world, because while we may have irrevocably changed this time, the fact is that it's had no effect whatsoever on the future."

Martin shook his head. "I still don't buy the idea that we aren't changing the future."

"If you don't believe me, look for yourself. You've got that fancy pocket computer of yours. Pop back to your time and see if anything has changed."

Walter and Margarita Banks watched as their son rooted frantically through the kitchen before finding a package of cling film.

Margarita asked him what was going on. Instead of answering he asked, "Do you have any heavy duty? This stuff's a little flimsy."

"In the cupboard under the sink," she replied. "Why are you wearing your Snape costume?"

Martin muttered, "It's Malfoy. You always get that wrong," but his parents did not hear him, partly because of the sound of many sirens coming from the front lawn. Martin grabbed two boxes of heavy-duty cling film and sprinted back to his room, shouting, "Thanks, Mom!" as he slammed the door. Walter and Margarita looked down the hallway at their son's bedroom door. They turned their heads when they heard an insistent knock on the front door.

They turned their heads again when Martin opened his bedroom door. He peeked his head out into the hall, looked at them and said, "Hi. Just checking, what's the capital of England?"

Margarita answered, "London." Martin retreated into the room again, slamming the door shut behind him.

Martin quickly scanned his childhood belongings. There were Star Wars toys, a few Power Rangers, nothing all that impressive. The one thing that stood out was a small painted plaster bust he had bought when he was twelve and he and his family had gone to Mexico to visit his mom's relatives.

Martin rematerialized in the meadow.

"Everything the way you left it?" Phillip asked.

"Yes, and I found what I'm going to put on the head of my staff!" Martin proudly held aloft the small painted plaster bust of El Santo, King of the Luchadores.

14.

They returned to Phillip's shop. Phillip gave Martin instructions on how to properly sand and varnish his staff (Step 1: don't make the obvious joke), and left Martin in the front room while he sat down at the crystal ball, typing furiously and mumbling to himself. Martin objected to using varnish in such an enclosed space, but Phillip said he couldn't very well do it on the street, and besides, the horrible odor of the varnish would add to the ambiance. Martin found that with a little effort the head of the staff fit nicely into the bottom of the hollow bust of Santo. The fit was snug enough that the bust would probably stay on the staff all by itself, but Martin threw some glue in for good measure. Martin also sawed off the bottom end of the staff, partly to make a flat base and partly because Phillip was adamant that the staff had to be five feet tall, not including the ornamentation at the top.

Phillip was still staring into the crystal ball, muttering things and sporadically typing on the Commodore 64's concealed keyboard, when Martin entered an hour later. "My new staff is drying. What next?"

Phillip didn't look up from the crystal ball. "Have a seat. We're ready for the good part. How's the temperature in here, Martin? Comfortable?"

"Eh, it's a little hot and stuffy, but not bad."

"Where do you usually put the thermostat in your home?"

"About seventy-eight degrees."

Phillip tapped a few keys, looked up at Martin, and theatrically hit enter. Instantly Martin was cool and comfortable. "Wow!" he said, instinctively looking for a hidden air-conditioning vent, though he suspected he wouldn't find one.

Phillip leaned back in his chair. "We've known about the file for a decade and we've been developing the shell program nearly as long. All wizards are free to explore the file and develop new shell functions as long as we share what we've found. I believe it's similar to what you'd call open source development."

Martin heard him, but he was still trying to get his head around the implications. "So, now it'll always be a comfortable temperature for me in this room?"

"Close. From now on you will always be a comfortable temperature everywhere. It doesn't matter if you go to Antarctica or Panama, your body will react like it's seventy-eight degrees with low humidity."

"Well, that's about the best thing I've ever heard."

"Isn't it? Of course, you can still get burned if you touch something hot, and you're still subject to sunburns, but in general, your sweating days are over. How many languages do you speak?"

"Two-ish. I speak English and I can get by in Spanish."

"Well, now you speak all of them. Turns out that what languages you speak is just another variable in the file. Near as we can tell, the program hears the words you intend to say and sends the hearer the words they need to hear. As weird as it seems, at the end of the day we're just two lines of code sending each other information."

Martin thought about this. "So, really there's only one language?"

"As far as the file is concerned."

"But … 'open' and 'abierto' are two different words."

"Yes, and if you actively choose to say 'abierto,' only those slated by the file to speak Spanish will understand it, but the file knows that you were saying 'open.'"

"So, if we went over to France, everybody would think I was speaking French?"

"Yes, and you'd hear them in English. Have you noticed that everyone's accent was thicker last night? That's why."

"You monkeyed with my file while I was asleep?"

"Just a little, to make today easier for you. Next question: how old are you?"

"Twenty-three."

"I'd ask you if you like being twenty-three, but you wouldn't know. You've never been older than twenty-three. I have, and I'll tell you, physically speaking, it's not going to get any better. It certainly beats being in your late thirties for all eternity." Phillip went back to hammering on his keyboard, then again, hit enter with a flourish.

"Are you telling me that I'm going to be twenty-three forever?"

"Physically, if that's what you want. You'll still develop mentally. If you exercise, you'll get stronger. If you don't, you'll get weaker. You can still get fat or go on a diet, but unless you go back in and edit the file, whatever you become, you'll be a twenty-three-year-old version of it."

Martin opened and closed his mouth a few times before words actually came out. "Are you saying that I'm immortal?"

Phillip let out a long breath. "Maybe. You still need food, water, and air. We found a way to make you not need those, but we don't suggest using it, even in an emergency, because you still feel like you need food, water, and air. If the only way to survive is to spend even an hour feeling like you're suffocating, I'm not sure death wouldn't be preferable. There was a person, I hesitate to call him a man, who did many things we didn't like and we had to send him back to his own time."

Martin asked, "That was Todd, right?"

"Yes. Todd." Phillip said it like the name was the vilest insult imaginable. "Anyway," Phillip continued, "one of the things he did was create a series of alterations he could make to somebody's file entry that would effectively make them a ghost. You'd be all but invisible, unable to touch anything, and unable to talk. All you could feel was hunger, thirst, and panic, because you thought you were suffocating. The only thing you could do, and this is the evil bit, was make spooky noises. We still don't know how he did it. You couldn't say a word, but you could go *Ooooooooooo* all day. The idea was that the person who was 'ghosted' would psychologically torture his friends and family trying to ask them for help."

Martin tried to imagine what that would be like, and then he tried desperately to stop.

"You need to eat, you need to drink, you need to breathe," Phillip continued. "You can still be killed. You can't be stabbed, beaten to death, or dismembered, but you can still be killed. Starvation, suffocation, drowning, and thirst, those will all still get the job done, but unless someone pulls you out of the shell, impact and puncture wounds won't. If you're not killed, though, yes, you will, in theory, live as long as you want. That's partly why I'm not bothered that I can't travel to the future. If I hang around long enough I'll get there anyway."

"You were able to make your Fiero indestructible, and they were pretty much made of Styrofoam. Does that mean . . . us?"

"Don't badmouth my Fiero. You're right, though: as long as you have full shell access, it will constantly monitor and update your file, meaning that you can't really be injured by conventional means. The meanest guy in town, or even Gert, can pound on you all day and you won't get a bruise. It'll hurt the whole time, but you won't be permanently injured."

"Cool!"

"Yes. It is! Took us years to figure it out, and a lot of mistakes were made along the way. At first we tried just stopping the decay rate, like on my car. The results were … sub-optimal. The body just keeps building on itself. Picture The Thing from the Fantastic Four, but instead of having the power of super strength, you have the power to experience constant pain. That brings us to an important point. When exploring the file, we wizards only experiment on inanimate objects and ourselves. We do not experiment on non-wizards; we only experiment on wizards who know what we're doing and give consent, and we never change a person's physical structure. "

"But I only discovered the file by accidentally making myself taller."

Phillip's eyes widened. "How much taller?"

"Two and a half inches."

"Well, you lucked out, my friend. Much taller and your spine might have stopped functioning."

"But you said we can't change our physical structure, and I've proved that we can."

"I didn't say that we can't, I said that we don't. I didn't mean it wasn't possible. I meant that if you do, we'll reset you to your original parameters, cut off your access to the file, and send you back to your time. We don't have a lot of rules,

Martin, but we take the ones we do have very seriously. What were they again?"

"Experiment only on ourselves or another wizard, and only if that wizard knows what we're doing, and we don't alter any person's physical structure, ever."

"Well done. Okay, Martin, I think you're ready to say the incantation and start learning to use your powers."

"Incantation?" Martin sneered. "You realize we aren't really doing magic, right? All this smoke and mirrors is great for the locals, but we don't really have to keep it up when we're in private, do we?"

"Yes, we do. Martin, if being a wizard is a mask you remove sometimes, it's only a matter of time before you forget to put it back on. You've got to live it all the time. Think of it as going undercover, if that helps. Also, more important, some of these bits of smoke and mirrors, as you put it, serve important functions. The shell we've written is always running in the background, monitoring the conditions of those we've authorized to use it."

"So it'll be spying on me?"

"You could look at it that way. You could also say that your television remote control is spying on your viewing habits. The shell watches, but it doesn't record. It just waits for certain signals, then it makes adjustments to your portion of the file based on those signals."

"Ah, and those signals are designed to look like spells and incantations."

"This thinking thing is slowly becoming a habit. So, if you're fully satisfied, may I please give you magical powers?"

"Of course," Martin said, chagrined. "I'm sorry I interrupted. Please, tell me what to say."

Phillip smiled and rose from his seat. "Splendid. Let's get you kitted out." He moved one of the loose folds of fabric that lined the walls. Behind it there was a small set of shelves. From them, Phillip grabbed a folded bundle of blood-red fabric, which he tossed to Martin. "Here, put these on. It's an old robe and hat of mine. They'll do until Gwen has finished yours."

Martin pulled on the robe. Thanks to Phillip's more generous proportions, the robe fit loosely, and pooled on the ground around his feet. The hat, which, like the robe, was blood-red with black trim, was also too large, and rested on his ears and eyebrows. The overall effect made Martin look like a small Druid child, dressing in his father's clothes and pretending he was going to a sacrifice just like daddy. Phillip took a second to admire Martin in his new ensemble. "Marvelous!"

"Really? I thought I looked ridiculous."

"Oh, you do. Marvelously ridiculous!" Phillip handed Martin his staff. "Now, hold my staff, and this is very important, *do not make the obvious joke.*" Martin took the staff and said nothing.

"Good. Are you ready, Martin?"

"Yes."

"Good. Repeat after me. Supren supren."

"Supren supren."

"Suben suben."

"Suben suben."

"Maldekstra dekstra maldekstra dekstra."

"Maldekstra dekstra maldekstra … dekstra?"

"Bee aye komenco."

"Bee aye komenco."

Phillip clapped. "It is done!"

"What was that?" Martin asked.

"I'm told it's a cheat code from a videogame called *Contra* that's a bit after my time, I'm afraid."

Martin thought for a moment. "Up, up, down, down, left, right, left right, B, … A. Yeah, start. Yup, that's totally the Konami code. What language was that, Latin?"

"No, these are the Middle Ages. There are people you've met here who actually speak Latin. All of our spells are in badly translated Esperanto. It's a universal language that was invented early in the twentieth century to foster international peace and understanding. It's perfect for our purposes because there are many resources to translate things into it and absolutely nobody speaks it."

"Nobody in this time."

"Nobody in any time. Seriously, William Shatner, and that's about it."

"But, you said the spells are badly translated."

"Yeah," Phillip said, looking a bit embarrassed. "If the spells were in perfectly constructed, textbook Esperanto, then we'd have to speak perfect Esperanto, so instead we use Esperanto vocab words, but with a caveman version of English grammar. Anyway, you've said the incantation. The shell is now active for you. To test it, try to move your head so your hat falls off."

Martin tried, but no matter how he whipped his head, the hat stayed on, despite being too large for his head. "Good," Phillip said. "Now reach up and take it off." Martin did, and the hat came off easily.

"So the shell is keeping my hat on?"

"Yes. Wind can't blow your hat off. Enemies can't knock it off. If you put your hat on, the only thing that can remove it is you."

Martin was puzzled. "That's a nice demo, I guess."

"Doesn't seem practical though, eh? Give me my staff back. I'll show you something." Phillip took his staff back. He reached into his pocket and produced a gold coin, which he set on the table next to the crystal ball. He held his staff in his left hand. With his right, he pointed at the coin and said, "Levi objekto." While still pointing, he raised his hand, and the coin floated in the air, staying perfectly aligned with his hand. He lowered the coin back to the table. He motioned to Martin. "Now you try."

Martin pointed at the coin, searched his memory, and said, "Levi objekto." He raised his hand. The coin didn't budge. "Did I get the words wrong?" he asked.

"No, you remembered the words just fine," Phillip said. He handed the staff back to Martin. "Hold this, put your hat back on, and try again."

Martin put the oversized hat back on his undersized head, held the staff in his left hand and pointed at the coin with his right, and said, "Levi objekto." He raised his hand, and the coin smoothly lifted into the air. Martin just looked at it for a moment. He raised and lowered his hand, and the coin moved with it. He had seen Phillip do the same trick, both with the coin and with that cursed goat, but it hadn't prepared him for the experience of doing it himself.

Phillip moved to stand beside him. "Push your hand forward, like you're gently shoving the coin away." Martin did, and the coin slowly glided away from Martin. "Now, pull your hand back, like you're pulling on the coin." He did, and the coin slowly glided back to him. "Make a stop sign with your hand." Martin did, and the coin sat motionless in the air.

"What now?" Martin asked.

"Have fun," Phillip answered.

Martin did just that. At his command, the coin explored every inch of airspace in the room. After a few minutes, Phillip asked, "It's pretty much the best thing ever, isn't it?"

"Yeah, it is!" Martin replied.

"You see, I registered you into the shell already, and now it's watching you, waiting for certain words or phrases—cheat codes, if you like. That's what we do. We research, design, and develop new cheat codes, which we share with the other wizards. It wouldn't do to have the codes just be words and phrases, though. If some local heard the Konami code, as you call it, and repeated it, they'd have access to all of the spells, and that would be bad. So, in order to use the spells, you need to have said the code, you have to know the commands in Esperanto, you must be wearing a robe with cuffs exactly two feet in circumference, and a conical hat no less than one foot tall. Also, you must be holding either a wooden staff five feet tall, not including ornamentation, or a wooden wand one and a half feet in length. Get any part of that wrong, and the shell will ignore you."

Martin played with the coin for a few more minutes. Finally, Phillip said "You can levitate things with your hand, or with your staff. It just depends which you point at your target when you say the magic words. Let's try something else. Say *kopio objekto*." Martin said it. There was a flash of blue light and then there were two coins.

"And that," Phillip said, "is why we don't have to work for a living." Phillip reached up and snatched one of the coins out of the air. "Now say *detrui objekto*, if you please." Martin did. There was another flash of light, and the coin disappeared.

"Where'd it go?" Martin asked.

"It didn't go anywhere. It's just gone. It no longer exists. That's the thing about being part of a computer program: the laws of physics no longer apply. Matter can be created or destroyed. That's why we train and screen people before giving them access. If you were to point at a person and say the spell, that person would be irrevocably gone and everything that person knows, including who had killed them, would be lost." Phillip stretched, yawned, and walked to the door that separated the crystal ball room from the shop. He stood silhouetted in the door with his back to Martin.

"Yup," Phillip said, "someone who has access to the shell can go anywhere, do almost anything, and if they kill someone, say the person who gave them the code, who would be the only person who could identify them, they'd be impossible to stop."

Phillip stood in the doorway for a long moment.

"Mm hm," he continued, "the only person who could identify them would be gone."

Another long moment passed.

"And in your case, Martin, that person would be me."

Slowly, Phillip twisted around to look over his shoulder at Martin, who was still standing there silently. Phillip smiled. "Well done! You've passed the most important test so far. You didn't try to kill me!"

"People actually do that?"

"Oh, yeah! Think about it. I've already made you functionally immortal. I've given you the ability to create money. I've shown you enough about flight to figure it out on your own. I've given you a hat, robe, and staff, and made it clear that if you took me out you wouldn't have to face the trials. Someone who isn't as decent as you might well be tempted to destroy me and get on with their lives."

"It didn't even occur to me."

"Dumb and decent can often look the same. It's depressing, but the truth often is. It's just as well. You're still in a safety mode. If you had tried to kill me, you'd have been knocked unconscious, and I don't think I need to tell you where, when, and in what state of dress you'd have woken up." Phillip walked back to the hidden keyboard and hit a few keys without bothering to sit down. He squinted into the crystal ball and nodded.

"There, the safety's off. Now... where was that ... thing." Phillip turned his back to Martin and rummaged around in the shelves that were now partially concealed by the drapes. He rummaged for a full thirty seconds, then stood up, faced Martin, and spread his arms wide.

"Congratulations! You've passed another test! You didn't kill me even after I explained in detail why you might want to! That clears up the whole 'dumb or decent' question." Phillip went back to the keyboard and hit a few more keys. When he finished he looked at Martin, who was studying him intently.

"Is this another test?" Martin asked.

"If you have to ask, then it probably is."

15.

Phillip and Martin spent most of the next two days practicing levitating and duplicating objects and going for long walks around Leadchurch. Phillip encouraged Martin to ask questions, but was careful in how much new material they covered on a given day. He said he wanted to keep Martin from getting overwhelmed. Martin would leave the embarrassingly oversized loaner robe and hat back at the shop. Without the rest of the ensemble, his staff seemed out of place, so it stayed back at the shop as well.

Occasionally one of the locals, as Martin now called them, would ask Phillip for some assistance. If they wanted money or food, he'd hear them out, and if he found them worthy he'd make their chicken into two chickens. If they wanted him to predict the future, he'd say something confusing and move along. If they were particularly hard up he'd say something confusing *and* make their chicken into two chickens. Martin noticed that the locals were falling into three distinct categories: people who wanted something and walked right up to ask, people who didn't want something right now but treated Phillip in a cordial manner, and people who clearly were up to no good, all of whom seemed to avoid Phillip like the plague.

"When I first got here," Martin said, "the first two locals I met were a couple of really tough-looking guys. We were on the road, miles from anyone else. I thought they were going to give me trouble, but they seemed terrified of me."

Phillip laughed. "These people have lived with us wizards in their midst for years now. They're all aware of the damage we can do if pushed. Think about how you got here, Martin. Think about all of us other wizards. We got here the same way. Part of why we all get along so well is that we're pretty much the same type of person. Only people who spend more time with computers than with people ever find the file, so we all share similar experiences and attitudes. Regretfully, some of us are still carrying a chip on our shoulder from the playground, and now that we have the power to get some revenge on bullies, some tend to take it too far. There's one spell that causes a thirty-foot-tall flaming demon to claw its way out of the ground and give your foe a wedgie. That makes a lasting impression."

"You're saying that the bullies are afraid of the geeks."

"Specifically, oddly dressed geeks who talk funny, and last night that described you perfectly."

"So we're allowed to use our powers as a weapon?"

"Only in self-defense. It seldom comes to that. As you've seen, we can make our homes and shops impregnable, and out here in the open we're unlikely to be taken unawares. If someone does grab me, I can always just say *eskapi*—"

There was a flash of blue light and Phillip was gone. Martin looked around. Everybody on the street was looking at him. Several very large men seemed particularly interested in the now unescorted wizard's apprentice, and started walking towards him. There was another flash of light, Phillip was back, and suddenly nobody was looking at them anymore. The large men seemed preoccupied with the sky, or the ground, anything but Phillip and Martin.

"Sorry about that. Anyway, I can say *that word* and I'll go to a safe place I set up in advance. In my case it's...."

"You know what," Martin interrupted, suddenly aware that people were paying more attention than Phillip might realize. "You can show me later."

That afternoon Martin multi-tasked, splitting his attention between the Esperanto vocabulary book from the 1930s that Phillip had given him and doing quick and dirty alterations on the loaner robe and hat. His own robe would not be ready for another week, and he'd decided he never wanted to be caught in public without the identifying markers of a wizard again. He sat in the shop, speaking gibberish and occasionally jabbing himself with the needle, which didn't break his skin, but still hurt. When he was done, he looked himself over, and he had to admit his handiwork looked pretty bad. He looked like he had had his tailoring done by an eight-year-old, but at least he didn't look like a victim.

He went into the crystal ball room to show Phillip his finished ensemble. Phillip agreed that the sewing wasn't great, but that Martin's staff had come out nicely. Martin had stripped off the bark, sanded the pale wood smooth, varnished and sealed the wood, and firmly affixed the six-inch bust of Santo to the top. The bust had a square base that included Santo's cape chain and collarbones, but cut off his shoulders. His thick, short neck led to his hand-painted mask. It was a dazzling metal-flake silver, like the body of a fiberglass dune buggy. The piping around the eyes, nose, and mouth holes was a flatter, duller gray. The eyes of the mask were canted at a fearsome, angry-looking angle, but the human eyes they framed looked kind and gentle. It was totally incongruous, and as such, perfect for Martin's needs.

Phillip took it all in and said, "You look like a crazy person."

"Good?" Martin said.

"Very good," Phillip said, "and you're just in time. We should really get going."

Martin wasn't aware that they were going anyplace that evening, and said so.

"You've been doing a great job, and I know that what with the consciousness-changing discoveries, police chases, time travel, and wizard training, it's been a stressful couple of weeks for you, so I figured it was time to have some fun."

Martin tried to picture what fun might be for someone with the kind of powers the wizards have. "Are we going to go flying, or teleport to a historical event?"

"We could do those things if you want. I was thinking we'd just meet a couple of my friends and spend the evening eating unhealthy food and playing board games."

"Let's do it!" Martin blurted.

Phillip smiled. "Let me tell them we're coming." Phillip gripped his staff in his left hand, and held his right hand at head height as if he were performing the Yorick speech from *Hamlet*. He said, "Komuniki kun Gary!" A glowing sphere of white light appeared in Phillip's outstretched hand. It pulsated and emanated an eerie warbling hum.

"Some of the guys call this spell 'the hand phone.' It's ringing," Phillip said.

After a moment, the sphere of light collapsed, changed shape, and became an image of a flaming human skull. It was completely flat, as if it were painted on a sheet of plastic. The flames moved, but not fluidly. It took Martin a moment of mental processing to realize that the image hovering above Phillip's hand was an animated GIF file projected into the world like an object.

A hollow, distant voice emanated from the flat flaming skull. "WHO HAS SOUGHT ME? I, WHO HOLD THE FATES OF…oh, hey, Phil. You still coming over?"

"Yeah, just wanted to let you know we're on our way now."

"Cool. See you then. The location code is *Gary la antaŭa korto*, got it?"

Phillip said, "Yeah, see you in a sec," and made a fist, causing the flaming skull to disappear.

Moments later, Phillip and Martin materialized in a small, dark clearing in a forest, near the side of a hill. The sun had not quite set, and the countryside beyond the forest was bathed in a golden glow. This chunk of forest, however, was dark and foreboding. What little light filtered in revealed twisted trees with gray bark and brown leaves. The underbrush was damp and smelled of decay. On one side of the clearing, a barely discernible path led into the woods. Trees hung menacingly over the trail, giving the impression of a claustrophobic tunnel. At the other end of the treeless area, the path widened, and the bordering trees provided less cover, as they all seemed to be dead or dying. Three wizards were already there. They seemed very happy to see Phillip.

"Gentlemen," Phillip said, "good to see you!"

Phillip introduced everyone. Gary was tall and thin with a short beard and large, mischievous eyes, wearing a black robe and hat. Jeff was small but muscular, with a narrow head, prominent nose, and small eyes. His robe appeared to be some sort of gray wool. Tyler was heavier, but by no means fat, with dark skin, short, black, curly hair, a friendly demeanor, and a striped purple and red robe. All three of them were smiling a little too broadly, almost to the point of laughing. Phillip frowned and looked down. He was standing ankle-deep in a puddle.

"GARY!" Phillip yelled.

"You shouldn't have let Gary know where you would be teleporting," Jeff offered. "Never smart."

"I used the location code he gave me," Phillip said, looking at his soggy boots.

"Like I said. Not smart."

There were spells that could be used to clean items, but nobody had come up with a better means of drying things than time and air, so Phillip was doomed to spend the rest of the evening barefoot, prolonging Gary's victory.

Tyler looked at Martin's robes. "Wow, Gwen's work is really slipping."

"Oh, you've all met Gwen?"

"Met, asked out, and got rejected by," Gary said.

"Yeah, that Gwen," Jeff said. "She don't like the wizards."

"She likes me fine," Phillip said, removing his waterlogged boots and socks.

"But you've never asked her out," Gary said.

"There might be a lesson in that," Phillip said, looking at Martin.

"I don't see the point in getting a woman to like you if you're not going to go out with her."

"No, Gary, you wouldn't," Phillip said.

"Anyway," Martin explained, "Gwen's still working on my robe. This is a loaner from Phillip."

Tyler looked at the robe again, then cocked an eyebrow at Phillip. "Blood-red with black trim? That's not your style."

Phillip shrugged. "I was in my necromancer phase."

Tyler nodded. "We all go through it."

"If you're lucky, you grow out of it," Jeff said looking at Gary, who was resplendent in his black robe.

When Phillip was convinced that his boots were clean, they proceeded into Gary's home. They had walked past the dead trees, around the corner of a steep hill, which blocked their view of what was ahead. They hadn't walked far, maybe a hundred feet, before a carefully calculated vista opened before Martin, revealing Gary's home. There was a small, perfectly round clearing at the base of a cliff. At the center of the clearing there was a stone plinth. On the plinth burned a fire so dark blue it was essentially black. The fire cast eerie shadows upward. Martin's eyes were naturally drawn to a twisting path cut into the rock. It switched back on itself twice before terminating about three stories up the cliff at a cave opening that formed the mouth of a ghastly skull. The hollows that formed the eyes of the skull glowed faintly red.

"Home sweet home," Gary said as he and Tyler lifted their staffs and flew to the skull's mouth. Jeff produced a wand and followed them, soaring gracefully through the air. Phillip left his boots and socks at the foot of the trail, put a hand on Martin's shoulder, and they both drifted effortlessly to the skull as well. The mouth of the cave was large enough for all five of them to stand comfortably.

"Welcome to Skull Gullet Cave, Martin. Come on in," Gary said, walking deeper into the cave. The cave entrance narrowed, then widened again into a chamber about thirty feet around, lit by torches set low on the walls that burned with a smokeless green flame. At the far end there was a massive throne made entirely out of antlers. Hundreds of sharp points jutted out at chaotic angles. It was the least comfortable looking chair Martin had ever seen. Next to it on a pedestal there was a massive, ancient-looking leather bound book, held at an angle, waiting to be studied.

"I just need to grab something really quick," Gary said as he hoisted the cover of the book open. Martin was surprised to see light emanate from the pages, illuminating Gary's face with a bluish glow. Martin was less surprised a moment later to hear the book make the classic synthesized bong of a Macintosh computer booting up. Gary lifted a dark gray, first-generation Apple PowerBook out of a hollow that was cut into the pages of the book. Gary held his staff in front of him and said, "Mother Love Bone." Lines of fire formed a rectangle on the cave wall. The stone inside the rectangle disappeared as the fire died out, revealing a room beyond. Gary led the others into the next room.

When compared to the cave's exterior and the first room, this room was shockingly normal by comparison. In one corner there was a roaring fire in a large fireplace, providing heat. There was a table with benches along both sides. There were three cushions on each bench to suggest where people should sit and help those people forget that they were sitting on a wooden bench. Light was provided by white balls of light that just hovered in the four corners of the room.

"I love what you've done with the place, but when people see this room, isn't the effect kind of ruined?" Martin asked.

"Nobody but other wizards ever sees this room," Tyler answered.

"If a lady wants to come home with me, I transport her directly to the bedroom," Gary said, motioning to a door in the back corner.

"And no wizard wants to go in there," Jeff added quickly.

Gary gave Martin the grand tour of the main room, but there wasn't really much to show. Martin was beginning to worry about the Spartan nature of wizards' lives. He didn't like the idea of spending the rest of his life living in barely furnished rooms and eating stew and porridge. As if reading his mind, Gary said, "So, who's hungry?" The answer was everyone. Martin was bracing himself for more stew when Gary said, "Martin, you're the new guy. What do you like, pepperoni, combo, or plain cheese?"

Martin sputtered, then said pepperoni. Gary took off his robe. Beneath it he was wearing torn jeans, gigantic loosely laced white high-tops, and a black t-shirt that said *Dokken*. He opened his PowerBook to reveal a small black and white screen surrounded by a two-inch-thick bezel, a small keyboard, and a marble-sized track ball. Gary typed a few words one-handed and disappeared. Less than a second later he reappeared holding three large brown boxes from Pizza Hut.

"I never get tired of the look on their faces when I pick up the pizza and walk directly into the bathroom," he said, chuckling.

"Aw, Gary, I told you not to take my food into the bathroom!" Jeff said.

"Relax! It's just a private place to teleport."

"Still, I don't need my pizza seasoned with bathroom air from 1992!"

"Martin, what's your favorite soda?"

"Diet Coke."

Gary muttered, "Wrong answer," as he typed a few more words and disappeared. Immediately he was back with two six packs of Diet Pepsi. The bottles were short and fat, like oversized hand grenades made of glass. The sight of the old font and logo briefly took Martin back to when he was a child. Gary put the drinks down. He said, "One more stop," then disappeared, reappearing with a fat stack of board games, paper plates, and a roll of paper towels.

While eating the best bad pizza Martin had ever tasted, and playing one of the most enjoyable games of Risk he had ever played, the five of them talked about a great many things.

They talked about their choice of staff ornaments. Gary had adorned his staff with large dolls of the band KISS, tied to the staff so they faced outward. If one of the locals asked what they were he would just say "The Demon, The Space Man, The Star Man, and the Peter Criss on Drums!" Tyler's staff was topped by the hood ornament from a Rolls-Royce. He didn't have a set explanation for its meaning, because a beautiful woman with wings speaks for itself. Jeff was the first wizard Martin had ever met who opted for a wand instead of a staff. He said, "It's easier to carry around, and I love me some Harry Potter."

They talked about where and when they were from. Gary was from Minneapolis, 1992. Tyler was from Montana, 2003. Jeff was from Delaware, and came from the year 2021. Martin was briefly delighted to meet someone from the future. He asked Jeff what happened in the years between Martin's time and his.

"A couple of presidents you've never heard of. A bunch of bands and movies you'd think are stupid. You'd freak right out if you saw my television. You'd love it, but you'd hate everything I watch on it."

Phillip saw that this answer didn't please Martin, and explained, "We don't discuss the future, not because it'll damage reality, but because it'll damage our friendships."

"It just leads to a fight," Tyler said. "Anyone from before your time looks like a time capsule. Anyone from after it looks like a privileged idiot. It's better to keep it vague. We figure if Jeff here had access to a computer and found the file, the future can't be too bad."

Jeff said, "I promise, if there was anything too bad, I'd tell you everything my federally mandated cranial implant will allow me to say."

"What? Federally mandated cranial implant?" Martin said. There was a moment of tension, then everyone but Martin laughed.

"That's the other reason we don't ask about the future. It's too easy to be made to look like a fool," Phillip said.

"Yeah," Gary added, "nobody wants to go through life looking like Ralph Wiggum." Everyone laughed but Phillip.

They discussed what they did with their spare time. Gary was a painter. Mostly he painted the kinds of images that would make great covers for heavy metal albums. Lots of bat wings and fire. Martin said that he bet living in the Middle Ages gave him lots of inspiration.

"Not nearly as much as I'd hoped," he said. "Turns out life here is just as boring as it is in the future. If I wanted to paint subsistence farmers I could have stayed in Minnesota. Tyler's getting a lot more inspiration out of this place than I am."

Martin turned to Tyler. "What do you do?" he asked.

"I write novels."

"Really?" Martin said. "Anything I've read?"

"Doubtful. I've only finished one, and it wasn't published. There wasn't really a market for a Gothic horror."

Gary broke in, "Especially one called *The Ghost of the Wolfman's Mummy*."

"It was called *The Curse*," said Tyler.

"And what was the subtitle?" Gary prodded him.

Tyler said, "*Of the Ghost of the Wolfman's Mummy*."

"*The Curse of the Ghost of the Wolfman's Mummy*," Martin repeated, trying to get his head around it.

Jeff said, "It answered the age-old question: what would happen if a werewolf bit a Pharaoh, who was then mummified, and whose tomb was defiled centuries later, causing him to come back to life and immediately get killed?"

"Turns out what happens is five hundred pages of confusion, gratuitous sex, and spooky growling noises," Gary said.

Tyler said, "It was a great idea! To defeat the ghost of the wolfman's mummy, you have to bring the ghost back to life."

"With a ritual that involves naked priestesses," Jeff interjected.

"Then gather all the funerary jars containing the mummy's organs," Tyler continued.

"By seducing them away from the beautiful, wealthy countess who bought them," Gary added.

"Then, once you've destroyed the jars..." Tyler pressed on.

"And had the sex to celebrate," Jeff said.

"...you still have a wolfman to deal with," Tyler finally finished.

"As sexily as possible, one would presume," Phillip said.

"Are you writing another horror book?" Martin asked.

"Nope. A fantasy novel. Living here's been invaluable. I travel around the countryside and ask people to tell me stories, then I write them up and weave them into my narrative."

"But Gary says it's mostly farmers around here."

"It is. I adapt their stories."

Gary said, "Instead of farmer, he writes *warrior.*"

"And instead of carrot, he puts down *goblin,*" Jeff added.

"And instead of grew, he writes *bludgeoned,*" Gary finished.

"But the point is I'm inspired by their stories!" Tyler said, defensively.

"Inspired to lie," Phillip said, not unkindly.

There was a long pause while Martin tried to decide how to phrase the question they all knew was coming next. Finally, Martin asked, "Do the farmers ever react badly to the fact that you're..."

"A black man in Medieval England?" Tyler finished for him. "They ask about it, but I tell them that I'm Moorish. They assume either I've been converted to Christianity, so I'm harmless, or I'm dangerous enough to survive in this country as a heathen. Either way, it ends the conversation."

Gary said, "The one here with the most interesting hobby is Jeff. He's one of the shell's most prolific contributors. Easily a third of the things we can do are directly thanks to him. What are you up to now?"

Jeff shrugged. "Still working on importation."

Martin was lost. "Importation? What are you trying to import?"

"In theory, anything that was created digitally, but I'm specifically trying to bring in assets from videogames. If they exist in a computer construct, and we exist in a computer construct, there should be a way to have us exist in the *same* computer construct."

"Yeah!" Gary said, pounding his fist on the table. "Then we'll get some dragons up in here!"

Tyler looked at Phillip. "What I want to know is what *you* do with your spare time. More to the point, what it is you keep on the second floor of your shop? Has he let you up there, Martin?"

"No, he hasn't."

"Why not, Phillip? What do you have up there?"

"Nothing," Phillip replied.

"Then what do you do up there?" Tyler asked.

"Nothing."

"I see. You go up there to do nothing, with nothing. Do you expect us to believe that?"

"No."

After a long pause, Tyler said, "Fair enough," and they got back to their game of Risk.

"So," Gary said, "I bet you're anxious to get your own robes, eh, Martin?"

Martin answered, "Can't wait."

"We go back for the first fitting tomorrow," Phillip said. "Until then he's welcome to wear my old robe. I don't really see the point myself. He's not doing magic in public yet."

"I dunno," Martin said. "I just feel safer if the locals think I have full wizard powers."

"Nonsense! You've lived your whole life up until now without people thinking you have powers, and you haven't faced the constant threat of violence. I don't see why it should be any different here."

"Because A) you clearly didn't go to my high school, and B) maybe I'm wrong, but I just get the feeling that there are some people around here who'd like to get their hands on a wizard who can't fight back."

Phillip shook his head. "Nonsense. You're just being paranoid. But if it makes you feel better to wear my old robes, I see no harm in it." The other three studied the game board in silence.

Time went by. Battle lines were drawn and redrawn. Tyler had a run of luck and wiped Phillip off of the map. Phillip congratulated Tyler and handed over his cards.

Tyler said, "Europe is the hardest continent to defend. Too many borders."

"Perhaps," Phillip said, rising from the table, "perhaps. Well, gents, I'm off to partake in the greatest pleasure the Middle Ages can afford a man."

Martin was confused until Jeff explained. "He's gonna take a whiz outside."

Phillip had explained earlier that bathrooms were a matter of personal taste for wizards. All of the wizards Martin had met so far were male, so they were comfortable urinating outdoors, but one's chosen mode of defecation was largely determined by one's comfort level. Phillip had facilities in his home similar to a modern bathroom. It was a small addition grafted crudely onto the back of his hut, and it resembled a classic latrine, except for three important factors: It had a modern toilet seat and lid, it had a roll of modern toilet paper, and it didn't have the horrible odor one expects in such a place. When Martin mentioned this, Phillip used his staff to shine a light down the hole. It was a deep shaft that was bone-dry all the way to the bottom. Martin asked if it was brand new. Phillip laughed, wadded up a ball of the bathroom tissue and threw it into the shaft. The ball fell down the shaft, then vanished into thin air a foot before the bottom.

"Where'd it go?" he asked Phillip.

"Where I wanted it to," Phillip answered.

After a moment's thought, Martin asked, "How deep is it?"

"Thirty feet."

"Why so deep?"

"To build up speed."

Phillip changed the subject, telling Martin about another wizard he knew (Tyler, as it turned out) who still kept an apartment in his original time. There was nothing unusual about that, but since he'd started living in the past, Tyler's apartment was basically a bathroom and a storage facility for bulk-purchased toilet paper, paper towels, hand soap, and garbage bags. He would commute back there every time he had to move his bowels. From his point of view, that meant every day or so, but since he always came back to the same moment he had just left, if you were in his apartment you would see him appear, use the lavatory, wash his hands, dry them with paper towels (cloth towels wouldn't have time to dry), and disappear. Then, less than a second later (but hours or days later for him), he would appear and do the whole thing over again. Then again, and again, and again. Tyler had been a wizard for four and a half years, so according to Phillip's math, Tyler's toilet had been in near constant use for something like five and a half days.

"His water bill is going to be astronomical!" Martin said.

"Yes, in something like twenty years," Phillip said.

Martin didn't know how Gary handled number twos, but when it came to urine, the answer was the forest outside, and that was where Phillip was going. The instant he was gone, Jeff, Gary, and Tyler's demeanor changed completely.

Tyler looked Martin straight in the eye and said, "You aren't wrong, Martin. Don't ever let the locals think you can't defend yourself. Most of them don't care about us one way or the other, but there are some who'd love to catch one of us unaware."

Martin was both alarmed and relieved. He told them about the few seconds Phillip had left him alone on the street, and how close he had come to getting attacked. They did not seem surprised.

"One time, I made the mistake of saying I'd broken my wand. A guy pulled a knife on me, like, immediately! Like he'd been waiting to do it for years!" Jeff said.

"What did you do?"

"I showed him that I'd glued my wand back together, then I showed him that it still worked. Then I showed him my back, from a great distance."

Tyler shook his head. "They need us, and they fear us. That's not the same thing as liking or respecting us."

"Why doesn't Phillip see that?" Martin asked.

"He doesn't want to, I guess. He likes almost everyone, and he figures almost everyone likes him. It's worked out pretty well for him so far. I don't want to be there the day it stops. Who knows, maybe it never will. It's hard not to like him."

Martin thought about the few days he'd known Phillip. In that time Phillip had publicly humiliated him, bounced him off of a tree at high speed, threatened him with prison and public nudity, and repeatedly accused him of not thinking, and yet Martin trusted Phillip, and considered him a friend.

"You said he likes *almost* everyone," Martin said.

Gary smirked. "You haven't seen him and Jimmy together yet, have you?"

"Look, Martin," Tyler said, "we're not saying you should live in fear. We're just saying to keep your guard up."

"Yeah, I get that," Martin said. He glanced at the door. The guys seemed to be leveling with him. He had a question he wanted to ask before Phillip returned.

"Guys, should I be worried about passing the trials?"

They all looked at each other. Tyler said, "You should work hard and do what Phillip says. He trained Gary, and Gary trained me and Jeff. Phillip knows what he's talking about. Do what he tells you, and take it seriously. That said, I think you'll pass."

"Yeah, you'll pass," Gary said.

"Because if you don't, we're totally gonna send you back to your own time, tied up and naked!" Jeff added, helpfully.

16.

The next morning it was time for the rough fitting for Martin's robe. Martin had spent most of the night before lying in his hammock, trying to figure out how to handle the Gwen situation. He listed the things he knew. She was the most attractive woman he had met in this time. She was also the first woman he had met in this time. Every attempt he had made to impress her had failed. Gary, Tyler, and Jeff had all asked her out and gone down in flames. She seemed to like Phillip, but Phillip made a point of not hitting on her. He toyed with the idea of hitting on her by not hitting on her. He would be friendly and professional, maintaining a façade of pleasant disinterest, all the while scheming to initiate a romantic relationship.

He plotted and schemed for a bit, but eventually realized that it would be a lot of work, and that he'd most likely mess it up and make her dislike him even more. Instead, he decided to give up. The Gwen thing wasn't happening, and he should just concentrate on his training. Instead of his big, complex bluff, he would just treat Gwen like he would any professional with whom he was doing business. He would be friendly and professional. It was just simpler that way.

Martin told Phillip he'd decided not to pursue Gwen.

"Splendid," Phillip said. "I'm glad you've chosen to follow my instructions. Although it's a shame about the lag time between when I tell you to do something and when you finally decide to do it." Phillip put a bowl of stew down in front of Martin. Martin started to dig in, but paused, his spoon hovering over the bowl.

"Is this still that same pot of stew?"

"It depends what you mean by *the same pot of stew*. Of course, it's the same pot, and it's still full of stew, but if you mean is it the same stew, that's been bubbling away in the pot for days on end, then the answer is also yes."

Martin put his spoon down. "Are you trying to kill me?" he asked, as politely as he could.

"If I were trying to kill you, you'd know it, because you'd be dead. Don't be such a baby. It's perfectly safe. It's been boiling nonstop for weeks! It's a whole lot cleaner than that bowl I put it in, that's for sure."

"That doesn't help."

"Look, I've added water occasionally, and thrown in more vegetables when I get them. This is how they do things here. Didn't you ever wonder how people survived without refrigerators? It was tricks like this. Also, letting the stew cook down over the course of days intensifies the flavors."

"Maybe so, but not all flavors are good," Martin said, eyeing the stew as if it might attack him.

"Look," Phillip said, "I told you not to go after Gwen, and after much deliberation, you decided to do as I say. I'm telling you to eat your stew. Sadly, we don't have time for you to decide that I'm right. We have to go and not hit on my friend Gwen."

Once Martin had half-heartedly choked down some stew, he and Phillip teleported to the street outside Gwen's shop. It wouldn't have been a long walk, but Phillip didn't have any customers lined up and he didn't like to let a day go by without some public demonstration of his power. Inside the shop they found Gwen talking to a peasant woman wearing what appeared to be a burlap coat. The woman was holding one arm straight out at shoulder level, and was pointing at it with the other hand. At first Martin thought she was doing some kind of tai chi move, but then he realized she was just complaining.

"The sleeves are too long. You don't have to be a bloody tailor to see that." She had a point. Her fingers were barely showing beyond the line of the cuff.

Gwen looked perplexed. "Are you hunching your shoulders?"

"Are you calling me a liar?"

Gwen held up her hands. "No, not at all. I'm sorry, I'm just mystified. Cloth shrinks, it doesn't grow. And even if it did, it wouldn't grow faster in one direction than in the other."

"Well, it is. I just bought this coat three months ago, and now it doesn't fit."

"We both agreed it fit fine when you bought it."

"Well, now it don't!"

Gwen thought a moment. "You live near to Sam, don't you?"

"We both live in Rickard's Bend. What's that got to do with anything?"

"Nothing, I'm sure. Look, I'm sorry for the trouble. Leave the coat with me. I'll hem the sleeves for free. Please come back in a week. It'll be done."

The woman handed Gwen the coat and left. As she passed Martin he heard her mutter, "Now to go settle up with that bloody cobbler."

"Tough morning, Gwen?" Phillip asked.

"Nothing I can't handle so far." Gwen looked pointedly at Martin.

Martin smiled. "Good morning, Gwen, it's good to see you."

"Uh, good morning, Martin. So, gentlemen, ready for the rough fitting?"

Gwen asked Martin to remove the blood-red loaner robe and hat. She unfolded a robe made of thin, off-white cloth, which she held up like a man helping his wife put her coat on. As Martin slid his arms into the robe, Gwen explained, "This is just a rough template I made to your measurements. Once this fits properly, I'll make the real thing out of more expensive fabric." Martin swung his arms around. "How's it feel?" Gwen asked.

"A little tight through the chest, but other than that, it feels good."

Gwen made a note. She pulled at the seams where the shoulders met the sleeves, held her measuring stick along the side of the sleeve, and took another measurement. "The shoulders aren't sitting quite right either."

Martin said, "It'll be fine. You know what you're doing. What fabric have you chosen?"

"I have a couple of ideas. I didn't want to settle on anything until I saw your staff – or are you the wand type?"

With great effort Martin let this pass without comment, simply turning to Phillip and asking, "Could you please hand me my staff?"

Phillip took the staff Martin had left leaning against the wall and handed it directly to Gwen. She looked at the small bust of Santo in his shiny silver mask. "Fearsome!" she said. "What is it?"

Martin puffed up a bit and explained, "That is the grim visage of the saint of the southern country. Destroyer of monsters and leader of men. He vanquished and later befriended the Blue Demon." It was the first time Martin had gotten to use the description he'd prepared, and he was pretty happy with it. Gwen seemed impressed.

Gwen put a conical hat made of the same flimsy fabric on Martin's head. They discussed how it fit. Gwen took a few more measurements and told Phillip and Martin to come back in a week for the final fitting, and if no further revisions were needed, they could take the robe home then.

As they left, the angry woman with the oversized coat came back in, now barefoot. Her leggings were stretching down past her heel onto her foot. She said, "You got me so angry talking about the coat, I plum forgot to mention that my leggings are too long as well!"

Martin and Phillip returned to the hut and worked until that time of the day when it was almost not the day anymore, but it wasn't quite night yet. The sun was still in the sky. It was low in the sky, but it was there. When it finally went down, the world would have a brand new night, with all the promise and opportunity that a night offers, but the world wasn't there yet. Before the new night could begin, the old day had to end, and it was grinding slowly to a halt. Birds were singing, quietly. Rabbits were mating, tiredly. People were doing their work, half-heartedly.

In Phillip's hut, he and Martin were just finishing up a discussion about transporting complex objects, a complex problem, which Phillip could tell was completely failing to hold Martin's interest. Phillip was annoyed by this until he realized that he couldn't remember what the last sentence he'd said was, because he'd been more interested in obsessing about Martin's lack of interest.

"Let's break for the day and have dinner," Phillip said.

"Great idea," Martin replied.

Phillip stood up, walked over to the stew pot, turned, and saw that Martin had walked the opposite direction, and was standing next to the door with his staff in hand.

"Where are you going?" Phillip asked.

"To get dinner," Martin answered.

"But we have stew here," Phillip said.

"That's why I'm eating somewhere else."

Phillip said, "What do you think you're going to eat?"

"Anything but stew." Martin left before Phillip could protest any further.

Martin didn't wish to eat any more stew, but he also wanted to stretch his legs and see more of the town. If he'd just said so, he was sure Phillip would have gone out for a walk with him, which would have been nice, but not as nice as going alone because part of his view of the town would have been blocked by Phillip, and he had seen Phillip enough.

Phillip's hut stood near the edge of town, so of the four directions Martin could walk, one led out into the woods, two led along the outskirts of civilization, and the last would take him into the heart of Leadchurch. Martin set a course for the center of town and started walking.

Martin knew that he cut an imposing figure in his borrowed blood-red robe and hat, carrying his staff with the fearsome visage of Santo staring out at the world. Martin tried to balance this by smiling and appearing friendly, but as he walked down the street, he found that the people who were still out milling around gave him a lot of room. They didn't seem unhappy to see him, just happier to see him from a distance.

Martin thought about his dinner options. He could go to the Rotted Stump and buy some food, but given the first impression he had made on the owner, he didn't like his chances of getting clean, unadulterated food out of that place. Frankly, he didn't like anybody's chances of getting unadulterated food from Pete, but he figured any food that Pete knew was going to Martin would probably be pretty adult by the time he got it.

Martin decided to turn right at the next intersection, then left at the one after that. Instead of walking directly to the center of town the same way he and Phillip had before, he would go via a slightly different route. Leadchurch was small, but there were still parts of it he hadn't seen. Martin wanted to fix that.

Martin thought, *There must be somewhere to buy some food in this place other than just the Rotted Stump.* He was sure he'd seen a guy selling fruit and vegetables out of a cart the other day. *Of course, he probably irrigated it with filthy water, but I can always wash whatever I buy with the local water, which is also filthy.* Martin realized that he hadn't thought this little expedition through very well.

He considered going back to his own time to get some real food. The problem there was that he didn't have full shell access, so he couldn't use whatever simplified tools the local wizards had developed for time travel. He could edit the raw file directly, which was possible, but difficult using his phone's tiny screen and twitchy on-screen keyboard, and time travel and teleportation were not activities in which one wanted to risk a mistake. His safest option was to use his app, which would always take him back to the exact time and place from which he last left, so that would mean raiding his parent's fridge, which would be awkward, given the fact that federal agents were laying siege to their house.

I could have something delivered. A pizza, or Chinese, or something, he thought. *I wonder if the delivery guy would fight his way past the Treasury agents if I promise to tip him an extra twenty.*

Martin was so delighted at the image of a minimum wage pizza deliverer elbowing his way past armed law enforcement officers that he forgot to pay attention to where he was going. He didn't collide with another person, or walk into a stationary object, but he suddenly looked around and realized that his surroundings had changed. The light seemed dimmer. The huts that lined the road were less well cared for, and many didn't seem to be structurally sound. The animals looked malnourished and what carts he did see were not in good repair. His fellow pedestrians were the most unsettling part. They weren't doing anything overtly threatening, but they were all watching Martin like hawks.

Stay cool, Martin told himself. *There's nothing to worry about. I'm a wizard, after all. Just keep walking, act like you belong here, and you'll be fine. Of course, I don't have all of my wizard powers yet, but none of these people know that. Someone would have to be pretty stupid to pick a fight with me. Or, a really, really good fighter. Or possibly both.*

A voice from across the street called out. "Hey! Hey you!"

Martin had never, in his life, had a sentence that started with "hey you" end in a way that made him happy. Despite this, he reflexively turned toward the voice, regretting it immediately. Across the street he saw a huge man, both tall and broad, built out of solid muscle in exactly the way that makes a man look terrible with his shirt off. Fortunately, he was wearing a chainmail vest. Unfortunately, his prodigious chest hairs were poking out through the mail, giving the viewer the impression that the chainmail was blurry.

Several other young men who were smaller than the big guy, but still larger than Martin, were hanging around. Martin had seen their type before. Really, anybody who attended public high school had. They were tough young thugs, looking for a good time, and the easiest way to find a good time, for them, was to make sure someone else was having a bad time.

Martin and the big man locked eyes. He gave Martin a look that said both, *How dare you look at me?* and *Yeah, you better look at me when I'm talking to you.*

He started crossing the street, walking directly toward Martin. Big patches of the man's hair were missing. Martin wasn't sure if they'd been pulled out in a fight or fallen out due to some awful illness. The big man smiled. Several teeth were missing, and Martin still wasn't sure whether to blame violence or disease. The man's nose looked like it spent more time broken than not.

The big man walked up to Martin, standing close enough that he couldn't be accused of touching him, but couldn't be prevented from it if he chose to. He kept his eyes locked on Martin, but turned his head slightly, as if talking over his shoulder to someone behind him. "Hey, boys, look who's here. This must be that new wizard we heard about."

The other punks filled in all around, surrounding Martin on both sides. They were all smiling. None of them looked friendly. One felt the fabric of Martin's robe. Another repeatedly flicked the point of Martin's hat. A third looked at the bust of Santo at the head of Martin's staff and made a face, growling at the masked *luchador*.

The big one said, "I hear the town wizard is teaching you. Is that right? Maybe you'd like to practice on us? Show us what you've learned. Does that sound like fun? I think it does."

Martin mentally ran through his options. His brain was in high gear, burning through ideas so quickly that it didn't even form words, just a stream of concepts.

He could try talking to them, but that's exactly what thugs like this wanted, to prolong things and make you squirm. He had his phone, he could use it to hover or teleport, but hovering was useless, and anyway, to teleport he'd have to pull the phone out and turn it on, which would just give them the opportunity to try to take it from him.

He'd have to use the powers he'd already been taught by Phillip. He was invulnerable. He could just let them pound on him until they got tired, but that didn't sound like fun. He could copy things. Of course, copying the thugs would be counter-productive, but he could copy a bunch of gold pieces and buy them off. He dismissed the idea immediately. It was cowardly, and would've just given them incentive to attack him again.

He could levitate objects. He remembered Phillip tormenting him with the flying goat.

Martin held his staff in front of himself, said, "Levi objekto," then shoved his staff forward with both hands. The big guy flew backwards and rolled to a stop in an undignified heap. Unfortunately, for every action, there is an equal and opposite reaction, and while there were ways to counteract this, Phillip had not yet seen the need to teach them to Martin, since he had only levitated very small objects.

The act of shoving the brute had also shoved Martin backwards even farther. He instantly realized what had happened, but was helpless to stop it. He slid to a stop on his backside. Looking up, he saw the smaller thugs, still standing right where they had been, but with a gap in the middle where Martin and their leader had flown away. Beyond the gang standing there with their mouths hanging open, Martin saw their leader, slowly lifting himself out of the dirt with murder in his eyes. One of the smaller gang members said, "He knocked down Kludge," in an awed voice.

Martin had to think fast. He had one power he could use as a weapon, and it seemed to have a fatal flaw, but perhaps he could turn it to his advantage. At the end of the street, directly behind the one they called Kludge, who was now on his feet, and walking toward Martin with terrible purpose, Martin saw a tall, sturdy looking tree.

Martin leapt to his feet, pointed his staff at the upper branches of the tree, and cried, "Levi objekto!"

The tree did not move. The thugs sneered and laughed. *Good*, Martin thought.

He hauled back on his staff as if it were a fishing pole and he was trying to land a marlin. If the tree had been floating in the air, this would have pulled it toward Martin with great force, but it was not. The tree was rooted to the ground, so instead of the tree being pulled toward Martin, Martin was pulled toward the tree

Martin streaked through the gaggle of punks, who flew in every direction. He hit Kludge directly in the chest with both feet, knocking him back down into the dirt. Martin's trajectory flattened, and he slid to a stop on the dirt road, barely managing to stay on his feet. He released the levitation spell and looked behind him.

The thugs were struggling to their feet. Kludge rolled over onto his stomach and looked up, locking eyes on Martin, who sprinted back to the main drag and nominally familiar territory. He turned right at the next intersection, and was back on the same street he and Phillip had used to walk into the center of town. From here, he'd be able to find his way back to Phillip's shop, Gwen's shop, or the lead church, but before any of those things, he knew he'd find the ramshackle fruit stand he'd been seeking for very different reasons just a few moments ago.

Martin was aware of several very heavy-sounding sets of feet running behind him. He knew the gang was chasing him, and he suspected they were gaining ground. As he got closer to the fruit stand, he saw the very thing he'd been hoping for. Pumpkins!

Martin slid to a stop. A calculated risk, but one he had to take. He aimed his staff at a large pumpkin, said, "Levi objekto," and raised the staff over his head like an axe. He saw that the pumpkin was obeying his command. He pivoted, observing that the gang was still about fifty feet behind him. They had been gaining, but now, seeing him standing his ground with a blunt object in his hand, and a heavy-looking gourd hovering above him, they screeched to a halt.

Martin leveled his staff directly at the leader, Kludge, and the pumpkin streaked straight at him. Martin aimed for his chest, specifically, for the two muddy footprints that marked where Martin had bounced off of him before, but Kludge turned and blocked it with his arm, the projectiles exploding in a cloud of pumpkin rind and guts. The rest of the gang shielded their faces from the residual flying seeds and goo.

Martin turned, levitating a second pumpkin, which he spun in an orbit around himself, swinging his staff like a Samurai sword. He picked out the second largest thug, then pointed his staff at him. The thug knew what was coming, and dodged, but the pumpkin still struck the smaller man behind him, knocking him off of his feet with an undignified yelp. After that everyone scattered. Even the man who'd just been struck crawled quickly then shambled to his feet before limping away as fast as he could. The only one left was Kludge, rolling on the ground, moaning.

Martin turned his back and walked casually to the fruit stand. He asked what he owed for the two pumpkins, paying the total from his coin purse. As he handed the gold to the fruit seller, he saw fear in the man's eyes. Martin turned to see Kludge, who was nearly on top of him, holding a large rock over his head. Martin stretched out his hand, and again said "Levi objekto." He lifted Kludge into the air, spinning and cursing. Martin braced himself against the pushback, and gently sent Kludge drifting away down the street and high into the air, as if he were a helium balloon and Martin had simply let go of the string.

Martin said, "Drop the rock."

Kludge shouted and cursed and threatened to do a lot more than that if Martin didn't put him down.

"Drop the rock," Martin repeated, before adding, "or I'll drop you."

Kludge dropped the rock.

Martin looked at him, floating in space, shouting obscenities. He drew Kludge in closer, so they could talk. *Really, he's a lot like the goat that Phillip levitated,* Martin thought. *He chased me around. He's unpleasant and nasty, but in the end, he's really no threat to me at all.*

He brought Kludge in close enough that he could almost reach out and grab him. Almost, but not quite. After trying several times, Kludge gave up, and simply hung there giving Martin the eye.

"This ain't over, wizard," he said. "Me and my boys'll be watching you. Count on it."

Martin smiled. "I hope you do watch, and I hope you pay close attention to what you see, because as long as you see me with this staff here in my hand, there's nothing you can do to hurt me."

Martin lifted Kludge high into the air, then sent him far into the distance toward the tallest building in town, the lead church. Kludge grasped the steeple with both arms, and Martin released him. Martin saw him slide down the steeple, heard faint distant yelling. He looked around, and for the first time saw that the street was lined with people who had seen the entire exchange. Martin thrust his hand into his robe pocket and grasped his phone.

He craned his head and peeked at the screen through the voluminous pocket's opening. While his app booted up he looked up and smiled at the villagers, who were still watching him silently, out of fear and shock. Martin glanced back down at the phone, chose the teleportation function, and estimated the location of Phillip's hut.

Martin looked up, smiled brightly, tapped the brim of his wizard hat with the head of his staff, and disappeared.

Martin reappeared at the far end of the road, about thirty feet beyond Phillip's hut. He quickly scampered to the door and ducked inside.

Phillip was still sitting at the table, reading an old issue of *Omni* magazine. He looked up and said, "Back so soon?"

Martin said, "Yeah, I decided stew sounded pretty good."

The next afternoon found Phillip and Martin in an empty field miles from town. The field was bordered on one side by forest and on the other side by the sea. Phillip was carrying what looked like an artist's easel and a large dartboard. "Today, we're going to talk about mystical rays and beams," he said, as he set up the target with its back to the sea.

"How long did it take you to get used to saying things like that without feeling silly?" Martin asked.

"I'm still working on it. Anyway, you already know how to levitate small objects and move them through the air. That alone is one of your most powerful defensive weapons. But in an actual fight, simply hurling heavy objects at people leaves something to be desired."

"It's not that impressive," Martin agreed. "I mean, making things float is cool, but everybody knows we can do that already, and at the end of the day there's not a lot of difference between throwing a rock at someone and *magically* throwing a rock at someone."

Phillip nodded. "That is one issue, but the more immediate problem is that it could kill them. If it's in self-defense that's one thing, but our goal is to prove that we have powers, not to prove that we are murderers. The beauty of mystical beams and rays is that you can make them look horrifically violent while being deliberately non-lethal." Phillip and Martin stood about a hundred feet from the target. "Okay, Martin, you're wearing a robe and hat. You've got your staff. What's the first rule of using your staff?"

"Don't make the obvious joke."

"Top man! Now, I want you to stare at the target. Concentrate hard on it. I want you to say *radion de ruga lumo* when you think you're ready."

Martin stared at the target. It seemed to loom impossibly large in his perception. He imagined it being obliterated by his will. He exhaled slowly, and when his lungs were almost depleted he said, "*Radion de ruga lumo.*"

An awe-inspiring amount of nothing happened.

Martin turned to Phillip and pointed at the target. "It's still there. What'd I do wrong?"

Phillip said, "Say it again."

Martin furrowed his brow. "Say what again, *radion de ruga lumo?*

A bright beam of light, the width of Martin's arm shot from Martin's pointing hand directly into the target. Martin gaped at it for a moment, then let out a whoop. He raised his hand to look at it and the ray angled into the sky. He aimed it back at the target. Then at the ocean. Then at a tree. Then at a rock. The whole time, he was giggling like a maniac.

"As I said," Phillip said, "the shell is always monitoring us. It's not just waiting for commands, it's also looking for signals. Of course, it won't let you do anything without a staff or wand, a robe, and a hat, but there are subtle clues as to your intent built into those items. The robe has two-foot cuffs because that's how the shell knows where your hands are. It watches for you to make a pointing gesture, and that's how it knows where to target things. It took us a few years to get the programming right. For a long time we could only shoot beams from our staffs and wands. You can still use your staff to shoot rays if you like. It can look very impressive, and can help with long-range accuracy if you hold it like a rifle. Also, if you think you're ready, you're welcome to stop shooting me with your beam."

Martin laughed and changed his aim so that the ray was no longer hitting Phillip in the chest. He aimed at the grass between them. The ray brilliantly illuminated a four-inch circle of grass, but was clearly doing no damage.

"I assume this is some kind of harmless learner's energy beam."

"Of course. Your hand is a glorified flashlight."

"Still, it's awfully cool. Thanks for showing me how to do this."

"You're welcome, Martin."

They stared at the spot of grass illuminated by the beam.

"Phil, would you show me how to stop it?"

"Sure, you know how already. What's Esperanto for stop?"

Martin laughed at himself and said, "Halti." The beam disappeared.

"Okay, now we're going to move on to something genuinely dangerous, so no kidding around."

"Gotcha."

"Good. I want you to carefully point at the target and say *radion de varmo* when you're ready."

Martin did as Phillip told him, and the target burst into flames. "I can't see the beam," he said.

"That's right. Simple beams like the ones we've been playing with usually either look cool or do something useful, but not both. If you want to accomplish something and look good doing it, you have to shoot more than one beam at once. You could tell the shell, 'Beam of heat and light and make a loud noise and surround me with sparkly stuff,' but that's a lot to translate into Esperanto on the fly. That's why the next thing we study will be making macros."

"Cool," Martin said. "Why isn't my hand burning?"

"We built a safety feature into the shell. The ray—all rays, actually—start three inches beyond your hand." Phillip pulled a long blade of grass out of the ground and touched it to Martin's pointing finger. It was unharmed. Slowly, he moved the blade away from Martin's finger, toward the target, and at the three inch point it burst into flames.

"Mind if I stop?" Martin asked.

"Feel free."

Martin said, "Halti." There was no visible difference, but he pointed at the ground and the grass was unharmed, so clearly the beam had stopped. He looked at the smoldering ashes of the target. "Sorry I destroyed your target," he said.

Phillip patted him on the back. "Don't be. I borrowed it from Gary."

Later that afternoon, Phillip and Martin sat at the keyboard of the Commodore 64. Phillip removed the crystal ball and put the monitor, an old eleven-inch color TV with a faux wood-grain exterior, up on the table so they could both see it.

Phillip said, "You remember the night we met, that display I put on before I sent you flying into the trees?"

"Yes. I remember that."

"Well, that was what we call a macro. I'm sure you're aware of the idea of a macro."

"Yeah," Martin said, "it's a simple program that allows you to execute several actions with one command."

"Exactly. That's all that was. I sat down in advance and thought up an entertaining series of commands and programmed the shell to execute them for me if I do certain things. In that case, I twirl my staff and quietly hum a few notes of *Ride of the Valkyries*. We all program our own macros. Some are useful. Some are for show. When we get together sometimes we have a duel to see whose macro is the most impressive. You could say it's like breakdancing for wizards."

"I could, but I like you, so I won't. What was that you hit me with, by the way?"

Phillip shrugged. "I can't tell you all of my secrets, but since you've experienced that particular beam firsthand, I suppose there's no harm in telling you that the active ingredient was a one-foot-wide column of wind."

"Wind?! I was blasted into the forest by *wind*?"

"Two-hundred-mile-an-hour wind."

"Yeah, I guess that'd do it. So, how do I make a macro?"

"It's just a matter of basic computer scripting. I'm sure it's nothing you can't handle on that pocket computer of yours."

Martin pulled out his smartphone, looked at it, and bit his lip. "Phil, I've done some programming and the thing is, I could probably write the macros on this, but it wouldn't be a lot of fun. This isn't really a computer. I mean, it IS really a computer, but in my time we really don't use these as computers."

Phillip looked confused. "What do you use them for, then?"

"They really haven't told you anything about the future, have they? This is my phone."

"A phone. You use it as a phone. You carry around a device that's the size of a deck of cards and is more powerful than a Cray supercomputer, and you use it as a *phone*?"

"I also play games on it, and watch a movie occasionally."

"You can watch movies on that?"

"Not many. I mean, I only have a sixteen-gig memory card in it."

Phillip muttered, almost to himself, "My Commodore has sixty-four kilobytes of memory and a floppy drive that stores one hundred and seventy K. You can double that, but you have to cut a notch in the disk." Then, loud and clear, Phillip said, "I kind of hate you right now."

"I guess that's why nobody tells you about the future."

"I guess. Anyway, that'll have to wait. We have some work to do this afternoon."

"What kind of work?"

"Nothing too taxing. Just a quick exorcism."

17.

Martin and Phillip teleported back to the shop so Phillip could grab a few things. He lurched around the room, picking up a couple of bottles, a small human figure made of twigs, and a dried dead frog, which he handed to Martin. "Here, take this."

Martin held the dead frog gingerly, dangling it by two fingers. "Why do I have to hold the frog corpse?"

"I wanted to see if you would," Phillip answered, looking at the frog and shuddering. "Ugh, disgusting."

Phillip walked into the crystal ball room. Martin followed. Phillip consulted a scrap of paper and punched some commands into the Commodore 64.

"I agreed to this exorcism a couple of weeks ago. That was before you showed up, of course."

"When you say exorcism, what do you mean?"

Phillip smiled, but didn't look up from his work as he talked. "I mean that some local thinks his son is possessed by a demon, and we've been asked to remove it."

"But there is no demon, right?"

"That depends on how you look at it. If you consider rebelliousness, sullenness, and liking things that their parents hate to be demonic, then yes, we live surrounded by demons."

"I didn't know wizards handled this sort of thing. I thought it was the church's department."

"It is," Phillip said, "and that's why we'll be working with my friend, His Excellency Father Galbraith, the Bishop of Leadchurch."

Martin was confused again. "I figured the church would be against the use of magic."

"It was, before we came along. Back when wizards were just crazy men with no powers and a mystical belief system that they couldn't really prove, the clergy was their sworn enemy. Kind of like two used car dealerships set up on the same street. Both sides claimed to have all the answers, but couldn't demonstrate that they were right without resorting to a lot of arm waving and suggesting that people *look around them* and *think about it*. They couldn't prove themselves right, so they channeled their energies into proving the other side wrong. Then we came along, with our irritating ability to prove that we had powers. We put the fake wizards right out of business, and the more practical-minded members of the church, Bishop Galbraith among them, decided that they had to find a way to explain our existence that was consistent with their belief system."

"How do they explain us?"

"They just say we were created by God."

"Fair enough. Why do they say God created wizards?"

"For a reason."

"Okay, I'm still with you. What is that reason?"

"The reason is … beyond man's understanding."

Martin thought about this. "That's not much of an explanation."

"No, but it is consistent with their beliefs. The advantage that religion has over magic or science is that man's inability to understand is built into the system, so if an explanation is confusing or unsatisfying, it strengthens the point."

Martin was clearly having difficulty with this conversation, and Phillip knew that they should not proceed until whatever was bothering Martin was settled.

"So, if the church is a sham, why are you working with one of the perpetrators?" Martin asked.

Phillip said, "I didn't say that the church is a sham." He put his bottles and dead frog down, then leaned against the counter, settling in for some good, solid explaining. "I said that they can't prove their belief system, and that the lack of proof is part of that system. It's all belief and no proof. You and I, we're both science guys. In science you question everything and prove ideas through experimentation. It's all proof and no belief. It's easy for us to sneer at the church for claiming the Earth was created in six days, five thousand years ago, when there's clear evidence that it's much older, but you and I can prove that the Earth is part of a computer program, and how long did it take to write that program? Five days, perhaps? How long has the program been running? Five thousand cycles, perhaps? Who programmed it? Maybe their initials are G.O.D. and they have a sense of humor.

"Even if none of those answers line up with the church's doctrine, what is our creator's reality based on? Is he in a computer program? Nobody has all the answers, because all the best answers generate more questions. The way I see it, religion is no more inherently evil than science is. It's just a matter of who's using it and how, and Bishop Galbraith is a good man. He's a gruff, cantankerous old fart, but a good man, and when our goals align, I'm happy to work with him. So, Martin, if you're ready, let's go forth as men of science and help a medieval Bishop exorcise a demon."

In front of a small farmhouse on the outskirts of town, an old man in black sat on a white horse and waited. His robes, leggings, shirt, and hat were all slightly different shades of black. Around his neck there was a rough leather thong holding a cross that appeared to have been hammered by hand from a chunk of raw iron. The fact that wristwatches weren't invented yet made it difficult to look impatient, but he managed. He squinted at the sun, which was high in the sky and partially obscured by puffy clouds. He looked at the shadows on the ground, which were stubby, dark silhouettes of the trees, fence posts, and sheep. He peered down the road, seeing nothing but heat waves and dust. He scanned the horizon, finding rolling hills, and occasional stone and thatch farmhouses like the one he was sitting in front of. He knew he wouldn't see what he was waiting for, but that didn't stop him from looking or from being irritated by not finding it.

Simple teleportation isn't much to look at. One moment the wizard isn't there, the next moment he is. Now that doing so wouldn't cause Martin to ask questions and jump ahead in the lesson plan, Phillip used a macro to add some razzle-dazzle to the process. Two indistinct hazes, about three feet off of the ground and roughly two feet apart, formed before the old man's eyes. A high-pitched, vaguely gurgly noise filled the air. The horse bucked a bit, because that's what one does in these situations. The sound grew louder. The two points of haze expanded into blotches of color and motion that took on the shapes of two men in robes and pointy hats. They remained unnaturally still as the sound and haze faded away, leaving them standing, holding their staffs at their sides, the older man's hand on the younger man's shoulder. When the haze had dissipated, and the sound faded away, the two men suddenly began moving, as smoothly as if they had never stopped.

"Star Trek! Nice!" Martin said.

"I thought you'd like that," Phillip replied.

"Yer late, wizard!" the old man yelled, climbing down from his horse.

Phillip looked at the sky, then spread his hands in a questioning gesture. "I said we'd meet when the sun was at its highest point."

The old man walked slowly toward them. He could clearly still get around, but it just as clearly took more effort than it used to. "Aye, and that time's past. I'm a busy man, you know. I can't flit about in the wink of an eye like you lot. It'll take me half the day to get back to my responsibilities in Leadchurch, and I don't have a young apprentice to help me."

"You have younger priests and several nuns," Phillip said, walking up to meet the old man halfway.

"True, but none of them are any help."

The old man and Phillip shared a laugh and a hug. Phillip gestured toward Martin. "Your Excellency, this is my apprentice, Martin."

Bishop Galbraith looked Martin over from head to toe. "Aye, Martin the Magnificent, I hear. Should I call you Martin, or Your Magnificence?"

Martin winced and bowed slightly. "You can call me whatever you like, sir."

"I will. You know, someone brought me in a piece of your transparent fabric. Said that any clothing made of the stuff would be indecent. Wanted to know why God would allow such a thing to exist."

"I'm sorry if I caused you any trouble," Martin said. He wasn't a religious man, but Phillip seemed to hold the priest in high regard, so Martin was inclined to be conciliatory.

"No, son, luckily the stuff tore easily. I told him it was the work of the devil, and like all of Satan's creations, was flimsy and useless."

"Well played," Phillip said.

"Thank you. Of course now there's a peasant wandering the streets, convinced that your apprentice is the devil's loom, but that's not my problem."

"Or mine," said Phillip. "So, Bishop, what are we walking into here?"

"Parishioners of mine. The Melick family. The father is Donald. A good man, but stubborn, old-fashioned, ignorant, domineering, and judgmental."

Martin made a note of the Bishop's definition of a good man.

"His wife," Bishop Galbraith continued, "is named Jan. A good woman. Smarter than she's given credit for. Excellent cook. Usually lets Donald have his way because it's easier that way. They have three daughters and a son, their youngest, Donald the younger. He's a good boy, fifteen years old. Of late, he's started acting differently. He's withdrawn and secretive. He misbehaves. He talks back and says things that sound like nonsense. His parents think he's become host to a demon."

"What do you think?" Martin asked.

Bishop Galbraith gave Martin a hard, questioning look, then looked to Phillip. Phillip shook his head slightly.

"Did you not hear me say that the lad's fifteen?" the priest said.

"He'll learn, Father," Phillip said.

The old man turned his back to them and started limping his way to the farmhouse's front door. Phillip glowered briefly at Martin, who shrugged in response.

Phillip gave Martin a last-minute coaching as they approached the door. "Say nothing. Nothing. Even if they ask you a direct question. You will listen and let me do my job."

"And what is your job?"

"Mostly, to stand back and let Bishop Galbraith do his."

The farmhouse was larger than average, but inside felt close and cramped. Mrs. Melick was what Martin's mother would describe as *plump and pleasant*. She welcomed them warmly and fussed over the Bishop and Phillip like having company was the best thing that had ever happened to her. Mr. Melick grudgingly got up when they entered. The rest of the room was taken up by three young women who were clearly the daughters of Mr. and Mrs. Melick. None of the girls was what Martin would call overweight, but the Melicks were a stoutly framed family, and farm work had made them more so. Mr. Melick introduced the girls as Kitty, Evie, and Maggie.

Martin saw Phillip's demeanor change as they entered the hut. He stood taller and looked more serious. He seemed to see everything. Bishop Galbraith's demeanor hadn't changed at all. Martin wasn't sure it could. The priest said, "I'm sure you're aware of Phillip. He's a powerful wizard."

"Oh, I'm aware of him, Father," Mr. Melick said, "though I'm not sure why you brought him along."

Phillip's nostrils flared, and his voice resonated. "I hold the forces of darkness at bay. I command spirits and demons. I have the power to send them back to the unknown dimensions in which they dwell."

Bishop Galbraith said, "You can see how that would be handy."

Mrs. Melick said, "I'm not sure this is really needed. He's a good boy, it's just—"

Mr. Melick turned to her as if a mosquito had bitten him on the ear. "You hush. I've told you it's needed. The boy's got a demon in him. It's the only thing that makes sense. The girls all agree, don't you?" He turned to look at the girls, who were standing together in a clump. They nodded vigorously, stopping the instant he turned his attention back to Bishop Galbraith. Mr. Melick invited the visitors to sit, then pointed at Martin. "Who's the lad?"

"He is my apprentice," Phillip said.

"Oh," Mrs. Melick said, lighting up as her maternal instincts kicked into gear, "that must be very exciting!"

"It is," Phillip responded.

Mrs. Melick looked directly at Martin. "Are you learning a lot?"

"He is," Phillip responded.

Mrs. Melick was taken aback. "Can he not speak?"

"No, he cannot," Phillip said.

Her large, wet eyes filled with large, wet sympathy. She put a hand on Martin's elbow so gently he barely felt it. Martin had never wanted to hug another person so badly in his life. "Poor lad. Why can't he speak? What happened to him?"

"I ordered him not to," Phillip answered.

Mr. Melick nodded, "Quite right. Young people should be seen but not heard. Isn't that right, girls?" His daughters nearly gave themselves whiplash while nodding agreement.

There were two benches, each of which seemed designed for four average people, or three full-grown Melicks. Mr. Melick sat about two-thirds of the way across one bench. There wasn't enough room for anyone to sit on his left. Mrs. Melick sat, perched on the far right end of the bench next to her husband. The guests were invited to sit on the other bench. Martin started toward the bench, but Phillip stopped him. "Stand back and watch," he whispered before he settled on the bench next to Bishop Galbraith.

Bishop Galbraith saw that the three daughters were still standing, and quickly stood himself. "Please. Ladies. Do sit as well." He looked around the room, but there was nothing else to sit on.

"They can't. You're sitting on their bench, but you are guests, and are welcome to it. Isn't that right, girls?" More nodding, but Mr. Melick didn't see it, because he didn't look.

Phillip looked at the girls, then the bench, then the girls again, and asked the question Martin wanted to ask. "Does young Donald sit on the floor?"

"Not in my house he doesn't! I'm raising him to be a man, not an animal!"

"Then ... does he sit on the bench with his sisters?" Phillip pressed.

"Why does it matter where the boy sits?" the elder Donald asked.

"I need to check for ... demonic residue."

"Oh, is that what that is?" The youngest sister blurted before every Melick in the room's eyes silenced her.

"When they were younger, the boy sat on the bench with his sisters, but they're all too grown."

Phillip tried to give the subject a rest, but after a moment, even Bishop Galbraith needed to know. "So, where does the lad sit?" the Bishop asked.

"He's young and has strong legs," Mr. Melick said. "Standing will help make a man out of him."

Phillip turned and made eye contact with Martin. He didn't need to say anything. In one sentence, Donald Melick had said it all. Bishop Galbraith asked probing questions, and in answering them, a clear picture of young Donald's life emerged. His father was a simple man. Not dumb, but simple. He loved hunting, fishing, and farming. He had married Jan and set out to create a son with whom he could hunt, fish, and farm. Three attempts left him with three daughters to feed via hunting, fishing, and farming, and still nobody (as far as he was concerned) to hunt, fish, or farm with.

When Donald the younger was born, his father tried to ensure that his son shared his passion for outdoorsmanship by talking about nothing else for fifteen solid years. The boy had not wanted for attention and love, though. It appeared his mother and sisters had loved him to within an inch of his life. Their father gave the girls permission to speak, and speak they did, at length, about how they all took an active role in raising their baby brother. Helping to feed him, to dress him, reminding him to stand up straight, say please and thank you, to not talk back, to respect his elders, to do as he was told, and above all else, to be grateful that he had so many people who cared about him.

"But no matter how much we correct him, he isn't grateful," Kitty, the eldest Melick girl, said.

Lately Donald had become quiet and sullen. He'd moved to an old shed out back. "I don't see why," Mr. Melick said. "I've worked damn hard to give him a nice place to stand in here. The worst of it is that he's taken to hanging around with those bastards."

"Which bastards?" the priest asked.

Phillip said, "Uh, I think he means The Bastards. They're sort of a gang. Only the leader Kludge and a few of his buddies are really scary. Most of them are just kids who hang out playing and listening to bad music." Martin had not mentioned his encounter with Kludge and his gang to Phillip, mostly out of embarrassment. Clearly, if Phillip's opinion was correct, Martin had met the worst of Kludge's clique. *Just my luck,* he thought.

Finally, Mrs. Melick asked Bishop Galbraith and Phillip, "What do you think? Is our little Donald possessed by a demon?"

Martin shook his head. Bishop Galbraith said, "Yes. I'm certain of it. Your boy is host to a demon."

Martin had expected as much. When Phillip opened his mouth, Martin anticipated an argument.

Phillip said, "I agree."

The shed was about thirty yards behind the main house. It looked small and leaky. Mr. Melick led the priest and the two wizards across the yard, past an impeccably manicured vegetable garden, to the shed. When they arrived, Mr. Melick abruptly opened the door.

A voice from inside the shed yelled, "I told you to knock!"

Mr. Melick yelled back, "And I told you it's my bloody shed and my bloody door, and I don't need nobody's permission to open it. Stand up straight, boy. You got visitors."

Donald came to the door. He had lank, greasy hair and an impressive collection of blemishes. His general bearing said that he didn't want to see anybody.

Mr. Melick invited Martin, Phillip, and Bishop Galbraith into the shed over his son's protests. He started to come in as well, but Bishop Galbraith stopped him.

"What transpires within these walls is not for your eyes."

"Why not? They're my walls, and the boy is my son!"

Bishop Galbraith was firm. "We cannot proceed if you remain here. Terrible forces will be unleashed. If you stayed, you would see things you could never forget, things that would shake you to your very core."

Donald the elder turned to go back into the house, but stopped after one step. He turned back to face Bishop Galbraith. His eyes softened and his eyebrows arched, making him look both concerned and puzzled. "You...you lot aren't going to hurt my boy, are you? Look, I know what I said, and I meant every word. I don't want to be so hard, but it's a hard world, and I...I don't want to see him hurt."

The Bishop put a reassuring hand on the man's shoulder. "I give you my word; we will not hurt the boy. Now, please leave us to it. Go back to your home and keep the ladies in there as well. We'll let you know when it's over."

Phillip made a show of producing a jar of mystery dust from his hat and then sprinkling the dust on the ground in front of the shed. Then he waved the figure made of sticks in his left hand and the dead frog in his right. Mr. Melick watched for a moment, shook his head, and went into the house, shutting the door behind him.

The Bishop turned to Phillip and said, "Please see to it that we're not disturbed."

Phillip dropped the frog and the stick figure on the ground. He walked to the nearest exterior corner of the shed, put his back to the corner, took three large paces, planted his staff firmly on the ground and said, "Nevidebla barilo timiga." He then walked the perimeter of the shed, maintaining his distance, and every few yards planting his staff again. When he had walked a full lap of the shed, he planted the staff again and repeated, "Nevidebla barilo timiga." Martin understood that Phillip had created a boundary of some sort. He asked if it would hurt anyone who tried to cross it.

"Heavens, no," Phillip said. "The shed will glow and they'll hear a random combination of screaming, growling, and chanting. The closer they get to the shed, the louder and brighter it will get." He told the Bishop it was done, and they all went back into the shed, closing the door behind them.

From the outside, the shed looked tiny, but it felt noticeably larger on the inside. It helped that it was practically empty. There was a pile of straw in the corner that served as a bed. There were some stout, round chunks of firewood that served as seats, Martin guessed. The boy's meager possessions, a knife and a candle, were on a broad, flat hunk of firewood that was acting as a bedside table. Along one wall, two chunks of firewood supported a rough wooden plank, on which there were a couple of interesting looking carved pieces of wood. Martin figured that firewood served the same purpose as stolen milk crates or mail bins in his friends' bachelor apartments back in his own time. Martin felt at home in the shed. It was like a modern teenage boy's room, only much more flammable. The boy, Donald, had retreated to his pile of straw, folding up his arms and legs in an attempt to disappear. He looked out at his unwelcome guests through a screen of his own greasy hair.

"Hello, Donald. It's good to see you again. I'm sorry about the circumstances," Bishop Galbraith started.

The boy grunted.

The priest continued. "I don't know if you've met Phillip or his apprentice. They're wizards."

The boy's eyes flicked quickly to Phillip and Martin. He grunted again.

"Mind if we sit?" the priest asked.

"You're gonna anyway," the boy said, in a surprisingly deep voice.

"No. This is your home, and we won't sit until you invite us to."

They all stood in silence for a few moments, then the boy said, "Sit if you want. I don't care."

The three men each found a piece of wood and had a seat. They sat in a vague triangle, the Bishop closest to the boy, Phillip behind the Bishop on his right and Martin slightly further back to the left. Once they were all sitting, there was another silence, which was broken by the boy.

"They think I have a demon. Do you think I have a demon?"

The priest turned and looked at Phillip, then looked at Martin. Phillip nodded. Martin looked confused.

"No," the priest said, "I don't think you're possessed. I think you have a father who forces the land to give him what he wants, and thinks he can force his family to do the same. I think you have three sisters who all think they're your mother. I think your mother loves you dearly, and sees that you're a good lad but there's only so much she can do because she's in the same family you are. I think you'd be happy to do your chores if they'd just leave you alone to do them. You'd likely spend more time with your family if they let you decide when. You'd probably tell them what you're thinking if they didn't constantly pester you to, then punish you for it when you do."

The boy said nothing. He just glared at the priest, not moving a muscle.

"Do I have it right?" the priest asked.

The boy blinked, then lunged forward. He seized the priest in a bear hug, and started sobbing violently, gibbering unintelligibly. Eventually he lost momentum and let go of the priest. Instead of going back to his pile of straw, he cleared off his end table and used it as a stool. He slumped sullenly and talked for a long time. He talked about his parents, his sisters, the other people in the village who were his age. The Bastards. Kludge's frightening personal habits. Girls, he talked a lot about girls. Finally, he ran out of steam.

Bishop Galbraith said, "Here's the deal. That lot back in the house thinks you have a demon. We're going to convince them we rid you of it. We're going to tell them that they have to make the shed more comfortable, and knock before they come in. We're going to tell them to tread lightly with you for a while, leave you alone if that's what you want. But we need you to promise to make an effort to be nice to your family. It's hard, but it will make your life easier. Any time you need to talk, you can come to me or Phillip. Tell your family that you're thinking of becoming a wizard or a priest. They'll like that."

"Can I become a wizard?" the boy asked.

"No," Phillip said, "sorry. You're either born with it or you're not. Your parents don't know that, though."

"Can I become a priest?"

"No," Bishop Galbraith said, to Martin's surprise. "Not yet, at least. Let's talk again when things have settled down with your folks a bit. We don't want you joining the church just because it seems like a nicer place to live."

Phillip rubbed his hands together. "Now that that's all settled, it's time for the fun part."

Bishop Galbraith chuckled. "Yes, I suppose it is. Shall I go, or do you think your apprentice is ready to help?"

"Oh, I fully trust him to do his part," Phillip said. "He'll probably be better at it than you or I."

Donald was not comfortable with the direction the conversation was going. "What are you talking about?"

"I'm kind of wondering about that myself," Martin said.

"We'll explain," Phillip said.

Bishop Galbraith turned back to Donald. He put a reassuring hand on the boy's knee. "Donald, the next five minutes will be very unpleasant. I think you'll enjoy it!"

Donald's family was sitting on their benches, looking concerned, when Martin burst in the back door. He looked like he was barely staving off panic. Everyone else turned to face him, but Mrs. Melick rose instantly to her feet. Martin looked frantically around the room.

"What do you need, lad?" Mrs. Melick asked.

Martin darted around the room, clearly hunting for something he couldn't find. "We need a plank, a platter. Something broad and flat. The Bishop needs it for his sacraments."

"Kitty!" Mrs. Melick snapped, "Fetch the good platter." The girl seemed too stunned to move.

"GO!" Jan Melick said, and Kitty leapt up from the bench and ran to the kitchen, which was really just a well-organized corner of the main room. "What else do you need?"

Martin squeezed his eyes shut and wiggled his fingers in an attempt to dislodge the information stuck in his brain. "Aah, ummm. JUICE! Or cider, or something like that! My master says the boy will need something to drink. Something nourishing that will give him back his strength."

"We have a jug of cider, but it's gone a bit hard."

"That will do," Martin said.

"Cider's not cheap, you know," Mr. Melick said.

"It will do," Mrs. Melick said.

"Been saving it. Letting it harden up," Mr. Melick said.

"It. Will. Do," Mrs. Melick repeated in a tone that said it would be the last time. Mr. Melick sighed heavily and told Kitty to bring the jug of cider as well.

A moment later, Kitty had the platter (a two-foot square wooden plank painted cheerfully, with handles carved onto the ends) and an earthenware jug with a stopper in the top. Martin took the platter, but Donald Senior had hoisted himself from his bench and taken possession of the jug. "Let's go," he said.

"My master told you, what is happening in the shed is not for your eyes," Martin said.

"No, your master said very little, and it's a good thing, because I didn't invite him here. The father told me, and I'm not listening. It's my shed and it's my cider, so I'm going to see what you're all up to!"

Jan Melick was furious. "It's your son, Donald!"

"That too. Let's go, apprentice. Time's wasting." Mr. Melick started toward the door. As Martin reluctantly followed him, he was stopped by Mrs. Melick's hand on his arm. She looked

Martin in the eye, and asked in a small voice, "Will he be all right?"

Martin stopped, and in his calmest, most serious voice said, "Your son will be fine." He followed Melick out the back door.

As Mr. Melick opened the back door a hot wind blew in. As they stepped out of the house, the wind was strong enough to make walking difficult. The wind seemed to be coming from the shed, along with horrible growling, howling noises. Every crack in the shed's structure seemed to ooze a harsh, red light. Under the other sounds you could just make out both Phillip and Bishop Galbraith yelling, the priest in Latin, Phillip in Esperanto. Mr. Melick stopped for a moment, shielding his eyes from the wind and light, then he ran into the wind toward the shed.

Martin shouted, "Wait! Wait! Let me go first!"

Donald jerked the shed door open, and for a moment he was blinded. When his eyes adjusted, he saw his son floating in the middle of the shed, a full foot off the ground. He seemed to be struggling mightily. His limbs were flailing. Red light was coming from his eyes, nose and mouth. He was throwing his head around as if he was yelling, but the only sound was an inhuman, animal roaring. He was enveloped in a glowing energy field coming from Phillip's staff. Bishop Galbraith held his crucifix toward the boy. A beam of white light shot from the crucifix, hitting the boy in the heart. All three of them looked at the door as if they had been caught doing something naughty. They saw Mr. Melick frozen in terror. The whole world seemed to pause for a moment, except Martin, who gently took the jug from Donald's hand and stepped well back.

The man gasped, "Son?"

The red light dissipated from the boy's eyes, nose, and mouth. He saw the concern in his father's face. He said, "Dad!" Then, the red light came back, the boy opened his mouth and projectile vomited with enough force to cover the distance between father and son without a single globule hitting the ground. Mr. Melick tried to run, sliding on the muck with which he was drenched. He ran straight for the back door of the house. He darted inside, and as the door slammed shut behind him, Martin heard the sound of four women shrieking.

The priest lowered his crucifix. The beam of white light did not lower with it. "Well, that went better than expected," he said.

As Martin came into the shed and closed the door, Phillip said, "Fino program," and all of the mystical light and sound faded away. Donald gently descended to the floor.

Martin looked at a patch of the fake vomit that had splashed off of Donald the elder. He looked at Phillip. "Stew?" he said.

Phillip shrugged. "It's what Monty Python uses."

Bishop Galbraith took the platter from Martin. "Well done, everybody," he said. "Particularly you lads. You both did well for your first exorcism. Now we move on to the most important part." Phillip took four of the pieces of firewood that passed for furniture and arranged them in a rough diamond in the floor. Then he took three more pieces, and arranged them in a triangle pattern inside the larger diamond. Bishop Galbraith placed the platter on top of the triangle, and put the jug of cider on the platter. The Bishop sat on one of the four chunks of wood that formed the diamond. He beckoned Donald to sit opposite him, and Martin to sit to his right. Phillip sat to the Bishop's left and removed his hat. He reached into his hat and one by one produced four drinking glasses.

"The Bishop and I are now going to teach the two of you," Phillip said, reaching into his hat one last time, "how to play pinochle." Phillip pulled a deck of cards out of the hat.

18.

"If you're going to make macros and use the shell," Phillip said, "I suppose you'll need a computer you can do real work on, not that *phone* that has more computational memory than every computer at MIT the year I graduated combined. Perhaps you should pop back to your time and get your computer."

"I can't," Martin said. "The last time I saw it, it was being dismantled by federal agents."

"And it only took you a week to get into that much trouble?" Phillip asked.

"All the trouble happened in the last two days. I spent the days leading up to that setting myself up for failure."

"Preparation is the key to success, or, in this case, the opposite," Phillip said. "I guess you'll have to get a new computer."

"Drat. I do hate buying brand-new computers," Martin said in a sarcastic monotone.

"I know, right? It's just a burden you'll have to bear," Phillip responded in kind.

Martin opened the settings dialog on the smartphone app. It felt like he had lived a lifetime since he created it. Back then it had seemed like an unnecessary detail to allow himself the ability to change where and when the phone was broadcasting from on the fly, but now he was glad he had gone to the trouble. He set the phone's time for a week before he fled his own time, applied the new settings, and opened the Amazon.com app.

Walter and Margarita Banks stood in their living room, trying to understand what was happening. Their son Martin was acting very strangely, there were sirens blaring from their yard, and someone had just pounded rather insistently on the front door. They looked at the door, then looked at each other, then looked at Martin when he stuck his head out of his bedroom door and said, "Hi. Just checking, what's the capital of England?"

Margarita answered, "London." Martin slammed the door shut again.

Whoever was pounding on the front door yelled, "We are federal agents! Open this door immediately!" Walter went to open the door, but made it only a step before Martin burst out of his bedroom again.

"Don't open the door! Not yet!" Martin said.

Walter froze.

"Have any packages been delivered for me?"

"Yes. You got two boxes from Amazon yesterday. They're in the kitchen," Margarita replied.

"Awesome!" Martin said, almost singing as he ran to the kitchen. Then he stopped. "Wait, what? Two boxes?"

His mother pointed at the floor next to the back door, and there were two boxes from Amazon. Martin could tell from the shape of the boxes which one he had ordered. The second box was a mystery.

The voice from beyond the front door shouted, "Open this door or we will break it down!" Martin knew that there was a limit to how much material he could reliably transport back in time, so the mystery box would just have to wait for another time, when he would probably know what it was anyway. He picked up his order and ran back to his room.

"What kind of trouble are you in, son?" Walter asked.

"No trouble, Dad. Everything's cool. Just don't open the door yet!" Martin said as casually as he could as he ran back into his room and slammed the door behind him.

Martin rematerialized in the crystal ball room of Phillip's shop hugging his Amazon.com box to his chest. Phillip had explained that transporting anything too large was a risky proposition. Large objects are usually just a collection of small objects held together by glue, screws, or clips, which are themselves just smaller objects. "More than one wizard has filled a suitcase with stuff, teleported, and materialized holding nothing but a handle."

"So keep it small?" Martin had said.

"Yes, and just to be safe, try to hug it when you teleport. Surround the item as best you can with your limbs. Make more than one trip if you must."

So hug the box Martin had, and the box seemed to make the trip just fine. Martin's favorite part of buying a new computer was unboxing and setting up the system for the first time. This time it was even better because he was experiencing it through Phillip's eyes, a man from 1984. The most advanced piece of hardware Phillip had ever seen, aside from Martin's phone, was Gary's 1994 Apple PowerBook. When Martin un-boxed the brand-new 2012 laptop that looked like it was carved from a single billet of aluminum, Phillip looked like his head was going to explode. Martin couldn't help smiling as Phillip read the specifications on the side of the box, his lips moving slightly as if he were a linguist trying to read the Rosetta Stone.

Phillip shook his head. "I understand all of these specs, but the numbers are all so large, I don't know what any of it means. What on earth can a person do with four gigabytes of RAM?"

"Upgrade it immediately," Martin answered.

Martin was delighted to see that the laptop had shipped with a partial charge on the battery, so Martin was able to boot it up and show Phillip how modern operating systems worked, how high-definition movies looked, what 3D games were, and how fast the computer could perform tasks. Phillip was visibly grateful, and insanely jealous.

"I could maybe get you one, if you want," Martin offered.

Phillip sighed. "No, I wouldn't know how to use it. I'd best stick with my Commodore. It fits my … you know, my computing style. Besides, I'll be able to get my own shiny new computer eventually, if I wait around long enough. That's the beauty of being immortal. You learn to appreciate delayed gratification."

Instead of learning the shell's scripting language, they spent the rest of that day setting up and optimizing Martin's new computer. Thanks to the shell, it was much easier to find the new laptop's entry in the file. All Phillip had to do was point at it and say *Statistikoj* and the entry came up on the Commodore 64's screen.

"*Statistikoj*? That means 'statistics,' doesn't it?' Martin asked.

"Yup."

"Does Esperanto ever remind you of Pig Latin?"

"Yes. By the way, Esperanto for Pig Latin is *porko latina*."

They set the laptop's battery to constantly be full, like Martin's phone. For internet access Martin simply used WiFi to tether the laptop to his phone so he could access the phone's 4G connection, a process that thoroughly confounded Phillip. Martin patiently talked Phillip through it as they went. He enjoyed playing teacher to Phillip's student, instead of the other way around.

The next morning, after a bowl of breakfast stew, they set up the laptop on the table in Phillip's house and settled in to get access to the shell. The shell was hosted redundantly on many corporate and government servers, just like the file itself. Because they knew what to search for, they found it pretty fast. They downloaded a version of the shell interface that was designed for Windows XP. It was badly outdated from Martin's point of view, but it worked in emulation, and was stable. The interface had large, cartoonish icons Martin could use to access the raw file, a sandbox for creating new powers and effects, a library of pre-existing powers and effects, and a graphical interface for combining them and assigning a trigger. Phillip was explaining how to stack several effects to create the illusion of a single, unified effect when Martin felt a sudden chill.

"Perfect timing, as always," Phillip groaned.

"Huh! I've got goose bumps," Martin said.

"Yes, so have I. Sit back, kiddo. You're about to see a textbook example of how many different effects can be layered to make an impression on your audience. In this case, to give the impression that the wizard is trying far too hard to impress."

A breeze blew through the room, seeming to blow inward from all four of the walls, converging on a point in the middle of the room. The wind formed a small whirlwind, which grew and darkened as more dust – far more than had been in the room to begin with – was drawn into the vortex. All light in the room dimmed until it looked like midnight in the dead of winter, rather than a sunny fall morning. As the light died, a glow emanated from the whirlwind, which had formed into the size of a man. There was a deafening sound, like a gas truck exploding but played in reverse, then the room was filled with nothing but white light and silence.

As Martin's eyes adjusted he saw a marble statue of an impressive wizard where the whirlwind had been. The statue held its staff aloft with its muscular left arm. Its equally muscular right arm was flexing mightily with its hand at head height, gripping a tiny, brilliant white star as if it were a softball. The statue's square jaw was set, and its facial expression spoke of a serene confidence and a terrible purpose. The statue's flowing hair was blown back as if it was standing directly in front of a fan. The light in the statue's hand pulsed orange, sending out a shock wave of fire that filled the room. Martin instinctively covered his face with his arms. Phillip did not flinch. As the shockwave dissipated, the marble burned away to ash, which fell but seemed to disappear before it hit the floor. As the ash crumbled away, it left behind a real wizard in the same pose. The arms were thinner. The jaw was weaker. The hair was limper. It was, however, the same wizard. His robes were a deep emerald green with gold trim. His staff was black, and as shiny as a piano. The figurehead was a small blue electric plasma ball, like teenage guys bought from mall novelty shops in the late 1980s. In an amplified voice with too much reverb, the wizard said, "Be not a-feared! I, Merlin, have appeared!"

Phillip groaned, then said, "Hello, Jimmy," without enthusiasm. "Would it kill you to knock?"

Jimmy smiled. "Hello, Phillip. Lovely to see you! I apologize for not knocking, but as you know, I put a lot of effort into my entrance."

"Clearly."

"Yes, and the whole effect would be spoiled if it was preceded by me meekly knocking on the door and asking if anyone was home. It wouldn't be nearly as impressive, now, would it?"

"Do I look impressed now?" Phillip asked.

"Why no, dear fellow, you never look impressed. That's part of your charm."

"What if, instead of knocking, you made three sonic booms, in the cadence of a person knocking?" Martin asked. "Then you could wait for an answer."

Jimmy's eyes widened. "That's a genuinely good idea! You must be this apprentice I've heard so much about. Pleased to meet you. You can call me Merlin."

Phillip muttered, "Or you can call him Jimmy, which is his name."

"Yes, thank you, Phillip. I must say, Martin, I'd heard you were clever. Lots of people tell me their ideas, but I rarely hear one I like. I'm impressed!"

"Yes," Phillip added. "Someday, when your ears are bleeding because you're being subjected to *shave and a haircut* played in sonic booms, you'll know you have yourself to thank."

Jimmy and Martin shook hands. Jimmy had a firm grip and a dry hand. He grasped Martin's right elbow with his left hand as they shook. He leaned in close to Martin's right ear, and quietly enough that Phillip couldn't hear, but without whispering, asked,

"Is Phillip treating you all right, Martin? Is he teaching you what you need to know? He's not making you do all of his housework or anything, is he, Martin?" .

"No," Martin replied quietly. "He's great! We're getting along fine."

"Good, Martin," Jimmy said, still shaking Martin's hand, leaning in close and almost whispering into his ear. "If there are any problems, Martin, I want you to contact me. Will you do that, Martin?"

Before Martin could answer, both he and Jimmy were startled by Phillip leaning in very close to Martin's other ear and grasping Martin's left shoulder. "Martin," Phillip said, in hushed tones, "is Jimmy acting creepy, Martin? Is he making lots of physical contact, Martin, and murmuring directly into your ear-hole? Martin, is he saying your name, Martin, much more often than any sane person would, Martin? Martin, it's almost as if he read a book on how to cruise chicks at a discotheque and, Martin, realized he could apply those lessons to everyone he met, isn't it, Martin? Martin, Martin, Martin?"

If Martin had been farther from Jimmy's face he'd have missed the look of irritation that quickly changed to a surprisingly genuine expression of amused good grace. Jimmy released Martin's arm and took a step back, laughing lightly and spreading his arms in a friendly, expansive gesture. "Now, Phillip, if you're not careful, you're going to give Martin the impression that we don't get along."

"We don't!" Phillip said, clenching his fists.

Jimmy quite deliberately looked confused. "Phillip, I've always gotten along with you just fine."

"Yes, Jimmy, you get along with me, but I don't get along with you, partly because you don't recognize that the word *we* refers to more than just you."

Jimmy laughed. "Oh, Phillip, you are a pistol."

"I wish."

After a profoundly uncomfortable silence, Jimmy said, "Well, I have other stops today. I'm out making the rounds, checking on projects." He looked directly at Phillip. "The chairman's work is never done."

"We won't keep you," Phillip replied.

"No, you won't," Jimmy said, initiating a second handshake with Martin. "If I can be any help, don't hesitate to ask. You'll be a fine addition to our community, Martin, I can tell."

Jimmy raised his staff above his head. Wind blew inward from the perimeter of the room again, converging on Jimmy, blowing his hair and making his robe flap like a flag. Jimmy spoke, but now his voice was louder, fuller, more epic. "And don't worry about the trials, Martin. If you do, you'll psych yourself out and fail, and that would be very bad!" The whirlwind converged and coalesced around Jimmy. There was a blinding light, a loud noise, and then silence. An idealized marble statue of Jimmy stood where the real thing had been, then it crumbled into ashes that disintegrated before they hit the ground. When the dust cleared all that was left was a scorch mark on the spot where Jimmy had stood. The scorch was in the shape of an M inside a pentagram.

Phillip rubbed at the mark with his boot. It wiped away easily. "It stands for 'moron,'" he said as he finished removing it.

"He seems friendly," Martin said.

"Yes, that's the problem with him. He *seems* friendly."

Martin knew that the wise move would be to leave it alone and get on with their day. He also knew that he wasn't going to do that. "It's obvious that you detest him."

"Obvious to everyone but him."

"Oh, I think he knows."

Phillip turned to face Martin, his eyes full of hope. "Do you think so? You think he knows how I feel? Oh, I hope that's true. Maybe he even feels the same way about me?"

"I think he may. What's your deal? Are you mad because he's Merlin and you're not?"

Phillip sat down at the table and slumped over, as if tired from the exertion of hating Jimmy. "No, I hate him because he's *not* Merlin. There is no Merlin and there probably never was. Look, when I came to this time, I knew I'd be disguising myself as a wizard, and hoped I'd be known as a good one. I thought that was a pretty good goal. Good enough for me, at least, but clearly not good enough for Jimmy. When Jimmy came back here, it was with the intention of making people recognize him as Merlin whether they wanted to or not, and he proceeded to scramble countless people's lives so he could bend reality to his will."

"You're angry because he changed the past."

"Yes, you could boil it down to that."

"But you're changing the past too."

"Yes, but on a much smaller scale, and for very different reasons. I made small changes in hopes of making a better life for myself and others. He made huge changes to create a much better life for himself and a slightly better life for everyone else maybe, if they were lucky, but if not, he's not really bothered."

A long silence passed as Martin tried to understand and Phillip tried to find a more elegant explanation. "Shortly after I got here, I decided the repository, *the file*, as you call it, would be much more useful if it had a simplified interface. I started working on the shell. I told Jimmy about it. He helped a little. When new wizards would turn up, he'd show them *our* shell that *we* made. Later on, I'd meet new wizards who had met Jimmy first, and they'd ask me what it was like helping Jimmy invent the shell."

"Ah," Martin said. "You want more credit."

"No, it's not about credit. It's about theft."

"Theft of credit," Martin said.

"Look," Phillip said, "the world can be described as a war between two sides. The problem is that everybody has a different idea of what those two sides are. Liberals versus conservatives, Star Wars fans versus Star Trek fans, people who see the world in terms of us-versus-them and people who don't. There are thousands of different *two kinds of people*. The way I see it, civilization is a war between people like me and people like Jimmy."

"Okay, who are the people like you, and who are the people like Jimmy?"

"Martin, did you ever play basketball?"

"Yes."

"Tell me, what's a foul?"

"It's when a player breaks one of the rules. Do it five times and you're kicked out of the game. Six, if it's the NBA."

Phillip smiled. "Good. The best way I've ever summed up the war as I see it is that one side, our side, sees a foul as being against the rules, and if you do it too many times you have to be removed. The other side, Jimmy's side, sees fouls as things you're allowed to get caught doing several times, and if you don't, you aren't trying hard enough."

"So you're mad at Jimmy because you think his side cheats at life."

"Partly. Mostly I'm mad because I'm pretty sure his side is going to win."

They spent the rest of that day covering the creation of macros, and they got a lot of training accomplished, but Phillip's mood never really recovered. It wasn't until the next day, after a good night's sleep, that his smile seemed genuine again. In fact, as Phillip roused Martin from the hammock, Phillip's smile seemed a little too genuine.

"Get up, me lad! I've got something special planned for you today."

Martin rubbed the sleep from his eyes as he carefully dismounted the hammock. "What is it? I was hoping to work some more on macros. I have a few ideas."

Phillip shrugged theatrically. "Well, we could spend the day at the computer if you'd rather and just leave learning to fly for another day."

"No, no," Martin said, quickly grabbing his staff. "If you think it's time to try flying," he continued, struggling to pull on his robe, "then I as the, uh, um ... student," he stammered, realizing that pulling on the robe would be easier if he weren't holding his staff, "should defer to your expertise," he said, setting down the staff, and successfully donning his robe, "and learn to fly today." Martin had gone from sleep to standing, ready to leave, in ten seconds and one run-on sentence.

"Now, now, don't be so hasty. You haven't had any breakfast," Phillip said. "Here, have one of these. It should tide you over until lunch." He handed Martin a palm-sized rectangle of something wrapped in cloth.

"What is it?" Martin asked.

"It's something I'm experimenting with. Are you familiar with the idea of a breakfast bar?"

Martin unwrapped it eagerly. "Yeah, in my time we tend to call them energy bars. I didn't know you had chocolate."

"I don't; this is much healthier. It's a block of dried stew."

It did tide Martin over until lunch, in that it made him lose all interest in eating. He and Phillip went outside. Phillip held out his hand, and Martin willingly put his hand in Phillip's. Martin just happened to look down the street, and happened to see Kludge, staring at him from a distance, but not so great a distance that he couldn't see Kludge smile at noticing that Martin had noticed him. Phillip held his staff aloft in his free hand and pointed its top, with the decorative glass bottle of Tabasco sauce, toward the sky. Phillip looked upward, said, "Flugi!" and they were soaring into the sky.

They flew about fifteen miles. In modern times that is not far, but in the Middle Ages, it was a huge distance. They flew over the forest until they came to a large clearing full of tall grass. In the middle of the clearing, two men in wizard robes were waiting for them. As Phillip swooped in for a landing, Martin could see that it was Gary and Jeff.

"Guys! Good to see you! I didn't know you were going to be here," Martin said.

"We wouldn't have missed it!" Gary said. "We wizards always come out for an apprentice's first flight."

"Where's Tyler?" Phillip asked.

"Dunno," Jeff answered. "He went out yesterday for some book research and hasn't come back. Some farmer's probably telling him a story about yams that he thinks he can make into a tale of high adventure. He loses track of time."

"He's gonna be bummed that he missed your first flight," Gary said. "It's a tradition."

"Yeah," Jeff said, "it's like when they launch a ship by breaking a bottle on its prow."

"But instead of a ship, it's you."

"And instead of a bottle, it's the ground."

"And there's no breaking involved. Just bouncing."

"Bouncing?" Martin asked. "I'm gonna bounce?"

Phillip shook his head. "Only if you crash."

"Which means yes," Gary added helpfully.

"Don't worry, though," Phillip said, scowling at Gary, "thanks to the various protective spells I applied to you, you can't be injured."

"Oh," Martin said, visibly relieved. "Good. As long as I can't get hurt."

"Oh, you'll get hurt," Jeff said, "just not injured. Your skin won't cut and your bones won't break, but you'll still feel pain if you run a knife across your skin, or you get poked hard with something sharp."

"Or if you fall screaming out of the sky at terminal velocity and land on the hard, rocky ground," Gary said, stomping on the ground to emphasize its hardness.

Phillip put his hand on Martin's shoulder. "Don't listen to them, Martin. They're just trying to scare you. Oh, they're not lying. You will probably fall, and bounce, and it will smart like mad, but they're just telling you about it to scare you. Now let's get you up in the air, shall we?"

Moments later, Martin was standing alone. The other three wizards were watching him intently, but giving him plenty of room. "All right," Phillip said, "we fly using our staff."

"Rule one," Martin said reflexively. "Don't make the obvious joke."

"Indeed," Phillip said. "Have you ever ridden a motorcycle?"

"Yes."

"How'd that go?"

"I crashed."

"This is gonna be GREAT!" Jeff said. Gary giggled.

"Ignore them," Phillip said. "That doesn't just mean today. In general, it's best to ignore them. Anyway, flying is a lot like riding a motorcycle in two ways. It's more about leaning than steering, and if you look at something, you're going to steer into it, even if you don't want to. Now, put your hand about half way down your staff and hold it over your head."

Martin did.

Phillip said, "Good. Now, think of the staff as your controls. Point the head of your staff forward and you go faster. Pull it back, you slow down. Tilt it to the left and you'll bank left. Tilt right, bank right. Tilt your wrist up and you'll angle upward. Tilt your wrist down and you'll angle down. It sounds like a lot to remember, but if you think of it like you're letting your staff lead you, it's very intuitive."

Martin said, "Kind of like riding a Segway."

Phillip and Gary said, "What?"

At the same moment, Jeff said, "Yes."

Martin asked, "How fast can we fly?"

"There's no theoretical limit, but the shell keeps us down to a hundred miles an hour, which, believe me, is more than fast enough when you're up there in the wind with nothing but a robe and hat for protection."

Martin took a deep breath, then raised the staff over his head. He held it there for a moment, then lowered it again. "Do I have to say *flugi*?" he asked. "It's the least dignified magic word ever."

"Right now, yes. Later you can make a macro and set any word you like, make sparkles trail behind you, whatever. During training we're focusing on basic flight, and to do that, you say *flugi*."

Martin raised the staff above his head again. He shook the tension out of his left hand, which was hanging by his side, paused a second to work up his nerve, and said, "Flugi."

Nothing happened. He was still standing firmly on the ground. He looked at Phillip, fearing that he was yet again being messed with. Phillip smiled and said, "Point the staff upward a bit. JUST A BIT! You want to start slow."

Martin tilted the head of the staff upward and he smoothly raised about thirty feet before he panicked and tilted the staff back, stopping all upward progress. He hovered there, oscillating between laughing, shouting, and being too stunned to make a sound. He had known intellectually that he was going to fly at some point, but now he knew that he was flying, and that was a different matter. He was sure it looked like he was hanging by one hand from his staff, but that was not how it felt. It didn't feel like he was weightless either. It felt as if every atom in his body had simply decided it was time to move in the same direction, and that direction just happened to be straight up. He looked down at Phillip, Jeff, and Gary. They looked delighted as they cheered Martin on.

Phillip raised his staff, said, "Flugi," and drifted up to meet Martin.

Jeff produced his magic wand, pointed it at the sky and shot upward with an eerie humming sound and distorted shock wave emanating from the spot where he had stood.

Gary whipped his staff around in an arc, chanting, "Mi estas mizera spektaklo ekstere." He held his staff aloft and rose slowly but forcefully on a pillar of black smoke so thick you could not see through it. Soon, all four of them were hovering there, thirty feet in the air.

"Okay," Phillip said. "You've got hovering down. Now it's time to fly. Remember, just sort of point your staff where you want to go. It's that simple."

Martin pointed the staff a degree or two upward, then tilted his wrist downward and he gracefully leveled off. His staff led and his body trailed behind. What had been pointing his staff upward now felt like it was leading him forward. He turned his head to look behind and saw the others following him. He experimented with some turns. He tried gaining and losing altitude. He swooped. He spiraled. He went as fast as he comfortably could, which wasn't all that fast with the wind in his eyes.

He shielded his face with his free hand and tried for a high-speed swoop. He swung down within a few feet of the ground, then gave it the spurs as he angled back toward the sky. He was fifty feet in the air and accelerating upward at a steep angle. Between the speed he was moving, the hand shielding his eyes, and the squinting in the wind, he nearly didn't see the duck.

Later, Phillip told him he probably would have missed the duck entirely if he hadn't reacted, but he had, involuntarily cringing and pulling his staff arm in to shield his face. In doing so he dropped the staff's air speed to nearly zero, then to full reverse, banked a hard right turn and stuck the staff into a steep dive all at the same time.

Martin's body cracked like a whip, flinging him out in front of the staff as he lost his grip. Without his hand to hold it the staff lost all power and tumbled to the ground. Martin's momentum flung him rear-end first directly into the now very startled duck. He and the duck fell earthward. For a crazy moment it seemed to Martin that he was sitting on the duck, which was horribly undignified for both of them. The duck seemed to agree, as it rolled between his legs and up the front of his torso, flapping wildly and quacking like mad the whole way. It bounced off of his face and for just an instant Martin was aware of a duck foot in his mouth, then the duck disappeared from his perception. Martin didn't know where it went and didn't care. He was more concerned with the ground, which was coming up to meet him quite eagerly.

As he tumbled, Phillip, Gary, and Jeff spun into his field of view, closing on his position very fast. Gary and Jeff seemed to be yelling something. Phillip was hurling his staff around like a lacrosse stick and shouting something as well. A blue ball of energy shot from the head of Phillip's staff and flew like a line drive, hitting the ground directly in front of Martin. He had just enough time to feel gratitude for Phillip for helping him when he needed it. Martin hit the ground full force. The pain was instant and blinding. He bounced into the air and had just enough time to curse Phillip before he hit the ground again, this time rolling to a stop. He lay on the ground, groaning.

Jeff and Gary landed. Martin raised himself up from the ground and looked around. The spot where he had initially hit the ground was marked with a glowing blue circle. Radiating out from that circle were ever larger concentric blue rings spaced a foot apart. Gary was counting the rings. "Twelve," Gary said, shaking his head sadly. That's four yards. Jeff, you guessed thirteen, you were over. I had nine and Phillip had ten, so Phillip wins."

"The duck slowed him down," Jeff noted bitterly. "Guess that means we both owe you a buck."

"No," Phillip said. "To be honest, I lost our other bet this morning. Martin didn't eat the stew bar."

19.

Day broke, and Phillip and Martin reluctantly got up and puttered around like men do when they're pretending to be awake. Phillip ladled the increasingly thick stew into a bowl, which he handed to Martin, muttering something about needing a good breakfast. Martin muttered agreement, walked to the privy, and with the door open, turned strategically so that Phillip could see, and poured the stew through the hole.

Now that breakfast was sorted, Phillip explained that the training was almost over. They only really had one more subject to cover, then it would be a simple matter of practicing what Martin had learned until they were both sure he was ready for the trials.

"The subject of the day," Phillip said, "is basic conjuring. Simply put, the creation of something from nothing. First, a little review. How do you copy an object?"

"You target it by pointing at it, either with your free hand, your staff, or your wand. Then you say *kopiu objekto* and a copy of the object will appear."

"Any object?"

"No. It has to be small, about two feet cubed is the limit, and mechanically simple. Solid objects work best."

"Because?"

"An object with moving parts is actually several objects working together. Copy a rock, you get two rocks. Copy a watch and you'll probably get a spare watch band."

"Well said. How about transporting things?"

"Well, all we've discussed is bringing stuff with us when we teleport. Our clothes, the things we're holding and the things in our pockets seem to come with us naturally, for some reason."

"Yes, the program has some way of organizing various objects defined in the file into units, but we've never quite cracked it. It's a bit embarrassing really, but all of us have been working for all this time, and yet....Anyway, you said you could hold things in your hand and bring them with you when you teleport. Can you bring anything?"

"No," Martin said. "Again, small, simple objects are best. If you do need to transport something larger or more complex, you want to keep it small, and hold it in such a way that you're ... well, enveloping it, I guess is the best way to put it."

"Indeed. Conjuring can best be described as copying something well after the fact, or transporting it from a state of non-existence. Now, when you copy something you have to target it by pointing, but when creating something out of nothing you need to define where it will be created, a set, predictable place for conjured items to materialize. So, Martin, tell me, what does a wizard need to wear for the shell to recognize him?"

"Well, we need a staff or a wand."

"For?" Phillip asked.

"Targeting, flying, and looking cool."

"Go on."

"A robe with sleeves that have a cuff circumference of two feet."

"Why two feet?"

"The shell looks for the cuffs to help it know where your hands are. Makes it easier to program energy beams and effects when you write a macro," Martin answered.

"Very good. What else does a wizard wear?"

"A conical hat that is no less than one foot tall."

"Do you have to be wearing it?"

"No, it can be in your hand or your pocket, but it has to be somewhere on your person."

"Correct. What does a magician use his hat for?" Phillip asked.

Martin smiled as he saw where Phillip was going. "For pulling things out of!"

"Top man! Yes, the shell looks for the hat and uses it as the default location to materialize created items. There are certain items we figured would be useful to be able to create at will, and we programmed them into the shell." Phillip held his hat so Martin could see that it was empty. He held it by the brim as if he intended to use it to carry things and said, "Krei monon." He reached into the hat and pulled out a gold piece. Then he said, "Krei sekigitaj bovaĵo," reached into the hat and pulled out a strip of beef jerky, which he handed to Martin.

"These are the things that we've hard-wired into the shell. You can use your staff to define and save a small item and program a macro to create it later. If the item is small enough it can be surprisingly complex. Krei rizo kaj fazeoloj ruliĝis en omleto!"

Phillip reached into his hat and pulled out a burrito. He said, "Enjoy your beef jerky," and bit into his burrito.

"You could make real food all this time?" Martin asked.

"Martin," Phillip answered, speaking with his mouth full, "have you ever once seen me eat any of that stew?"

With the basics out of the way, the following days were made up of practice, review, and practical application. Macros were created. Miss Abigail's goat got moved from one pasture to another a few times. The foundations of a life in Medieval England got made for Martin. He spent an afternoon creating a tidy war-chest of gold pieces. The lesson he learned in his own time still applied here—having a ready supply of money was as potent a form of magic as any. Martin and Phillip looked around Leadchurch for a cottage Martin could buy after he passed the trials. They didn't find anything that excited Martin, but it was fun to look.

Finally, the day came to pick up Martin's robe and hat. When Martin and Phillip entered Gwen's shop, they found her sitting at her work table, stitching the hem of a tunic. On Gwen's left there was a small stack of two or three neatly folded garments. On her right was a massive pile of garments in various contrasting shades of earth-tone and oatmeal. As they entered she tied a knot in the thread she had been pulling. The sleeves of her dark gray cloak were pushed up on her arms, giving the impression that she was putting in some serious effort. She folded the tunic she had just finished and put it atop the larger pile.

"You've been busy," Phillip said.

"Busy, but not profitable. These are all free alterations, and this is just the first batch. That loudmouth Sam starts putting on weight and his waistband can't accommodate his belly anymore, but he can't accept that, so he says his pants have gotten longer. I agree to fix them, really just to get him out of my shop, and he tells everyone who'll listen. Next thing you know his entire village comes in one by one doing their best Sam impression and I end up hemming an entire village's worth of clothes for free."

"And you'll get to deal with them all again when they come in to pick up their garments," Phillip said.

"No, when I'm done I'm just going to go out to their village and get it over with in one trip," she said.

"Would you like some help?" Martin asked. "I could transport you and the pants magically. It might take a few trips, but with both of us carrying pants it shouldn't be too bad. It'd be a lot faster than driving your cart out there, and I really could use the practice."

Gwen smiled, which made Martin smile, which made Phillip smile. Martin's eyes darted over to Phillip. Phillip quickly frowned and furrowed his eyebrows at Martin. Martin looked away quickly. Gwen nearly laughed out loud.

"Thanks for the offer," Gwen said. "It's sweet of you, but the last thing I need is any of these people thinking I have wizards helping me do my work. I have a hard enough time getting them to pay a fair price as it is."

"What I don't understand is, if this is everyone in the village's clothes, what are they wearing now?" Phillip asked.

"Their other clothes," Gwen answered. "Most of them own two full outfits, and they were very clear that they'll want me to work on the other when these are done. I told them I'd charge for the second set. That should cut down on the bulk. Anyway, enough about my problems. I bet you gentlemen are here to pick up the robe." She put down her work and exited to a room at the back of the shop, leaving the two wizards alone for a moment.

"How many shirts do you think you could've carried per trip?" Phillip asked.

"I wouldn't want to try more than two or three."

"It would take many trips. You'd have had to spend quite a bit of time helping Gwen."

"Yeah," Martin said. "Probably."

"I could have shown you a way to move them all at once."

"I wouldn't have used it."

"Martin, you're not dumb. Not at all," Phillip said smirking in spite of himself.

Gwen returned carrying a bundle of the same rough cotton his fitting robe was made of. For a moment he feared that his finished robe was made of the same cheap material, then he realized that the final robe and hat were simply wrapped in it for protection. Gwen sat the bundle on a bare patch of her work table, stepped aside, looked at Martin, and with a flourish motioned to him to unwrap the package.

Martin unfolded the covering and lifted the robe so he could see it. The primary fabric was a highly reflective silver color with little flat pieces that reflected a surprising amount of light integrated into the weave. It sparkled and glittered as if Gwen had made the robe from the hide of a skinned disco ball. The trim was a lighter, less reflective fabric that matched the trim on Santo's mask. Martin was delighted. As he held it up, Phillip grabbed Martin's staff and put the bust of Santo up against the robe. The colors were an almost perfect match. Phillip gave Gwen a questioning look. She shrugged and looked at Martin.

"Gwen, it's perfect!" Martin said, holding the garment up to the light.

Gwen smiled at Phillip. Phillip shook his head and said, "Well done."

"I was worried it might be too flashy, but from what I saw on Martin's first night in town, I didn't think *too flashy* would really be a problem."

Martin hastily shed the red loaner robe and hat. Gwen held the new robe by the shoulders so Martin could easily slip it on. It fit perfectly and instantly felt like a part of him. The silver hat sat easily and comfortably on his head. The cone of the hat did not flop over completely, but instead bent back slightly. Unlike Phillip's brimless hats, Martin's hat had a three-inch brim, the color of his robe's trim. Martin spread his hands wide and looked down at himself. Gwen directed him to the mirror, which was really a highly polished sheet of metal, but it did the job.

"What do you think?" she asked.

Martin said, "I look bitchin'!"

"That's good," Phillip explained to Gwen.

Martin wanted to strut back to the shop, but Phillip had insisted that Martin teleport them instead. They thanked Gwen, then paid her a great many gold pieces. The fabric was not cheap, but she knew wizards were good for it. Martin put one hand on Phillip's shoulder, and held his staff aloft with the other hand. In his most impressive tone of voice, Martin said the magic words, "Transporti al Phillip butiko," and they were standing in the front room of Phillip's shop.

"Good. The shell is recognizing the robe and hat. Gwen does excellent work, but nobody's perfect. It's always a good idea to test a new robe before you try to do magic in public. Try shooting a beam."

Martin pointed at a dead squirrel in a jar of yellowish fluid on the shelf and said, "*Radion de ruĝa lumo.*" A ray of red light shot from his hand, illuminating the jar, which was unfortunate.

He moved his hand around, watching the beam track with the direction of his finger. After a moment Martin said, "Halti," and the beam stopped as if someone had flipped a switch. Martin then tested the hat by producing two burritos for their lunch. As they sat in the crystal ball room, enjoying their meal, Martin asked what was next in the training schedule.

"Well, I've shown you all of the basics. Now we concentrate on getting you ready for the trials."

"How long do you figure that'll take?" Martin asked between bites.

"Two days."

"That's pretty specific," Martin said as best he could while chewing.

"Very specific," Phillip said. "Your trials are scheduled for two days from now."

After Phillip had administered the Heimlich maneuver, Martin immediately started yelling, or would have if he'd caught his breath enough. Instead, Martin gasped emphatically.

"What do you mean the trials are scheduled for two days from now?!" he wheezed.

"I don't know how to state it any more plainly than you just did," Phillip answered. "In two days, we are going to go to London. Jimmy, as the chairman, will throw a party in your honor, all the while referring to himself as Merlin. Try to enjoy the party. There will be many wizards you haven't met, pretty much every wizard in Europe. There'll be food and drinks, and many top-notch insults will be hurled at Jimmy, by me. At the end of the dinner, you will show everyone the most impressive macro you can come up with. The next morning, you will face the trials. By that night you'll be a full-fledged wizard."

Martin smiled and said, "Thanks!"

"Or naked and hogtied in the back of a squad car."

Martin sneered and said, "Thanks."

Martin spent most of the next two days at Phillip's house, hunched over his laptop. Phillip would occasionally stop by to quiz him on his Esperanto, or to take him out for a quick practice flight, but most of the time was spent with Martin working on his macro and Phillip away at the shop, staying out of Martin's way. At one point Martin had a question, and rather than just calling Phillip, he decided to stretch his legs. He teleported to Phillip's shop.

After he materialized in the front room, the one designed to look like a shop, Martin thought about how easy it would be to become lazy as a wizard, and how much he looked forward to it. His eyes landed randomly on a small, ornate box, sitting among the other random objects Phillip had placed on his shelves solely for their ability to look mysterious. The box was about five inches long, made of wood, and its proportions were similar to a coffin. It sat on tiny, carved, clawed feet. Its hinged lid and sides were decorated with carvings of dragons. He called Phillip's name and got no reply. He tried again. Still no response.

Humming quietly to himself, he moved cautiously into the crystal ball room, around the table, and faced the door that led upstairs, the door that no person could open or enter but Phillip. He knocked, and waited several seconds. No reply. He knocked again.

Martin decided Phillip wasn't there. As he turned his back to the door upstairs, he noticed that the shelf built into the crystal ball table that usually held Phillip's beloved Commodore 64 was empty. He looked into the crystal ball and saw that the TV was also missing. Martin was so engrossed in peering into the crystal ball, he didn't hear the door behind him open.

"Can I help you, Martin?" Phillip asked.

Martin jumped, then tried to sound casual. "Uh, I, uh, I just wanted to get out of the hut. I thought I'd come see what you're up to," Martin said.

"I'm not up to anything," Phillip said as he stood framed by the open door, drying his hands on a modern hand towel. He was wearing his powder blue robe, but not his hat. The forbidden staircase stretched off into darkness behind him.

Martin pointed to the empty shelf where the computer had sat. He could see a rectangular patch that was free of dust. "Why'd you move the Commodore?"

"No reason," Phillip said.

"Oh," Martin said, as if that explanation simply hadn't occurred to him. The two men stood, looking at each other in silence for a moment.

"Well," Phillip said, "you'd better get back to studying and working on your macro. Tomorrow we go to London, and the day after, you face the trials. I'd hate to have to strip you naked, tie you up, and send you back to your time. Especially the first two parts. Never pleasant." Phillip started closing the door as if Martin had already left. Martin raised his hand and cleared his throat like a schoolboy with a question.

"Yes, Martin, what is it?" Phillip said, now just poking his head through the partially closed door.

Martin held up the small wooden box he'd taken from the shelf. "Mind if I make a copy of this to use? It's your box, so I thought it'd be polite to ask first."

Phillip looked down at the box. For a moment all irritation drained from his face. "Ooh, that's the perfect size, isn't it? Make a safety copy or two if you like, but the box is yours. It's a gift.

Take it and go home, Martin." With that, Phillip closed the door firmly. Martin knew not to knock again.

Martin spent the rest of the day working on his macro. Phillip had told him that the wizards would expect to see what they liked to call a *salutation* – the set of effects used at the beginning of a duel, or when feeling threatened by the locals, to show that everybody knows they've got a powerful wizard on their hands. The night he and Phillip first met, the light show that ended with Martin flying backwards into the forest had been Phillip's salutation.

Wizards also used their salutation as a means of both entertaining and demonstrating their power and creativity. Phillip had often called it the wizard's form of breakdancing. It was a dated reference, but Martin thought it fit.

Martin asked Jeff some questions about his work on importing video game assets into the real world. Specifically, Martin wanted to know about displaying and animating three-dimensional assets in space and playing audio files. Later, he asked Gary about smoke, light, and particle effects. He had seen that Gary had a good grasp of the subject. Also by not asking any one wizard all of his questions, he had a better chance of keeping his macro a surprise. He spent the rest of the day searching the web for code snippets and existing animations to speed up the process. He ran a simulation or two, and was happy with the results.

Phillip returned from the forbidden zone above his shop at dusk, acting as if nothing had happened. They dined on burritos from Phillip's magic burrito hat. Phillip had many other food choices he could produce, but a selection of specialized burritos is all the variety most men need. After dinner, they went for

a fly and found themselves back at The Rotted Stump, the inn
where they'd first met. When they went in, Martin noted that the
place looked exactly as it had when he first arrived, and yet it felt
totally different. It seemed less hostile, less frightening. He figured it was partly because he was more familiar and comfortable
with this era now, and partly because he knew he could level the
whole building with a few words of Esperanto.

Pete was behind the bar, wearing what appeared to be a
Windbreaker made out of used cling film. He had collected all of
it from the patrons and had Gwen help him fashion it into a shirt,
but it was devilishly hard to put on and take off, so he cut it up
the front and used it as a jacket. He said it still turned inside out
every time he took it off, but he just wore it inside out the next
day, and because it was transparent, nobody could tell. Gert was
also there. She greeted Martin in the friendliest way she knew
how. She cracked her knuckles.

Phillip tried not to look too proud when, without any urging,
Martin apologized to Pete and to Gert for the scene he'd caused
on his first night in town, and asked if he could do another trick
to make up for it. He pointed to an empty flagon that was on the
bar in front of Pete and said, "Kopiu." He repeated this fifteen
times and fifteen more flagons appeared on the table. Then he
removed his hat and produced enough gold to pay for enough
beer to fill all of the flagons. He announced that the next round
was on him, then he leaned in close to Pete and said, "Feel free to
keep all of the flagons."

Pete replied, "You gonna help me wash them?"

"Do you wash the ones you already have?" Martin asked.

"Good point."

20.

The next morning, Martin woke early. He lay in his hammock, listening to nothing. He didn't often hear nothing. He had discovered that living in a medieval town was not much quieter than living in a modern town. Sure, cars make a lot of noise, but so do hooves, and while in a modern house the road noise is filtered through modern windows, in the past it came through either rough, single-glazed glass or a simple hole with wooden shutters. It was quiet now, because it was early, barely dawn.

Martin wasn't totally awake, but not totally asleep either. He was in that hazy, semiconscious state where the dreams of the night before dovetail with the reality of the day ahead. That time where you find yourself thinking how unfortunate it is that your lower half has been replaced with the body of a crab, and how difficult it will be to explain to your boss that you couldn't come in to work because your pants are now impractical.

Martin opened his eyes a crack. A light streamed in around the edges of the window shutters. Phillip was in his bed, snoring lightly. The light illuminated the dust that hung in the air, swirling lazily in space. Martin thought about how in a dark room you couldn't see anything, and in a brightly lit room you only saw large things, but in a room with very little light, you could see very little things, like dust. As the sun rose, more light came in, and he watched the dust slowly spiraling in random patterns as the shaft of light got larger and brighter.

Martin opened his eyes all the way, then immediately squinted. There was clearly a void in the dust, next to Phillip's bed. It was barely discernible, but dust was flowing around the empty area. The void was irregularly shaped and appeared to be moving. It seemed still toward the floor, but there was a churning quality about the upper part of the void. Martin lifted his head so he was no longer looking at it sideways. He squinted harder, and for just a moment, the dust seemed to form the outline of a person leaning over Phillip, as if he meant to attack. Martin gasped. The form turned suddenly to face Martin, who recoiled in shock and fell out of his hammock.

Martin hit the ground and cursed loudly. He looked up and saw that the form was gone, if it ever really had been there. Phillip was sitting upright, looking at him. "What's wrong with you?" Phillip asked.

"I, uh, I fell out of bed," Martin sputtered.

"Yes," Phillip said, rubbing his eyes. "That's just a symptom, not the root problem, but whatever."

Martin chose not to tell Phillip what he'd seen. Bad enough that he'd had a silly half-dream and freaked himself out. No need to make it worse by telling everybody about it. Still, Martin was unusually quiet that morning, partly because of the strange start his day had had, and partly because he was nervous about the trials. Phillip did his best to calm Martin's nerves.

"Look, there's no point in freaking out about the trials and ruining your day," Phillip said.

"I know," Martin agreed.

"Freak out tomorrow. That's when the trials are. Today is meant to be a day of fun. Possibly your last."

Martin didn't think that Phillip's best was terribly good.

They ate their breakfast, had a conversation about the infinite adaptability of the humble burrito, then ran through a quick checklist of all the things they would need for the trip. It was not a long list. Wizard robes, wizard hat, wizard staff, completed macro, and a positive attitude. Martin asked if he would need his laptop.

"No," Phillip said. "Remember, many wizards are from a time before useful portable computers. The trials were designed in such a way that directly accessing the shell is not needed. Besides, you've got your pocket computer. If anything, you've got an advantage, not that it'll help."

Martin spent a couple of hours going over his macro a few more times. He was certain it would work. He asked Phillip to quiz him on the things he'd need to know to pass the trials. Phillip asked him some Esperanto vocabulary questions and quizzed him about the finer points of conjuring and flying, but Phillip didn't seem terribly concerned. Martin thought this was either encouraging or maddening, though he wasn't sure which.

Finally, Phillip seemed to get bored and asked, "Ready to go, Martin?"

Martin said that he was, but he was not sure of it. Phillip could sense his hesitation. "Buck up, Martin! Two days from now, you'll be a fully trained wizard with full shell access. Or you'll be in jail. The point is, you'll know. All the uncertainty will be over."

Martin asked, "Have I told you that I'm going to miss your little pep talks?"

Phillip said, "No, you haven't."

Martin said, "There's a reason for that."

Phillip put a reassuring hand on Martin's shoulder. "I have every confidence in you. You'll be fine."

Martin shook his head, and started to thank Phillip, but Phillip interrupted him. "Either way. Transporto londono kvin!"

An instant later, they were standing in a pasture. Martin did not react well. Sometimes, people will forget what kind of beverage is in their glass. They'll get it in their head that they have a glass of milk, when in fact it's soda. If they take a drink without looking, the pleasant mouthful of pop will, for a moment, taste like the most messed-up mouthful of milk in history. Martin had expected city, and instead got a mouthful of pasture. It was a pleasant enough pasture, but Martin had expected a city.

"I thought you said we were going to London," Martin said.

Phillip smiled. "We're in London. This pasture, those woods, that river bank over there, especially that river bank, all of it will be London. If we stand right here, a little under a thousand years from now, we'll be standing in front of a really good curry stand I know, and it'd be a good thing, because by then we'll be hungry."

Martin looked around. The landscape was dotted with cottages. There were people in the distance tending to sheep, working in their gardens. A relatively busy road, by medieval standards, led off into the woods. More people were headed toward the river than away from it. Martin had never really been one for agriculture, but it was all very picturesque. "Okay," he asked, "so why'd you pick this spot? What's your point?"

"I wanted you to have a moment to prepare yourself for what London is at the moment. You've grown up with pictures of Big Ben and Buckingham Palace. I wanted you to be prepared for the fact that none of that is here. When I showed up, all there was that was recognizable were the beginnings of Westminster and the Thames."

Martin shrugged. "Well, at least there's something recognizable."

"There was, back in the *pre-Jimmy* period of English history. Now it's been replaced by Camelot and the river Jems."

Martin was confused. "Why'd he change the river to Jems?"

"It's spelled James."

Martin was starting to see why Phillip hated Jimmy.

Phillip held his staff aloft, preparing for flight. "Shall we?" he asked.

Martin followed suit, and soon they were flying through the air. Martin was deliberately lagging behind, allowing Phillip to lead. They skimmed over the farms and fields, toward the river *James*. In the distance, beyond the trees, crowded along the far bank of the river, Martin saw what he had to assume was London, or as it was now known, Camelot. From a distance it looked a lot like Leadchurch. Actually, it looked like ten Leadchurches packed in together. For Martin's entire life, he had thought of cities as places where there were tall buildings, but aside from one notable exception, there were no tall buildings to be found. The technology simply wasn't there yet.

Phillip swung in a low, lazy arc around the city. Martin followed. Chaotic patterns of narrow streets and squat, mostly brown buildings spread out below him like a field of wooden blocks. The one exception was a large building next to the river, slightly to the left of the city's central mass. The building was surrounded by a wall that was at least three stories tall, and seemed to be covered in highly reflective gold. The building itself was not just a castle. It was *the* castle. It couldn't more obviously be a castle. It bristled with parapets, towers, arrow slits, sky bridges, and buttresses, all covered in the same shiny gold leaf as the outer wall.

Phillip led Martin to the castle, losing altitude as they went. They barely cleared the wall and landed lightly in a large square just inside the main gate. The road came in through the gate, then made a circle around a large reflecting pool, past the formal entrance to the castle, which looked like the gaudiest casino in Las Vegas had been covered in gold leaf and the greeters replaced with knights in hammered gold armor. Beside the entrance, a golden carriage waited for the royal family. It was hitched to four white stallions, presumably because gold stallions weren't available, not that it mattered. Everything within the walls was tinted gold by the reflected light from the castle and the walls.

There were several buildings inside the golden keep of Camelot, not just the castle. Maintaining a facility of this size required infrastructure, which added to the size of the facility, and inevitably, the whole thing gets out of hand. Martin could see that what from a distance had appeared to be a simple, ridiculously ornate golden castle behind a golden wall was in fact a small golden town surrounding a golden castle inside a golden wall. The guards at the castle entrance were serene and regal, but all around there were workmen, stewards, groomsmen, maids, valets, and craftsmen, all milling about in gold-accented livery, looking at the ground, lest they be blinded. The only people looking up at the castle were the tourists, though Martin supposed they were called pilgrims in this time. There were many of them though, milling about. Pointing. Squinting. Buying surprisingly expensive paintings of themselves in front of the castle. "Jimmy had a massive tax levied on gold paint," Phillip explained.

"Wouldn't it be the king who levies taxes?" Martin asked.

"Ah, you're right. Let me rephrase that. Jimmy had the king tax gold paint. Probably just added it to his daily monarch-do list."

"Jimmy really has that kind of power?" Martin asked.

Phillip shook his head. "Martin, look at that statue. You tell me who's in charge."

Martin was aware that there was a grand golden statue of some sort in the reflecting pond, but he hadn't looked directly at it for fear of being blinded. He removed his hat, mumbled some Esperanto, and pulled out a pair of sunglasses with round, green lenses and metal frames, which made Phillip smile.

In the center of the reflecting pond stood an intricately detailed statue, approximately two stories tall. It featured an older king (King Stephen, it would turn out), handing a spectacularly ornate sword (Excalibur, which Jimmy had made, then claimed he'd found in a lake, Phillip explained later) to his son, then-Prince-now-King Arthur (who was, understandably, willing to change his name from Eustace). Standing behind and between the king and his son with a fatherly, guiding hand on both of their shoulders, was an unmistakable likeness of Jimmy. Not Jimmy as he was, but Jimmy as Jimmy pictured himself. Idealized Jimmy. He stood a full head taller than the king, and towered over the prince. With his sunglasses, Martin could make out that Jimmy's robe had a *Merlin* name tag stitched into the right breast, as if he were a mechanic. Jimmy's hat and parts of his head and shoulders were quite severely tarnished and stained.

"What's up with Merlin's head?" Martin asked.

Phillip shrugged, and with a trace of a smile, said, "Ask someone who lives here."

Martin stopped the next person to pass, a porter carrying a crate.

"Pardon me, sir, I'm new to … Camelot," Martin said, with some effort. "Can you please tell me why the wizard's head is stained?"

"That's the miracle, innit?" the man said.

"The miracle?" Martin asked.

"Most every day since the statue was put up, the wizard's head produces a miracle from thin air."

"Really? Every day?"

"Indeed!"

"When? Will it be soon?"

"Don't know," the porter said. "The schedule's not very regular."

"Regrettably," Phillip added.

"What comes out of the statue?" Martin asked. "Blood? Tears? More gold?"

"Unspeakable filth," the porter answered.

After a long, uncomfortable pause, Martin asked, "What kind of filth?"

"Unspeakable filth, like I said."

Another pause.

"Yes, but, is it mud? Is it gore?" Martin asked.

The porter thought a moment, then said, "One could call it muck, I suppose."

"Muck."

"Yes. Unspeakable muck."

"It's excrement, isn't it?"

"Um, yes."

"Feces."

"Yes."

"Human..."

"YES! YES! It's unspeakable...human...muck."

"And it just appears?"

"Yes. It seems to just come from the point of Merlin's hat."

"Then it kind of...trickles down," Martin finished.

"No," the porter said, shaking his head. "It don't trickle. It comes down forceful. Like it fell a ways."

"Perhaps thirty feet?" Phillip offered.

"Could be," the porter agreed.

"And nobody knows where it's coming from."

"We've kinda stopped asking, to be honest. When it first started a few people went up with ladders to try to get a closer look. They regretted it."

"And it's always muck?" Martin asked.

"Mostly," the porter said. "There'll also be some mucky paper. On rare occasion it'll be something different. Word is, one morning last week it was something that smelled like stew."

Martin looked at Phillip, his eyes wide. Phillip thanked the porter for the information and sent him on his way. After a moment, Phillip said, "Amazing, eh?"

"Amazingly immature," Martin replied.

"Most acts of protest are. The headlines after the Boston Tea Party didn't refer to the participants as *several erudite gentlemen*, now, did they?"

"Why doesn't Jimmy stop it?"

"He can't. It's not like there's a visible doorway to my outhouse hovering over the statue. Stuff just appears there at unpredictable times. He can't come to me directly because he doesn't know I'm the one doing it. He could narrow it down to all the wizards who hate him, but in truth, most wizards hate him, at least a little."

"And he knows that?"

"Knows? He's proud of it. He puts it down to jealousy. All he can do to stop the automatic vandalism is remove the statue, and he won't do that, ever. It'd be admitting defeat. Instead, he planted the idea that he might have done it himself as a lesson in humility."

"If you dislike him so much, why did you all make him the chairman?"

Phillip spat, "We didn't make him the chairman. He made himself the chairman. His first act as chairman was to appoint himself chairman. There were only three of us at the time, so we didn't think much of it. I thought he was joking, but every wizard who's shown up since then has been introduced to 'our chairman, Jimmy,' and that's that."

After a long silence, Martin said, "You have to hand it to him."

"I don't hand it to him, but I make sure he gets it, all the same."

Phillip led Martin into the castle. Martin expected the guards to make some attempt to stop them, but the men in the gold armor stood stock still as the wizards walked past. "They know we're guests of Merlin," Phillip explained.

"Well, I'm always happy not to get hassled, but still, you'd think they'd have at least shown that they noticed us."

"Well, there are guests of Merlin, and there are *guests of Merlin*," Phillip explained. "If we had arrived with Merlin, I promise you, they'd have tripped over each other racing to lick our boots. If a wizard comes to Camelot without Merlin, or, indeed, unannounced, we're still allowed in because they assume we're here to meet with Merlin, but they kinda take on the same attitude as a high-level executive's secretary. You're not as important as their boss, and they control your access to their boss. Therefore, by the transitive property of dominance, they're more important than you."

"But they just let us walk in. They didn't even take our staffs. Don't they know how dangerous we could be?" Martin asked as they walked through a massive, gold-leaf-encrusted, ornately carved, marble-floored chamber. It would be the main hall of any conventional public building, but here seemed to function as a cloakroom.

"No, they don't," Phillip said. "They think Jimmy is the most powerful wizard in the world, and in a sense he is, but only because he has influence with the king. They think we stay in line because any wizard who starts any trouble will be immediately exterminated by the mighty Merlin." Phillip leaned in closer and lowered his voice. "If they knew we're just a bunch of dorks essentially living on the honor system because we know we have a good thing going, well...it really wouldn't change much of anything, but still, we don't want them catching on."

"But they'll stop us if we try to go somewhere we're not supposed to," Martin said.

Phillip stopped walking. "They don't have to, Martin. We can't go anywhere we're not supposed to. You know the second story of my shop?"

"Where you go to do nothing."

"Yes. The reason you've never come up to interrupt the nothing is that you can't. Jimmy...sorry, Merlin, knows the same trick. There are many rooms in this castle that only he, the royal family, and their staff can enter. There are others that only he and the royals can go into, and I'd bet that while there are no rooms he can't enter, there are probably rooms the king himself can't see the inside of without Merlin holding his hand."

Martin looked around. "Where are the places we can't go, then?"

"What do you want, a sign? A velvet rope? No, the guy these people know as Merlin doesn't want to *warn* people that they can't do things. He wants to *remind* them that they can't do things. He wants people to try to go through an arch and run into an invisible wall. He hopes they're carrying scalding hot soup when they do it. Merlin never wants the locals to forget that he is Merlin, that magic is real, that he can control it and that they can't. You'll see. Everything he does is designed to constantly remind them, including having this room built."

With that, Phillip led Martin out of the large, impressive marble-and-gold-leaf anteroom they had been traversing. They walked through a massive arch, festooned with innocent-looking cherubs and less innocent-looking nymphs. From a distance, Martin hadn't formed a clear image of what was beyond the arch. He saw more marble flooring, a gold railing, people walking to and fro and an indistinct wall in the distance. As they walked through the arch, and the full majesty of the room they were entering dawned on Martin, he fell silent. Phillip, despite his disgust for Jimmy and all things Jimmy-ish, also went quiet as they entered the famous great hall of the castle Camelot.

Martin had gotten used to mentally adding various comments about Medieval England to the end of declarative statements.

Gwen's an excellent tailor, *for someone trained in Medieval England.*

Gwen's a really cute girl, *considering she lives in Medieval England.*

I'm spending an alarming amount of time thinking about Gwen, *seeing as if I don't concentrate on the trials I might get kicked out of Medieval England.*

The great hall of the castle Camelot was the first thing (aside from Gwen) he'd seen that would have been equally impressive no matter what time or place he saw it. It was the kind of room that is often described as a *shoebox* by architects who didn't get the contract to design that kind of room. The hall was at least a hundred yards wide, and twice as long. Two rows of graceful stone columns ran down the sides of the hall, leaving a large strip of the center of the room open and uninterrupted. The arch that Martin and Phillip had used to enter was in the middle of one end of the hall, raised about three stories off of the floor. On either side of them, staircases lead off to the four tiers of walkways that stretched to the far end of the hall. Clearly, these were meant to support spectators.

The floor was a vast sea of inlaid marble and other decorative stones. Some of the people milling about clearly had places to go; others clearly did not. The floor seemed relatively empty, but a floor that size would. Martin noted that rather than the reflective gold leaf that decorated most of the castle, the majority of the gold in the hall was a relatively dull gold paint, except for the far end of the hall. That wall was hung with massive tapestries, richly woven with decorative strands of golden thread. Shiny golden stairs led up to the top of a tall, shining gold dais. A massive golden throne sat, flanked on either side by smaller, slightly less impressive golden chairs. Both sides of the room were lined with massive glass windows (larger than Martin would have thought possible in any time) that let in a tremendous amount of light. The ceiling was at least two hundred feet above the floor and was a thicket of surprisingly modern-looking metalwork, all painted gold.

Martin gaped at it for quite a while before finally asking, "How is this possible?"

Phillip shook his head. "Same way everything we do is possible. Magic. It took six years from the time King Arthur, who was twelve at the time, by the way, decreed that this place would be built. During that time, Jimmy spent three hours a day just creating gold, some to pay for the construction, some to use as construction materials. Most of this is just wood and stone covered with gold leaf. That stuff goes pretty far. When the workmen didn't know how to make the main hall, he taught them about buttresses. When they didn't know how to span the distances, he taught them to make I-beams. When the metal turned out to be too weak he taught them to make steel, and when the steel took too long to smelt, he just went ahead and made a bunch for them."

Martin was impressed. "Good for the craftsmen. They learned a lot."

"Except that he only told them as little as possible, and that magic is what made it all work. Poor buggers killed themselves building the greatest building in the world, and they're convinced that Jimmy deserves all the credit. He warned them that any other buildings made with these methods would be cursed, and just to sell the idea he destroyed a few churches while they were still under construction. Look, Martin, I don't want to just stand here saying bad things about Jimmy. Sorry, that's not true; I do want to, quite badly, but I won't. Jimmy is smart, he's resourceful, and he can be quite charming. At one time, I considered him a friend. Just remember, the only way anybody ever profits from an encounter with Jimmy is if Jimmy doesn't care enough to bother to prevent it."

Phillip gave Martin a quick tour of the main hall, which took over an hour because of the distances involved. The tour ended at the middle of the room. Most of the floor pattern was gigantic rectangular patches of polished gray stone set into the white background. Each large rectangle had long, narrow rectangles running up their longer sides. "The gray parts are banquet tables," Phillip explained.

"Do you mean they symbolize banquet tables, or that that's where they put banquet tables when they need to?" Martin asked.

"Neither. I mean that the large gray slabs are tables and the thinner slabs next to them are benches. Jimmy has a macro on the floor. He says the right trigger phrase and the slabs rise up and form tables and benches."

This confused Martin. "I thought the shell couldn't manipulate anything too large or complex."

"They're just slabs of stone. There's nothing complex about them. As for being too large, you're right that you wouldn't be able to take one back to your time with you or anything, but as for levitating, as long as the object is one homogeneous piece, it's possible."

"Ah," Martin said, "it's because it's all just one thing. If I tried to lift a tree, I'd probably just strip off the bark."

"Or rip off a single leaf, which won't impress anybody," Phillip added.

Martin continued, "But if I lift a boulder, it should work fine."

"Yes. Kind of. But not really." Phillip clarified. "If the boulder is one solid mass of stone with no impurities to speak of, yeah, you're good, but if there is a vein of a different stone, even just a slightly different type of the same base material, it'll crumble like a dirt clod."

"So, how did he get such large chunks of pure stone?"

"Same way most of us learn about sex: trial and error. He teleported out to the quarry every time they'd chisel a slab off the side of the mountain, and he'd try to lift it. If it hung together, it became a table. If it shattered, it got used for smaller bits."

Martin smiled and shrugged. "Phil, you say that like it's a big waste of time, but I bet the workmen who were saved the trouble of breaking up the big slabs of granite with chisels didn't mind."

Phillip's eyes widened. He set his index finger in *making an important point mode*. He got so far as to say, "But it's all…." before he was interrupted.

"Ooh," Jimmy said from between Martin and Phillip, "he is a perceptive one, isn't he, Phillip?" Both Martin and Phillip jumped. Neither of them had thought that anybody, let alone Jimmy, was anywhere near them. They both turned quickly, and were perplexed to find that they were right. Nobody was within thirty feet of them. Jimmy's voice laughed. It was a small laugh, mostly sympathetic, but with an undercurrent of smugness.

"I'm over here, gentlemen," the voice said, still from an empty spot between them. They continued to look around them, confused.

After a moment, Jimmy spoke again. "Oh, damn. Sorry about that." There was a pause, then, faintly, from a great distance behind them, they heard, "I'm over here." They turned and saw Jimmy standing in front of the dais, hundreds of feet from where they stood. He was recognizable only by his green and gold robes, and the small dot of light emanating from the plasma ball at the top of his staff. Jimmy spread his arms wide and said something else, but from that distance, it was hard to make out.

"I'M SORRY! WE CAN'T HEAR YOU, MERLIN! YOU'RE TOO FAR AWAY!" Phillip yelled. He did not look sorry.

Everyone in the entire hall was now looking at the three of them: the two wizards standing out in the open vastness of the hall and the most famous wizard in the world, standing at the far end, apparently struggling to be heard. If Merlin was irritated or worried, he didn't let on. He simply took a single step forward. He stepped forward slowly, like he was absent-mindedly drifting around the room while thinking about something else. His back foot lifted from the ground before his forward foot touched down, and in the intervening second, he covered the entire distance between himself and the other wizards. He didn't fly so much as he floated with great speed. When his forward foot did touch down, there was no sense of any unusual weight or momentum. He simply had taken a single step forward, and had arrived where he was going. It was a powerful demonstration of the casual, effortless use of tremendous power. Martin remembered what Phillip had said about Jimmy's need to constantly remind people what he could do.

"I said, welcome to Camelot, Martin." Jimmy smiled and extended a hand, which Martin shook. It was a good, solid handshake and a natural, toothy smile. "Phillip has given you the tour, I see. What do you think?"

"It's amazing!" Martin said.

Jimmy held the handshake and the smile slightly longer than expected. After a moment he said, "But?" he seemed amused, not irritated. If anything, his smile brightened.

Martin laughed nervously. "It's all a bit...."

"Vulgar?" Phillip offered. "Hideous? Repugnant?"

"Much," Martin said.

Jimmy smiled at both Phillip and Martin. Martin smiled back. Finally, the handshake ended, punctuated by a firm slap on Martin's back. "You're not wrong, Martin. Walk with me." Jimmy turned and started moving toward the center of the hall. To Martin's relief, he didn't traverse the entire distance in one step as before, making it difficult to keep up. To Phillip's disgust, he instead simply levitated several inches above the ground and floated forward at a walking pace, robes flapping behind him as if he were standing on the shore of a wind-swept lake. The marble floor seemed to distort beneath him and smooth out behind him as he moved, like the wake behind a boat. Martin walked beside him, listening. Phillip followed behind, glowering.

"You see, Martin, despite what some people may believe, I'm not in charge here. I serve at the pleasure of the king," Jimmy said, looking down at Martin from his elevated height.

"King Eustace," Phillip said.

"Indeed, although he prefers to be called Arthur."

"At your suggestion," Phillip added.

"Exactly! As Phillip says, I make suggestions, but the king makes the decisions. I just try to help. I'm a consultant. They wanted a castle. I suggested a location. They wanted it to be the greatest castle of all time. I showed them how it could be done. They wanted it covered in gold. I made that happen. They wanted their names to be remembered in myth and legend. Can you think of a better way to accomplish that than to use the Arthurian myth?"

"*Use*," Phillip spat. "You mean *hijack*."

Jimmy stopped, still hovering, and pivoted as if he were standing on a turntable to face Phillip. Martin would have expected him to look irritated, but he seemed delighted. "Yes! Phillip's right, Martin. *Hijack* is a good description of what we did to the Arthurian legend. It's an ugly word, but really, *use* isn't much better. Before you think too ill of me, Martin, let me show you something." He pivoted again, to face the spot they'd been walking towards. The exact center of the hall was marked by a massive inlaid medallion. A perfect circle of polished granite twenty feet wide was set into the floor. The circle was decorated with intricate scrollwork and inlaid floral motifs. Like moons orbiting a planet, thirteen granite circles two feet across were spaced evenly around the circumference of the medallion.

Everyone in the hall had watched the wizards since the moment Jimmy joined them, but Martin was suddenly far more aware of it. All conversation had stopped. The world was holding its breath. Jimmy took a deep breath, and for a moment Martin thought of him as Merlin.

Merlin said, "Ronda Tablo supreniro," and tapped the circle closest to their feet with his staff. Blue tendrils of lightning similar to those in his novelty store plasma ball shot from the tip of his staff and filled the two-foot circle of granite set into the floor. The sparks radiated to the edge of the circle, tracing its outline on the floor. The light continued along the edges of the thirteen smaller circles, then leapt to the medallion in the center until all of the circles were outlined in blue light. A sound filled the air, like a two-ton slab of stone sliding against another two-ton slab of stone, recorded, amplified and played through a speaker carved from a two-ton slab of stone. Slowly, all of the circles began to rise. As they rose, the circles were revealed to be the tops of pedestals, their sides bowing inward gracefully toward the middle, like stylized hourglasses. The thirteen smaller columns stopped rising, and were about a foot and a half tall. The central medallion stood taller than the other columns, and was similarly bowed inward, but rather than flaring back outward simply stopped at its narrowest point.

The hall was steeped in reverent silence, so it was particularly grating when Phillip said, "Nice card table you've got there."

Jimmy ignored him. As the people in the hall got back to their business, Jimmy turned to Martin. "What do you think?"

Martin walked forward and put his hands on the table. "It's the round table."

"It's *a* round table," Phillip corrected him. "It's not *the real* round table."

"It's *a real* round table," Jimmy corrected Phillip. "The other round table, the one Phillip's referring to, never existed, so I ask you, Martin: Isn't this *the real* round table?"

"But it's not the authentic round table," Phillip said.

"It is authentic," Jimmy said. "It's what's really here. The fact that reality doesn't match what you want or expect isn't reality's fault. Besides, authenticity is overrated. When you were a kid playing in your backyard, who did you pretend to be, Han Solo piloting the *Millennium Falcon*, or Buzz Aldrin going to the bathroom in his astronaut pants?"

Martin, still running his hands over the table's polished surface, said, "But the table's just furniture. The king and the knights were the point, and they're different."

"I bet their names sound familiar, though," Phillip said.

"I only suggested changing three of their names. Lancelot, Galahad, and Gawain, and to be fair, Gawain's original name was

Dwayne, so that was a lateral move. Phillip's got a valid point, Martin. I'm not proud of everything I've done. I've bent reality to fit a work of fiction just to make the royal family happy. I had good reasons, though. A happy king doesn't start wars out of boredom. I've given them this castle because a wealthy king doesn't start wars out of greed. I made them legends because a living legend doesn't kill out of jealousy. "

"He gives them what they want, and in return they do exactly what he tells them," Phillip said, "because if they ever stop, he might stop, too."

"I'm not forcing anybody to do anything, and I put it to you, Martin: whom have I hurt?"

"You may not tell them that they have to do what you say, or else," Phillip said, staring directly at Jimmy, "but when was the last time they didn't do what you told them to?"

Jimmy, who had faced Martin through the entire conversation, and didn't change that now, answered, "I'm fortunate that the king seems to hold me and my advice in high esteem."

"Yes," Phillip said. "The level of the esteem in which you are held is amply demonstrated by that statue out front!"

Although neither man spoke for the next five seconds, they were the most eventful of the entire day, as the facial expression equivalent of a chess match played out, with Martin as the spectator.

At the mention of the statue, Jimmy, for the first time, seemed genuinely irritated. For an instant, Phillip looked quite pleased with himself. Jimmy seemed unsure if this was because he had gotten in a good insult, or if Phillip knew something about the continued vandalism of his likeness. *Was it a confession,* he seemed to wonder, *or is he just laughing because someone else has gotten one over on me?*

Jimmy gave Phillip a suspicious, questioning look. Phillip doubled down on the smugness, with a side order of slightly confused innocence, as if to say, *what are you looking at me like that for? I know nothing about how your statue is regularly anointed with feces.* This did nothing to answer Jimmy's unspoken questions, so he did what he always did when unsure of himself: he feigned confidence. He smirked and almost imperceptibly nodded his head. It was very convincing. For a moment Martin thought Phillip was caught.

Phillip clearly knew that Jimmy was bluffing, and he chose to stand pat with the smug, confused innocence, now with *more smug!* This, Martin saw, was a masterstroke. To laugh, smile, or even nod would be an admission of guilt. To blanch, flinch, or look away would be just as big an admission. To continue with no change in expression would have told Jimmy that he was trying not to betray any information, which would have told Jimmy everything he wanted to know. To remain innocently confused, but get slightly smugger told Jimmy, *you think you know something. I know what you think you know. I know if you're right or not, and I'm never, ever going to tell you.*

"Well," Jimmy said, turning back to Martin. "I must get back to my business. It was good to see you again, Martin." Jimmy tapped the stool closest to him and the round table and stools silently sunk back into the floor.

"Goodbye, Jimmy," Phillip said.

"Goodbye, Martin," Jimmy said. "I'll see you tonight." Jimmy turned and in a single, graceful step was at the golden dais at the far end of the hall. In another step he was at the top of the dais, next to the throne. He paused there, turned, and looked at Phillip as he stroked the back of the throne of England, then he glided around a corner and disappeared into a hole between the tapestries Martin had not noticed before.

They watched him leave, then Phillip said, "It may surprise you to know this, Marty, but I really do hate him."

"He makes some valid points," Martin said.

"That's a big part of why I hate him. If he were wrong about everything I could just dismiss him as a moron, but he's not. He's smart, probably smarter than I am, so I have to take him seriously."

21.

Finally, the time of the feast arrived. As the guest of honor, Martin turned up last. As he entered, he quickly counted around twenty people in attendance. As they walked to the banquet table, Phillip told Martin that almost every wizard in Western Europe was there, but it did not look like a lot of people. Part of the problem was that the party was being held in the great hall of the castle Camelot. Only one of the numerous rectangular slabs that he knew could rise to be used as banquet tables had been lifted. It looked tiny, all the way at the far end of the hall, and the assembled wizards were all huddled together at one end. They could have spread out far enough to not hear each other and only used half of the table. Martin had never been one for parties, but he knew there was a chance that by this time tomorrow he'd be sitting in the back of a squad car, hopefully wearing a bathrobe, so he was determined to enjoy this night. As they approached the table, all of the wizards stood and applauded. Jimmy floated out and met them well before they got to the table. Martin surreptitiously tapped his staff three times on the floor as Jimmy approached.

"Martin, welcome," said Jimmy, putting a hand on Martin's back and leading him toward the head of the table. Martin could see that two seats had been saved for them—a large, ornate, onyx seat with a high back at the head of the table, and an empty spot on the bench to the right of the chair. When Martin started for the bench, Jimmy stopped him.

"Martin," he said, not unkindly, "what are you doing?"

"Well, that chair's, you know, at the head of the table, and I just figured, since you're the chairman...." Martin trailed off.

"Nonsense! Martin, this is your banquet! You're the guest of honor!" Jimmy said, guiding Martin into the fancy stone chair. "Tonight, you get to sit in my chair!"

Martin settled into the seat. It was the most comfortable ice-cold slab of stone he had ever sat on. He looked around for Phillip and made eye contact with him as he settled into the only seat still available, on the bench at the far end of the group. Phillip clearly seemed to find the seating arrangement funny, so Martin didn't worry about it. Gary and Jeff were at the far end of the group with Phillip. They immediately fell into serious conversation.

Every other person was a stranger, but they had certain things in common. They were all men between the ages of twenty and forty. Most had facial hair, some so thick and unkempt that Martin feared they were home to rodents, others so scraggly that they barely earned the name *beard*. Here was a group of guys that would look right at home at a table in the cafeteria of the Googleplex, the Microsoft Redmond campus, or a science fiction convention, but they were in Medieval England, dressed as wizards, and they were all looking at Martin. Jimmy introduced Martin to the wizard seated to his left, an Asian man in his thirties wearing a spectacular red silk robe and hat, both embroidered with dragons. His staff leaned against the table next to him. It was some sort of highly polished driftwood with a claw carved into its top as a figurehead.

Jimmy said, "This is Wing Po, mysterious sorcerer from the East."

Wing Po extended his hand and in a thick New Jersey accent said, "Hiya! You can call me Eddie." Martin shook his hand. A profoundly awkward silence descended on the table. Everyone was looking at Martin, and Martin was looking back at everyone.

"Hi, everyone," Martin said. Nobody said hi back, but there were nods of acknowledgment all around.

"Uh," Martin continued, "thanks for coming." Everyone was offering encouraging looks except Phillip, Gary, and Jeff, who were just enjoying the show.

Jimmy put his hand on Martin's wrist and said, "Martin, you don't have to say anything."

"Oh! Good! Thank you," Martin replied.

"But you can if you want to," Jimmy said. "Go ahead." Everybody seemed to lean in, expecting to hear something good, particularly Phillip, Gary, and Jeff.

"Um," Martin said, "I, for one…am hungry. Let's eat!"

The assembled wizards approved of this. Jimmy clapped his hands. Servers in gold uniforms accented with contrasting slightly shinier gold trim brought out a variety of roasted animals, boiled vegetables, and breads that seemed to be made up entirely of crust. An empty earthenware mug was placed in front of each wizard. As all of the other servers hustled out of the hall a single steward with a large jug entered and started to pour the contents of the jug into Martin's cup, but Jimmy stopped him.

"Steward, this is a solemn occasion," Jimmy said. "Leave us in peace and see that nobody enters this hall until we emerge. Go now. We will have no need of your intoxicating drink." The steward bowed deeply and hastily, and then nearly ran out of the hall. When the door had shut with a thud that reverberated throughout the massive room, Jimmy removed his hat and reached inside, saying, "We're more than capable of supplying our own." He pulled out a bottle of Scotch and set it on the table with a satisfying clink. The wizards started removing their hats and producing their beverages of choice. Martin pulled out a bottle of Diet Dr Pepper. Jimmy tilted his head and squinted at him.

"I'll save the booze for after I've demonstrated my salutation," Martin said. Jimmy seemed to approve.

After that, the assembled wizards did the most reassuring thing they could do. They ignored Martin and ate.

There were only men at the table, as women tended to find the climate of Medieval England a bit more favorable for wizards than it was for witches. Martin remembered that Phillip had told him the women who found the file tended to go to Atlantis, either right off the bat or immediately after training. Martin had asked if any of the men ever went to check it out. "Go to see a society governed by women who chose to go somewhere we weren't? No, we've never sent anyone to go look around. We're afraid we might not like what we find."

The wizards all knew each other. They gathered regularly, but thanks to teleportation, they were able to live in small clusters spread all over Western Europe and into Russia. Only a few chose to live very far from any other wizards.

Anybody who's attended a large family holiday meal would recognize the pattern of the conversation. There were small pockets of tentative conversation, followed by chewing noises. Then there was genuine lively conversation about unimportant topics. Those conversations picked up steam as the eating wound down. Less successful conversations died off, killed by more successful conversations, and soon there was a nice mix of talking and laughter as the men at the table started to remember all the reasons that they liked each other. The key, any good host knew, was to intervene before everyone started remembering why they *didn't* like each other. Even his most virulent critic (Phillip) would agree, Jimmy was a good host.

Jimmy rose from his seat, which for Jimmy meant floating straight up into the air, gliding sideways so he was no longer over his chair, then stretching out to a standing position. Once all that was accomplished, he took Martin around the table, introducing him to everybody and making some small talk.

Martin later reflected that eighteen is just about the optimal number of new people to meet at one time, if your goal is to not remember anything specific about any of them. He had already met Eddie/Wing Po, who lived in London/Camelot with Jimmy/Merlin and was his best friend/assistant.

The Paris contingent had the most elaborate robes and staffs. There were four of them, named Daniel, Stephen, Mitchell, and Greg. They were all Americans. They talked at great length about French girls in such a manner that it was clear they did not know what they were talking about.

The guys from Norway, Magnus and Magnus, had little bits of fur on their robes as trim, which wasn't necessary, as the shell made sure they were never cold. They were from the late nineties, and had both chosen their names to honor the world's strongest man, Magnus Ver Magnusson. Their interests included Vikings, heavy metal, and fulfilling stereotypes. Martin suggested that they should talk to Gary, but they knew Gary already, and derided him as being "too glam."

There was one guy named David who lived in Russia. Martin asked him why he chose Russia, and he replied, "Russian women." That was all he said, but he said it in a way that left Martin sure that David knew exactly what he was talking about.

Jimmy and Martin had worked their way down the right side of the table, reaching the rest of the England contingent: Phillip, Gary, and Jeff.

Jimmy said, "And I know you've already met Gary and Jeff."

"Yeah," Martin said while shaking hands. "Still no Tyler?"

Gary shrugged. "Dunno. He disappears from time to time, but this is the longest he's ever been gone."

Jeff added, "Weird part is, the guy doesn't answer his hand! It's not like him. Maybe he's spending some time up in the future. His plumbing may have finally given out!"

"Well, I'm very disappointed that he's not here," Jimmy said. "I do prefer to have everybody attend these banquets."

"And by *prefer*, he means *demand*," Phillip said.

"It makes it nicer for the new wizard," Jimmy continued.

Phillip also continued. "And by *new wizard*, he means *Jimmy's ego*."

Jeff looked puzzled. "It makes it nicer for the Jimmy's ego?" he quoted.

"Yes," Phillip assured him. "The Jimmy sometimes refers to himself in the third person and uses the definite article. That's just the Jimmy's way."

Jimmy said, "The Jim . . . I do not." Jimmy put his hand on Martin's shoulder and teleported the two of them to the other side of the table, rather than walking all the way down and around the empty two thirds left at the end. They continued working their way up the table.

Carl, Felix, and Theodore lived in various parts of Germany, and seemed to communicate entirely through inside jokes. Fred and Louis lived in Spain. "Isn't that a little close to the Crusades?" Martin asked.

Fred gave a knowing smile. "It's right in the middle of the Crusades."

"It's where the action is!" Louis said. The two went on to describe *the action* as if it were a particularly exciting football game. Martin was relieved when Jimmy ushered him on to the next group.

The last five wizards chose to live in Italy. Specifically Tuscany, because why wouldn't they? They were Ross, Lenny, Ron, Sergio, and Kirk. It was clear immediately that Sergio and Kirk did most of the talking, and Sergio's part was largely urging Kirk to be quiet. It turned out Ron had attended the University of Washington, and discovered the file only a couple of years before Martin. It was strange to think that he and Ron had probably passed each other more than once without taking any notice of each other, and now they were finally meeting, hundreds of years in the past and on the other side of the globe.

The introductions were over. The meal was eaten. The drinking had just started building momentum. It was time for the entertainment, and at a party thrown by Jimmy, that could only mean one thing.

"SPEECH! SPEECH!" Eddie shouted, striking his knife against his earthenware mug with a dull clunking noise. Martin and Jimmy looked at each other, both seemingly caught off guard. Martin reluctantly started to stand. Jimmy put a hand on Martin's shoulder and pushed him back down into his chair as Jimmy rose to speak.

"Friends," Jimmy said. There was a cough from the far end of the table.

"And Phillip."

"Thank you," the distant voice said.

"We are here," Jimmy continued, "to welcome a new member into our family, Martin, a young man with tremendous potential, who was brought here, as we all were, by his abilities, his cunning, his willingness to do things others would not consider, and his desire to become something that others would not consider possible. Something more than what he was. A wizard.

"Now he's here with us, and we call upon him to demonstrate the power he has earned, by learning to not just use and understand computers, but by finding the file, having the grit to use the file, and by listening to his betters... or in this case, the person his betters allowed to train him."

Jimmy paused while someone made a strangled choking noise at the far end of the table.

"Now rise, Martin, and show us your salutation, for in the morning you face the trials, and then you will truly be a wizard."

Martin rose and started to thank Jimmy, but Jimmy, oblivious, cut him off. "Or we'll strip you naked, truss you up like a turkey, and send you back to your time, where a prison cell awaits."

Martin didn't thank Jimmy after all.

He and Phillip had discussed the purpose and theory of the salutation at length. Initially, Phillip had described it as a display wizards put on to demonstrate their powers. It's one thing to tell the non-wizards that you have magical powers, but one often needed to do something ordinary mortals couldn't to seal the deal. The salutation also sent a message to other wizards. As it had evolved, every part of it had taken on new layers of meaning. What you said to trigger it, how elaborate it was, how much thought you put into transitions, what imagery you used, what impression you gave the witnesses – all spoke volumes about who you were and what you thought was impressive. Do you create fire or flowers? Unicorns or demons? Do you dissolve in an elaborate light show, or just wink out like an old-timey camera trick? Do you use props and stagecraft, or just say *abracadabra*?

"Don't say *abracadabra*," Phillip had told him. "I'd rather you made the obvious joke than hear you say *abracadabra*."

Martin did not say *abracadabra*. Instead, he said, "For this, I'll need the assistance of the imp I've captured to do my· bidding." With his left hand he held his staff, with its silver and gray bust of El Santo. With his right he reached into his pocket and produced the small, carved box Phillip had hastily given him as a gift. He had painted it with silver and gray highlights, to match his robe and staff. He held the box in front of him and swung the hinged lid open with his finger. From most angles, the lid appeared to open on its own. As the lid opened, a flickering, uneven light came out of the box and washed Martin's face. Martin could see his smartphone wedged into the bottom of the box with some wooden shims to keep it from rattling around. Martin smiled and muttered into the box as if he were talking to a treasured pet. "Wake up, imp. There's a good imp. I'll call you Tyrion! Yes I will!"

There were a few laughs, but Martin could tell they were laughing with him, not at him. Everything Martin had done so far was just preamble. Now it was time to get to the serious part. He said, "starigis la scenejo," and immediately it looked as if Martin had dived head first into the box. His head shrank and disappeared into the box, followed by the rest of him until only his hands, still full size remained at the ends of his stretched and contorted arms which looped around and terminated into the box. Then Martin's arms and hands followed, dragging the base of the box with them. The box itself warped, twisted, and disappeared into itself, leaving only the ornately carved lid, which slammed shut, buckled, shrank and vanished.

In the middle of the cavernous hall, four feet above the very spot where Martin had tapped his staff three times at the beginning of the party, a small light winked in and out of existence with a faint pop. When the light disappeared, the box was left in its place, hovering in midair. Its lid opened and a thick white smoke poured out and fell heavily to the floor. Instead of spreading when it reached the cold marble, it coalesced into a pillar that grew and thickened until it solidified in the form of Martin, still holding his staff and peering into his box. To Martin's surprise there was actually a smattering of applause. He smiled, then closed the imp box, placed it back in his pocket, planted his feet and held his staff over his head with both hands, and looked at the floor.

In a loud, deep voice, he said, "EH NEEEK CHOCK!"

Silvery lines of pure energy traced the contours of Martin's form. The lines formed a pattern similar to the mortar in a brick wall. When the line pattern had covered him, the contours of Martin's body warped and flattened until he appeared to be a brick sculpture of Martin, but instead of bricks, he was made of copies of his imp-box. For a moment all was silent, then Martin exploded.

There was no fire, no smoke, not even any noise to speak of, just boxes, flying and tumbling outward and then orbiting each other. They formed a thirty-foot sphere of swirling, multiplying boxes. They spun chaotically for two revolutions, then reassembled into another statue of Martin, three stories tall. Because the boxes were still the same size, this statue was more recognizably human shaped than the one before. The boxes were not touching each other, but were floating in a three-dimensional pattern. For just an instant, when the statue stood still, the wizards could see Martin, suspended inside the statue's massive torso.

It silently towered over the wizards as they sat, gaping in their seats. The huge staff it held level above its head was also constructed of imp boxes. The head of Santo looked large enough that a grown man could hide in it. Another brief round of applause started, but stopped dead when the statue raised its head. With a strange combination of ponderousness and speed, the statue's left hand pushed the staff, which spun like a helicopter blade, pivoting on the blindingly fast brick fingers of the statue's right hand. The hall filled with a deafening roar of wind until the statue's right arm came down to the statue's side, stopping the staff's spinning and slamming its base into the floor with a sound like a sonic boom. The statue looked straight ahead and let go of the staff, which stood balanced for a moment, then it collapsed into a pile of boxes, which spread into a lumpy rectangle at the statue of Martin's feet. The rectangle sharpened and solidified into the unmistakable shape of an immense sheet of corrugated cardboard and a massive dual-cassette boom box with four huge speakers.

The statue looked down at the table of speechless wizards and jerked its chin upward sharply, as if to say *Wazzup?* The giant statue bent sideways at the waist. With a massive finger, it hit a button on the top of the boom box. The great hall was filled with the familiar hiss of a cassette player until the inevitable finally happened. The boom box played Herbie Hancock's "Rockit."

As loud as the giant boom box was, it was nearly drowned out by cheering and laughing as the statue started to do the robot. Once it had demonstrated its mastery of robotics, the statue dove forward, did a serviceable version of the worm, then hoisted itself into a headstand and swung its legs around wildly for a moment before doing a headspin. The headspin transitioned seamlessly into a backspin, which ended with the statue lying on its side on the cardboard. It was facing the wizards, its head supported by its arm and its upper leg bent at the knee in a posture of simulated relaxation. With its free arm the robot formed a gun with its thumb and forefinger, which it aimed at the table of wizards. As Herbie Hancock hit a large downbeat on the drums, the statue "shot" the finger gun and in an instant the statue, the boom box, and the cardboard all collapsed into splinters that fell to the ground and disappeared.

All of the wizards were applauding and cheering except one. The cheering only got louder when they realized that the wizard who wasn't applauding was Martin, who had been standing next to Jimmy since the moment the statue started dancing.

The rest of the night was a blur of drinking and laughing. The only serious moment occurred when Jimmy pulled him aside and asked him about his plans.

"I haven't made any beyond trying to pass the trials tomorrow," Martin said.

"Look, I know you and Phillip are friends," Jimmy said, "and I know that Phillip and I aren't, but if you don't have anything to do in Leadchurch, I hope you'll consider coming here to Camelot. I could use a man like you."

Martin looked at Jimmy, then looked around at the opulent palace Jimmy had essentially created through sheer force of will. "What on earth would you possibly need me for, Jimmy?"

Jimmy patted him on the back. "In theory, no one wizard is more powerful than any other, but you'll learn that just because the shell gives everyone else the same powers you have doesn't mean that they can do the same things you can do. You have something very rare, Martin. Showmanship. You know what most of these guys' salutations are? They fly and they glow and they shoot energy beams. If I'm lucky they swing their staff around a bit while they do it."

Martin remembered Phillip's display the night they met. Jimmy had just described it pretty well.

"What you did tonight was the first really original thing I've seen in a very long time. None of these guys could have done it. They don't have flair, like you do."

"Gary has flair," Martin said.

"Yes," Jimmy admitted, "but he has no taste. He's all hellfire and bat wings. It's impressive, but nothing I can use. I can use you, Martin. Think about it. You don't have to decide tonight, but when you get bored in Leadchurch, and you will, you can always come here and help me make the world better."

Sometime around 1:30 in the morning, Martin learned the best thing about wizard parties, which is that because wizards can teleport, they can sleep in their own beds no matter how drunk they get or how far away the party was. Unfortunately, they still were susceptible to hangovers, and Martin woke up with the worst one of his life. The swaying of his hammock made him feel vaguely ill. The light coming in the windows made his brain feel as if it was on fire. The slightest noise was agony. For a moment, while he was still only half awake, he thought he heard a very distant, hollow noise that sounded almost like growling, which was a new one, but he figured it was the blood rushing through the veins in his ears.

He carefully dismounted his hammock. He groaned lightly as his feet took over the task of supporting his weight. The groan was barely a whisper, but it was enough to cause Phillip to gasp, "Keep down that racket!" Then Phillip winced at the toll his own voice had taken on his head.

Martin attempted to say he was sorry silently, by squinting at Phillip and waving his arms vaguely, then he shuffled into the bathroom to go deface Jimmy's statue.

Over the next hour the two men moped and groaned their way back into the world of the living. The quality of life in Medieval England had improved drastically since Martin had learned to pull black coffee, real food, and over-the-counter pain medications out of his hat. Of course, all of the food items he could access were gifted to him by Phillip. He wouldn't be able to set up macros to retrieve his own favorite items until he had unlimited shell access and the ability to come and go to and from the future without the imminent threat of arrest.

He'd figure out how to deal with the feds later. Today, his only priority was to pass the trials. He'd have felt a lot better if he knew what the trials were, but nobody had been willing to tell him anything.

Martin spent the morning going over vocab, quizzing himself on technique, and generally making himself more nervous. Phillip spent the morning reading a dog-eared paperback of *Ender's Game* that he'd borrowed from Jeff. After a couple of hours of this, Phillip's hut was filled with the warbling chime sound that Martin had anticipated and dreaded in equal measure.

Phillip smiled at Martin and said, "Well, Martin, that's the call. You ready?"

"I really don't think so," Martin answered.

"Good." Phillip raised his right arm and held his hand as if he were palming a softball. The chiming sound died and a glowing blue image of a calligraphic letter M appeared in Phillip's hand. "The hour is nigh!" Jimmy's voice bellowed. "Is the initiate ready to face the trials?"

"Yup," Phillip said with aggressive informality.

"EXCELLENT! Bring him forth to the great hall of the castle Camelot to be tested and judged!"

"Uh huh. Will do," Phillip replied. The uppercase M in Phillip's hand hovered there silently for a long moment, then disappeared.

"Does he do everything in the great hall?" Martin asked.

"Wouldn't you?" Phillip stood up, smoothing out his robe. "Well," he said, "I guess it's about that time. Do you have to use the bathroom before we go?"

"No," Martin said. "You?"

"No," Phillip said. "Let's just get this done."

Martin hesitated. "Um, Phil, I just want to say, no matter how this ends up, I really appreciate everything you've done for me."

Phillip put a comforting hand on Martin's shoulder. "You're welcome, Martin. And don't worry; you're going to do fine."

Martin smirked. "I know, because if I don't, you'll send me to prison naked."

Phillip looked wounded. "I wasn't going to say that, Marty."

"Oh, I'm sorry."

"But it's true. We'll totally do that to you. TRANSPORTO RONDA TABLO!"

In an instant they were standing in the center of the black granite disc that marked the center of the great hall of the castle Camelot. The disk was raised as it was when being used as the round table, but the chairs remained recessed into the floor, giving the overall effect that Martin and Phillip were standing on a raised pedestal for examination. The hall was dim, despite the massive windows that lined its sides. Martin saw that there were huge curtains drawn over the windows, blocking most of the light. All of the wizards he had met, dined with, and entertained with his avatar's break dancing the night before were there, arranged in a curved row, facing the platform where he and Phillip stood. As his eyes adjusted, Martin could see that one of the wizards on the end seemed to be holding some rope. At the middle of the line, one wizard stood taller than the rest, because he was hovering five inches above the floor.

"Who comes to face the trials?" the hovering wizard asked.

"With all due respect," Phillip said, "you know exactly who it is, and I'd appreciate it if you didn't waste his time with your idiocy, Jimmy."

"That wasn't very respectful," Jimmy said.

"No, but it's all the respect you're due. Now get on with it!" Martin recognized Jeff and Gary's laughs coming from the end of the line of wizards.

Jimmy took a moment to compose himself, then continued. "Are his skills adequate to the challenges that await him?"

"You know they are, or I wouldn't have said he was ready, would I?" Phillip answered.

"All right then. Phillip, you've done your duty. Leave your apprentice to his fate."

Phillip clambered down off of the platform and walked slowly to the end of the shadowy line of wizards. As he reached his spot, he said, "Hello, Gary. Jeff. You brought the extra scratchy rope, I see." Muffled laughs and shushing followed.

"Martin, do you feel ready to leave your life as an apprentice behind and take on the powers and responsibilities of a wizard?"

Martin gave Jimmy a look that he hoped read as determination, and said, "Yes."

A long moment passed. Nobody moved. Nobody spoke. If someone had told Martin that the birds outside had stopped flying in midair, he would not have doubted it. Finally, Jimmy said, "Okay."

Martin looked at all of the other wizards. They all looked at him. He looked back to Jimmy and said, "Good."

Jimmy replied, "Yes, good."

Martin looked at Phillip, who held up his hands and mouthed the word *what?*

They're messing with me, Martin thought. *They're trying to put me off balance. Then, when I'm vulnerable, the trials will begin.* He bent his knees, transferring his weight to the balls of his feet. He hunched his shoulders slightly, put his empty left hand out in front of him for balance, and held his staff slightly behind so he could whip it forward with force if need be. For another long moment all was silent, and Martin was at the center of the universe, a coiled spring, ready for whatever happened next.

Eventually, Martin realized that nothing was going to happen. He stood up straight again and asked, "Okay, what's going on?"

When the wizards were done laughing, Jimmy explained, "It's over, Martin. You're in."

"What?! But ... the trials!"

"Were last night," Jimmy said, "if you must call them that. Look, Martin, the point of the trials is to make sure that you know what you're doing and that you can be trusted. Phillip has lived with you and trained you, and he says you're okay. We all met you last night and you didn't set off anybody's warning bells, so, you're in."

Martin sat down on the edge of the round table. He didn't know if he was more relieved or angry. "So it was all a lie?"

"No," Phillip said as he walked to where Martin was sitting, "it wasn't all a lie. It was mostly a lie. In a sense, the trials began when you and I met, and the final test was your macro last night. You got off to a rocky start, but you paid attention, you learned, and you took the whole thing seriously."

"What if I hadn't?" Martin asked. "It's happened before. Phillip told me about a trainee who failed a few years ago."

Mitchell, one of the three wizards from Paris spoke up. "Yeah, I had an apprentice who seemed all right at first, then I caught him *practicing* his powers on animals. Nasty business."

"What did you do?"

"I called Jimmy," Mitchell said, "and told him about it. He had me tell the guy that he was ready for the trials. We had a dinner just like last night. He showed us his macro, which I'm not going to describe to you because there are some things you can't un-hear. It's bad enough we had to see it. Anyway, after that we were unanimous that he had to go. The next morning we told him he'd failed and we used the shell to make it so that no integrated circuit would function within ten feet of him."

"That's how you keep him from using the file!" Martin said. "I'd wondered about that."

"Yeah, unless he figures out how to access the file from an abacus, the world is safe. Then we sent him back to his time...."

"Yeah," Martin said, waving his hand. "Hogtied and naked so the police would get him. Are you sure the police were looking for him?"

"Oh yeah," Mitchell said. "No question. The fact is, the police are looking for almost all of us."

Many heads nodded. Gary said, "It turns out that bank fraud is surprisingly hard to get away with, even if you create the money out of thin air."

Jimmy nodded. "Not surprising, really. At the end of the day all a bank really does is track money. It makes sense that they'd be pretty good at it."

By this time all of the wizards had walked over near where Martin was sitting. Fun is fun, but they knew they had put Martin through the wringer, and they wanted to make sure he was all right, partly because they'd all been there themselves and partly because few things are more dangerous than a wizard bent on revenge.

"So, Marty," Phillip said, "you haven't said yet if you'll join us."

Martin shook his head. "Are you kidding? Phillip, how can you ask me that? Of course I'm going to join you! Even if there wasn't unimaginable power in it for me, and even if the feds weren't waiting in my time to take me to jail, I'd stick around just to help do this to the next sap to come along."

That was when everyone knew that Martin was truly one of them. There were many handshakes and back slaps. Jimmy congratulated Martin then excused himself and his assistant Eddie, saying they had pressing business elsewhere. Gary made a pizza run and the remaining wizards generally had a pleasant afternoon. They all found Martin to be a little quicker to laugh now that the pressure was off.

Slowly, wizards started making their excuses and going back to their homes. Finally it was just Martin, Phillip, Gary, and Jeff left to clean up.

"I wish Tyler were here," Gary said.

"He'd have enjoyed this," Phillip agreed.

"That, and he has all those paper towels in his apartment," Gary said while attempting to scrape some melted cheese off of the granite table with the edge of a cardboard pizza box, leaving a smear of oil behind.

"You could go to your time and get a roll," Jeff said.

"Yes, but we both know that's not going to happen," Gary said. He piled all of the pizza boxes on the stone floor, aimed his staff at them, and said, "Flamo sur." There was an intense gout of blue flames. The pizza boxes completely burned away in less than a second. With nothing left to feed them, the flames took on the shapes of demons and rose to the ceiling and dissipated. For just a moment Martin could see that the spaces between the flames took the shape of a man waving his arms frantically, as if in agony. When the flames were gone, Martin said, "That was a touch overdramatic."

Jeff smiled. "Like you should talk."

Jeff and Gary said goodbye and disappeared into thin air. "How do you think he made the areas between the flames look like a person?" Martin asked.

"Hmm," Phillip said. "I didn't even notice that."

There was nothing left for Martin and Phillip to do but go home themselves. *Home* meaning *Phillip's home*, which became all too obvious to Martin quite quickly. They rematerialized in Phillip's hut and Phillip rubbed his hands together and said, "I expect you'll be anxious to get out on your own."

Martin didn't know how to react. "Phillip, I hope I haven't done something to make you think I'm anxious to leave."

"Oh, Marty," Phillip said in a chummy sort of way, "I didn't say *think*, I said *expect*. There's a difference. So, where will you go?"

"I ... I guess I'll get a place of my own," Martin sputtered.

"Splendid idea! When?"

"I dunno. Tomorrow morning?"

Phillip shook his head and put an arm around Martin's shoulders. He said, "Martin, don't stay here for me." Martin clearly heard a comma that wasn't stated, but was there nonetheless. *Martin, don't stay here, for me.* Martin suddenly realized that Phillip had shared his entire existence with Martin, and now he wanted it to himself again. Martin couldn't blame him.

"It's a bit late to try to find a shack of my own," Martin said, "but I bet Pete has a room at the Rotted Stump he'd rent me until I find a place."

"I bet he does. You might even be able to pay him in cling film! I'll tell you what. You go get a room, and then I'll help you move your things."

"All I have is my laptop."

"I'll help you move your thing."

Martin had set a teleportation waypoint for the Rotted Stump. He suspected Pete, Gert, and the others would be pleasant company if he stopped trying to impress them all the time, a quality, he now realized, that they shared with pretty much all of humanity. He uttered some Esperanto and appeared outside the Rotted Stump. A friendly conversation and a small transaction later, he was the temporary owner of a room with a bed in it. When he reappeared at the hut, Phillip was waiting. Martin grabbed his laptop. Phillip handed him his bundle of street clothes, wrapped in his old Hogwarts robe. Martin had nearly forgotten them, but realized immediately that he'd want them if he ever went back to his own time.

Neither of them was a particularly emotional guy, so their goodbye couldn't help but be awkward. A poorly worded *thank you* was followed by an inelegant *you're welcome* and punctuated with a stiff, uncertain hug. When the hug finally ended, Phillip said, "I'm happy to have you as a friend, Martin, and even happier to lose you as a roommate."

What would have been a cutting remark just fifteen minutes before made them both laugh now. Then Martin teleported to his room on the second floor of the Rotted Stump, and he was on his own.

That night, Martin lay in bed and considered his next move. He could do anything he wanted. He just had to figure out what he wanted. He didn't know what he wanted to do with his life in the long term, but that could wait. Near-term was all he needed to worry about tonight. The noise from the tavern coming up through the floorboards made it clear that his first order of business would be getting a place of his own. His first impulse was to stay in Leadchurch. All of his friends were here, and there was close proximity to Gwen. Then again, Leadchurch was a pretty small place, and as he said, all of his friends were here. It was a pretty high wizard saturation for such a small town. Then it struck him that he didn't actually know where Gary's cave was. He'd assumed it was close, but he'd never asked. For all he knew, the cave was clear up in Scotland. For the first time, it really struck home with Martin that, thanks to teleportation, the entire world was really just down the hall. He could literally set up shop anywhere and it would make no difference. Martin thought about all he knew of this version of Medieval England, and realized that the most interesting place he knew of was Camelot. Martin was a city boy, and Camelot was where the action was. He didn't have to worry about Jimmy getting angry because Martin was moving in on his turf, because Jimmy had invited him. He didn't know how Phillip would react, but it wasn't like he was siding with Jimmy. He was just moving to the capital to see things for himself.

The next morning, Martin used the hand phone spell to call Jimmy. He told the glowing M in his palm that he was going to stay in Camelot for a while (it took some effort not to call it London) to see if he liked it. Jimmy was delighted, and said that he'd have Eddie find a couple of prospective places to look at.

The following day, Eddie had three places to show Martin. Eddie explained the various features of the buildings, resplendent in his red silk robe with gold embroidered dragons as he showed the sizes of the rooms and the proximity to various shops and inns. Martin amused himself with the notion that it was like having Ming the Merciless as a Realtor. He mentioned this to Eddie. Eddie laughed, then pointed out in his thick New Jersey accent that Martin was wearing a silver robe and carrying a stick with a *luchador* head on it. Martin thought, *It's amazing how quickly we get used to weirdness when it's our own weirdness.*

He settled on a building in a bustling area on the east side of town. It had been used mainly for storage. It had a smallish room facing the street, and then a very large room with a high ceiling in the back. Eddie had suggested it because it would give Martin room to work on large-scale macros, and Martin couldn't help but agree. It didn't take Martin long to pull enough gold from his hat to buy the place outright.

After Eddie left, Martin looked at his new home, and realized that he had no furniture of any kind. He made a quick list of all the stuff he'd had in his old apartment, then he asked himself how much of it he'd really needed. The answer was, "not much of it." He decided that the first things he needed were a table, a chair, a bed, and some bedding. Chairs and tables could be procured here in Camelot, but the comfort level of the standard issue straw and scratchy blanket bed he'd used at the Rotted Stump had not impressed him, and he had no intention of spending the rest of his life sleeping in a hammock.

In the Bankses' living room, chaos reigned. Walter and Margarita Banks could tell from the cacophony of sirens, pounding noises, and yelled threats that their quiet suburban front yard was crawling with law enforcement officers, many of whom would soon be coming in. Their youngest son Martin had burst in unannounced and sprinted into his old bedroom, emerging several times in quick succession to model his old Halloween costume, mutter about Draco Malfoy, demand Saran Wrap, and ask geography questions. Then he'd demanded a package that he said he'd ordered, but seemed surprised to see. Now he was back in his room.

The pounding at the door was getting louder. Through the sirens they could hear a man's voice yelling, "We are federal agents! We are pursuing a suspect and we saw him enter these premises! Open this door immediately or we will break it down!"

"One moment! I'm coming!" Walter yelled. He and his wife Margarita exchanged bewildered looks and Walter started toward the door.

"NO, DAD, STOP!"

Margarita and Walter looked down the hall. Martin had come out of his room again. He was standing in the hall wearing a silver sequined bathrobe and a pointy hat. He was carrying a long pole with his old souvenir bust of what Margarita had always called *that stupid wrestler* perched on its tip.

"Martin, baby, what's going on?" Margarita asked. "What have you done?"

"Nothing," Martin said as he lurched three steps down the hall and threw open the door to the linen closet. "I haven't done anything," he continued as he grabbed a small stack of sheets and pillowcases. "I especially haven't done any of the things those men are going to tell you I did." Martin yanked a blanket down from the top shelf, clamped his staff against his body with his left arm, slammed the closet door shut with his foot, and quickly went back to his bedroom, shouting, "Thanks for everything! See you later! Dad, you can open the door now!" The bedroom door slammed shut behind him.

Martin rematerialized in his new home, holding a pile of laundry in one hand and his smartphone in the other. He hastily threw the laundry down on the pile of his old street clothes, hoping that would keep them relatively dirt-free. He put down his staff, took a breath, then touched the screen of his phone with his thumb and disappeared again. A moment later he reappeared, bear-hugging the mattress from his childhood bed, which was rolled up like a giant burrito.

It still had all of its bedding attached, as if he had simply pushed the fully made mattress over on itself, stood it on end, threw his arms around it and hastily teleported out of there, which is exactly what he had done.

He let go of the mattress. It unfolded and fell limply to the floor, creating a low *whump* noise and a noticeable cloud of dust.

Martin said, "I'm home."

22.

Two days later, Martin's place was coming along nicely. He had a nice flat table to set his laptop on and a chair to sit on as he used it, and use it he had. He'd taken a page from Phillip's playbook. He set up exclusionary zones that kept anyone from entering his building if he wasn't there. He poked around the shell and found that most of the food items he'd want to replicate were already programmed in. That saved him some labor, and the trouble of getting a stew pot, although he figured he'd have to get one eventually if he was going to have anyone come visit. He had already tweaked his macro to make it less of a show-piece, and more of a practical display of power. The people of this chronologically polluted version of Medieval England were much more sophisticated than he had originally suspected, but he still doubted they'd be impressed by his ability to do the worm. He was working on this and that when, for the first time on his own, he heard the eerie, warbling chime that meant that the hand phone was ringing.

Martin held his hand up in front of his face and said, "Hello."

A crudely animated image of a flaming skull filled Martin's hand, and Gary's voice filled the air. "Hey Martin, oh...huh. You're still using the default icon."

"Oh! I hadn't even thought about that! What is the default icon?"

"The words *default icon*," said Gary's disembodied voice.

"Yeah," Martin said. "I gotta fix that."

"Yeah, well, do it later. I need you to come to my place right now. You know how to get here?"

"Yeah, don't use any coordinates you give me."

"You're smart, Martin, but I promise. No funny business. This is serious. Just use the location code Skull Gullet Cave."

Martin took a moment to make sure he was presentable. He put on his hat and grabbed his staff, and moments later he was standing in the massive stone mouth that marked the entrance to Gary's home. He found Jeff waiting for him.

"Come on back," Jeff said, beckoning Martin deeper into the cave. They passed through the carefully designed set, through the concealed door and into Gary's comparatively pleasant apartment. Inside, Gary was sitting on a bench next to Gwen, who was gripping a mug with both hands and looking off into the distance. They both had their backs to the table. As Martin and Jeff entered, Gary nodded subtly to them, and tilted his head toward the other bench on the far side of the table. Taking his cue from Jeff, Martin nodded back and silently took a seat across the table from Gwen and Gary. After a moment, Gary turned sideways so he could address Jeff and Martin and still observe Gwen, who only moved occasionally to sip from her mug.

"She showed up here about a half hour ago," Gary said. "She was really worked up about something, and wasn't making any sense. She said I was the closest wizard she knew. I hitched her horse and wagon and brought her inside. When I finally got her calmed down, she told me why she was freaked out, and I got worked up and didn't make any sense for a while. Then I called you two, and now you're up to speed."

"Why didn't you call Phillip?" Jeff asked.

"I tried. Got no answer. He's probably up in his attic, *doing nothing*." Sadly, it went without saying that Gary had tried to reach Tyler, and failed.

"How'd Gwen know where you live?" Martin asked, and immediately regretted it. Any other time he'd have been tortured a bit for asking, but Gary wasn't in the torturing mood, or, perhaps, for the first time he actually was.

"I've invited her here more than once," Gary said. "You can't blame a guy for trying."

"Actually, women *can* blame a guy for trying," Gwen said without turning to face any of them. "We do it all the time."

"Okay, so come on, what is it?" Jeff asked. "Gwen, what happened?"

"There's a farmer who's been complaining that my garments get longer over time."

"Oh yeah, uh . . . Sam! Right?" Martin said. "Got his whole village convinced. Gwen ended up altering a ton of clothes."

Gwen nodded. She still hadn't turned to face them, instead staring into her drink. Jeff watched the back of her head as she spoke. Martin's eyes drifted to the hood of her favorite cloak, possibly the only one she owned, for all he knew. The hood tapered to a point down near the small of her back in a decorative flourish. *It's weird, the things we notice at times like these,* Martin thought.

"I got all the alterations done," Gwen said, "so I loaded the wagon and went to deliver them."

There was a long silence, punctuated by Jeff saying, "And?"

"They were dead."

Martin and Jeff looked at each other, then at Gary, then at the back of Gwen's head. Martin hadn't known that it was possible for the back of someone's head to look upset, but Gwen's did.

"Sam and his family?" Martin asked.

"Yes," Gwen said, "and his neighbors, and every other person in his village. Everyone, Martin. Everyone's dead."

Gwen was remembering what she had seen and was understandably starting to lose it again, so Gary took over. "It's a little village about an hour's ride away. Not on any map. It's called Rickard's Bend. I'd say about a hundred people, give or take, live there."

"I don't get it. How does a whole town die? Were they attacked by animals or something?"

"No," Gwen said.

"Were they attacked by raiders?" Martin asked.

Gwen stood and turned to face them. To Martin's surprise, she was not crying. She didn't even look close to tears. She looked close to murder. She said, "I don't know what happened to them, but I came here because I thought you lot might."

A few minutes later they materialized on a hill on the outskirts of Rickard's Bend. A cluster of seven or eight smallish buildings with stone walls and thatched roofs stood on either side of a wide dirt road. The countryside was a random collection of gently rolling hills dotted with farmhouses and grain fields. A smallish river cut through the landscape toward the town, then predictably bent, right about where Martin figured some guy named Rickard had found it.

It would have been quite idyllic, if not for all the corpses.

At first Martin didn't see them. It was obvious from a great distance that the town was completely still, which was eerie enough. Then, as they walked closer, they could see what looked like people having naps leaned up against trees, or in front of buildings, or face down in the middle of the road.

Once they got within touching distance of the buildings, there was no doubt in any of their minds, or noses, that everyone was dead. Gwen was handling it better than the three wizards. Of course, she'd seen it before. None of them were forensic scientists, so there was little scientific about their actions. They yelled to see if anyone would answer, but they neither expected nor received any reply. Martin strained his ears, but all he heard was the sound of a dog growling somewhere far away.

They walked around in a daze, looking at the dead bodies and exchanging confused looks with Gwen. When Gwen wasn't looking, they'd exchange alarmed looks with each other. There was no sign of any violence or bloodshed. It reminded Martin of things he'd read in history class about poison gas attacks. An entire village, caught in the act of living its life, killed in one stroke. There was evidence that it hadn't been an entirely normal day. Upon close inspection, certain patterns emerged. Martin very badly wanted to look at a member of the village he had seen before.

"Hey Gwen, where does that guy Sam live?" Martin asked.

Gwen pointed to a farmhouse a mile or so down the road, sitting on the crest of a hill. "That's his house, if you want to go look. He has a wife and two little girls." Jeff, who happened to be standing closest to Gwen, put a hand on her shoulder. She smiled sadly at him. "Would you like to magic us there?" she asked all three of them at once.

"No," Martin said, "I think I could use a walk and some fresh air."

Gary quickly said, "Agreed."

Gwen shrugged and started walking down the road towards Sam's house. Jeff gave the other two wizards a knowing look, then kept pace with Gwen, and started a conversation that the other two couldn't quite make out.

Gary immediately got to business. "Martin, see anything weird about the bodies?"

"Mmm hmm," Martin said quietly. "Sam was right. All of their pants are too long. They all seem to have really stubby arms and legs."

"Yup. That's not all. Call me crazy, but it looks to me as if most of them died right after removing their shoes."

Gwen and Jeff were well ahead of them now, walking along the side of the road, next to the now vacant buildings. Martin and Gary were following, engrossed in a conversation neither liked.

"That's why I want to see Sam," Martin said. "I've met him. I know how tall he is … was."

"If I didn't know better, and I don't," Gary said, "I'd say someone was trying to make Hobbits."

"I agree," Martin spat. "This is clearly the work of a wizard."

A voice from behind said, "That's what we thought. NOW!"

A large piece of timber swung out from behind a building and caught Jeff on the back of the head with a loud crack. At the same instant, Martin felt a brutal impact on his left hand that sent his staff flying, and another blow to his head that plunged him into darkness.

23.

Martin didn't wake up so much as he gradually became less unconscious. At first he didn't know who he was, where he was, or what he was doing. Then he figured out that he was Martin Banks, he was in Medieval England, and that he was struggling at the ropes with which someone had tied him to, respectively, Jeff, Gary, and a tree.

It was dusk, and Martin was seated on the ground with his back resting against the tree trunk and his legs stretched out in front of him, bound together with heavy rope at the knees, ankles, and the arches of his feet. Although he could see only their feet in his peripheral vision, he knew Jeff was on one side of him and Gary was on the other, both in the same position. Their arms were all intertwined as if they were out for a grand day in a musical in the 1930s. Martin's hands were bound together by a length of rope that was pulled tight just to the point of causing him constant discomfort. Another thick rope lashed Martin's back to the tree, another held his neck to the tree, and a final thick and well-used rope was tied tight around his head, holding his mouth open, effectively gagging him. *Whoever has us,* Martin thought, *it's someone who isn't suffering a shortage of rope.*

Martin could feel Jeff and Gary struggling just like he was. They were helpless, lashed to a tree beside one of the buildings that used to make up the town of Rickard's Bend. Whoever attacked them was wise to take them by surprise, disarming them of their staffs, and Jeff his wand, immediately. Without their staffs, the shell wouldn't recognize them as wizards and allow them to use their powers. On the bright side, no matter how hard his captors tried, unless they put on a very specific robe and hat and knew some Esperanto, they'd never get the staffs to do magic for them either. Also, the staffs were unbreakable, thanks to the shell, so that was something. Martin could feel that his hat was still on his head. Glancing down to his robe's pocket, it looked like his imp box was still there, meaning his smartphone would still be inside. The staffs, and to a lesser extent the wizards themselves, were being guarded by a single person. He appeared to be young. A teenager, Martin figured. The guard was standing with his back to Martin, watching what was going on in the distance, and Martin couldn't blame him.

There was a massive bonfire surrounded by young men. There was a sort of band playing something approximating music. One guy was pounding on a crude drum and another was playing some sort of stringed instrument that was completely drowned out by a huge bruiser blowing with all of his might into some sort of horn. Martin knew instantly that it was Kludge. He sounded awful, but Martin didn't want to be the one to tell him that. Many other young males were gathered around the bonfire. Some were dancing. Some were fighting. It was hard to tell which was which. Martin thought it actually looked like a pretty good party until two guys hauled the body of a dead villager into view, then chucked it onto the fire.

Martin was relieved to see Gwen, sitting on a stump, well away from the fire but also far away from the wizards. She didn't seem to be tied up, and nobody seemed to be threatening her at the moment. She didn't look happy either, sullenly examining her measuring stick, probably as an excuse to not make eye contact with her captors. Martin had attended many parties and seen many attractive girls do the same thing.

Martin took stock of the situation. He, Gary, and Jeff were helpless. Gwen was surrounded and outnumbered. Their captors had demonstrated a willingness to use violence, and he hazily remembered them saying that they blamed wizards for what had happened here. All in all, Martin thought the situation was grim, but not hopeless. If he could get one hand free, he could get to his smartphone and with one button press he could escape. Once he was gone, he'd have the time to plan and prepare, and come back for the others.

No, actually, if I press that button, I'll be deposited back at my parents' house right as the cops bust in, he realized. *I'd probably still be tied up. At least I'd be dressed. That's something, I guess.*

Martin made a mental inventory of the smartphone app's other functions, and cursed himself for not having reprogrammed it to do any of the new things he'd learned. Still, he could teleport. It wasn't a one-button process, but if he got a few seconds and a free hand, he could put several hundred yards between himself and his captors. That would buy him time to teleport somewhere useful. Then he could come back and rescue the others. First things first, though. He couldn't do anything until he was at least partially untied, and that would mean talking to the guard, gaining his confidence, and conning him into offering some assistance. *Time to turn on the old Martin Banks charm,* Martin thought, and then winced at how bad it sounded, even in his own head.

Martin cleared his throat, which, with the rope in his mouth, sounded like he was gagging. Then Martin said, "Hello," which, with the rope in his mouth, also sounded like he was gagging. Then Martin gagged.

The guard heard the third gagging noise and jumped. The guard turned, as if he was afraid of what he would see when he looked at the wizards. At first it was hard to see the guard's face because of the lack of ambient light and the bright bonfire silhouetting him, but once his eyes adjusted, Martin was shocked to see that his guard was Donald Melick, The Younger, the boy he had recently helped exorcise.

Donnie cringed. Then he looked back to the bonfire and all of the young men there, and cringed again. He backed toward where the wizards were bound to the tree, watching the gang around the fire the whole time. Finally, he crouched next to Martin and quickly turned to face him.

"I'm so sorry about this," he said. "I wanted to tell them that I knew you, and that you were all right, but that would've been … dumb."

Martin couldn't argue with that.

"One of the guys is from this village. He came out to threaten his family, maybe steal some food. He comes running back to Kludge and says everyone's dead and they all look weird. Well, Kludge says he doesn't believe it and he wants to see it for himself."

Maybe we were wrong about this Kludge person, Martin thought.

"So four or five of us get here, and it's like he said. Everyone's dead. Kludge says it's the best thing he's ever seen."

Nope, Martin thought.

"Someone said that it didn't look like there was any fighting, so it must've been magic that killed everyone, and Kludge starts talking about how he's never liked wizards, or anybody else, but particularly wizards. He says he won't have anybody going around wiping out towns and not inviting him. He got everyone all worked up. They wanted to go find the first wizard they could and do something awful. Well, I know you and Phillip are okay, so I said that'd never work. I told them that wizards are dangerous. It was pretty easy to convince them, since we were surrounded by the bodies of folks killed by a wizard. I told them the only way we'd ever get the best of a wizard would be to catch them by surprise. I just about had them convinced to give it up, then we saw you lot appear on that hill over there, and, well, you looked pretty easy to surprise."

I bet we did, Martin thought. *They probably had just enough time to hide before we got our bearings. In retrospect, explicitly telling Kludge that my staff made me undefeatable was probably a bad move.*

"Once you were knocked out, a couple of the guys wanted to kill you straight away, but Kludge says we should tie you up and let you sit awhile."

He wants us to sit here and worry, Martin thought. *Now I understand this Kludge guy. I know how he thinks.*

"He says he wants to give time for your flavors to meld."

Martin made a mental note to stop assuming he understood anybody.

Donnie looked furtively over his shoulder at the chaos around the bonfire. Kludge appeared to be playing the drum and the horn at the same time by hitting the drum with the horn. It would have been quite impressive if it hadn't sounded like a small animal being kicked repeatedly.

Donnie said, "The guys tried to use your staffs to make magic, but it didn't work, so now they're just carrying them around, trying to look all fearsome and impressive. That's not working either."

Now that he was looking for them, Martin could see that a couple of the brutes near the bonfire were wielding his staff with its bust of Santo, and Gary's with its KISS action figures. There was one guy with what might have been Jeff's wand, or might have just been a stick—it was hard to tell unless you could get close enough to see the word *Wonderboy* carved into its shaft.

Donnie took his eyes off of the fire, and leaned in closer to Martin. "Look," he said quietly, "Kludge told me to tell him as soon as you lot woke up. I'm really sorry about all this. I'm going to try to think of a way to get you out of it, but I have a family, and Kludge knows where they live. I'm only still hanging around with them so I can fade away slowly instead of just not showing up one day. You understand, don't you?"

Martin gagged as affirmatively as he could. Donnie looked equal parts pleased and worried. He reluctantly rose to his full height, turned his back to the three helpless wizards, and yelled, "Oi! Kludge! The evil wizards is awake! Can we kill 'em now?"

He glanced down at Martin, who was glaring up at him. "Sorry. I had to make it convincing." Then he kicked Martin.

Kludge couldn't hear anything over the sound of his own demented horn playing, but one of the oafs yelled in his ear and the music stopped abruptly. Kludge approached with the slow, deliberate gait of a man who enjoys the fact that people don't want him to approach them. Somewhere between fifteen and twenty more thugs followed behind. Martin assumed that when word got out that Kludge had captured three wizards, like-minded flunkies had started coming out of the woodwork. None of them seemed to have swords or knives, which didn't surprise or comfort Martin. Swords were designed to kill quickly and easily. Kludge seemed like the type who'd rather do it the slow, difficult way with tools he crafted himself. An old-fashioned purveyor of artisanal pain. A man who takes his time, and pays attention to the details. A man who hurts people for the love of the craft.

Gwen rose from her seat and had walked half the distance to where Martin sat before one of the thugs thought to grab her arm and *force* her to walk to where Martin sat. Soon, the thugs had crowded around, leaving about a ten-foot clearing around the wizards to form a natural stage for Kludge to do whatever he intended to do. Donnie was still standing nearby. He was trying to act like a proud bird dog that had presented his master with a dead pheasant, but Martin wasn't fooled. The boy wasn't a very good actor, but he was good enough to fool Kludge.

"Well, well, well," Kludge said. "Looks like our guests have finally decided to wake up!" Kludge was alarmingly tall and broad. His scraggly black hair had grown in a bit since the last time Martin was this close to him. He reached into the crowd and snatched Martin's staff from one of the gang. Kludge was wearing a chainmail shirt he'd most likely stolen from someone who had learned that an armored shirt doesn't save you from a punch in the face. Just standing next to him on the street had intimidated Martin. Sitting on the ground, tied helplessly to a tree at his feet, Martin was terrified. Kludge loomed over them like death itself, and he clearly knew it.

"Where's their girlfriend?" Kludge asked. Gwen was shoved roughly to the front of the crowd. She stumbled, but caught herself before she fell. She didn't look at the wizards. Martin thought she probably didn't want to give Kludge and his buddies the satisfaction, or perhaps she didn't want to give them an idea where to start.

Kludge stooped down to one knee, leaning a bit on Martin's staff. Even then, he towered over the wizards. "Sorry we had to be rough with you three, but we couldn't have you turning us into toads or nothing. It stands to reason that if you could do any magic all tied up and gagged like that you would have by now, so that means we've got you, and if you want to go back to your homes and hang upside down like a bat or whatever it is you freaks do, you're gonna have to do what I say. Now, I'm gonna have the runt take one of your gags out, and whichever one of you is lucky enough to get to talk is going to tell me how to do what was done to the people in this here town, and if you don't, I'm gonna do something pretty bad to this young lady here."

Martin glanced at Gwen. The thug standing behind her was a head taller, and a full Gwen-width wider than her on each side. He had the dull eyes and broad smile of a born follower. He was the type of person who mistook being large for being tough, being tough for being strong, and being strong for being smart. He saw that Martin was looking their way, so he put a hand on Gwen's shoulder. It was a reassuring gesture, in that it was meant to reassure Martin that he had no qualms about doing any number of things that Gwen would not like. She had pulled up her hood. Only her mouth, set in a grim scowl, was visible. Her hands were slowly working their way up her measuring stick. *Poor thing,* Martin thought. *She's probably not even aware she's doing it. I've got to think of a way to get her out of this. She was just in the wrong place at the wrong time.* It was a nasty jolt to Martin when he realized that *the wrong place* was in close proximity to wizards, or more specifically, *him.*

Kludge looked at the three wizards, deciding whose gag he would remove. He poked whoever was tied on Martin's left with

Martin's stolen staff. Martin couldn't turn his head, and could only see the man on his left's boots, but was not surprised to hear Gary's voice. *If I were going to pick someone to tell me how to use magic to hurt people, I'd go for the one wearing black too*, he thought.

After a deep breath, Gary said, "Let's get something straight. If you hurt the girl, we tell you nothing!"

Kludge smiled. He had a few teeth missing, and the condition of the ones he had gave the impression that the missing teeth were the lucky ones. "If we hurt the girl, you'll tell us nothing... voluntarily. If we hurt her enough, one of you might crack. If none of you talks, then we move on to you. We hurt you enough, I bet it'll loosen someone's tongue. If not, we move on to the dandy," Kludge said, then kicked Martin, who was now regretting his shiny silver robe and hat. Kludge looked at Jeff with great relish. "By the time we get around to this one, I'm betting he'll be ready to talk."

"He won't talk," Gary said. "None of us will, and you'll spend hours torturing us for nothing."

Martin rolled his eyes. He didn't blame Gary. Martin couldn't think of anything better to say, but threatening these guys with the prospect of having to spend a lot of time hurting people was like threatening an avid golfer with hours and hours of playing golf.

Kludge kept his eyes on Gary, but tilted his head toward Gwen and the slab of beef with his hand on her shoulder, and said, "Percy, hurt the girl."

Everyone's eyes, Martin's included, turned to Gwen, who was holding her measuring stick tightly with both hands. Because her hood was pulled up, Martin could not see her eyes, but she clearly did not want what was about to happen. The bully behind her grinned like a delighted child as he put his other massive hand on her other shoulder and started to squeeze and twist.

There was a sickening dry snap followed by a ripping noise. Everyone who heard it winced involuntarily.

Martin's impulse was to look away, but he couldn't. He was frozen with disbelief at what he was seeing. Gwen had snapped her measuring stick in half, then in one smooth, clearly rehearsed motion, hooked her thumbs into the sleeves of her cloak and pulled them apart, ripping a seam that had held the sleeves tight to her arms. With the seam destroyed, the cuffs widened to a loose flare. When Gwen held the two halves of her measuring stick up in front of her, it was clear to Martin that they were now two magic wands. For the first time, it occurred to Martin that the exaggerated taper of the hood on Gwen's cloak might not be purely decorative.

Later, Martin, Jeff, and Gary would discuss Gwen's salutation. The whole idea of a salutation is to make it plain to anyone who sees it that you do have magical powers, and that you should not be messed with. They all agreed that Gwen's was probably the best salutation they had ever seen, and what made it so effective was its subtlety. All salutations were triggered by a specific action or phrase. It could be anything. Phillip hummed a tune, Martin (in a failed attempt to amuse Phillip) yelled the magic words that Apache Chief from *Super Friends* would use to grow huge.

Gwen shouted, "NO!"

Once triggered, a good salutation would demonstrate the wizard's power by doing something that normal people could not do, and which could not be faked. Phillip flew. Martin grew into a giant statue.

Gwen emitted a single, blinding pulse of white light, like a human-sized flashbulb. At that moment Percy, the thug who was touching her, flew twenty feet back and bounced off of a wall. The salutation itself made no sound. The people watching made plenty of noise on their own.

After the initial flash of a salutation was complete, most of them employed some continuing effect to remind onlookers of the wizard's fearsome power. Phillip hovered in the air and emitted a blue glow. Martin, now to his embarrassment, had break danced.

Faint but unmistakable waves of energy were radiating from Gwen with blistering speed. It looked as if anyone who got their hand too close would see the flesh ripped from their skeleton. Her hood had tipped back slightly. Her face was visible. She had murder in her eyes. She aimed the wand in her right hand at Kludge and muttered something under her breath. Kludge immediately shot into the air, shrieking like a little girl and dropping Martin's staff as he went. He hung helplessly in the air above the heads of his awestruck gang. One of the thugs made a halfhearted move toward Martin's staff, which was now lying on the ground, but all it took was Gwen silently pointing her second wand at him and he sheepishly withdrew back into the group.

"Now," she said quietly, through gritted teeth, "you idiots are going to untie these idiots, or I throw that idiot into the fire."

The bravest of Kludge's gang said, "Girly, you can kill Kludge, but you can't kill all of us before we swarm you."

Gwen tried to answer, but couldn't be heard over Kludge screaming threats and obscenities at his gang. She sighed, and with a flick of her wrist caused Kludge to gain altitude. His voice became more distant and more shrill.

"As I was about to say, yes, I can kill all of you where you stand, but I didn't say I was going to kill anyone, not even him. I'm going to throw him on the fire, then get the wizards out of here whether you untie them or not, leaving you all here with an angry, burned Kludge who's looking to take his pain out on someone, and who knows that none of you did anything to save him when you could."

They looked up at Kludge, who was still raining down curses on their heads. Immediately, the mood of the crowd shifted, and it was clear to all that Gwen was going to get her way. Donnie leapt to untie the wizards before anyone told him to. Martin picked up his staff. Jeff and Gary were given their wand and staff back. Gwen maneuvered Kludge so that he was floating over a tall tree. She stowed her second wand in her pocket and put her hand on Jeff's shoulder. He put his hand on Gary's shoulder and Gary put his hand on Martin's.

"All right," Gwen said, "we're gonna go now. Consider your-selves warned. Next time any of you gives any wizard a hard time, we won't be so gentle."

Martin quickly grabbed Donnie, put him in a headlock, and touched his staff to the young man's temple. Martin yelled, "Yeah, and to make sure none of you primitive screwheads tries to follow us, we're taking this runt hostage, see?"

The crowd of thugs listened to Martin in silence, then turned in unison to see what Gwen would say to that.

She shook her head slightly. "Ugh, whatever."

She looked up at the still-screaming Kludge and said, "Faligis," which caused him to fall quickly into and then slowly through the tree, bouncing off the branches as he went. While everyone was watching that, she said, "Transporti al plumba pregejo," and the five of them disappeared.

Not far away, the lead-covered chapel that gave the town of Leadchurch its name was an island of tradition and tranquility. Its thick walls and solid foundation gave a sense of peace and solace to the faithful, who were sitting in the pews, communing with the Almighty. Their faith, like their church, was unchanging and serene. Then four wizards and a hostage materialized in front of the altar and immediately started yelling at each other.

"How long have you been a wizard?" Martin asked.

"That's a stupid question!" Gwen said.

"Yes, it is," Gary said to Martin before turning to Gwen and saying, "Answer the stupid question!"

"I started about a week ago," Gwen said, sneering. "I figured if you fools could do it, I might as well give it a shot. By the way, none of you carries a secret wand hidden somewhere in your clothes? Really?"

"I have one," Jeff said. "It's in my pants."

"Don't make the obvious joke," the other three said in unison.

"No, really. It's one of those old-school collapsible pointers. I just couldn't get to it because he tied us up." Jeff pointed his wand at Donnie, who asked politely if he could be released from Martin's headlock.

Gary asked, "How'd they know to take our staffs away anyhow? We don't go around just telling people our weakness!"

"Where are we?" Martin asked, changing the subject. He'd walked past the church, but had never seen the inside.

"We're in the lead church," Gary said before asking Gwen, "Why on earth did you bring us here?"

A voice from the back of the pews bellowed, "I'd like to know that myself!"

The authority in the voice made all four of the wizards freeze. It also made Donnie freeze, but he was already in a headlock, and was fairly immobile. Silently, they looked to the back of the room and saw a flustered looking nun standing next to Bishop Galbraith. A moment passed, then all five of them started frantically explaining all at once.

The bishop listened to the unintelligible chatter for a moment before shouting, "This is the Lord's house and I am his representative here on earth, and I swear if you don't all shut up and behave yourselves, I will see to it that you meet him personally!"

They all went to Bishop Galbraith's quarters to discuss things like mature adults, because an older authority figure had ordered them to.

"Why on Earth did you decide to take a hostage?" Gwen asked.

"Oh, I know Donnie. He's a good guy. He just got caught up in the wrong crowd. Isn't that right, Donnie?"

Donnie nodded a little too quickly, as if he thought he might still be caught up in the wrong crowd.

"Well, now you're free of them," Martin said. "Lie low for a few hours, then go home. If Kludge or any of his friends ever shows up asking questions, tell them that we were flying low over some trees and you jumped for it and hid. Then tell them that you don't want to hang around with them anymore because not one of them lifted a finger to rescue you."

"But what if they're out there trying to save me right now?" Donnie asked. After a long silence, he said, "Yeah, right. Never mind.

Donnie thanked the wizards, made his excuses, and got out of there. After he left, Bishop Galbraith gave Martin a look that said, *I'm impressed, but don't expect me to ever tell you that.*

With the hostage issue off the table, the next order of business was explaining to Bishop Galbraith why they were there. He sat behind his desk as they stood, like naughty children meeting with the principal. They explained what Gwen had found in Rickard's Bend and how she had brought the others in to have a look. They told him how they had ended up in the clutches of Kludge and his band of oafs. They glossed over who had teleported them to the church. They all knew it was best to discuss that when the Bishop was not around. Instead, they discussed why they'd come to the church at all.

"It seemed like the safest place to hide out and come up with a plan," Gwen explained.

"On account of churches having to offer sanctuary!" Jeff said.

"I don't have to offer you anything, son," the bishop snorted.

"It's the last place Kludge would ever come looking for us," Gwen said.

"Yup, 'cause the church hates us wizards!" Jeff said.

"I do not hate, boy. Not wizards, or anyone else. Though there are some wizards that I dislike, more so by the minute," the Bishop replied. "No, Kludge won't come looking for you here at my church because doing so would mean coming to my church, and he'll look everywhere else before he resorts to that. Besides, I expect you don't plan to stay here very long."

"You're right," Martin said. "Rickard's Bend has to be dealt with. We've got to figure out exactly who did that, and how we can stop them from doing it again."

It was clear, even to the Bishop, who hadn't even been there, that the mass killing at Rickard's Bend was the work of a wizard. Martin and Gary had remained silent about their speculation that someone was trying to make Hobbits.

"So then," Bishop Galbraith said, "is there a wizard any of you know who is capable of this? Someone who's secretive? Some wizard who is probably in this area and has had time to himself to do something of this scale?"

Gwen and the Bishop were silent. They had nothing to say. Martin, Jeff, and Gary were also silent. They had something they didn't want to say. They looked at the floor. They looked at each other. They looked at Gwen and the Bishop. Gwen and the Bishop looked back at them, and they quickly looked at the floor.

The Bishop bared his teeth and blurted, "Out with it!"

Martin sighed and reluctantly said, "Well, there's Phillip."

An eternity seemed to pass. The room was silent. The only sound was a faint, distant dog, snarling at something. Martin wondered if there were any friendly dogs in this town. Finally, the Bishop spoke.

"Well, it's clearly not Phillip. Who else?"

Martin, Gary, and Jeff shrugged at each other. Martin said, "I don't want to believe it either."

"Good," Bishop Galbraith said, "I give you permission not to. Who else could it be?"

Martin said, "Phillip fits perfectly! He lives nearby. He's as powerful a wizard as anybody. He has a whole floor of his shop that nobody's allowed to see. He disappears up there and refuses to talk about what he does. I hate to say it, but it fits."

Gwen gave Martin a long, penetrating look before saying, "He's right."

Martin was relieved.

"It's not Phillip," Gwen continued. "Who else could it be?"

Martin reflected on the fact that his feelings of relief were increasingly fleeting.

"Look," Martin said, "I'm not saying Phillip did it."

"Nobody is, so let's move on," the Bishop said.

"But," Martin said, "we have to rule him out."

"Fine. He's ruled out. Who else could have done it?" the Bishop said.

Martin sputtered uselessly for a moment, then composed himself. "I don't want to think that Phillip did this. I don't believe he did this, but we have to be sure."

"I am sure," the Bishop said. "I've known Phillip for ten years. That's a lot longer than I've known any of you." The Bishop paused and looked at Gwen. "Actually, I've known you a little longer than that, haven't I?"

She replied, "Something like that," and actively avoided eye contact with anyone.

"Well, I've known Phillip a long time, and while I don't like what you wizards do, I like Phillip. I trust Phillip. I know he'd never hurt another person, and he'd never take the chance of accidentally hurting another person, and if you, his apprentice, don't understand that, then I have to wonder if I can have the same faith in you. Now, if you ask me, and I notice you haven't, I'd say you take a good long look at that weasel Merlin up in Camelot. He can't be trusted."

Martin wasn't surprised to hear Merlin/Jimmy's name/names brought up, but he didn't think much of it. Jimmy was capable of wrongdoing, but only small, silly wrongdoing. He was far too obvious a villain to try to get away with anything truly sinister.

No, this was obviously the work of the last person you'd suspect, and that meant they had to investigate Phillip. Martin looked around the room for support and found none. The Bishop was yelling at him. Gwen was glaring at him. Gary and Jeff were silently staring at the floor. Even the angry dog in the distance seemed to be growling louder.

"Listen to me," Martin said. "I know that Phillip would never deliberately hurt another person, even if that person was trying to hurt him. It's not in him. But he is human, Father. We wizards are only human, and it's entirely possible that Phillip has made a mistake. I don't think he has, but none of us can honestly say that we know he hasn't, and if we don't at least go and ask him, everyone in this room will always wonder, and that's not fair to Phillip."

In the long silence that followed, Martin noted that everyone in the room seemed to have gotten angrier, which he took as a sign that he had won the argument.

24.

Although he had been argued into submission, Bishop Galbraith refused to take part in confronting Phillip, so the wizards set out for the shop on foot. They could have flown or teleported, but it was only a short walk, and none of them, even Martin, was looking forward to getting there. Gwen was in front, and to the outward observer would have appeared to be leading. In reality, she didn't want to walk with the others, and was trying to put some distance between herself and them, which can be a form of leadership. They walked in terse silence. The only attempt at conversation did not go well.

Martin quickened his pace to catch up with Gwen, and in a hushed voice asked, in as non-accusatory a manner as he could, "So, why didn't you tell anyone you were a wizard?"

She answered, "I figured anyone who really deserved to know could figure it out on their own."

It wasn't worded to be a specific criticism of Martin, but he took it as one, and he wasn't wrong. "But Gwen, if you're deliberately hiding something, you can't be mad at me for not finding it. You have to give a guy some clue!"

Gwen stopped dead in her tracks, causing Martin to step out in front of her then stop awkwardly. Gwen looked at Martin's dazzling reflective silver robe, the robe she had made for him, then looked him in the eye and said, "Plastic sequins were invented in the 1960s." Gary laughed. Gwen started walking again, faster and angrier than before. Martin watched as she left, and as Gary and Jeff walked past. He looked down at his robe, let out a heaving sigh, and followed behind.

Finally, they reached Phillip's shop. They entered, filing into the decoy storefront. Martin knew that they'd be unable to enter the next room, with the rune-covered drapes and the crystal, unless Phillip was in there already, so he was not surprised when he tried to push through the curtain and found it as immovable as a brick wall. Martin yelled Phillip's name a few times. There was no sound. Gary attempted to call Phillip on the magic hand phone, and got no answer. Martin said he'd check to see if Phillip was at home.

He disappeared, then a few seconds later he reappeared, shaking his head. "No, not there. He's gotta be upstairs."

The four of them just stared at each other in impotent silence until Gwen rolled her eyes, looked at the ceiling and yelled, "Phillip, it's Gwen! They know I'm a wizard!"

A moment passed, then they heard Phillip's muffled voice say, "I'll be right down."

"Phillip knew?" Martin asked.

Gwen said, "He's not an idiot."

There was some crashing and banging from upstairs, then the sound of heavy, annoyed footsteps coming down the stairs. Finally, Phillip emerged through the curtains into the shop. He nodded to Gwen and said hello, then he turned to Martin and asked, "What tipped you off? It was the sequins, right?"

Gary laughed, and Martin turned on him. "You didn't figure it out either."

"Yeah, but I didn't really care enough to try."

Gwen asked Martin, "What's your excuse?"

Martin turned back to Phillip. "No, it wasn't the sequins. It was when she saved us by scaring off the thug who was threatening to torture us to death."

Phillip looked at Gwen, who nodded.

"Yeah, I suppose that'd be a bit of a tip-off. How'd they get your staffs away from you?"

"They crept up and pummeled us from behind," Jeff said.

Gary added, "We were a bit distracted by all the corpses."

They went on to describe how Gwen had found the now-defunct village of Rickard's Bend, and brought in the other three while still trying to maintain her secret. They told Phillip about their many attempts to reach him and their arrival at Rickard's Bend. They described in great detail the condition of the bodies they found. The stunted limbs. The lack of shoes.

Phillip shook his head slightly and muttered, "Hobbits."

"Yes, clearly, Hobbits," Gwen said.

Martin was surprised, since neither he nor Gary had mentioned this theory to her. Then he made a mental note that he needed to stop acting surprised when Gwen knew things.

By this time they had all moved into the crystal ball room, and were sitting around the table. Martin noted that the Commodore 64 was not in its usual spot on the secret shelf in front of Phillip's seat, which meant Phillip was using it elsewhere, most likely upstairs.

Phillip ran his fingers through his hair and said, "Okay, so, this is awful. We have a wizard somewhere who tried to turn an entire village into Hobbits, killing everyone in the process. We'll have to work together to deal with this. Any suggestions as to what we should do now?"

Gary, Jeff, and Martin looked at each other. Gwen looked at the table in front of her. Martin steeled himself and said, "I think the logical first step, Phillip, would be for you to tell us what you're doing upstairs."

After a predictable amount of shocked, angry stammering, Phillip downshifted into angry, offended yelling. "You can't honestly think I would do something like this! I'd never dream of such a thing!"

"I told him you didn't do it," Gwen said.

"And I agreed," Martin said, "but you're clearly up to something, and a whole village is dead. Think about that, Phillip. You didn't have to look at it like we did, so take a second to internalize it. An entire village of innocent people, killed in one stroke. And it was clearly done by a wizard who was trying to turn them into Hobbits! We wizards have to police each other because nobody else can do it. You're the one who taught me that."

"Oh, I taught you that, did I? Not surprising, since I taught you everything!" Phillip's voice rose to a high, wounded whine. His eyes looked like they might pop out of his head. "Martin, I took you in! I'm the best friend you have! I'm your bloody mentor! Does it really seem likely that I'd be a mass murderer?"

"No, Phil, it seems highly unlikely. That's why we have to consider it. You could say that you're the last person I'd ever suspect!"

Phillip shook his head. "Oh, Martin, is that it? I seem too nice and too harmless, so I must be hiding some sinister secret, like we're nothing but two-dimensional characters in some bad novel?"

"I genuinely hope not," Martin said.

"Yeah, I bet. Look, kid, what I do upstairs is my business, and that's just going to have to be good enough for you. Now get out of my shop." Phillip rose and pointed at the door. Martin did not stand, nor did any of the others.

Martin spoke in a low, sad tone. "Phillip, I really am sorry. I don't for a second believe that you would do this, but I'm not the only person who has noticed that you disappear upstairs and refuse to talk about what you're doing up there."

"I disappear into the bathroom and I don't want to talk about what I do in there. Does that mean I'm doing something wrong in there, too?"

Martin kept his voice flat, but arched his eyebrows. "Do you really want to discuss your bathroom?"

Phillip sat down hard in his seat. He looked around the table. "If I kick you lot out of here, you're just going to go to Jimmy, aren't you?"

"We don't want to," Martin said.

Phillip sneered and shifted his focus to Gary, who shrugged and said, "Just show us what you're up to, man. We won't tell everyone. We'll just take a peek, then we can get on with finding who did this."

Jeff said, "We'll be in and out. We won't touch nothin'. We'll be like a cool breeze, blowin' through your attic."

Phillip looked at Gwen, who was still looking at the table. He asked her, "What do you think?"

She lifted her gaze and looked him in the eye. "I think you should show us what you've been up to and be done with it."

Phillip shook his head. "You know what's sad? I was almost ready to show you anyway."

Phillip led them through the curtain and up the stairs. The steps were dark, rough-hewn, unfinished wood. The outer wall was unfinished stone; the inner wall was wood. The first five steps led to a landing where the staircase bent ninety degrees to the right. The first few steps, those that might be seen from the curtains, were the same as those before, but beyond that it was too dark to see. Phillip stopped, looked at Martin, sighed in an exasperated manner, then flipped a plastic light switch on the wall.

Once his eyes had adjusted, Martin could see that the remainder of the steps were a beautiful, long-grained hardwood that had been treated with some sort of finish which had made them glossy and turned them the color of honey. The outer wall was still stone, but the inner was slightly off-white plaster, with a subtle bumpy texture. Phillip continued up the stairs. The others followed. As their heads rose above the level of the floor, they were able to see the room they were entering. It took a moment to fully comprehend what they were seeing.

The entire upstairs was one large room. The floor was covered in the same beautifully finished hardwood as the stairs. Tasteful track lighting and a skylight illuminated clean, white plaster walls. A sofa made of chrome and white leather sat near a black leather lounge chair and matching footrest. Between them was a coffee table made of glass and white-washed concrete. The walls were decorated with a palm tree rendered in neon, and thin black frames supporting angular paintings of beautiful women with smooth white skin, thick black hair, and perfect bodies. There was also a stereo the size of a small kitchen appliance with speakers as tall as Martin, and a full-sized arcade cabinet that said GORF. Phillip made a beeline for the corner, where a small glass-and-concrete dining table and chairs sat next to a built-in wet bar. Phillip pulled the cap out of a bottle of whiskey and poured himself a drink without offering one to anyone else.

Gary whistled and said, "I'm totally doing my cave up like this!"

Phillip said, "Well, be sure to let Martin know what you're up to, or you might get accused of mass murder."

Martin took no notice. He was preoccupied by what he saw beyond the seating area. A large roll-up door was built into the wall. In the corner there was a work table with the Commodore 64, modem, and tiny TV, displaying the file. In front of the door sat a nearly mint condition white Pontiac Fiero. Nearly mint because the tail lights were not fully assembled. A set of screwdrivers and a drinking glass with screws lying in the bottom told Martin exactly what Phillip had been doing when they demanded that he come downstairs.

Martin approached the Fiero. It was smaller than he remembered them, but then, he hadn't seen one since he was a child. He slowly circled the car, drinking in all of its contours. He bent to look in the window like a teenager peering into the interior of a floor sample at a Ferrari dealership. It looked complete and pristine. Martin knew there were limits on what could be transported back in time. His flimsy kid-bed mattress was about the upper limit of what was possible. Clearly, Phillip had painstakingly disassembled his beloved car, transported the parts here piece by piece, and reassembled it with great care; more care than was probably taken when it was assembled in the first place.

Martin stood up and looked at Phillip, who was still behind the bar on the far end of the room. "This is amazing!" he said. "Why didn't you tell me? I could've helped!"

Phillip said, "That's the point. I wanted to do it myself. There's a certain pride in looking at something big and complex and knowing you did it without help."

Even if Martin could argue with that, he wouldn't have. A minute ago, seeing what was in this room had seemed like the most important thing in the world. He was willing to suffer any consequences to make it happen. Now he had seen what was here, and it was great, far better than anything he had hoped, and infinitely superior to what he'd feared. Now all that was left was to deal with the fallout and try to repair the damage. Looking at Phillip, and the faces of his friends, he saw how much damage had been done. In that moment, Martin couldn't imagine what he'd been thinking just a few moments before.

Gary was sitting in the lounge chair. Gwen sat on the couch. Jeff was studying the GORF machine with great intensity. None of them were looking at Phillip.

Martin had taken the lead in making the mess. He'd have to take the lead in cleaning it up. He walked around the nose of the car and slowly approached the bar. Phillip watched him silently, holding the glass of whiskey in his hand. When Martin reached the bar, Phillip silently reached beneath it and pulled out another glass. He glanced at Martin and poured a second glass of Jack Daniel's. He picked up the glass, looked Martin in the eye, then quickly downed it himself. He sneered at Martin as he slammed the empty glass down on the bar.

Martin said, "I think I speak for everyone when I say that we're sorry we did this."

"I know I am," Phillip said.

"But, Phillip, you get it, right?" Martin continued. "I mean, I know you're mad, and you've got good reason, but you see why we had to do this?"

"No. Honestly, Martin, I don't. I don't understand why you couldn't take my word. All of you, I mean, okay, Martin's only known me a little while, but I've known all of you for years! I thought we were all friends! But the first time someone kills a hundred or so people, you lot are the first to turn up at my door with pitchforks."

Gwen turned on the couch to look at Phillip. "None of us wanted to believe it, Phillip, but you're the only one we knew who was keeping a secret."

Phillip smiled as he said, "Really? Gwen? I'm the only one you know who was keeping a secret?"

Gwen flushed and quickly turned away.

"You're the only one we knew who was *obviously* keeping a secret," Jeff offered.

Phillip looked poised to yell some more, but stopped. Instead he finished his first drink, looked into the empty glass for a moment and said, "You mean I'm the only one who was keeping a secret badly."

"Well," Martin said, "it isn't easy when you've got some jerk living with you."

"Agreed."

Jeff turned away from the GORF machine. "Oh come on, Phillip! That isn't fair! We all thought...."

Phillip put up a hand to signal surrender and silence Jeff. "We can argue about that later. We have more important business. Somewhere, there's a wizard who's killed innocent people, and now that we know who it isn't, we have to figure out who it is."

"So," Martin asked, "what do we do now?"

"As much as it pains me," Phillip said, "I think we have to go tell Jimmy."

None of them seemed happy with the prospect. Phillip was the only one who was openly hostile toward Jimmy, but Martin was Jimmy's biggest fan in the room, and even he would describe his attitude toward Jimmy as *wary*. Nobody spoke. The only sound was a distant dog growling.

"Man!" Martin said, "What is the deal with that dog?"

"I know, right? How long can a dog growl before it just says forget it?" Jeff said.

Gary laughed. "It's all, *gaarrrraarrrr, arrraaaarrr … grrrrrrrr*, like all the time!"

"How long have you been hearing it?" Gwen asked. "I heard a dog growling back in Rickard's Bend. It can't be the same dog, can it?"

Phillip shook his head in disgust. "Oh, yes. Proper bunch of detectives you are." He hastily grabbed his staff, which had been leaning in the corner behind the bar, and stepped around the end of the bar, across the room to an empty patch of floor in front of the Fiero. He planted the tip of his staff on the floor, then with his other hand pointed to the spot where the staff intersected with the floor.

He cast his eyes around the room, then said in a loud, clear voice, "Okay. Stand here, and stay there until I say to move." Martin started walking toward the spot to do as he was told, but stopped dead when Phillip glared at him and shook his head. Phillip pulled his staff away and slowly backed off from the spot he'd indicated as if it were radioactive. In three quick steps he was at his computer. With his left hand he pointed his staff at the spot he'd indicated. With the other he typed some commands. A few excruciating moments passed with nothing but the sound of clacking keys and Phillip muttering. Finally, Phillip's shoulders slumped and the muttering gave way to cursing. He looked at the empty spot on the floor and said, "Hold on. Just another second," then typed in another command and hit enter.

Tyler appeared, gasping for air, eyes bulging. He immediately fell to his knees. Gary and Gwen had watched with interest, but now they leapt to their feet. Jeff abandoned the arcade console and ran to where Tyler, breathing deeply and moaning, knelt on the floor. Phillip pulled off his hat, said, "Enboteligita akvo," and produced a bottle of mineral water. He handed it to Tyler, who gulped it down at an astonishing rate.

Martin remembered his first morning in Medieval England, when Phillip told him the dos and don'ts of wizarding. Particularly the part about getting "ghosted." Being made invisible. You didn't need food, air, or water, but your body didn't know it. You could still see and hear. You could still move around, but you couldn't interact with anything heavier than a mote of dust floating in the air. The real torture was that you couldn't talk, but you could make faint spooky noises, so any attempt at communicating would only torment and repel those you tried to contact. Martin knew Tyler had been missing for at least a week. Starving, suffocating, and dying of thirst for a week, surrounded by people who would love to help him, but didn't know he needed help. Martin couldn't imagine anything worse.

Tyler finished the bottle of water. He remained kneeling on the floor, breathing deeply. He opened his eyes, reached out, and took Phillip's staff. He said, "Mia bancâmbro," Esperanto for *my bathroom,* and disappeared.

Yup, Martin thought. *That's worse.*

They sat in a sullen, guilty silence while they waited for Tyler's return. Phillip poured everyone a drink.

Finally, Tyler reappeared. Nobody said a word, nor would they until Tyler broke the silence. He walked to Phillip, who was standing by the bar. He handed Phillip's staff back to him, then hugged him for a very long time. Finally, Tyler released the hug and said, "Thank you."

Tyler turned to the rest of the group, who were seated but stood up as soon as Tyler returned. Tyler nodded to Gwen and said, "Gwen. A pleasure, as always." She returned his greeting. He turned to Gary and Jeff, his two best friends, and in a genuine outpouring of heartfelt emotion said, "Damn you idiots! You morons! Ngaah! I'm so mad at you two … Mbraaaagh!"

Clearly, words alone couldn't express what he was feeling. He shouted inarticulate rage noises at Gary and Jeff for a while longer. By the time he was done, Phillip had produced another bottle of water, which he handed to Tyler. Tyler sat heavily on the couch and took a drink.

"I've been growling at you idiots for *twelve days*," Tyler said between gulps of water. "You've both read my book! I'd hoped spooky growling would make you think of me at least once in all that time."

Martin turned to Gwen, and said in a low voice, "Tyler's an author. He wrote a book called *The Curse of the Ghost of the Wolfman's Mummy*. The monster would make a spooky growling noise."

Gwen nodded and said, "I know. I've read it. Phillip loaned me a copy."

That meant that Martin was the only one in the room who hadn't read the book. He thought, *I really do have to stop assuming that Gwen doesn't know things.*

Tyler turned to Martin, fresh anger in his eyes. "And you, the new kid. You looked right at me TWICE! I know you saw me. One time you were so scared you fell out of your stupid hammock!"

"That was you?" Martin said.

"Yes, Martin, the ghostly apparition trying desperately to get Phillip's attention was me. I'd given up on ever getting through to Ren and Stimpy over here, and thought I'd try to get the attention of the one sensible adult I know. Thanks again for finally saving me, Phillip."

"You're welcome," Phillip said as he settled into the lounge chair. "I'm just sorry it took us so long." They all apologized. Even Gwen, who hadn't really done anything. Tyler waved his hand dismissively, which was as close to an *apology accepted* as they were likely to get.

Martin pulled a bar stool over and had a seat. Gary and Jeff followed suit. Gwen sat on the lounge chair's matching footrest. After what he'd gone through, the least they could do was let Tyler have the couch.

"So," Phillip said, "how'd it happen?"

Tyler told them that he'd gone to Rickard's Bend to do some more research for the fantasy novel he was working on. When he got there, he bumped into Jimmy. Jimmy had asked why he was there, and had reacted with great interest when he learned that Tyler was writing a novel. They talked about the books they'd read and the movies they'd seen. Finally, Jimmy had told Tyler that he had a project he was working on, and that he would welcome Tyler's opinion.

There were several knowing looks at this. Even Jimmy's greatest detractors had to admit that he was not without his talents, and one of them was making whomever he was talking to feel like the most important, talented, and valuable person Jimmy had ever met.

Tyler continued, telling them how he had gone to Camelot with Jimmy, and how Jimmy had shown him plans to gradually remake the people of Rickard's Bend into Hobbits.

"He asked me if I had any input, as an author," Tyler said. "I told him that he was a monster."

"And that's when he ghosted you?" Phillip asked.

"Ooooh yeah. He ghosted me but good. I turned my back to walk away and he flew up behind me, pressed his staff to my back, and said the words. At first, all I could do was struggle to breathe. I felt like I was dying nonstop until I got acclimated."

"How long did that take?" Martin asked.

"Hours. I don't know how many. Then I got used to it."

Gwen said, "It's a good thing the craving for air gets better."

"I didn't say it got better," Tyler said. "I just got used to it."

They all considered this for as long as they dared. Martin broke the silence, turning to Phillip and asking, "What do we do now?"

Phillip stood. He looked at the other wizards and said, "We take Jimmy down. We'd better call everybody and get them up to speed. We want to do this right. And by *right*, I mean *in as public and humiliating a manner as possible*."

25.

Thirty minutes later, the clearing beneath Skull Gullet Cave was full of wizards. They had called every wizard in Europe except Jimmy and Eddie (a.k.a. Wing Po). They'd excluded Jimmy for obvious reasons. They had no direct evidence that Eddie was involved, but they had no evidence that he wasn't either, and they chose not to risk telling him. They kept it quiet by telling everyone they were planning a surprise for Jimmy, which, Phillip pointed out with palpable glee, was true.

Skull Gullet Cave was chosen for the meeting because it was large enough to accommodate everyone, and the mouth of the skull made a fine amphitheater. Phillip stood in front (because he was the most well-known and respected wizard present), next to Gwen (to explain that she was a wizard, and to tell what she had found in Rickard's Bend), Tyler (to explain about Rickard's Bend, and to tell about his ghosting), and Gary (because he insisted, and it was his cave).

As the wizards started arriving, Martin found a quiet moment to speak with Gwen privately. He leaned in close. "Gwen, can I ask you a question?"

Gwen tensed, but said, "Yes."

Martin bit his lip, then asked, "In your salutation, how did you throw that lummox off of you like that? That was really, really cool! I considered trying to do something like that in mine, but I couldn't figure out an elegant way to program it.

You'd have to differentiate between you, your belongings, and the person you want to repel. I just can't figure out how you did it."

Gwen smiled, and actually laughed a bit. "Oh! Uh, it's actually really simple. You know the exclusion zones we use to seal off certain places? They only act on people, and you can make them not apply to yourself, right? Well, I make a cone-shaped exclusion zone underground beneath my feet. Then I make it move up over my head really fast, and any person who isn't me, but is standing inside the radius of the cone, gets thrown off."

Martin stared at her, mouth agape. She thought he was amazed, and that was part of it. He was also tremendously turned on.

"Wow," he said. "That's so simple! That just never occurred to me! Really, nice work!" He couldn't think of anything else to do, so he shook her hand. He started to walk away, then turned back to face her. "Can I ask another question?"

"Sure," she said.

"What year are you from?"

She laughed again. "Twenty-fourteen. Born in ninety-two."

Martin smiled. "Huh, so I'm a little older than you."

She shook her head. "I've been here for ten years, so technically I'm older than you. I was just born later."

Martin smiled again. "Huh. That's right, isn't it? Cool!" He turned, and walked down to the clearing. Gwen watched him go.

Martin and Jeff stood in the clearing with the rest of the wizards. Phillip thanked everyone for coming, apologized for the false pretenses, and promised them that they'd all understand why it was necessary soon enough. He started by announcing that Gwen was a wizard.

"I told all of you that I was the first one to show up in this time and place, but that's not quite true. Gwen, whom you all know, since she made all of your robes, had already been here for a month when I showed up. She swore me and Jimmy to secrecy because a female wizard is called a witch, and the locals have something of an attitude about witches."

Heads nodded in agreement. One voice at the back said something about her weighing the same as a duck, but nobody was in the mood. Phillip opened the floor for questions about Gwen's wizardiness before moving on to business. Most of the questions centered on her tailoring business. She explained that she took measurements and made patterns the old-fashioned way, but went to the future to buy fabric. Also, on harder sewing jobs, she'd use a sewing machine. She had the powers of a wizard, the standing in the community of a craftsman, and the freedom to walk the streets without people asking her to magic their problems away. It had all been quite lovely until Rickard's Bend.

Her description of what she found there sucked all of the air out of the room. She told the story of how she had brought Martin, Jeff, and Gary out to have a look, and she explained that she'd had to break her cover to get them away from Kludge's gang. She concluded by saying that it was clear to them that the villagers were killed by a wizard, and that the wizard had embarked on a secret plan to make Hobbits.

This comment produced several raised hands. Gwen called on one of the Norwegian death-metal wizards.

"Um," he stammered, stalling a bit, "sorry, but I have to ask. Phillip, what have you been doing upstairs in your shop?"

Phillip bit his lip. Gary announced, "We already checked on that. He's been transporting and assembling a car one piece at a time."

Most of the hands went down. Phillip made eye contact with Martin, who could only shrug.

Gary continued. "It's a Pontiac Fiero."

The rest of the hands went down. The wizards from Italy tried to hide their amusement, but not very hard.

Phillip explained briefly that the others had come to him, and that during that conversation, they figured out what had happened to Tyler. Phillip turned the floor over to Tyler, who just barely managed to keep his composure as he told the assembled wizards how he learned Jimmy's plan and was ghosted for it. That was all it took. By the time he was done, everyone present was of a like mind.

There was some discussion, but the consensus was that Jimmy had violated the only three rules they had. He had altered people's physical structure, he had done so on helpless locals who had not given their consent, and he had used his power to ghost Tyler, which everyone agreed was unspeakably cruel without really having to discuss it.

Phillip summed up. "So, we know what was done, and we know by whom. We can't let this stand. If we don't stop him, we're just as responsible as he is. We have to go to London, confront Jimmy, and put an end to this once and for all. We must police ourselves, because no one else can. We'll give him an opportunity to explain himself. I doubt he'll have a valid excuse, because I can't imagine what a valid excuse would be. More likely, he'll try to fight us, but he can't possibly ghost everyone, and if he manages to get a few of us, the rest can neutralize him and undo the damage."

"It's not going to be easy," Phillip continued. "Many of you like Jimmy, and it's going to be hard for you to take him down. I despise him, and as such, I will have a hard time pretending not to enjoy every second of his downfall and humiliation. That's my burden to bear."

The sun was high in the sky, and in the splendid courtyard in front of the golden palace of Camelot, people were going about their daily business. Workmen worked, guards guarded, and everyone was squinting, as was their custom on a sunny day.

The light reflecting off of the golden castle Camelot, the giant gold-covered gates, the massive golden statue of the old king, the young king, and the wizard who advised them, and the polished gold adornments on the staff's uniforms combined to give the impression that to be at Camelot castle was to stand in the center of the sun. People's vision was so impaired by the unceasing glare that most of them didn't even notice when twenty-three wizards wearing sunglasses suddenly appeared out of nowhere linked hand to shoulder like a sideways conga line.

The wizards separated themselves from one another and strode purposefully to the castle's entrance, Phillip and Tyler in the lead, flanked by Martin, Gwen, Gary, and Jeff. Martin asked Phillip, "So, what's the plan?"

"I'm gonna win," Phillip said. "I'm finally gonna beat him, and I'm gonna taste his defeat. Then I'm gonna chew his defeat. Then I'm gonna open my mouth wide and make him look at his gross chewed-up defeat, and he will be disgusted by it, as I am by him."

"Damn right!" Tyler added. "And I think I might kick him in the nuts."

Martin considered this, and said, "Good. I'm glad we have a solid plan."

The castle had no door, as such. The massive open archway led to the opulent antechamber, which in turn led to the great hall. Guards in gold-encrusted uniforms flanked the gold-encrusted arch, defending it with gold-encrusted swords. The guards made no move to prevent the wizards from entering. Phillip sneered at them as he walked through the arch and ran face-first into the invisible field that kept any wizard from entering the castle without Jimmy's permission. Tyler, Martin, and Gwen also walked into the field. The other wizards walked into them, or each other. Over the sound of grumbling and cursing, one of the guards said, "Merlin is expecting you. Please wait here and you'll be escorted to his chambers."

The wizards spread out, straightening their robes and regaining their dignity as best they could. After a moment, Eddie appeared in the antechamber.

"Gentlemen. Gwen. Welcome to castle Camelot. Do come in."

His lack of surprise at seeing Gwen carrying a wand was telling. Martin looked at Gwen askance. "Eddie knew about you?" he asked.

Gwen was at a loss. "I didn't tell him."

Eddie had sharp ears. He smiled and said, "Merlin tells me everything."

Tyler asked, "Oh, does he?" About twice as loud as he probably intended. Phillip put a steadying hand on Tyler's shoulder.

In a dry tone, Phillip asked, "Did he tell you that he killed an entire village full of people?"

Eddie's smile faded. He looked confused, then his expression soured, and he mumbled, "Oh, Phillip." He composed himself, then with forced joviality said, "Merlin will be ready to see you all in a moment. Please follow me."

The wizards spent the next ten minutes exploring the most opulent waiting room in all of England. The seats were veritable thrones. Instead of magazines, there were *tomes of arcane knowledge*, which Martin recognized as books of magic tricks from the early twentieth century. Some of them were in English, featuring men in tuxedos holding playing cards and pigeons. Others were in Chinese, and featured men in silk robes holding chrome rings and pigeons. It occurred to Martin that one way or the other, stage magic was the art of manipulating the pigeons. He considered sharing this idea with the other wizards, but he knew nobody was in the mood.

While they waited, Eddie sat at a large desk in the corner. When they first arrived, he told the wizards to make themselves comfortable. Then, Eddie held up his right hand to use the magic hand phone to make a call, but put his left hand up to his ear, as if to press an earpiece. Merlin's flaming M icon appeared in his hand and Eddie said that the wizards had arrived. Nobody heard the reply. Then Eddie said in a worried tone that they had said something about killing a village. More silence followed, but Eddie seemed reassured. He ended the call and told the assembled wizards that it would only be a few minutes.

After a minute or two he tried to engage Gary in conversation, but Gary asked him if he was proud to be the world's first receptionist, and with that, Eddie picked up on the ugly mood in the room and stopped talking.

Ten minutes later the large, ornately carved golden doors opened, and Jimmy invited everyone into his office. The wizards angrily stormed into Jimmy's office, but as the door was only wide enough to accommodate two wizards at a time, *storming in angrily* was almost indistinguishable from *filing in politely*.

Although nobody had mentioned it, everyone was waiting to see Jimmy's reaction to Tyler. Everyone expected a satisfying mix of shock and guilt. Everyone was disappointed.

Jimmy saw Tyler and took on the attitude of a man who has just bumped into an old friend who he knows has been in the hospital.

"Tyler," he said, "I'm so glad to see they finally brought you back." He looked to Gary and Jeff and rolled his eyes dismissively. "I always knew they'd get the hint eventually, but I had no idea it'd take them so long! If it had gone on too much longer, I was going to step in and rescue you myself."

Tyler kicked Jimmy in the crotch as hard as he could. The speed and ferocity of it made every man in the room cringe. Every man but Jimmy, who mentioned that he had anticipated this eventuality and had created an exclusionary zone one foot in diameter around his genitalia. He explained that no one could get anywhere near that part of his body without his permission. He arched an eyebrow at Gwen. He had to speak up to explain all this, over the sound of Tyler grunting with exertion as he fruitlessly kicked Jimmy's nether region over and over again. Finally, after several more kicks, Tyler stopped. Clearly, Jimmy's words had finally sunk in.

"Satisfied?" Jimmy asked.

Tyler kicked him in the shin. Jimmy grimaced in pain, hunched his shoulders and hopped as he rubbed his bruised shin with his hands. "For now," said Tyler.

Jimmy's office was about the size of a tennis court. It had marble floors, gold leaf columns, a high ceiling painted to look like the sky, and large stained-glass windows—the standard Jimmy design scheme. In one corner there was a desk, a predictably oversized gold rectangle of hardwood so covered with tiny ornate carvings that from a distance it read as a bumpy, popcorn, ceiling texture. In another corner there was an equally ornate altar. Clearly, this was where Jimmy stood to do magic in the presence of non-wizards. Martin wondered which of these two pieces of furniture hid Jimmy's computer.

In the middle of the room there was a large conference table. There was something acutely bumpy in the middle of the table, covered with a sheet that covered the table's entire surface and hung over the sides.

Jimmy tried to do his customary glide step over to the conference table, but his newly acquired limp spoiled the effect. "Gentlemen, Gwen," he said, "I understand that you're all upset. I don't blame you one bit. Particularly you, Tyler. I haven't been honest, and I've done more than one thing of which I'm not proud. Mistakes were made. Grave mistakes. But I'm confident that when you see why I did it, you'll understand. Please, gather 'round."

The wizards approached the table. Everyone, even Phillip, had intended to give Jimmy the chance to explain. Nobody expected him to be able to justify his actions, but he was entitled to try. Eddie nosed his way through the group to stand next to his best friend and boss.

"As you all know," Jimmy said, "when I first arrived in this time and place, I found primitive conditions and ignorant, super-stitious people."

"And me and Gwen," Phillip added.

"Quite," Jimmy agreed. "And may I say, Gwen, I'm delighted that you've finally decided to come out in the open and join the rest of us. Anyway, back when it was just the three of us, we made a sincere effort to keep from exposing the native people of this time to our modern ideas and conveniences. Phillip, would you like to tell them how well that worked?"

"They all know that we discovered contamination from time travelers who had gone back even farther than us," Phillip fumed, "and that our actions weren't affecting the future. So what?"

Jimmy smiled benevolently. "So, I decided there was no reason I shouldn't make life better here for everyone. I devel-oped a three-phase plan. Phase one was to introduce little niceties like eating off of plates with forks instead of eating with daggers and stale slabs of bread. I introduced basic sani-tation. I was careful to do this in such a way that the natives thought they were inventing it themselves. The castle we're standing in was phase two. I've stabilized the government, raised the kingdom's standard of living, and given the people leaders they can look to with pride." Jimmy looked intolerably pleased with himself. Eddie also looked intolerably pleased with him.

Jimmy continued, "I had hoped to put off going public with the final phase of the plan, but I'm afraid Tyler forced my hand, which is fine! It's really no problem. I apologize for ghosting you, Tyler, but I had no choice. I still had a couple of details to shore up before I could unveil phase three.

"Phase three is designed to give the people the life they always wanted instead of the life they always get. When life gets hard, too hard to face, people often turn to movies, television, or books. They, *we*, retreat into a world of fantasy. I am going to improve life for every sentient being on Earth by making reality a little more like fantasy.

"As you all know," Jimmy continued, "one of the few truly sacred rules we have is to never alter a living person's physical structure, because, of course, you will most likely kill them. However, a few of us have proven, mostly by accident, that if the changes made are small enough, the subject can continue their life unharmed, and in some cases, unaware that anything happened to them at all. I have devised a plan whereby I can use small, incremental changes over a prolonged period of time to improve the physical condition of every man, woman, and child in this country."

Jimmy whipped the sheet off of the table, revealing a three-dimensional relief map of the British Isles. The cities were delineated by small stylized models blown far out of scale to the land itself to make them stand out better. Camelot was a recognizable golden model of the castle, but most of the other cities, towns, and villages were less recognizable.

Jimmy produced a pointer and indicated London, now Camelot, and most of the main island. "In this area, people will remain largely unchanged. I have a plan to make them a bit taller, more muscular, and overall healthier, but there will be no drastic changes. This area will be the kingdom of man."

Jimmy pointed to a small area near the border with Scotland. "As we all know, this area has many rather dense forests. I have chosen this area to be the kingdom of the Elves. The people of this area will be much taller and thinner, with larger eyes. I can't make them take to the trees, but I plan to encourage them with financial incentives. I know the Elves will be a bit too far away to enjoy on a regular basis, but marbled throughout the kingdom of man, there will be occasional pockets of Hobbits to work the farmland and generally add local color. In the final phase, Scotland, being quite mountainous, will of course be home to the Dwarves." Jimmy lowered his pointer and radiated smugness while everyone else tried to fully comprehend everything he'd said.

Finally, the thick, velvety silence was broken by Eddie. "Remember when I said that he tells me everything? I was mistaken."

Phillip said, "So what happened at Rickard's Bend, then? Something go wrong with your Hobbits?"

Jimmy sucked at his teeth, then said, "Yes, regrettably. My encounter with Tyler left me so shaken that I accidentally skipped a step in their transformation plan and, well, you all know what happened then. Anyway, it was a most unfortunate accident, and I certainly don't blame Tyler for it."

Martin rubbed his eyes and took a deep breath. *He doesn't understand*, he thought. *He honestly does not get how wrong he is.*

Phillip cleared his throat and finally, for the record, said, "Jimmy, you're a bastard."

Jimmy seemed more confused than insulted. "Does trying to improve life for everyone make me a bastard, Phillip?"

"Yes!" Phillip shouted. "If you don't give them any choice, it does!"

Jimmy said, "Well, Phillip, if you want to eat a hamburger, you have to kill a cow. If you want to make a chair, you have to kill a tree. I want Elves and Hobbits, and I haven't killed anyone to make them, deliberately. I do feel very bad about Rickard's Bend."

"Good!" Phillip said. "You should! But, even if you hadn't killed an entire village, you'd still be wrong! What if all of these people you're *helping* don't want to be Dwarves and Elves? Did you ever think about that?"

Jimmy rolled his eyes as if he thought Phillip was being terribly silly. "Phillip, of course they won't want to become mythological creatures *at first*. Change is always scary! Once they see what they've gained they'll change their minds. When the Dwarves start pulling up all the gold that I'll keep magically feeding into their mines, when the Hobbits find out that life in Hobbitown is like a perpetual Oktoberfest held in Amsterdam, when the Elves start to notice that they have a life span of hundreds of years, though, actually, I'll probably have to tell them about that up front. The point is, they're all getting something in return."

"But they weren't given a choice," Phillip said. "You took that upon yourself, and you chose to murder over a hundred people and endanger ... well, I'm not sure. How many people have you endangered?"

Jimmy thought. "If you're referring to the experimental villages I've modified as a proof of concept, there are two more. That brings me to the next point. When Tyler reacted so badly to my Hobbit village, I knew I needed to speed up certain parts of the process so I could really show you what I'm trying to do. Look, I know you're planning to exile me and cut me off. I have the right to a proper defense. All I ask is that you all come with me and let me show you my work. I promise, you won't regret it."

Jimmy took his staff in hand, lifting it so the glowing blue plasma ball was slightly above head height, and offered his shoulder to Phillip. Phillip grimaced, then put a hand on Jimmy's shoulder. Jimmy looked to Martin, who followed suit, and in a moment everyone in the room was linked.

Jimmy said, "Regardless of how this all comes out, I want to thank all of you for trusting me. Transporto al armeo post alpha!" As soon as they heard that, every wizard in the room regretted having trusted Jimmy.

The wizards appeared in an empty field just outside Camelot's fortified golden walls. The sky was still bright and clear. The sun was still blindingly bright, reflecting off of the golden city wall, which they were facing. Behind them was about a half mile of open field with forest on the far edge. Between them and the wall were at least five hundred soldiers. They were standing at attention, wearing golden chainmail. Rows and columns of them stretching off to both sides, and back into the distance until the last row of soldiers stood with their backs to the wall. They were all quite tall, and their skin had an ashy blue pallor. Jimmy took a single, graceful step that covered the forty or so feet between the wizards and the soldiers. He landed lightly and spun theatrically, his arms stretched wide. His green and gold robes swirled around him. He waved his staff over the heads of the soldiers with a flourish. "Feast your eyes upon the king's fearsome army of Orcs!" Jimmy bellowed in triumph.

The various wizards said various things under their breath, but Phillip summed up their feelings with a single word. "Crap."

Jimmy spun around again to look at his handiwork, turning his back to the wizards. "I know, right?" he said, putting his left hand on his hip and leaning heavily on his staff. "That chainmail is real gold, you know. Took me forever to produce all those little gold rings."

Martin was straining to process the full meaning of everything he saw. Some part of his mind gave up and decided to just take all of the problems one at a time. He was a bit surprised to hear himself yell, "You can't make armor out of gold! It's too soft! An axe'll go right through it!"

Jimmy looked back over his shoulder at Martin, and for a moment he looked concerned. Then he shrugged and said, "Ah, oh well. I can always make more."

Gwen asked, "More gold rings, or more soldiers?"

"Either," Jimmy answered. "And please, call them Orcs."

"No! Never! They're not Orcs! They're not!" Phillip shouted.

"Well, not yet. To be honest, they're only about ten percent of the way to their final form. I don't dare change them any faster." Phillip motioned to the soldier nearest to him. "You. Step forward."

The soldier lumbered forward. He was at least a foot taller than Jimmy, and his movements were slow and deliberate.

"They're still adjusting to their new size," Jimmy explained. "Show them your teeth." The soldier bared his teeth, large slabs of yellowed calcium with livid red gums, and more than a little blood gathered in the spaces between the teeth. "It's quite painful, unfortunately. Not just because of the growth, either. As they get used to their new teeth, I'm afraid their cheeks and tongues take quite a bit of abuse. I deadened their pain receptors to compensate. As an added bonus, they know that if I'm unhappy the pain comes back. Keeps them obedient."

Jimmy turned back to face the wizards, spreading his arms wide. "Well? What do you think?"

Phillip said, "It's inhuman."

Jimmy said, "Yes."

"No!" Phillip said. "This, this...*Jimmy*! This is inhuman! This is the worst thing ever! Even I didn't think you were capable of this! Jimmy, you have to stop! You have to change them all back!"

"Oh, Phillip. I can't do that. If I did, all my hard work would be wasted."

Phillip didn't shout, but his voice had a hint of madness to it. "Jimmy. You will undo everything you've done, and then we will decide on your punishment!"

"And if I don't?" Jimmy asked.

"Then we will undo what you've done and punish you."

Jimmy shook his head. "That's not much of a choice, but you never were a very good negotiator, were you, Phillip?" he chuckled, but when it was clear that he was the only one who saw anything funny, he stopped. He took a long moment to gauge the mood of the wizards who stood as a unified block behind Phillip. "Okay, I'll tell you what. If any of you agree with Phillip, stay there with him. If you understand what I've done, and see that it was the right way forward, then come stand with me."

Nobody, not even Eddie, moved to stand with Jimmy.

"I see," he said. "Alrighty then, Phillip. If what I've done is a terrible crime for which I must be punished, then I suggest you get on with it." He laid his staff on the ground and crossed his arms in front of himself, as if waiting patiently for a police officer to handcuff him.

Phillip walked forward. He removed his hat and muttered, "Ŝnuro, kvar metrojn," to produce some rope. As he reached into his hat, he said, "Well, Jimmy, I won't pretend that I'm not going to enjoy this." Phillip reached his hand into his hat and grasped, but got nothing but a handful of air. He tried a couple more times, perplexed. He was puzzling over this when he walked face first into the invisible exclusion field between him and Jimmy. Phillip bounced off of the wall, sprawling backwards onto the grass, yelping with surprise.

Jimmy said, "I must admit, I enjoyed that quite a bit as well." He bent down and picked his staff back up. Martin and Gwen ran to Phillip's side, as he lay on the ground five feet in front of where Jimmy stood. Phillip sat up, feeling his nose to see if it was broken.

Jimmy said, "You'll find that the entire city of Camelot is surrounded by an exclusion field, the largest ever attempted. That's what I had to rush to get finished when Tyler turned out to be such a wuss. You're going to love this part—the magic phrase that activated it was 'Alrighty then, Phillip.' You see, I always knew you'd turn on me someday."

"I turned on you years ago!" Phillip cried from his seated position on the ground.

"You think I didn't know that? You didn't hide your hostility very well, Phillip."

"I didn't hide it at all! I've been openly hostile!"

"Well," Jimmy sniffed, "don't think for one minute that I was fooled by your false friendship."

"I hate you! I hate you! I've hated you openly for years!"

"And finally, the truth comes out!"

Phillip shouted inarticulately for a while, too mad to care that he was giving Jimmy just what he wanted. Finally he stopped, and hoisted himself to his feet, picking up his staff and hat.

"You won't be needing those," Jimmy said. "I've disabled the shell on that side of the field. If any of you had come over to stand with me, you'd still have your powers and full access to the shell, but instead you're cut off. The shell will ignore you as long as you're out there. So, pretty much for the rest of your lives."

Martin shouted, "You won't get away with this, Jimmy!"

"I've already gotten away with it. It just took you cretins this long to notice. And my name is *Merlin*!" Jimmy composed himself, then continued. "Of course, since the shell doesn't work at all out there, I can't use magic against you either."

None of the wizards on the wrong side of the barrier was surprised when Jimmy continued, "So, I'll just have to sic my Orcs on you instead!"

Phillip was in a full rage. "They aren't Orcs, you idiot! Just because you call something something, doesn't make it ... it!"

Jimmy shook his head. "Oh, Phillip. You've always lacked imagination, as that last sentence proved."

26.

The wizards quickly discovered that having free access to all of the food, shelter, and money you could ever want, and the ability to teleport and fly, was not conducive to good cardiovascular health. They didn't know for sure if disabling the shell had rendered them just as prone to injury as a non-wizard, but not one of them chose to stick around and find out. The wizards ran less than a hundred feet before most of them were winded. Also, due to the unevenness of the field through which they were running, most of them almost immediately pulled, wrenched, or twisted some part of their anatomy. Martin was among the most physically fit among them, but that was only because he had arrived most recently. The wizards were running for their lives and were doing a terrible job of it.

Luckily, the Orcs weren't doing much better. At Merlin's order, all five hundred of them advanced on the now-powerless wizards, but they moved clumsily, grumbling as they did. Clearly, the process of turning into Orcs was even more uncomfortable than Merlin had let on. This was good, because it meant the wizards had some chance of escape. It was bad in that it meant that if they were captured, the Orcs would be in the mood for revenge.

Martin noticed that he was pulling away from the pack, and he fought his natural instinct to widen the gap. Instead, he took the opportunity to slow a bit and look behind him. The little band of wizards had a lead on the Orcs, but Martin knew it wouldn't last. The wizards had accelerated well, but they couldn't keep it up for long, and while the solid wall of Orcs was slow, he saw no reason to believe it would get any slower. Martin looked to the tree line, still hundreds of yards away. He didn't think the wizards would make it. Several of them were already clutching at their sides. Even if they did reach the forest, there was no reason to think that the Orcs wouldn't chase them into it. Really, the forest would most likely just split the wizards up and make them easier to capture.

Martin felt his imp box with his smartphone inside rattling around in his robe pocket and beating against his left hip as he ran. It was maddening. His robe, his hat, his staff, his phone. All of them had been so powerful just ten minutes ago, but now they were as useless as if the shell had never existed.

Hang on, Martin thought. *My phone could do stuff before Phillip told me about the shell. That's how I got here!* He risked turning around and running backwards for a moment.

"Hey, Phil," he yelled. "He said he disabled the shell, right?"

Phillip was badly winded and losing speed. He spoke between huge gulps of air. "Yeah … so … what?"

"He didn't say he disabled the file, just the shell."

"Yeah … it's really … hard to … cut someone … off from the … file. We … can … do it, … but it takes … a lot of doing! … You can't rush it."

Martin didn't say anything; he just dug out the silver imp box and showed it to Phillip. Phillip looked puzzled for a moment, then started screaming, "DO IT! DO IT NOW! DO IT!"

Martin flipped the lid of the box open. The smartphone's screen glowed invitingly. He pulled up the app and looked at the options. He could go back to his own time, and be arrested like a civilized person. *No thanks.* He could teleport himself away and watch from a distance as his friends got beaten to death. *Not much better.* That left one option. He pressed the hover button, and immediately bobbed two feet into the air. He heard a ragged cheer come up from the other wizards, but he was more concerned with the bone-jarring vibration he'd never bothered to fix. Also, with his feet no longer touching the ground, he was quickly losing speed. Phillip must have noticed this too, because he grabbed Martin's sleeve and started pulling him through the air behind him.

"Okaa-ay," Martin said, sounding like a goat sitting on a paint shaker. "I provvved it wwworksss. I'mmm gonnna ssstop n-n-now."

Phillip yelled, "Don't you dare! I've got an idea!" He maneuvered Martin's vibrating body so that he was skimming along two feet above the ground, head first and face down like Superman. Martin was wondering what Phillip had in mind when he felt Phillip jump into the air and land with his knee in the middle of Martin's back. Martin let out a pained yell as Phillip started kicking the ground, propelling them forward, riding Martin like a scooter. Martin started to complain, but Phillip cut him off, saying, "P-p-pipe downnn. Youuu ooowe meee onnne!"

"Okaaay! Whooo elssse hasss a p-p-pocket commmputerrr thaaat caan accesss the reeposssitorrry fiiile?" Phillip yelled. A disappointingly small number of voices answered. Martin couldn't be sure, but he thought he heard three. Gwen and Jeff were two of them.

"Rrright," Phillip said, "weee neeed aaaa divvverrrsion! Ideasss?"

An endless moment passed, then Jeff said, "You know what? I think I got somethin'! I gotta stop running to do this. Keep going, no matter what happens to me!"

Gary yelled, "Done!" All who knew him realized that this was what passed for an expression of concern from him.

Martin was still being used as a hoverboard. He hung his head down so that he could have an unobstructed but inverted view behind them. He saw that the wizards had opened a lead of about a hundred feet. He could also see that Jeff had stopped running, and turned to face the groaning, limping mass of Orcs. His head was bowed, and he was clearly operating some sort of electronic device, but Martin couldn't see what it was. As the Orcs closed the gap, Jeff raised his eyes to meet them. They were about thirty feet away when he made the final key press.

Martin could hardly see the Orcs. His view was obstructed by a massive army of demons. They were ten feet tall with pinkish-red skin on their top halves. Their legs were brown fur, and ended in cloven hooves. Their snarling, animalistic faces were framed by large curled horns. Their fists glowed green with arcane energy. There were hundreds of them, standing between Jeff and the Orcs, lined up like hellish Rockettes. In the gaps between the demons' arms and legs, Martin could see just enough to get a sense of the panic in the Orc ranks. One instant they were jogging toward the wizards, the next they were sprinting away. They continued to grumble, but much more emphatically.

It struck Martin as odd that the demons were facing the wizards, with their backs to the Orcs, but he was willing to accept that. The wizards did not need to be told to stop running. They stood in the tall grass a few hundred feet from the tree line, gasping for air and clutching their sides. Phillip lifted his knee from Martin's back. Martin vibro-floated a few feet while he poked at his smartphone, then he dropped to the ground and lay there, grateful to be alive and stationary. After a moment he got up and joined the other wizards, who were watching Jeff's demon army chase off the Orcs.

Martin watched the battle as he walked around the back of the clutch of wizards. Now that he was standing upright, the demons looked familiar. It helped that they still appeared to be facing Martin, even as they chased the Orcs back to Camelot. Martin wondered why they were running backwards, but then he realized that some of them were running sideways, and that they were all moving in an odd, herky-jerky manner. Martin smiled, then moved ten feet to his left, still watching the demons. They all rotated to face him no matter where he was, like animated cardboard cutouts of demons. Martin laughed, then yelled, "Jeff, Doom?"

"Yup!" Jeff replied. "They're called *Barons of Hell*. They were level bosses from the first game. They showed up again in Doom II, I think. I don't have all the frames imported or the sounds. I didn't think I'd need 'em yet." Jeff turned to Gary. "I was gonna give you one as a pet for Christmas."

One of the Magnuses from Norway said, "I will buy ten. Name your price."

The demons didn't run very fast, but neither did the Orcs. Jeff had time to enact a few more subroutines, enabling the demons to turn sideways, and to throw green fireballs, which seemed to enable the Orcs to run faster. A few Orcs were hit in the back by fireballs, and were too scared even to notice that the fireballs had no effect. The terrified Orcs crowded through a side portal in the city wall like five hundred Three Stooges, slamming a portcullis down behind them. "Can you make more of those?" Gwen asked.

"How many you want?"

"Enough to make sure the Orcs stay inside for a while."

"Sure," Jeff said. "The hard part was writin' an emulator so the game's code would run out here. Now that I've done that, I can make as many as we need. They'll just wander around, attacking anything that moves." Jeff hit a few buttons, did some thumb typing, and suddenly the field was full of Barons of Hell, wandering about and throwing green fireballs at random. The only sound was the chirping of birds and the wind rustling the trees.

"Like I said, I haven't imported the sound files yet," Jeff explained.

"Clearly, Jimmy didn't stick around to watch his Orcs dispatch us, or else he'd have retaliated by now," David, the wizard from Russia, said as a demon punched him ineffectually in the back of the head.

"Agreed," Phillip said, his back aglow in pixelated green fire from repeated fireball strikes. "We need to get back into the city."

Martin looked at his smartphone, wedged into its decorative box. Two demons were standing on either side of him, silently struggling to kill each other through him as if he weren't there. "I can transport myself in there, no problem, but I've never tried to take another person with me, let alone twenty."

Gwen pulled out a smartphone as a demon walked through her, possibly attempting to kick her. Martin assumed from the phone's shape and the logo that it was an iPhone 6. She squinted at the screen, saying, "I can transport anyone with this, but I don't have a UI, just the raw file. I'll have to do it one person at a time, and I'll need the hard coordinates of the exact landing spot. Anybody have some safe coordinates inside the city memorized?"

After a conspicuous silence, Eddie looked at her phone, noticing the logo on the back. "Apple? They're still in business?"

Jeff said, "You're from the early nineties, aren't you?" His portable, from just a few years after Martin's time, appeared to be two sheets of glass glued together into a rectangle. The back sheet of glass was opaque; the front held the display. Martin didn't see a logo, which probably meant it wasn't made by Apple.

One of the Germans had a Palm Treo that looked like it was designed by a committee of lowest bidders. Martin didn't think it would be as much use as Gwen's iPhone.

By this time, the wizards had formed into a loose huddle, and the demons had surrounded them, pelting their backs with a constant barrage of 16-bit fireballs, the fusillade illuminating the wizards' faces with an eerie green light.

"Okay," Phillip said. "Martin, get in there and keep Jimmy occupied. I doubt he'll ghost you, at least not right away. He'll want to play with you, maybe turn you to his side. Try to get him talking. Whatever you do, try to do it in public. Jimmy wants people to think he's a hero, so he won't do anything too underhanded if people are watching. I know the coordinates to my shop by heart. Transporting a car one piece at a time takes a lot of trips. Jeff, Gwen, and Felix will send us all there one by one, and we can use my computer to figure out the coordinates and do a group transport to come help you."

"Your computer is a Commodore 64. I don't think the help will come very fast," Martin said.

"Hey, don't knock it. I could have a VIC-20."

A mournful voice from the back of the pack said, "Hey! I love my VIC-20!"

Phillip continued, "You up for this?"

"Why not?" Martin answered. "What's the worst that can happen?"

"He could kill you."

"See, that's noth … wait. What?"

"He could totally kill you," Phillip reiterated. "There's a spell that would take you out instantly. The only challenge for Jimmy would be remembering the right words."

"Oh yeah," Tyler said. "If you don't use a spell that often, the words just go bye-bye."

Gary said, "Yeah, but if it's something as important as killing Martin, I'm sure Jimmy'd have the words written down."

"Obviously," Jeff agreed.

"Phillip, why didn't you tell me there was a spell to kill people?" Martin sputtered.

"If you were me, and you were training you, would you tell you that you could easily kill you at will?"

Martin asked after a moment, "*You*, meaning *me*, or *you* meaning *you*?"

"Either way," Phillip answered.

Martin asked, "Why am I doing this again?"

Gwen put her hand on Martin's arm and looked him in the eye, calming him instantly. "Martin, when he finds out the Orcs failed to kill us, he'll probably just do the job with the shell, and we won't be able to defend ourselves. Someone's gotta get in there and distract him until the rest of us can find our way in, and your phone's the only device that can do it that quickly."

OFF TO BE THE WIZARD

Phillip said, "Just go in and get him out in public. Keep him occupied, and we'll be there as fast as we can."

Martin opened the imp box and pressed the glowing screen of his phone a few times. His eyes darted to Gwen's just in time to see her look away. He looked at Phillip and said, "I love this plan! I'm excited to be a part of it. Let's do it!"

Phillip said, "*Ghostbusters*." He smiled, part out of admiration, part because he was delighted to get a pop culture reference for once.

Martin pressed the screen of his phone and disappeared. He reappeared standing roughly where Jimmy had stood when he turned the Orcs on them. He was on the other side of the barrier. The wizards watched as Martin flew into the air, then swung around, and accelerated toward the castle.

"Do you think he can do it?" Gwen asked.

Phillip smiled. "His job is to draw attention to himself and get into trouble. I don't think he's capable of *not* doing it."

27.

Before Martin flew to the castle, he wheeled around to get a look at the wizards. They were a small clump of people, surrounded by a chaotic mass of enraged, two-dimensional demons. He noted that Phillip and Gwen were both watching him.

Martin turned toward the castle and accelerated. He had full shell access and the use of all of the macros in the system. As he flew low over the rooftops, he muttered, "Ĉi tiu iras al la dek unu," the trigger phrase for a macro he'd found while researching his salutation. It was a bit of Gary's handiwork. Anything he said now would be amplified to the approximate volume of a speed-metal concert.

Martin shouted, "MEEERRRLINN!" in the angriest-sounding voice he could muster, and repeated it every few seconds, almost like a siren. He wanted Jimmy to feel the same feeling in the pit of his stomach that he himself had felt when he was being chased by the federal agents, what felt like years ago. He streaked across the medieval skyline, a silver blur, shrieking Merlin's name with eardrum-shattering intensity. Not a single living thing was unaware of him. Countless items were dropped as people put their hands to their ears and looked to the sky, just a moment too late. He was moving too quickly to track easily. All eyes turned to where Martin had just been.

Martin slowed as he approached the castle, then stopped so suddenly that he nearly lost his grip on his staff. He swung for a moment as his body's momentum spent itself. Finally, he settled to a standing position, hovering fifty feet in the air above the front courtyard. The guards stood their ground, but they didn't look happy about it. Martin let out another ear splitting "MEEERRRLINN!"

The guards seemed to hear a sound too faint and distant for Martin to pick up. They looked behind themselves, then parted. Jimmy, looking very small, slid into view, covering a space of several yards in a single step. With a second step he glided through the arch and stopped in front of the castle entrance. He cleared his throat, then in a voice much calmer, but every bit as loud, said, "MAAARRTINN! Good to see you. Do come in!"

Martin had designed his salutation to be modular. In this situation, the parts where he transported himself to the stage area, transported himself away unseen, and watched the statue break dance autonomously would not be needed.

A good key phrase for a macro should be something that is memorable in times of stress, but that you're unlikely to say in normal conversation. Martin said, "Groovy." Immediately, lines delineating the rectangular shapes of boxes started tracing the contours of his form. As he fell from the sky, his body divided into hundreds of silver boxes which dispersed, swirled, multiplied, and re-formed into a thirty-foot-tall version of Martin, which landed heavily in a three-point crouch, holding its staff above and behind it with its right arm.

Only the boxes that made up the hands, feet, and staff had any mass. The rest looked solid, but were without substance. Suspended at the point of center mass, Martin floated, mimicking the three-point crouch. Any motion Martin made, the statue made. Martin had tested it with a doll-sized test version of the statue, but he'd never tried it at scale, and was nervous about his ability to walk. He avoided the problem by flying. He launched himself straight at the entrance, and Jimmy. He barreled forward, the statue skimming only a few feet above the cobblestones. His massive right hand grasped Jimmy and lifted him roughly. Since he was entering with Merlin, the shell didn't stop him as he streaked through the arch and tumbled gracelessly through the antechamber. He ground to a stop in the great hall, his massive feet sliding on the marble floor. As he stopped, he flung Jimmy with great force toward that far wall. He knew that with the shell enabled Jimmy would not be damaged. It would hurt, but Jimmy had earned some hurt. As he let go, he heard Jimmy say something. It sounded like *groovier*, which made no sense.

As Jimmy hurtled forward, his body glowed blue and shattered into hundreds of glowing blue plasma balls. The spheres swirled and multiplied before reforming into a forty-foot-tall statue of Jimmy. Giant Jimmy hit the far wall, but with most of the force dissipated. He came to a rest standing with his massive feet on either side of the throne.

"How do you like my new macro?" Merlin asked. "I made it myself from parts I found in the shell. Oh, and I want you to know that I appreciate you calling me Merlin."

"Yeah, I was being sarcastic," Martin groaned.

Back in the center of the writhing mass of silent demons, the wizards were making slow progress. Gwen, Jeff, and Felix were transporting wizards to Phillip's shop as fast as they could, but with text editors and access to the raw file, it was a slow process. They had to work with each individual wizard to find their entry, then manually enter the coordinates for Phillip's shop. It would have been difficult work in a quiet study. Standing in a field being silently attacked by ineffectual demons and working on tiny smartphone screens made it much harder. Hearing Martin's shouting, followed by silence, had made it nearly impossible.

Phillip did some quick math. Assuming twenty-two wizards, taking at least thirty seconds to transport each, then using his computer to dig up safe transport coordinates (it wouldn't help Martin if his rescue brigade materialized in the middle of a wall), he figured it would be well over five minutes before they got him any help. Phillip listened for a moment. In the distance he heard crashing noises and amplified grunts.

They had to get help to Martin faster.

"How many have we transported so far?" he asked.

Gwen was peering at the phone's screen. One of the Parisian wizards was standing closer than he really needed to, looking over her shoulder to help isolate his file entry. She answered, "Four," without looking up.

"Okay, change of plan. Jeff, Felix, keep sending people to my shop. Gwen, you're going to send me to the shop, then you'll follow. I have an idea."

Martin could see Jimmy suspended in the torso of Giant Jimmy. Martin had to admit that the matrix of glowing blue plasma balls made for an impressive statue, especially when it was sprinting across the massive gold-and-marble expanse of the great hall of the castle Camelot, intent on doing him harm. Martin barely managed to get Giant Martin up on one foot and one knee before Giant Jimmy was on top of him. Martin put up his hands, catching Jimmy's as they came down with tremendous force. Martin held Jimmy at bay, the two massive forms held in stalemate. Within their giant effigies, Martin and Jimmy could see each other, one looking through a screen of floating plasma balls, the other through a field of silver boxes.

"You didn't create that!" Martin said, straining to hold Jimmy at bay. "All you did was take something I created and change it!"

"Yes! I changed it into something new," Jimmy said, bearing down with all of his strength. "Something better, that I made."

"I created this macro! I came up with the idea! I invented the control scheme. I animated the transition!"

"Yes, and I thank you for your assistance," Jimmy said, with an innocent expression that Martin thought just might be genuine.

Martin shifted his weight to the right and let all of the strength go out of his arms. Jimmy fell forward and rolled to the side and away from Martin. As he clumsily got Giant Martin up on his feet, he hissed, "You have no originality!"

"That's ridiculous!" Jimmy said, as he rolled on the ground.

Martin stood over him brandishing his staff and shouted, "This castle. The Hobbits. The Orcs. My macro. Even your name! Everything you do is a copy."

Jimmy sprawled on the ground, flailing wildly for a moment before managing to maneuver Giant Jimmy into a low crouch. "And I was the first person to put it all together!"

Martin thought, *I gotta keep him occupied, and get him out in public if I can.* He glanced around the hall. People were starting to gather in the doorways and outside the gigantic windows that lined the walls. He took a clumsy step backward with his right foot to adjust his stance and said, "There's more to innovation than just putting other people's ideas together like LEGO bricks." He adjusted his grip on his staff, holding it near its base with both hands. He swung it like a baseball bat with all of his force, aimed squarely for the real Jimmy at the core of Giant-Jimmy. Jimmy saw it coming and took a single step backward. Being Jimmy, that single step took Giant Jimmy all the way to the back of the hall, leaving Giant Martin to cope with the momentum of the swing. Martin spun clumsily, lost his footing, and fell to the marble floor.

"You make a valid point," Jimmy said. "My innovation wasn't to do what everyone else did. My innovation was to do it better."

Phillip appeared in the secret upstairs annex of his shop and was immediately horrified. Four wizards had been sent there before him with the instructions to use his Commodore 64 to try to find a safe teleportation point into Camelot. The first wizard to be transferred, David the Russian ladykiller, had made a beeline for the computer and was hard at work. The next three wizards, the two Magnuses and Sergio from Italy, had clearly decided that David had matters well in hand, and that the best thing they could do was make themselves at home. One Magnus was trying to pry the coin box of Phillip's GORF machine open to see if there were any quarters. The other was draped over Phillip's white couch like a slab of melted cheese, his boots kicked up on the armrest. Sergio was sitting in the driver's seat of the Fiero, inspecting the interior with an amused scowl on his face.

"You! Feet off of my couch!" Phillip shouted. "You! Out of my car!"

Sergio muttered, "Gladly," but didn't seem to be hurrying to comply.

Phillip turned his attention to the GORF machine. "Magnus, you can make all the gold you could ever need! Why would you even bother trying to steal from me?"

Magnus looked at Phillip and said, "I dunno. It's what'cha do, isn't it?" He turned his attention back to trying to jimmy open the coin box.

Gwen appeared. Phillip spun around and said, "See why I tried to keep this a secret?"

Gwen held up her hands and said, "You're preaching to the choir."

Jeff and Felix were still sending wizards over, so it was no surprise when Kirk appeared. He spun slowly in awe, then said, "Wow! It's like I'm watching an episode of *Miami Vice*!"

Couch Magnus said, "Really? I think it's kinda dated and sad."

"That's what I meant," Kirk replied.

"Okay, Gwen," Phillip said, "now we have to get to my hut."

"Do you know the coordinates?"

"Not off the top of my head," Phillip said as he ran to the roll-away garage door built into the wall. "If I did, we'd have just gone straight there. We have to get there as soon as possible, and we can't get the coordinates because my computer is occupied." He hefted the door up on its rollers. It slid smoothly along tracks on the ceiling, exposing a mass of sturdy look-ing oak planks. He backed up, took a moment to gather his strength, then ran into the planks with his shoulder, causing them to break free of the door frame and tip forward at hinges built into their base. The planks stopped with a dull *whump*, forming a ramp between the second floor of Phillip's shop and the crest of the steep hill behind it. Phillip opened the passenger door of the Fiero and made an inviting motion with his other hand toward Gwen, like a doorman helping a lady into a cab.

"Can I offer you a ride in my car?" Phillip asked.

Sergio, still in the driver's seat, said, "Cool. Where are you going to sit, Phil?"

Martin had to admit, Jimmy had improved on his macro. Not only was Giant Jimmy larger, stronger, and flashier than Giant Martin, but Jimmy's signature glide-step was a superior means of locomotion when compared to Martin's technique of flailing his arms while struggling to maintain his balance. Jimmy was playing with him. He would drift effortlessly from one corner of the great hall to another and Martin, standing in the center of the room, would laboriously turn to face him. A few times Jimmy cut diagonally across the room, forcing Martin to defensively leap out of his way, then clamber back to his feet. It was all the more embarrassing for Martin because of the spectators. Looking at the windows and doors, it seemed to Martin that the castle's entire staff was watching Jimmy make a monkey of him. *Not bad*, he thought, *but if we're ever going to draw a proper crowd, I need to get him outside.*

Giant Jimmy was bouncing lightly on the balls of his feet. Martin could just pick out Jimmy's face peering out from between the glowing blue orbs. Since he had written the macro to begin with, he knew that the spheres that made up Giant Jimmy were transparent from Jimmy's point of view, much like the boxes that made up Giant Martin were to him.

"You should've joined me, Martin," Jimmy said, moving gracefully across the far end of the great hall. "I really could've used someone with your skills." Jimmy launched Giant Jimmy at Giant Martin with surprising speed. Martin ducked, barely evading Giant Jimmy's arm as Jimmy attempted to clothesline Giant Martin on his way across the room.

Martin smiled bitterly and turned toward Jimmy while remaining in his crouch. He made a show of looking over Giant Jimmy from head to toe, then said, "Seems to me you already did."

"Why is everyone so hung up on who came up with an idea? In the end, nothing could be less important! It's who utilizes an idea that matters. Inventing isn't nearly as important as using."

"What an eloquent way to sum up your world view."

Jimmy said, "Thank you," and launched Giant Jimmy at Martin again. This time, since Giant Martin was hunkered down in a crouch, Jimmy swung his giant staff at him like a hockey stick. Martin sprung into the air. Giant Martin mimicked the movements of Martin's actual limbs on a much larger scale, and in the process multiplied the forces involved. Since the only parts of Giant Martin that had mass were the hands, feet, staff, and Martin's comparatively tiny real body suspended inside Giant Martin's torso, that meant that a leap that would make Martin fly two feet into the air sent Giant Martin rocketing into the gold-plated rafters of the great hall. He tried to grab the rafters, but only managed to give himself an awkward spin as he fell back to the floor a hundred feet below. He landed on his side, then struggled to regain his footing. Giant Jimmy was again standing at the throne end of the hall, bobbing lightly with bent knees, the way actors do when they are playing a ninja. Martin could hear the people watching laughing at him.

"That was not meant as a compliment," Martin said.

"The best compliments seldom are," Jimmy replied.

"You lied to me, Jimmy. When you asked me to join you, you said you wanted to make a better future."

"And who's to say I haven't?"

"The Orcs!"

Jimmy laughed. "That's just silly! The Orcs don't talk, or at least they won't when they're finished."

Martin righted himself and faced Jimmy, ready for the next attack.

"You really don't get it," Jimmy said, as if he was only now understanding Martin's confusion. "Martin, nothing we do affects the future at all. We've proven that. Not only is there no reason not to change things, knowing what we know, it's our moral *duty* to change things. I talked the king into ordering people to boil their water and to discard spoiled food. I got slavery outlawed. You don't hear Phillip complaining about that, do you? Sure, the Hobbits and the Elves are a bit silly, but if we're going to improve the world, why shouldn't we have fun doing it? Think of the possibilities! I plan to put an end to the Crusades. Then I'll prevent the Inquisition. Imagine a Renaissance where someone with unlimited funds lets Da Vinci build whatever he wants. Where

Michelangelo is never without a commission. What if, when the new world was discovered, the Native Americans had horses and guns? Let's find out! Picture World War I with armored blimps! What if Adolf Hitler's parents had an unfortunate accident, and he got adopted by a nice Jewish family? I have seen the future, Martin, and it's a better past!"

After a moment's thought, Martin said, "Jimmy, I won't be a part of this!"

Jimmy said, "And you've convinced me that you shouldn't. Well done," and hurled Giant Jimmy at Giant Martin with all of his strength. Giant Martin was standing flat-footed in the middle of the hall, holding his staff at waist height with both hands. Jimmy was aiming high this time, and it was clear to everyone that Martin would not be able to dodge. Jimmy's aim was spot on, and Giant Jimmy's left fist flew with staggering force into Giant Martin's face. Since Jimmy had forgotten what he was doing, and punched one of the many parts of Giant Martin that had no mass, his fist streaked through Giant Martin's head as if he had punched a cloud of smoke. Martin, meanwhile, reversed his right hand's grip on the staff, took a single step backward with his left foot, and, as Giant Jimmy flew past, swung the giant staff, the bust of Santo on the end acting as a counterweight, and struck real Jimmy in the small of the back. The blow added a substantial amount of momentum to Jimmy's already out-of-control trajectory, sending him screaming and flying toward the entry hall. Spectators dove to the side as Giant Jimmy skidded and tumbled through the antechamber and back out into the courtyard.

Martin said, "I'm glad we've come to an agreement." He pointed his staff forward, and Giant Martin flew out of the great hall.

+>=·=<+

The streets of Leadchurch were not particularly full, but still, the sight of a white Pontiac Fiero tearing through at speeds of up to forty miles per hour had caused a great many people to scream, then dodge, then scream again.

Inside the car, Phillip looked like a kid in a candy store, and Gwen sounded like a mother who didn't want to buy any candy.

"What in the world? Why is the music so loud?" she asked.

"It isn't!" Phillip explained, cranking on the wheel. "It seems loud because the speakers are built into the headrests! Isn't it awesome?"

"It might be if you were playing something good," Gwen said, gripping the dashboard for dear life.

Phillip steered the car sideways through a sliding turn while explaining, "That's *Genesis*! It's called 'That's All'! It's a song of love and loss and a relationship turned sour!"

"Does Phil Collins write songs about anything else?"

"He doesn't have to. He's so good at writing good songs about bad relationships, to do anything else would be a waste of talent! It's a great song! In the video the whole band was dressed up like bums."

As a chicken bounced off of the windshield, Gwen asked, "Why? What do bums have to do with this song?"

"You know," Phillip said while the car skidded to a stop in front of his home, "I'm not sure." The car had scarcely stopped before Phillip threw the door open and ran into his house, taking his staff, which had lain across both of their laps and out of Gwen's window.

Gwen followed, taking the time to look around at the frightened villagers, eyeing the Fiero like it was a vicious beast, which they probably thought it was. "Don't worry," she said. "It can't hurt you." She remembered Phillip's driving, then added, "When it's still. It can't hurt you when it's still. If you see it moving, run and hide."

Gwen entered Phillip's home and found him hastily untying the knots that fastened a heavy canvas hammock suspended in the corner. "What are you doing?" she asked.

One end of the hammock came loose and fell to the floor. Phillip lunged to the other end and started to work on the knots, mumbling, "Martin's been using this tarpaulin as a hammock, but I need it now." A few seconds later, the hammock was no more, and Phillip had a tarp tucked under his arm. He scurried over to a trunk that sat in the corner near the cold fireplace. He rummaged furiously, let out a triumphant shout, and came up with a coil of rope.

"All right," he said. "We're ready to go!"

"Where are we going?" Gwen asked.

Phillip squinted, set his jaw, pointed to a door that was not the entrance, and said, "To the bathroom."

Gwen grimaced, and said, "Ewwwww."

Giant Jimmy ground to a stop in the front courtyard of the castle Camelot after tumbling through the entry arch and sliding for some distance. He had just enough time to get up on all fours before Martin was on him again. Jimmy had demonstrated that the giant forms flew more gracefully than they walked. It was a lesson Martin took to heart.

Giant Martin barreled out of the castle, skimming the ground, and grabbed Jimmy with his free hand as he passed. As Jimmy left the ground, Giant Jimmy went with him, mimicking every move Jimmy made. Martin shot up at a forty-five degree angle. Almost instantly they reached an altitude of a hundred feet, and Martin employed the first maneuver he had learned, albeit by accident. He pulled his staff arm inward, as if to shield his face. The staff's air speed dropped to nothing, then to full reverse, as it had the day he learned to fly. Again, Martin's body cracked like a whip. This time he kept his grip on the staff, but he deliberately let go of Jimmy. Giant Martin hung in space from his hovering staff and watched as Giant Jimmy splatted against the inside surface of Camelot's golden wall, then slowly slid down to the ground.

Martin adjusted his pose to look a little more heroic and floated, waiting, while Giant Jimmy groaned and rolled on the ground, stunned. Jimmy crawled over and sat heavily on the ground, his back resting against the wall. Clearly, hitting the wall had knocked the fight out of him. Martin looked around. The tops of the walls were lined with the soldiers enjoying the best view in the house. The gate held back a sizeable crowd, not that any of them had any interest in getting closer. Martin felt a small pang of sympathy for his adversary. Jimmy wanted to be important, and who couldn't relate to that? Jimmy was learning the hard lesson that the things we do to make ourselves feel big end up making us look small.

Giant Martin drifted in closer. "Had enough, Merlin?"

Giant Jimmy's shoulders sagged. Jimmy laughed. "Yeah. I've had enough."

"Good. Let's go inside and wait for the others."

Giant Jimmy's hand slowly went up. Jimmy said, "In a second. There's just one thing I want to do." He made a fist and thrust it toward Martin, shouting "Ŝraŭbo vi!" Something, a force field, a shock wave, a wrecking ball, *something* hit Martin with tremendous force. As he flew helplessly through the air, he was dimly aware that Giant Martin had dissipated. His body hit the wall of the castle just above the entry arch and fell to the ground below. As he rolled on the ground, struggling to catch his breath, he saw the blue mass of glowing orbs that formed Giant Jimmy closing on him fast. He felt the giant hand close around him, and then he was streaking across the courtyard again, hitting the far wall and falling to the ground.

"Such a waste," Jimmy said as he rushed toward Martin again. Martin was lifted and thrown again too quickly for his brain to process the sensations. As he sailed through the air, hit the castle wall, and fell to the cobblestones below, he heard Jimmy still talking.

"And now you learn the central truth of your friend Phillip's life. He never really does anything." Then Martin was streaking through the air, into the wall, and down to the ground again. "He watches," Jimmy continued, "while other people do things and he complains about it. Sure, he felt just as strongly as you did that I needed to be stopped." Martin sailed across the courtyard again. He was getting to where he was hardly aware of it. "But you're the one here getting used as a racquetball, and where is he? Somewhere far away, probably saying something snide." Jimmy threw Martin again, with extra force this time, as if he were throwing

Phillip … at Phillip. "He's perfectly happy to let others take all of the risks, but he resents anyone who claims the rewards."

Martin lay, a crumpled mess, on the ground. He was stunned and in great pain, but some part of his brain knew that he was not injured. Giant Martin was gone, but his invulnerability remained. Perhaps other things still worked. He lifted his staff into the air and said, "Flugi." A different part of his brain was not at all surprised when nothing happened.

Giant Jimmy stood over Martin, giving him time to realize just how doomed he was. Martin employed the only means of escape his brain could provide in its current state. He crawled.

Martin scarcely noticed when Jimmy deactivated Giant Jimmy, landing lightly on the ground next to Martin, who continued crawling, his head slowly clearing, while Jimmy followed.

Jimmy explained in a calm voice, "While your friends have spent the last few years sewing robes, building cars, and making their homes look like Ozzy Osborne album covers, I've spent my free time creating shell commands that only I can access."

Martin continued crawling and groaned. "You all agreed that you wouldn't do that."

"Which is often your first hint that you should do something." Jimmy shook his head, casually stalking. "It's just so sad."

Martin asked, "What is?" Martin collided with something. He looked up. He had crawled directly into the stone rim of the pool that surrounded the golden statue of the old king, the young king, and Jimmy. Every part of Martin that he could feel, hurt. He flopped over and sagged onto the ground, leaning against the rim of the pool.

Jimmy looked down at him. "Martin, you've thrown your life away. You must see that! There's no way this can end well for you, and what did you do it for? Nothing!"

"Some things are just wrong, Jimmy."

"Yes, and destroying yourself for no good reason is one of them!"

Martin shook his head. "Jimmy, you killed a town. A *town*, Jimmy, dead. You did that! For what? Because you like Tolkien? Your Hobbits died, your Orcs are in constant pain. God knows how the Elves are doing."

"They're fine."

"You'll forgive me if I don't take your word for it. Jimmy, you've killed or injured hundreds of innocent people! That's why I came here, and that's not nothing!"

"Yes it is, Martin. Yes it is! Look around you!" Jimmy gestured toward the crowd beyond the gate and the soldiers watching from the top of the parapets. They still had a large audience. Their now non-amplified voices could not be heard from the distances involved, but they were still in plain sight. Martin and Jimmy were having a private conversation in front of a massive audience.

"Look at them, Martin. They don't know the truth, but you and I do. They aren't real. They aren't people. They're lines of code. They're information, and not very much of it. They're algorithms, created automatically by another algorithm to accomplish who knows what for we don't know who! What could be more unimportant? What could be more insubstantial? They're not real, and nothing done by them or to them could possibly make any difference."

"They're just as real as you are," Martin spat.

"Yes! Exactly! I'm not real either, and neither are you! Nothing any of us does matters, so why are we arguing about what I've done? Nobody else seems to understand this like I do."

Martin smiled. "Which is often your first hint that you're wrong."

Jimmy shrugged, then pointed his staff at Martin as he lay prone on the ground. "I can see I'm not going to change your mind, so I have to decide what to do with you. The way I see it, I have three options. I can strand you in your own time, which in your case means jail. I can let you stay in this time, stripped of all powers. It'll be a hard life, subsistence farming, but you'll have your freedom and you'll enjoy all the improvements I make to this timeline. Or maybe it'd be more humane to just kill you now. You wouldn't suffer, and you'd serve as an example to everyone else. What do you think, Martin? Prisoner, peasant, or ..." Jimmy pursed his lips. His head turned up and to the left, lost in thought. Finally, he said, "Death."

Martin laughed. "You couldn't think of a word for death that starts with P, could you?"

Jimmy laughed as well. "No, I couldn't, but as we've established, it doesn't really matter."

A voice said, "Passed away!" Both Martin and Jimmy looked to the top of the statue. The golden muck-covered head of Merlin was draped with what looked to be a tarp. A rope draped down off of the statue's head, over the shoulder and down its front to the water. The other end of the rope seemed to disappear into thin air a few feet above the statue. Phillip stood on the statue's shoulder, holding the rope with one hand and his staff with the other. He looked pretty pleased with himself.

Martin was surprised to see Jimmy smile. "Phillip! I really should have guessed it was you vandalizing my statue. It's about the right maturity level. I should be mad, but I'm just too delighted at the symbolism of you appearing on that statue's head along with all the other crap. Tell me, how'd you climb down a rope carrying your staff?"

"I had Gwen drop it down to me when I was almost to the bottom."

"Ah," Jimmy said. "Is she coming as well?"

"Soon enough," Phillip said, before saying *flugi*, and using his staff to glide down to the ground, forming a triangle between himself, Jimmy, and Martin.

"I'm glad you're here, Phillip. You're just in time to watch me dispatch your sidekick."

"I'm not his sidekick," Martin protested. "If anything, he's my sidekick!"

"Yes, of course," Jimmy said. "Everyone remembers how Batman was Robin's trainee."

When Phillip and Jimmy were done laughing, Phillip said, "I can't let you do that, Jimmy."

For a long moment, Jimmy and Phillip stared at each other, their faces illuminated by the cheesy plasma ball at the end of Jimmy's staff. Jimmy broke the silence. "You can't let me do it, but you can't stop me from doing it, either. You won't ghost me. You won't kill me. You can't hurt me. You can't stop me."

"I dunno," Phillip said. "Maybe I've learned to be a little more like you."

"Phillip, if that's true, I've already won."

Phillip looked at Martin, then looked back to Jimmy. "You're right, I won't ghost you. I won't kill you. I can't injure you. But I can hurt you." With shocking speed, Phillip swung his staff with all of his might. The head of the staff traced a graceful arc, striking Jimmy on the bridge of the nose. The bottle shattered on impact, and while the shards of glass could not pierce Jimmy's skin, the ten-year-old Tabasco sauce it held easily penetrated the membranes of his eyes, nose, and mouth.

Jimmy dropped his staff and clutched at his face, then shrieked, gasping and coughing. He stumbled and fell to the ground, writhing in helpless agony.

28.

An hour later, every wizard in Europe had managed to find his way back into Camelot. With that many people working on the problem, and Eddie to act as a guide, it didn't take long to reinstate the shell, deactivate all of Jimmy's macros, and remove the exclusion field from around the city.

That all handled, it was time to turn to the task of punishing Jimmy. Phillip made no effort to hide his glee. When he was asked to try, he pointed out that his obvious enjoyment of Jimmy's punishment was an important part of said punishment.

They gathered in Jimmy's office.

The only surprising bit was Eddie. He was angrier than anyone. He'd acted as a glorified secretary for years, hoping that someday Jimmy would let him in on his amazing plans. Then, all in one day, Eddie found out that the great man had shared his scheme with someone else on a whim, that the plan itself was abhorrent and immoral, and that his mentor and closest friend was all too happy to see him torn to shreds by fake Orcs with all of the other wizards.

The wizards engaged in some heated deliberation in Jimmy's former office while Jimmy was stored safely on the floor of his former waiting room hogtied, naked, with a gag in his mouth. Finally, they brought him in to share their thoughts. The model of the new Europe was removed from the conference table. Jimmy was placed there instead. Jimmy's face was still stained red and streaming tears, but he'd regained some of his composure.

They could easily send Jimmy back to his original time and place, but they had to make sure that he received some punishment for what he had done once he got there. Nobody was surprised to hear that Phillip had some ideas.

Gwen's levitation spell was used to hold Jimmy helpless in midair.

Phillip climbed up on the table behind Jimmy. He removed his hat and pulled out two fat grease markers, one green, the other yellow. Phillip took his time, writing *Brazil* in large green letters, then used the yellow marker to write *#1*.

"I looked up the day you left your time, Jimmy. Did you know that on that exact date, there's a massive rally in Buenos Aires to show support for the Argentinean national football team? Seems they were about to play their arch-rivals, the Brazilians. Have you ever been to Argentina? It's a lovely country full of strong, healthy, passionate people, most of whom hate the Brazilians with the intensity of a thousand suns." As Phillip clambered down off of the table, Tyler spoke.

"I wanted to ghost you, for at least as long as you ghosted me for. They all talked me out of it. Instead, we've pumped up your magnetic field so strong that any electronic device within ten feet of you will stop functioning, just like we did with Todd."

Tyler walked up close to Jimmy, savoring the only satisfaction he was likely to get. "You can't use a computer, you can't use a phone. If you try to get anyone to help you, it'll be by writing a letter or speaking to them in person. Either way, you'll sound insane. As you know, we've reset your stats to the original factory settings. You're aging again. You're able to get hurt. For Todd, we all figured that was a sufficient punishment, but you have a talent for getting people to do what you want. That's why we're stranding you in South America. You don't speak Spanish, do you? No, no you don't. You will spend the rest of your life an illegal immigrant in the penal system of a foreign nation where you don't speak the language and everyone thinks you're insane, but you'll remember your time as Merlin. It's not quite like being a ghost, but it's close enough for me."

Eddie ungagged Jimmy, leaving him hanging in space. Jimmy knew better than to struggle. He was stuck, and any attempt to unstick himself would just entertain his captors. He looked at Phillip and said, "We'll meet again, you know."

Phillip stepped forward and pointed his staff at Jimmy. "Yes, in eight hundred years or so. Anything you want to say before we send you to your fate?"

"Yes—"

"Too bad," Phillip said, and sent Jimmy on his way.

Eddie led Phillip, Martin, and Gwen to the private chambers of the royal family. They weren't surprised to find that while they were very luxurious by medieval standards, they were a hovel compared to Jimmy's accommodations. King Stephen had died long ago. King Arthur, a thin young man in his early twenties with a confused manner and large, questioning eyes, shared his quarters with his mother, the regally passive Queen Matilda.

Eddie explained that Merlin was gone. King Arthur nodded, and asked what that meant. Eddie explained that Merlin had left and wasn't coming back ever. The king nodded, squeezed his mother's hand, thought for a moment, and asked, more emphatically, "What does that mean?"

Eddie explained that Merlin wasn't going to be around to help him, and that life would go back to the way it was before Merlin arrived.

Arthur said, "But ... I wasn't the king before he arrived."

It was clear that without assistance, the monarchy would fall. That wouldn't be so bad, except that it would drag the rest of Europe into decades of bloody warfare with it. It was a terrible mess, but the wizards couldn't in good conscience just stand back and watch as the Merlin-vacuum destroyed the fledgling western civilization. It was decided that the wizards would elect a new chairman to act in the wizards' interests, and to help prop up and guide the royal family into self-sufficiency. When time came to pick a chairman, everyone wanted to know what Phillip thought, which said more than a vote ever could. Phillip had no interest in living in Camelot, so his first act as chairman was to order Martin to act as his liaison to the royals, with Eddie's assistance.

Martin argued, but Phillip was firm. "Martin, we all have to do our part. I don't want to be chairman, but that's what everybody wants, so I'm doing my duty."

"Yes, but...."

Phillip cut him off. "As chairman, I order you, Martin, to do your part. It just so happens that *your part* is to do the vast majority of my part."

The wizards split into two groups, one to go talk to Jimmy's attempted Orcs, the other to go talk to the Elves. The Orcs were delighted to hear that they would be turned back to normal, but less happy to hear that it would take several weeks. The group that went to talk to the Elves reported that the only manifestation of Jimmy's work so far was that the entire town was thinner, so they were happy to leave things as they stood.

That night, the wizards held the largest victory party of all time, when measured in terms of area. There were still only about two dozen of them, but they had regained the ability to teleport, and having gone without it for the afternoon, they all felt like using it. The party started in Jimmy's former office, but soon some wizards wanted to see Phillip's rec room, and others wanted to check out Skull Gullet Cave. Eventually, teleportation points were defined for several of the wizards' larger homes, and the event took on the feeling of a party held in a mansion, where one drifts from room to room, only in this case, the rooms were spread all over Europe.

The hardest part about throwing a party for time travelers is finding music everyone can enjoy. Everyone is invariably convinced that their artist/genre/format of choice is infinitely superior to all others. After making the obligatory rounds to see where everybody else lived and show them his empty storage facility, Martin settled into Phillip's '80s-themed attic for the duration, but now it was getting late, and Phillip was loudly explaining that Thomas Dolby had recorded more than one song. Martin decided he needed some air.

Martin stepped through the open garage door and across the heavy wooden ramp that led to the hill behind Phillip's shop. He found Gwen, sitting on the ground, fiddling with her wand and looking at the stars. Martin sat next to her. There were many things he missed about his own time, but he knew that if he ever went back, he would miss the medieval night sky. He knew it was the same sky, but it really wasn't. The lack of any light source brighter than a campfire meant that even here, on the outskirts of a medium-sized town, the sky was a spectacular vista of stars, far more than a city boy like Martin had ever realized were there. In his original time, a sky like this was a luxury he'd have to travel for hours out into the middle of nowhere to get. Here, on any clear night, he could just step outside and see the whole universe.

After a period of time Martin carefully calculated to seem nonchalant, he tore his gaze away from the sky, and looked at Gwen. He opened his mouth to speak, but she beat him to it.

"I'm going to Atlantis. I'm leaving tomorrow," she said, in a tone that left no room for questions.

Martin wanted to say *I'm sorry you got outed as a witch*, but he didn't want to say *outed*, or *witch*, for that matter. *Female wizard* sounded stupid. *Lady wizard* was even worse. He tried to come up with a word that meant "witch," that didn't have any insulting or demeaning overtones. He couldn't. In fact, after some thought, he couldn't think of a word that meant *female* that men hadn't imbued with some belittling shade of meaning. Finally, after a much longer silence than he had intended, he simply said, "I can understand why. Frankly, I'm not sure why you stuck around here to begin with. You're a wizard. Why hide that and pretend to be a tailor?"

Gwen said, "I wasn't pretending to be a tailor. I am a tailor, Martin. It's a fair question though. I came here because I'd read a lot of fairy tales when I was a girl, and I wanted to see what the reality was like. I decided to stay here because it was a lot better than I expected. I mean, the food, water, and sanitation aren't great, but we have ways around all of that. As a peasant, I'm powerless, but I'm just as powerless as a peasant man, so that's a kind of equality. It's a pretty good time to be an independent woman, as long as you can defend yourself, and nobody gets it into their head that you're a witch. Of course, I don't know if that's the way it always was, or if that's just our influence. Atlantis isn't just far away, it's also long ago, if you see what I mean."

"I'm really sorry to see you go, though."

She turned and graced Martin with the saddest smile he'd ever seen. "I'm sorry to be going too, but 'Most famous witch in Medieval England' isn't a title that comes with a lot of benefits."

Martin knew this was true. He kept his eyes on the stars and considered his next words carefully. "I've known you a while, but it's like I just really met you today."

"Yes," Gwen said. "It is."

"And that's my own fault," Martin continued.

Gwen laughed gently before saying, "Yes, it is."

There was a long pause while Martin test ran several next sentences in his head, before finally settling on the safest course of action.

He turned his head to look at Gwen and said, "Well, I guess this is goodbye then."

She looked back at him and said, "Yes."

They looked at each other for a moment, then Martin asked, "Would you mind if I kissed you goodbye?"

Gwen smiled, and said, "No."

Martin was thrown high into the air, silver robe flapping in the wind. He landed on the roof of Phillip's shop, where he slid limply, flopping off the side and falling into the valley where the side of the hill met the wall of the shop. Gwen, radiating with glowing power, cursed herself and shut off her macro. She stuffed her wand into her pocket before rushing to Martin's side. He was lying silently in the gutter, not moving. She tried to roll him over, but the fall had wedged him into the dirt crevasse, and now that she was close to him she could see that he couldn't extricate himself because he was laughing too hard. He finally regained his composure enough to get up, but as soon as he made eye contact with Gwen, they both started laughing again.

They didn't make another attempt at a kiss goodbye. They both knew that this was a much more fitting end to their relationship.

29.

Walter and Margarita Banks were living a nightmare. Their son Martin was acting crazy and running from the law. He was holed up in his childhood bedroom, but he kept reemerging for non-sensical reasons, and the authorities were threatening to break down the door.

"One moment! I'm coming!" Walter bellowed, more out of alarm than any anger he might have felt. He gave his wife what he hoped was a reassuring look and got one back from her in return as he started toward the door.

Martin once again came out of his old bedroom and shouted, "No, Dad, stop!" He was wearing a shiny silver muumuu of some sort and a matching Wee Willie Winkie night cap. He had mounted his old bust of Santo the Mexican wrestler on a pole. It was clear to Walter that his boy was insane.

"Martin, baby, what's going on?" Margarita asked. "What have you done?" It broke Walter's heart to hear her sound so distraught.

Martin said, "Nothing! I haven't done anything." He grabbed an armload of linens, all the while yelling, "I especially haven't done any of the things those men are going to tell you I did." Martin awkwardly carried the bedding and the wrestler on a stick back into his bedroom, saying, "Thanks for everything! See you later! Dad, you can open the door now," as he went.

Walter knew what he had to do. There was no doubt in his mind that his son needed help. He opened the front door and said, "He's in his bedroom. This way."

Walter walked quickly to Martin's bedroom door and knocked firmly. The hall had instantly filled with men in dark suits and uniformed police officers.

"Martin," Walter said, "the police are here, and some men from…." Walter trailed off.

One of the men in dark suits said, "The U.S. Treasury."

Walter and Margarita, whom he could barely see at the back of the crowd of officers and federal agents, exchanged a look that only those who have been married for a long time can understand. Walter looked at the doorknob, then asked the agent closest to him, "Do you have a nail? If he locked the door, we'll need a nail." The agent glared at him.

"Martin!" Walter shouted in as calm a voice as he could muster. "We're coming in." He tried the knob and it turned easily. He opened the door, and the officers rushed in past him, but not before he saw that Martin was not in the room. He and Margarita watched as the officers flipped the bed, noting that the mattress was missing, which was odd. They looked in the closet, but Martin wasn't there. They opened the curtains, but there was a uniformed officer standing outside who insisted that he'd stood there the whole time, and had not seen anybody in a silver robe dive out the window. The police seemed confused and angry as they searched the rest of the house, but the Treasury agents just seemed irritated. After a few minutes, the two agents who appeared to be in charge arrived. They introduced themselves as Miller and Murphy. Agent Murphy did all of the talking. He had a quiet, kind manner. He gently asked them questions, the answers to which were almost always "no."

"Did he tell you what he was up to?"

"Do you know where your son went?"

"Do you know how he went there?"

After a couple of hours of this, the police announced that Martin was not there, and the Treasury agents announced that they knew that already. Agent Murphy left a business card. He made a point of saying that Martin had not hurt anybody, and that they didn't think he was dangerous, but if he did make contact, to please call the number on the card.

Walter and Margarita Banks stood on their front lawn and watched the law enforcement officers drive away like they were watching relatives leave after a holiday dinner. The squad cars drove down the street, around the corner, and hopefully, out of their lives. Margarita mentioned that it looked like someone had driven a car into the big tree at the end of the road. Walter reflected on the little things you notice when you're upset. They kept their arms around each other as they walked back into their home, closing the door behind them.

They didn't have time to sit down before the doorbell rang. Margarita opened the door without bothering to ask who was there. When the door opened, Martin was standing on the front step. He had gotten a haircut and had shaved. He was wearing a nice dark gray suit, but no tie, instead leaving his dress shirt's collar open to the first button. Behind him, on the street, there was a taxi idling. Margarita gasped.

Martin said, "Mom, I'm so sorry."

She pulled him inside and hugged him to within an inch of his life. His parents wanted an explanation, but knew they weren't going to get one. Martin promised that he hadn't broken the law, and that it was all a big misunderstanding which he intended to straighten out. In the meantime, he wouldn't be around much, but they could always call him. He'd never be far from his phone.

"You know my old mattress, and all that bedding I took?" Martin asked. "You're not gonna be getting that back. Sorry. Do you still have that second box from Amazon I ordered?"

Walter shook his head. "No, the cops took it. What was in it?"

"Nothing important. There's a company that makes modern computers that look exactly like an old Commodore 64. I'd bought one for a friend. I can just go buy another one before I go back."

"Go back where?" Margarita asked.

Martin answered, "Home."

Martin walked out of his parents' house and got into the cab. He and the cabbie talked for a moment, and then the cab pulled away and turned left at the end of the block, disappearing from view. A man sat on his bicycle at the end of the street, next to the now-damaged tree. He made a note of the exact time of departure, the license number of the cab, and direction of travel. He scribbled furiously into a tattered notebook with a small greasy stub of a pencil.

He let the saddle of his long-suffering bicycle support his weight. The worn-out toes of his off-brand sneakers rested on the sidewalk more for balance than to carry any load. He was in his sixties, but looked terribly haggard. A ragged fringe of gray hair ringed his deeply sunburned bald spot. His skin was deeply creased and leathery. He had the gaunt frame and unhealthy demeanor of a man who had gotten far too much fresh air and exercise.

The man finished his notation and closed the notebook. He slung his backpack off of his shoulders and opened it. It contained a little food, a few articles of clothing (mostly socks and underwear), and a great many cheap notebooks. No two were the same brand. Their labels were printed in a mix of English, Spanish, and Portuguese. All of them had a range of dates, stretching back to the nineteen-eighties. He placed his notebook in with the others, zipped the bag closed, and put it on his back where it belonged. He started riding down the sidewalk. He instantly became graceful once in motion. He had clearly had plenty of practice riding his bike.

A woman driving a huge SUV was trying to pull out of a parking lot. She stopped short of the sidewalk to let the man ride by. As he passed in front of her truck, the engine died. The man on the bicycle looked at her briefly, but kept moving. The woman cursed. She'd only had the vehicle for a few months. She really didn't want to have to deal with a tow truck and a mechanic tonight. She turned the key and was tremendously relieved when it started easily. She looked at the traffic, trying to find a place to jump in. She saw the man further down the street, still riding his bicycle.

He's lucky, she thought. *I bet his bicycle never breaks down.*

ALSO BY THE AUTHOR

Help is on the Way: A Collection of Basic Instructions

Made with 90% Recycled Art: A Collection of
Basic Instructions

The Curse of the Masking Tape Mummy:
A Collection of Basic Instructions

Dignified Hedonism: A Collection of Basic Instructions

The Basic Instructions Desk Calendar

ACKNOWLEDGMENTS

First and foremost, this book would not exist without the assistance, encouragement, and tolerance of my wife, Missy.

I'd also like to thank Allison DeCaro, Jen Yates, John Yates, Philip Nolen, and Rodney Sherwood for their feedback and support.

I'd like to thank Ric Schrader for putting up with my continued abuse, and Scott Adams for having pointed out to the world that I exist.

After the first edition of *Off to Be the Wizard* was published I received assistance from Marshall Gatten, Debbie Wolf, Mason Wolf and from Neil Robert. They helped me improve my book, and for that I am grateful.

Thanks to David Pomerico and everybody else at 47North.

Last, I'd like to thank the readers of my comic strip, *Basic Instructions*, whose support made the writing of this book possible.

ABOUT THE AUTHOR

 Scott Meyer grew up in the small town of Sunnyside, Washington. He began his career in humor by working as a standup comedian and radio personality, a highlight of which was participating as the opening act in Weird Al Yankovic's "Running with Scissors" tour. Following a long stint touring the United States and Canada, Scott settled down in Orlando, Florida, where he works on his ongoing comic strip, *Basic Instructions. Off to Be the Wizard* is his first novel.